Not Far Away

CONTEMPORARY NATIVE AMERICAN COMMUNITIES
Stepping Stones to the Seventh Generation

Acknowledging the strength and vibrancy of Native American people and nations today, this series examines life in contemporary Native American communities from the point of view of Native concerns and values. Books in the series cover topics that are of cultural and political importance to tribal peoples and that affect their possibilities for survival, in both urban and rural communities.

SERIES EDITORS

Troy Johnson, American Indian Studies, California State University, Long Beach
Duane Champagne, Native Nations Law and Policy Center, University of California, Los Angeles

BOOKS IN THE SERIES

Inuit, Whaling, and Sustainability, Milton M. R. Freeman, Lyudmila Bogoslovskaya, Richard A.
    Caulfield, Ingmar Egede, Igor I. Krupnik, and Marc G. Stevenson
Contemporary Native American Political Issues, edited by Troy Johnson
Contemporary Native American Cultural Issues, edited by Duane Champagne
Modern Tribal Development: Paths to Self-Sufficiency and Cultural Integrity in Indian Country,
    Dean Howard Smith
*Native American Studies in Higher Education: Models for Collaboration between Universities and Indigenous
    Nations*, edited by Duane Champagne and Jay Stauss
Spider Woman Walks This Land: Traditional Cultural Properties and the Navajo Nation, by Kelli Carmean
Alaska Native Political Leadership and Higher Education: One University, Two Universes,
    by Michael L. Jennings
Healing and Mental Health for Native American: Speaking in Red, edited by Ethan Nebelkopf
    and Mary Phillips
Rachel's Children, by Lois Beardslee
A Broken Flute: The Native Experience in Books for Children, edited by Doris Seale and Beverly Slapin
Indigenous Peoples and the Modern State, edited by Duane Champagne, Karen Torjesen,
    and Susan Steiner
Native Americans in the School System: Family, Community, and Academic Achievement, by Carol J. Ward
Indigenous Education and Empowerment: International Perspectives, edited by Ismael Abu-Saad
    and Duane Champagne
Cultural Representation in Native America, edited by Andrew Jolivétte
Social Change and Cultural Continuity among Native Nations, by Duane Champagne
Drinking and Sobriety among the Lakota Sioux, by Beatrice Medicine
American Indian Nations: Yesterday, Today, and Tomorrow, edited by George Horse Capture,
    Duane Champagne, and Chandler C. Jackson
Not Far Away: The Real-life Adventures of Ima Pipiig, by Lois Beardslee

EDITORIAL BOARD

Jose Barreiro (Taino Nation Antilles), Cornell University; Russel Barsh, University of Lethbridge; Brian Dippie, University of Victoria; Carole Goldberg, University of California, Los Angeles; Lorie Graham (Blackfeet), Suffolk University; Jennie Joe (Navajo), University of Arizona; Steven Leuthold, Syracuse University; Nancy Marie Mithlo (Chiricahua Apache), Institute of American Indian Arts; J. Anthony Paredes, Florida State University; Dennis Peck, University of Alabama; Luana Ross (Confederated Salish and Kootenai), University of Washington

Not Far Away

The Real-life Adventures
of Ima Pipiig

Lois Beardslee

A division of
ROWMAN & LITTLEFIELD PUBLISHERS, INC.
Lanham • New York • Toronto • Plymouth, UK

AltaMira Press

A division of Rowman & Littlefield Publishers, Inc.
A wholly owned subsidary of The Rowman & Littlefield Publishing Group, Inc.
4501 Forbes Boulevard, Suite 200, Lanham, MD 20706
www.altamirapress.com

Estover Road, Plymouth PL6 7PY, United Kingdom

British Library Cataloguing in Publication Information Available

Library of Congress Cataloging-in-Publication Data
Beardslee, Lois.
 Not far away : the real-life adventures of Ima Pipiig / Lois Beardslee.
  p. cm. — (Contemporary Native American communities ; 22)
 ISBN-13: 978-0-7591-1118-9 (cloth : alk. paper)
 ISBN-10: 0-7591-1118-9 (cloth : alk. paper)
 ISBN-13: 978-0-7591-1120-2 (pbk. : alk. paper)
 ISBN-10: 0-7591-1120-0 (pbk. : alk. paper)
 1. Indians of North America—Social conditions—Fiction. 2. Indian women—Social
conditions—Fiction. 3. Racism—Fiction. I. Title.

 PS3602.E255N67 2007
 813'.6—dc22

                                                                    2007014208

Printed in the United States of America

⊚™ The paper used in this publication meets the minimum requirements of
American National Standard for Information Sciences—Permanence of Paper
for Printed Library Materials, ANSI/NISO Z39.48-1992.

Contents

Introduction

In Ojibwe one might say that historical information tends to be shared by *ogemagiigadawuk*, and that morals and stories tend to be shared by *dibaazhi-maaduk*, and that some people are good at being both. I cannot lay claim to either title, however, because the Ojibwe culture does not permit one to apply those terms to oneself. They imply something larger than mere repetition of information. They are cultural emblems for the speaking of higher truths. They are behavioral constructs that one is expected to strive toward; and judgment is left for others to give and take those titles at will.

This book is about the impact of post-*Brown v. Board of Education* white flight upon Native Americans in rural northern Michigan. The topic is such a heavy one that I've chosen the unusual format of blending nonfiction with fiction. The stories that wrap themselves around the fictional character of Ima Pipiig are rooted in humor, beauty of culture, and racism. Traverse City, Michigan, and its surrounding bedroom communities provide me with ample sources of all of these. But to truly understand the pervasiveness of the racism that underlies Ima Pipiig's daily activities, one must confront the horrific statistics and behaviors that frighten many of northwest Lower Michigan's citizens, and especially its educators, in even very small doses. Therefore, I have interwoven Ima Pipiig's stories with several essays of nonfiction. The fiction and the nonfiction are intended to enhance one another. They brush precariously close. This fiction is rooted in reality. It provides insight into the emotional damage and socioeconomic lack of choices that real people experience as a result of cold, hard truths, those both statistical and unacknowledged. Nonfiction can be unemotional and lets one avoid the psychological consequences of real faces, real people, real personalities, real innocence, and real guilt. Statistics can be gathered with careful omission, to avoid actual

1

transmission of knowledge and to avoid confronting real faces, real people, real personalities, real innocence, and real guilt.

The nonfiction essays in *Not Far Away* create a factual milieu within which one can appreciate Ima Pipiig and her idiosyncrasies. There are repeat themes, but the material bears repeating. It is the stuff that does not make its way through most contemporary information filtering systems. *The Real-life Adventures of Ima Pipiig* are my own real-life adventures, as well as those of my family, neighbors, and friends. The names have been changed, to protect the innocent (me) from lawsuits by the guilty (them, and sometimes me). I make no apologies for Ima Pipiig. She is, above all, a woman of integrity.

I do not like writing about ignorance, racism, hatred, and abuse. I prefer writing about beauty. But, as a Native American living in twenty-first century America, I experience the former as much as the latter. So, sometimes writing-to-fight-evil takes precedence over reveling joyfully in my everyday experiences and in my family and culture. Writing about racism is especially difficult because it is the part of my day that I want to tuck away into the folds of my brain tissue, the ones that absorbed the first mailing address I ever had, along with the pain of surgery and childbirth and a couple of phone numbers that I wrote down last week and tucked away for safekeeping god-knows-where. Unfortunately, racism is the part of my day that I need to relive several times a day and to deal with in a new format several times a day. Racism is born and raised in various environments of ignorance and itself gives birth to even more ignorance in an endless cycle that results in cultural and socioeconomic monocultures that are as deadly and prone to species extinction as any virus or insect pest on any new continent. Ignorance, racism, and hatred are the potato blights of my human community. I treat them with reverence, washing them from my conscious memory periodically, in order to rest from the burden of trying to nurture my own family and culture within their ever presence. And I spend free time and vast amounts of energy on preventive measures, knowing better than to hope for a cure, but tired and wanting of respite, as the very burden of dealing with racism is an extra drain upon my resistance to the disease.

Racism sneaks up in the oddest, least expected ways. Racism rarely wears white hooded robes today. It is lithe and subtle. It floats about on the air, as common as house dust. It is as present as a mold spore. It is so much a part of the very makeup of our lives that we no longer need hoods. Racism is the air that we breathe. We have chosen rejection of "others" over celebration of diversity. Racism happens when I talk to my son's third grade teacher. It happens when I interact with university personnel. It happens when I go to some restaurants and stores. It happens when I answer the telephone. It happens when I listen to the radio or read a magazine. It happens when I pick up a book that my child has brought home from school.

So I speak out, because if I don't, I see no future for myself in my old age; I see no future for my children. So I speak out, because if I don't, my children will be burdened with the gargantuan task of trying to make a future for their own children in a system that is so painfully broken that it is killing Indian people. So I speak out, because I want to whittle away at that burden, to ease the task for those future parents who are now my beautiful and much-loved children.

Here I am, trying with all my might to write about ignorance, racism, hatred, and abuse. But I keep circling back to beauty (my children). You see, those of us about whom the dominant culture is ignorant are beautiful. If we are locked out, rejected, and feared, and the very foundations of our self-esteem and our cultures are destroyed, we are not the only losers. You lose, too. People who are schooled and brought up without access to diversity are destined to function in a limited domain. Eventually, they will have to step out into the integrated world, or they will have to let it in. That beauty, diversity, can be interpreted as a predator at the door, or it can be welcomed as a gift. I hope for the latter. Right now, my children and I are tap-tap-tapping at your door, and I am telling you—we are beautiful.

Because I have been honing these arguments for several years, some of the essays in this book have already been published elsewhere. "F-ed by the V-Monologues" first appeared in *News From Indian Country* and *Ojibwe Aking* in the spring of 2004. "Shiigawk" and "The Shirt" appeared in *The Glen Arbor Sun*. "The Throw-away People" was incorporated into a temporary collage that was exhibited at the Leelanau Historical Museum in Leland, Michigan, to accompany a series of works on the theme of mothers and children that was displayed with a Mary Cassatt pastel drawing. "The Lecture They Want to Hear" was presented in 2005 at a fund-raiser for independent media in Traverse City, Michigan. Several essays and chapters in this book have been read for live audiences or on public radio.

The Real-life Adventures of Ima Pipiig

$\mathscr{I}$ma Pipiig lives in Sleeping Bear County, one of the wealthiest counties in the state of Michigan, one of the wealthiest counties in America. Located in the northwest corner of the lower peninsula of Michigan, the county is named after the Sleeping Bear Dunes National Lakeshore, a national park that was carved out of an old state park. Additional bits and pieces of nearby land were acquired, until a patchwork quilt of public and private land was created. The result was less valuable for the environment and the wildlife than it was for well-connected real estate developers. It is the public land of the National Lakeshore that attracts white-flightists to the constantly increasing number of small lots that have eaten up the agricultural landscape. It is the white-flightists who have transformed Ima Pipiig's ancestral home into an exurb, a high-income suburb, of Twin Bay City, Michigan, the largest city in the region. They have also transformed Ima Pipiig's relationship with her home and her community. Ima Pipiig perceives the new community as a bastion of homogeneity, with little acknowledgment of the original Native culture. Ima Pipiig battles various forms of racism each and every moment of each and every day. But the people of Sleeping Bear County do not want to acknowledge this.

The region was, earlier in Ima Pipiig's lifetime, remote and quasi-wild, a mix of woods and marginal farmland, with ample beaches and shoreline, but with poor roads or electrical trunk lines. It seemed to be a magnet for intellectuals. Harvard faculty and award-winning authors summered and rubbed shoulders with old homesteaders and even with the Indians. It was a place where differences sometimes disappeared for brief bits of time, while people enjoyed one another's intellects.

Eventually the region, along with its special gifts, was discovered by developers and the hordes that fled northward away from the loss of industrial jobs, poverty, disputes over forced integration, and other urban plagues of their own making. Twin Bay City, the largest city in northern Michigan, was a convenient magnet, with institutional facilities and services that had been designed to serve a scattered population.

Northwest Lower Michigan College, the local junior college, once attracted exceptional faculty and produced students of an exceptional nature. Today, it is, by Ima Pipiig's standards, an ersatz educational institution with an ersatz, typical-small-town-middle-America-exurban artsy-fartsy museum that purchases canned exhibits that the rest of ersatz, typical-small-town-exurban artsy-fartsy museums purchase all across America. The exceptional staff of the college has been replaced by unexceptional white-flightists, and the institution cranks out unexceptional white students who perform unexceptionally well in the institutional white jobs that wait for them.

The national park and the other public lands of the region are no longer flanked by farms and wooded hillsides. One may canoe for a half-mile on an inland lake, portage into another otherwise inaccessible lake, expecting beauty and solitude, only to look up at hillsides covered with upper-middle-class mansions, permanent outdoor floodlights intact. There is a tackiness to the parkside development that makes it incomprehensible to Ima Pipiig how visitors could imagine this as pristine. She understands that the park visitors and the new residents come from places where another family's property is only a few feet from their own home; but she does not comprehend this, because she thinks she would die if she were forced to live that way, and she is haunted by the transition of hundreds of miles of open land into suburbia. Her need to be isolated is exacerbated by the social isolation she feels in her community, where Indians are expected to live up to people's stereotypes and are, in general, undesirable entities on a landscape of summer vacation fantasies turned into year-round homes for the affluent and the fortunate.

The visitor's center at the National Lakeshore is full of cute books full of Indian legends written by white people, for the expectations of white people, for whom two acres is a vast and wild place, and for whom Indians are of value only if they are dead and long gone and as vacant from the surroundings as are unbroken habitat for wild wildlife. It is a place where the new exurban/suburban residents, in their desire to live in a wild and dangerous place, with the convenience of a convenience store, a police department, cable TV, and the Internet, fantasize that they have surely, surely seen wolves or mountain lions, even where little bobcat footprints are magnified by melting snow. Their piss smells the same, you know. . . . They can't tell the difference . . . but Ima Pipiig can tell. She can tell by the size and spacing of the scratch marks on the old dead cedar logs in the swamps where she once hunted grouse with Lester. She can tell by the few days of sunny weather preceding her finding of those fat paw prints. She can tell by the advance of realtors from the suburbs of Detroit who have wounded two or three deer and think that they are wild men of the woods. And she can tell by the advance of the subdivisions upon her own farm, her own home, her own shrinking habitat. She can tell by the presence of three-or-four-or-five-hundred-thousand dollar homes with ten—Jesus, count them ten—fucking cats living in the basement just across the road from the public land. Supplemented predators upon the songbirds, thinks Ima Pipiig, angrily. And, damn, don't you people know that the songbirds breed in such great numbers because they are essential fodder for the predaceous hawks and owls that follow them up and down this coast? *Jeesus, I mean Jeeesus, what are you guys doing messing up this tiny little patch of surviving habitat with housecats?* She thinks it but does not vocalize it. But they don't get it; and Ima Pipiig gets it.

Ima Pipiig is an endangered species. She has been part of this habitat of the Great Lakes for thousands of years. The species she eats, the species she depends upon to scatter seeds, the species who depend upon her to keep them under control or scatter their spores, they have grown up, evolved, matured with Ima Pipiig's family for so many generations that they are intertwined. Symbiotic. The biologists call it symbiotic. But there are no biologists among the real estate developers on the zoning boards adjacent to the national park. There are no biologists among the well-paid professionals in the ersatz junior college and the marginally functional public schools. Ima Pipiig is a biologist. She is a biologist like a pike is a biologist, like a snowy owl is a biologist, like a mouse is a biologist. Ima Pipiig is a biologist who sees Indians as part of the ecology of the Great Lakes and who sees Indians as an endangered species.

Ima Pipiig will plead for the life of the bear who uses her farm as only part of its habitat before the zoning commission full of real estate developers who want to make a quick buck because they have bought up or inherited acres and acres of Sleeping Bear County in the exurbs of Twin Bay City, Michigan, which has always been a suburb of Detroit, Michigan, and Evanston and Chicago, Illinois, and all of the suburbs of both of those cities that were affected by *Brown v. Board of Education*, when Thurgood Marshall got those judges, time and time again, to say, "Hey, integrate! Mix yourselves up with those who are darker than you, because they are as essential to your environment as are the frogs, the bass, the walleye, the trout, the bear, the caribou, the deer, the elk, the moose, the wildflowers, the bacteria, the fungi . . . " But they did not listen, because brown people were closer to them than the frogs, the bass, the walleye, the trout, the bear, the caribou . . . and they could not imagine anything as like themselves as wild and an essential part of the habitat. So Ima Pipiig suffers for survival in bits and patches of habitat surrounded by subdivided former farms and woodlots bought up or inherited by white people from Detroit, Michigan, and Evanston and Chicago, Illinois, and all of the suburbs of those cities that were affected by *Brown v. Board of Education*, when Thurgood Marshall got those judges, time and time again, to say, "Hey, integrate! Mix yourselves up with those who are darker than you, because they are as essential to your environment as are the frogs, the bass, the walleye, the trout, the bear, the caribou, the deer, the elk, the moose, the wildflowers, the bacteria, the fungi . . . " And Ima Pipiig understands that these people behave this way because their own ancestors were torn from their own ancestral homelands within which they had evolved generations ago, but she does not comprehend this.

Ima Pipiig once got a letter in the mail, from one of those new environmental institutes founded by some of those new white-flightists. She knew the type. Her friend, Dave-the-world's-best-mechanic, had a father-in-law who saw them coming. He'd had bumper stickers printed that said, "We don't give a damn how you did it downstate." He passed them out among his friends, and they became so popular that he had to have a second printing made. The people who didn't get it, who never understood the bumper sticker, they were the ones who founded the Northwest Lower Michigan Multiple Land Use Society. They had one goal, and that was to find themselves jobs in the exurb into which they had chosen to insert themselves, at the expense of the indigenous species: the bobcats, the fish, the snakes, the snails, mollusks, bacteria and fungi, the wildflowers, the songbirds, the predators, the old Indian tales, and the old Indians . . .

Ima Pipiig had thrown the letter in the trash. It invited her to work for free. They *all* invited the Indians to work for free, because the letter-writers had all grown up in the cities downstate, where black slavery was legal in the form of underemployment, and asking someone who had to prove their humanity to work for free was the status quo. Ima Pipiig, Indian that she was, could not possibly have something valuable to offer in the way of opinion; and she would be included as a token representative of her people, at great institutional sacrifice on the part of her superior white benefactors who were providing her with a table and chair and using her name and ethnicity to get state funding. She would no doubt respond to their letter, because she recognized their superiority and deferred to their superior white judgment, because they had, after all, come from cities where people knew the value of habitat in two acre blockettes with mostly-white subdivisions ringing them like crown jewels set in the precious shiny metal of suburbia. So they asked her to volunteer for the day of events they had planned. Ima Pipiig had followed her instincts and had thrown the letter in the trash. At least there were a few British thermal units to be gained for this downing of a northern tree . . . because Ima Pipiig did not think that mailing out hundreds or thousands of fliers to raise money for the jobs and semirural enjoyment of white people only and ones who thought they were environmentalists by doing it justified the death of one single old growth tree. Ima Pipiig understood how these people thought that they had to use up resources from somewhere else to save the resources close to their chosen homes; but she didn't comprehend it.

But her friend, a museum curator . . . a nice one, whose ancestors were local homesteaders who had originally "displaced" the Indians and who understood the difficulty of surviving in this place before the onslaught of yuppie-induced highways and medical centers . . . told Ima Pipiig that they really were nice people trying to do a good thing, because they were bringing together farmers and large landowners and waterfront property owners and conservationists and scientists and environmentalists and educators and artists and writers. And Ima Pipiig was all of these things. The museum curator friend gave Ima Pipiig another copy of that stupid letter and urged Ima Pipiig to send in her name as someone who was interested in possibly participating in those symposiums for a day. And Ima Pipiig filled out the stupid form letter, because she did not want to offend her friend . . .

And the response that Ima Pipiig got back was offensive.

It was dictated by form letter to Ima Pipiig that she would be a participant in their day of celebration of themselves—she was to demonstrate "Indian crafts" for people to look at during their lunch break. Cute as hell. Indian-fucking-crafts. Ima Pipiig did not do Indian-fucking-crafts. She was one of the finest Native American artists alive. She was an educator, and she had done her undergraduate work at Oberlin College, a private liberal arts college in Ohio, where she had graduated cum laude or summa cum laude or one of those damned things that was not in Ojibwe and didn't mean diddly-squat to Ima Pipiig or her elders, even though she had obediently studied Latin and had excelled at it. And she had obtained postgraduate degrees and had done post-postgraduate work. And she had taught and worked in museums, universities, public schools, and other settings. . . . She had taught math and science and rocket trajectories and sociology and the value of the rare and special Woodland Indian *art forms* of the Great Lakes that were dying out because of the economic abuse of Indian people. She did not do Indian-fucking-*crafts*. Not even for nice white people who were trying to do the right thing.

Nobody had contacted Ima Pipiig to ask her what she had to offer, or how, or even *if* she wanted to participate in whatever their agenda would turn out to be. She was, after all, an Indian. So she was supposed to demonstrate Indian-fucking-crafts for the *real* participants to look-down-and-paw-at-with-greasy-hands during their lunch break. No opportunity to speak. No opportunity to woo. No opportunity to share her experiences or her lifetime of farming, logging, hunting, banding birds on the local islands, preserving miles and miles of waterfront property and ancient timber, earning undergraduate and graduate degrees, teaching, developing educational materials, writing fiction and nonfiction, preserving endangered traditional art forms, and being an Indian with cultural ties to the region that went back thousands of years. . . . Just a silent–fucking–crafts–making–stupid–Indian–as–lunchtime–entertainment. The important people were on the discussion panels—large property owners, waterfront property owners, farmers, longtime residents, historians, educators, environmentalists, innovators. . . . And Ima Pipiig could understand why all of these puffed–up–with–themselves white newcomers would assume that Ima Pipiig could not possibly be any, let alone all, of these things; but she could not comprehend it.

2

Kool-Aid

$\mathcal{W}$hile she dipped and swished at the white five-gallon bucket, Ima Pipiig fantasized about addressing the audience: "I'd like to answer that one question about Indians that has been on everybody's lips . . .

"Why is Kool-Aid the official beverage of powwows, spiritual gatherings, and other Indian events?"

The water bug she chased was dark and shiny, smaller than a ladybug, and faster than a speeding bullet. It cruised around in the top centimeter of the water bucket adjacent to the kitchen cupboard taunting her until she approached with the small aluminum saucepan that served as the water dipper. Then it dove down the depth of the full four gallons or so that had been heaved up the steps to the cabin that sat tilted precariously on the glacier-smoothed boulders that provided the only high and dry ground on her scant acreage. The keenness of the bug dumfounded her, and she felt as helpless against the small creature as she did against society in general. Eventually, getting the bug out of the bucket became a moot point, one that would require more calories than a bugless bucket was worth; so Ima Pipiig made a false dip, chasing the bug downward, then passed again, filling her dipper several times.

The water was to be boiled on the small propane stove, for at least a minute, five would be better, she supposed. This was to eliminate the giardia, the intestinal virus that inhabited the lake water. It was carried by sport fishermen and beavers in their feces. Neither was particularly careful about whether or not they despoiled her family's drinking water. It was just as easy to blame it on the beavers as on the fishermen. After all, the hairy critters had lodges all around the lake. The beavers were, in fact, Ima Pipiig's only neighbors. The village on the railroad where her distant Cree cousins rented out cabins to the sportsmen was at least an hour and a half away by boat and by car.

The road to the remote inland lake, now the domain of multinational logging corporations, had been part of a small network of roads that serviced Indians and white miners. Now it was heavily washboarded from the logging trucks, its corduroy base of cedar logs exposed to the air and rotting. The five miles to "civilization" could be traveled only at a snail's pace. Sometimes the wild-eyed moose that ran along the open roadway ahead of the truck, thinking, mistakenly, that they were being chased, would travel faster than the family's vehicle. That was fine by Ima Pipiig and Lester. If the truck crept up on a bull moose too quickly, it would sometimes stop, turn, lower its head, and threaten with its antlers. Lester wasn't so sure he could outrun a moose in reverse, and he didn't relish the thought of backing into an oncoming logging truck, blazing along at breakneck, shock-absorbed speed, knowing that it had the right of way over mere civilians and their tiny cars.

Here, in the confines of the Chapleau Game Preserve, the largest game preserve in the world, timber harvesting had become king, and the Crown had given forth the northern Ontario resources that time and distance had preserved for the creatures of the woods, the moose, the bear, the ravens, the eagles and the hawks—and, well, the Indians. Because Indians were, to the consumers and profiteers of ancient resource mismanagement, no larger than the small black beetle that Ima Pipiig confronted in her water bucket in today's challenge for potable water.

After the water was cool, after it had become room temperature in the warm, poorly insulated wooden structure, Ima Pipiig would make Kool-Aid for the kids. It would be a weak Kool-Aid, barely sweet and somewhat pink . . . just dark enough to cover up the boiled water fleas and the odd organic materials that existed in the water of a shallow lake. She did this as her mother had done. And she did not explain to her children that the family had once had access to the clearest, coolest, cleanest water on the face of the earth, on both sides of the U.S.-Canadian border that had once never existed for this family . . . that they no longer owned those precious shorelines . . . that they had been taken away and sold to the highest bidders—the developers, the railroads, the loggers, the shippers, the government officials, and eventually, anybody with a good enough job to afford a summer cottage. But not the Indians.

So her children developed a taste for Kool-Aid. Weak Kool-Aid, warm Kool-Aid. It didn't matter. Strong Kool-Aid over ice became for them a delicacy, as it had become for Ima Pipiig. And in a changing culture in which the traditional Indian teas were looked upon as boorish and trashy, but juices and milk were either too expensive or hard on an aboriginal digestive tract, Kool-

Aid became a beverage of choice, a symbol of Indianness. Ima Pipiig giggled at this odd symbol of snobbishness as she mixed the Kool-Aid and sugar into the big glass jar. She screwed on the lid that kept out mosquitoes, dust, and mice, and she shook the big jar. Then she dished up big slabs of wild blueberry pie, three inches thick, solid and perfect, with a golden crumbled crusting of rolled oats and brown sugar on top. She kicked open the green wood of the screen door at its wobbly base and stepped outside, old ceramic plate and glass of Kool-Aid in hand. Then she skittered between the jack pines and the blueberry bushes that pushed forth from the immense boulder that was her summer home, stepped gingerly down the steep, smooth rock face where it touched the water, and settled in to watch her children swim with the beavers. One young beaver swam close to Ima Pipiig, blew water from its nostrils with an insistent sneeze-like puff that sprayed her toes, blinked several times, then dived, flapping its tail loudly at the conclusion of its dive. Ima Pipiig was startled and rocked backward. The kids guffawed and pointed, and while she had their attention, Ima Pipiig held up the plateful of big pie, nodded toward the house, and called out, "Kool-Aid's ready."

• 3 •

Solstice

$\mathcal{T}$here had been a break in the heat. For this they were both grateful. They were freshened. They were able to accomplish more in an hour, more in a day full of long daylight hours, more in the time they spent fighting the clock, to get enough done to justify collapsing, exhausted. Lester had finally finished sawing the last of the hardwood logs he had cut last winter, the shortest ones, the ones he saved for the end, because they would be the easiest to stack on top of the piles of evenly, perfectly spaced rough-cut green lumber boards that towered in the barns.

And now, as a light breeze passed through the western doors of the big barn, wrapped its way around the outermost stack of lumber, found the low spot where a stack of ten-footers waited for more boards, and exited the southernmost doors of the big barn, Lester held a wobbly ladder steady for his wife. As she slipped her lean, fifty-year-old frame upward, past the wobbly ladder top, finding toeholds among those protruding boards that were a few inches longer than their designated piles, he held his long arms outward, near to her, near enough to stop her from a fall, but distant enough not to startle her as she concentrated on her climb. And she saw this loving gesture out of the corners of her eyes, just as she saw it every time she made this climb, every year, each time these same woodpiles in this same corner of the barn grew too high for anyone's comfort level. So Ima Pipiig froze this image in her mind, to store away in a reserve of precious memories that she would need to fortify her through the low spots as she lived out and managed the rest of her life.

She enjoyed this time they spent together, silently stacking lumber in the big barn, especially now that it was cool. They got themselves into a wordless pattern there, once they figured out which board went where first, then next, then last, layer upon layer, until Ima Pipiig realized that the boards upon which

15

she stood had become stacked so high that the air was ten degrees warmer, way up in the rafters of the big barn. And she wished she had a T-shirt on under her baggy sweatshirt. The sweatshirt was now too hot for the task, but she needed the cloth to protect her torso from the scraping and gouging of the long boards, the two of them hefting and sliding them into place, he reaching up and out as far as he could, she doubled over, hopping about on top of the boards, dancing from one to another as the empty space above the height of a man's head was transformed into cool, wet, solid lumber. The rough-sawn boards were fuzzy and soft to the touch, but dense and hard to maneuver.

Eventually the next layer of boards balanced upon the front-end loader of the big, green tractor was too long for these piles. Ima Pipiig swung her legs over the edge of the pile, while Lester guided her feet to the top of the wobbly wooden ladder, and she eased her way down, using the tall woodpile for support. She followed Lester out the western doors of the big barn, around and past the deep green of the poison ivy that had sent runners around the corner and over the concrete, growing upright and healthy from nothingness, as though from the healthiest soil, reaching upward like those stacks of lumber. These barns were full of life.

A few feet past the tractor was a smaller barn, long and low, once a chicken coop, long ago scrubbed clean, with rows of "windows" roughly sawn in its sides, to let the breezes in to pull the moisture of the northern Great Lakes from the stacks and stacks of long boards. Ima Pipiig climbed up the ladder, and rolled herself on top of the sixteen-foot-long maple two-by-twelves. They were stacked to the height of her shoulders, and Ima Pipiig was still amazed that she and Lester had stacked them without help. It seemed each time that she lifted her end of the board that there really ought to be another full-grown man there to help them with it. But the boy was only nine-and-a-half now, not able to concentrate on a task that involved the danger of a heavy board and barns full of things to duck under and around; and his body was growing—it was not a time to subject it to hard labor from which it might not recover. Ima Pipiig was content to listen to him singing in the springtime grass outside, between the buildings, as his sister had done years before. She remembered the feeling of her muscles rebounding after moving each and every one of those exceptionally heavy green pieces of lumber, the long, wide ones, the ones they did first, so that they could stack them on the bottoms of the piles. She remembered the distinct sensation of the disks rising back upward between her spinal vertebrae after setting down each and every one of those exceptionally heavy green pieces of lumber, the long, wide ones, the ones they did first, so that they could stack them on the bottoms of the piles.

Ima Pipiig spaced out her knees and palms on the long boards, careful not to rest painfully on the sharp-edged spaces between them, careful not to nudge the carefully spaced boards, so that they would dry even and straight, careful not to put too much pressure on the outside of her left knee, the spot where she had banged the kneecap against an old metal bed frame years ago, and where she knew that a sharp piece of bone lodged in the tissue, but that she never spoke of and learned to live with . . . And she thought of the bones of Negro slaves, brought up from their vast colonial graveyards in America's south and east, the bones that told stories of short lives of hard labor, of torn ligaments and burdens too heavy for young growing bodies and burdens too heavy for young, healthy bodies and burdens too heavy for middle-aged bodies; and Ima Pipiig wondered how her own body would measure up on one of those anthropological autopsy reports. Would the physical anthropologist of the future assume that she had been a slave? A slave to what? A slave to a racist economy that kept her underemployed? Would the physical anthropologist determine that this woman had come from an uneducated caste of laborers? Why, she wondered, didn't all of her college degrees manifest themselves in the wear and tear of her muscles, her long bones, her spine? And Ima Pipiig was concerned that the lessons of wear and tear upon the human flesh and bones and psyches of the brown and black slaves of the New World did not speak louder to the dominant culture that kept people like her underemployed and doing work that was just a little bit past what her body could comfortably endure.

Then the boy called her name. "Mom!"

She took the weight off her left palm and swatted a mosquito against her hair. There was not enough room between the lumber and the ceiling for her to sit upright. She winced and readjusted the knee.

"What?"

"Can you tell where I am?"

"Outside the barn."

And then his voice echoed. "Can you tell where I am now?"

"Inside the barn."

"Just my head."

"Stay out of the way. Your dad's bringing a board."

They were shorter now, and narrower, small enough for Lester to lift off the forklift alone, even though they were too long for the short piles in the other barn. He gently placed one on the outside of the pile, careful not to disturb the stickers, the one-inch-by-one-inch wooden spacers used to let air travel between the boards and to help them dry straight and even. This made their barn-dried lumber more valuable than the kiln-dried lumber from the big building supply companies. Finish carpenters loved working with Lester's wood.

He was back again, with another board, which he slid over the other; and then Ima Pipiig helped him shift it into place next to the other one, with exactly three inches of space in between. It had to be exactly three inches. He got kind of grumpy if it wasn't. And they slid and shifted those boards into place one by one, until they reached the middle of the pile, where Lester couldn't reach anymore, and then Ima Pipiig was up on top of that pile alone, receiving the boards through one of the rough "windows" in the wall, shifting and grunting and shoving those boards until they went all the way back to the interior wall of the old chicken coop, with exactly three inches in between them, not two-and-a-half inches at one end and three-and-a-half inches at the other end, but three inches exactly between them, all the way down the length of each and every board. Then Lester would hand Ima Pipiig a pile of stickers, one-by-one-inch-by-eight-feet long, and the middle-aged woman would scramble on her hands and knees and line them up perfectly perpendicular to the green lumber, each lined up exactly above the one below it, barely finishing before Lester would arrive with a new board at the window. And she took it from him as quickly as she could, to relieve his spine from the burden of lifting the boards alone, because she loved the man, and she loved his spine.

The two of them worked like that, saving the shortest and lightest boards for last, until the pile had grown to the point that Ima Pipiig was crawling on her stomach along the boards. Then Lester watched her scramble down the pile of boards, from shortest to longest, like the broad steps he had once seen outside the Lincoln Memorial in Washingon, D.C., and she disappeared out one of the rough "windows" in the back wall of the chicken coop, diving head first into a row of peach trees. When she reappeared next to the tractor, they kissed, as they always did when they finished one phase of a project. Then Lester carried the wobbly old ladder back to the first barn and guided his wife up the side of the shortest stack of green lumber.

The short stack was in the middle between two higher stacks, and Ima Pipiig felt safe up there, using the adjacent lumber piles for balance and support. It was scary when she had to walk her end of the board close to the outer edge of the pile. From there she could see the sharp metal protrusions of various pieces of farm equipment, resting on cement blocks over concrete. She did not even try to imagine what it would feel like to fall onto that concrete and protruding steel. Instead, she kept her center of gravity away from the ends of the boards. As the center pile upon which she was standing increased in height, the sides of the piles that gave her a feeling of comfort receded. She had to duck from the beams of the massive ceiling joists. The barn was tall, and cherry tanks that could hold a full ton of fruit and water stood along a far wall, stacked twelve and sixteen feet high, placed one upon another with a forklift last summer, when the barn was empty, when the trucks with their burdens of pallets of lumber and the harvesting equipment and the cultivators and the snowplow and the cement blocks and the unnamed tractor attachments with deadly protrusions had all sat outside in the rain and the sun for a few weeks. Now the barn was full, full to the rafters, and Ima Pipiig stood upright to relieve her bent back, slipping her armpits over a rafter for security and support. Lester was climbing up the old ladder now with each heavy, green board, and she was scurrying to the end of the pile each time, trying to rescue man and board and spine.

They had never intended for it to be this way, both of them working so hard all the time. When they were younger and first in love, they did not imagine one another with scars and calluses, hobbling sometimes from working too hard . . . still in love. And they did not imagine that they would ever be too tired to make love.

Her mind was wandering by the time he said they were done. Done for the wood-sawing season. Done for the wood-stacking season. She peered over the edge of the stack, upon careful placement of this last of the heavy, green boards. Even Lester had given up trying to space them equally and perfectly, once he was sliding his end into place above his head, from the top rung of the old ladder. The steel monster below, the one with the protrusions waiting for gravity to impale her upon them, it was the stump-puller, the one Lester had designed and welded to fit onto the front-end loader of his favorite tractor, the big one with tires the height of a man. Normally, she never paid any attention to the stump-puller, except when she was stacking lumber. Then it took on a personality.

Years ago, in her childhood, a second cousin, an Ojibwe from northern Ontario, married a blond woman named Jessica. Jessica Lundergunder or somesuch. She was not merely blond. She was very blond. Her eyebrows were white. Her eyelashes were invisible. The rims around the lower edges of her eyes were pink, like on a domesticated rabbit. And the part down the middle of her long, straight, wispy hair was pink. She was from Chicago. Or maybe from near Chicago. It might as well have been Mars. Ima's cousin, Tommy Wewemitigo, was enthralled with her, smitten. She was his blonde. And she was from Chicago. And she was willing to forgo all of the modern conveniences of urban living to make a life with him, up in "da bush." She was even willing to become a Catholic.

Jessica Somesuch appeared to be in love with Tommy as well, or at least in love with the idea of marrying an Indian and bearing authentic Indian children. She hung a dream catcher from the rearview mirror of her rust-free Chicago sedan, followed Tommy to summer powwows, and proudly donned the dance regalia that Tommy's mum and aunties stitched to fit her sturdy frame. She was built a bit like a barrel, round about the middle with little skinny legs, and she twirled like a top among the dark women of the dance circle. Her enthusiasm pleased the older relatives immensely, and the relationship was sealed by a priest come autumn, in a tiny Indian church at the edge of the village. Jessica had taken several photographs of the church for family and friends back home, asking Tommy and all of his relatives, close and distant, to gather at the base of the wooden cross outside, the one that culminated in an eagle's head, with a cross member of outstretched wings.

Ima Pipiig remembered sitting in a back pew with her brother. She was thirteen. He was twelve. It was an age of skepticism. By the last quarter of the twentieth century, quite a few barrel-shaped blondes had found their way into the Indian communities of the northern Great Lakes. Most of them found their way out after a few years, often taking their brown-eyed offspring with them, leaving the rest of the community wondering what would become of their now-distant Chicago cousins. Some of them would show up decades later, after a few of the Ojibwe bands on the U. S. side of the border installed casinos and offered various services and payments.

It was Ima Pipiig's brother who first pointed out that the blond women all looked like they were related, like maybe they had been cloned in a laboratory in the southern netherworlds of North America that lurked somewhere below the forty-fifth parallel, someplace exotic, where they had frost less than eleven months out of the year, someplace where they experimented with crossbreeding women with albino piglets. And the name that he coined for each of these sturdy, pink-skinned blondes was *Helga*. *Helga the Stump-puller.* It caught on like wildfire among his seven older sisters and the other young women of the Indian communities that were beginning to be threatened by the fact that their men were being snatched up by women with golden hair. As she stared down at the piece of farm equipment resting on its concrete blocks, Ima Pipiig recalled her brother poking her ribs from next to her in the pew, and at the appropriate time in the ceremony giggling so hard that he jiggled, whispering, almost spitting into her ear, "Thou shalt pull stump."

Ima Pipiig had never told Lester about the Helga the Stump-puller thing. She thought that as a blue-eyed blond, he might find it in poor taste. And some things are best just left quiet between cultures, even among lovers.

"Yoo-hoo! We're done." Lester was waiting to help his wife climb down the side of the stack of lumber, arms outstretched, like a spotter for a lizard descending a rocky cliff.

"How high do you think that pile is, Les?" Ima Pipiig asked her lover, expecting him to say twenty feet, a hundred and twenty feet, maybe a million.

"Oh, only about eight feet."

"I don't believe you. You always underestimate."

"Fine. Get a tape measure."

"I'm too tired. All right, I believe you . . . But I think you're lying."

He laughed, and as they always did when they finished a project, they kissed. She slid ahead of him, past the stump-puller, and Lester remarked, "You didn't even fall on Helga."

Her brother must have blabbed.

Ima Pipiig went back to the house to urge the boy to bathe, and to cook, to wash some dishes, to ignore a pile of laundry. Lester cleaned up the sawmill and shoveled up the sawdust, so that the grass would grow. She would miss the screech and lurch of its engine in the distance as he put it into gear every evening until dark. She always knew he was there and safe, as long as she heard the sawmill. It was dark by the time Lester returned to the house, by the time she finished cooking, by the time either of them were off their feet, allowing flesh and bones respite from the realities of the economy of the early twenty-first century. The three of them fell asleep together in one bed, the man and boy watching a movie about vampire-biker-chick-aliens-from-outer-space, and Ima Pipiig wondering how other people celebrated summer solstice, the longest day of the year.

· 4 ·

Indian Boarding School

Ima Pipiig was like a sparrow hawk dodging past a plate-glass window. There was nothing in her early hawk training to prepare her for this phenomenon. Trees. Clear, crisp leaves moving in the breeze, then gone, a glare, loss of bearings in dive and space.

She had grown up in a loving family of sparrow hawks, demure, part of the food chain, honest in their own role in nature. Loving parents who chased down hundreds of chipping sparrows and the occasional young gull as a special meaty treat for their brood. These were good things, and this was a good life.

But they needed more, they were told, these loving parents. They needed to provide more for their children—a *different* life way, a *different* set of values, a *new* way to dive and dip and follow the breezes. The toughest part was the glass, reflective, fleeting, shiny but deadly.

• 5 •

Not Far Away

$\mathscr{B}$eing an Indian in northern Michigan has never been easy. The Great Lakes have always been a source of resources to be tapped by non-Indians ever since their discovery by non-Indians. The area was, after all, being exploited by Native peoples themselves, but not to the extent of overexploitation for export on the scale that would set hold in ever-expanding circles after colonization. Our populations had not yet reached that point. Perhaps we would have gotten there by ourselves without the introduction of the fur trade. Then again, maybe not. The land itself was a desirable resource and continues to be. The lumber alone removed from this region exceeded the value of all the gold of the great California gold rush. The mineral wealth removed from the shores of only one of the lakes, Superior, exceeded the wealth of the great California gold rush as well.

All of that brings us to the present, where waterfront property and the notion of a "safe" suburban lifestyle with plenty of public land nearby has given northern Michigan's real estate a value once again exceeding that of all material goods removed and squandered in previous generations. The rural inconveniences that characterized the areas where beleaguered remnant Native populations clustered in shuddering, desperate survival camps have been replaced by newer, faster roads and automobiles, better health care facilities for those who can afford them, easier shopping, and ease of communication. These things have not merely arrived with the new land rush; they have exacerbated it. Unfortunately, some Native populations are, in part, still clustered in shuddering, desperate survival camps; and there is a mistaken notion that they are survival camps of the victims' own making, that economic exclusion and psychological battering are options chosen by their recipients.

A key concept here in reference to this new, northern suburban lifestyle is "safe." What constitutes "safe" to the thousands upon thousands of people who have moved into the area in the last three decades, and who continue to do so? And for whom is it safe?

In his book *Jim Crow's Children* (Penguin Books, 2002), constitutional scholar Peter Irons describes the impact of *Brown v. Board of Education* and subsequent federal mandates for school integration on urban and suburban communities throughout the United States, as whites continued to fight forced interaction with minorities. He eloquently describes the frighteningly rude, crass, ignorant, and self-serving manner in which citizens and agents of government alike professed their objection to contamination of white culture and violation of the status quo. His descriptions and quotes ring painfully familiar to me, as they echo the arguments and expositions I hear fifty years later, today, in my own northwest corner of Michigan's lower peninsula. It is no coincidence that the huge influx of people from Detroit and Chicago into northern Michigan began in the 1970s, after busing was implemented to rectify white flight from cities into new suburbs. Those among the fleeing who could simply took bigger steps and eventually demanded services and facilities to accommodate their growing numbers. So the communities of northern Michigan grew.

However, I fear that the growth might have been an unbalanced one. The interaction and hiring patterns of a frighteningly high number of my new neighbors have made me wonder if a disproportionate number of racists and xenophobes haven't made their way north. Did a larger percentage of open-minded individuals choose to stay in the cities precisely because of that diversity? Did they manage, through all of the hype, fear, and poverty, to see beauty and value within the folds of layer upon layer of differences around them? Or, did the initial white-flightists establish a preculture, complete with a set of socioeconomic status quos and an educational system that was doomed to teach racism, fear, and hatred of others, indeed, a system that defined itself by the concept of "other"—a lesser other, an other that it was acceptable to exploit, evict, even destroy if necessary? Are these my new neighbors, those whose convenient right to xenophobia at the expense of others was sanctified by the Milliken Decision of 1974, much to the disdain of Thurgood Marshall? Is it possible to distinguish between so many of them and the lumber barons, vicious mining bosses, and union-busters of the late nineteenth and early twentieth century?

In some educational psychology textbooks, popular theories suggest that understanding of exceptionally abstract concepts, including fairness and equal rights, is related to brain development and that only 20 percent of the population actually reaches that level. It is a notion that relates the ability to comprehend civil rights with high intelligence, and it matches IQ in its bell curve mapping, with the loftiest thinkers far to the right of the curve in decreasing frequency. It leaves much of the human race, and especially my neighborhood, open to a plethora of bad jokes. There is an optimistic side of me that suspects that ignorance may be the culprit in the apparent lack of brain development among racists and abusers. It may well be an issue of nature versus nurture; and if we fail to nurture interaction between cultures that is a win–win situation socioeconomically, we promulgate interaction that is exploitive and abusive and therefore destined to failures and shortcomings.

Hoping that our educational status quo can be repaired and brought into an equitable norm is what keeps me functioning as an educator, in spite of insults, threats, assaults, and exclusion on the part of many of my white "colleagues." These issues are sacred cows. Good academics don't talk about them. And good Indians don't talk about them. Acknowledging them might embarrass the beneficiaries of the status quo. That's why Indians who are not good Indians are often ignored. Or punished.

That's why I chose to stop being a good Indian. I'm not sure when it happened. I think it has been a gradual process. It happened when I discovered that I would be excluded from equal work at equal pay. It happened when my daughter was threatened by a white elementary principal. It happened when my son brought *Little Black Sambo*–type children's literature home from school. It happened when I answered the telephone last week. It happened when I spoke to someone from the National Park Service yesterday. I know that my choice to abandon my good Indian role for one as a not-so-good Indian has been a result of lack of ample reward for keeping quiet about the position of underling that several white-dominated institutions in America, including education, have designated for me at this time. There is a certain point below which people cannot survive, both physically and mentally; and at that point, they rebel against the status quo.

By the standards of the late twentieth and early twenty-first century, I'm obviously not a good academic either. I'm proud of that. If I were a good academic Indian, I'd tell you that a coyote made me say that . . . or a trickster. But I *am* the coyote. I *am* the trickster. College graduate. Good student. Overachiever. Mistake maker. Indian. Woman. Parent. No fantasies, no superhuman ethnic hero dying to save the white guys. No soft and gentle Indian girl in buckskin braiding flowers. No traditional stories or even your own distorted translation of our traditional stories. Just the truth as I live and see it. I do not apologize for being some of these things and for not being others.

At a job interview for the position of Native American educational liaison at a school district bordering a local Indian reservation, I was asked, "What sorts of programs would you suggest for Indian children who are perfectly

capable of showing up at school regularly and of learning but who simply refuse to do so?" The first thing I suggested was that we quit blaming several
hundred Indian families for the inappropriate teaching methods of a couple of
dozen white teachers, and that integrating the staff, revising the teaching materials, and providing staff training in how to interact with people they perceive as "other" might be good places to start. A white lady is currently the
Native American educational liaison at the school district bordering that local
Indian reservation. She is, after all, comfortable with the status quo. She is, after all, comfortably encased in the pay scale and retirement benefits of that status quo. The Indian students, however, face a status quo and future built upon
their role as America's most underemployed, no matter how well they perform
in an educational setting. They know this because every day they are bused
into an institution that never has hired and never will hire a minority in a position of authority, or even as a janitor, for that matter, as long as public dollars keep flowing into the pockets of the institutional participants.

The northwestern part of Michigan's lower peninsula is an especially
beautiful place. A hilly, but tillable landscape rolls out in layer upon layer on
the horizon, creating a warm (for the northern regions of the Midwest) microclimate on the downwind side of Lake Michigan, which runs north to
south for hundreds of miles of clean, sandy, swimmable coastline. Because
Lake Michigan takes so long to heat up in the springtime, crop-killing early
frosts are less likely here than inland. The growing season is a bit longer, too,
because the great lake's heat-holding mass delays autumn frosts. The hills and
microclimate have lent themselves especially well to fruit farming, especially
cherries, and the region remains the nation's, and one of the world's, great-
est producers of sweet and tart cherries. Wine grape plantings have been increasing in number, hand in hand with a swelling population of suburbanites seeking ways to "minifarm," or to enjoy agriculture in ever-smaller bites
of real estate. Grand Traverse, Little Traverse, and Sleeping Bear Bays provide calm, protected coastlines for cities and towns, along with numerous
harbors and marinas. The low spots between the hills are filled with water,
creating additional miles of developable waterfront property, view lots, and
desirable suburban homes.

State and federal public land is plentiful, more abundant than in any other
state east of the Mississippi, and includes Sleeping Bear Dunes National
Lakeshore, a blend of preserved habitat and somewhat tacky adjacent developments that hover over the park fringes like view-lot vultures. Some people see
the area as a public-land ghetto full of small lots with big backyards at the taxpayers' expense, a form of exurban sociopathy, where people who are used to
ten feet of personal space on either side of them mount their snowmobiles,

leave their tiny lots, and terrorize the old homesteaders. It is a community that needs to grow into itself and resolve some of its problems.

The region attracts people from all over the world, including celebrities, such as Michael Moore, Tim Allen, Madonna, and retired politicians. It was once the favored retreat of Al Capone and other Chicago gangsters. Owners of ancient waterfront cottages along the Leelanau Peninsula often joked that, "Al Capone (probably) slept here." Leelanau, the peninsular county jutting north into Lake Michigan due west of Traverse City, which is currently the largest city in northern Michigan, had long been a retreat for intellectuals and the wealthy. However, it had also maintained one of the largest populations of Native Americans east of the Mississippi River, in a state that ranks in the top ten in terms of Indian population.

The Indians who remained in the area, often in the face of forced removal, were the Anishinabe, *first people*, and included mostly Ojibwe (Chippewa), Odawa (Ottawa) and Potawatomi. They spanned both sides of the U.S.-Canadian border, originally surrounding almost all of the Great Lakes, making up the second-largest Indian tribe in North America, fusing gently into the Cree, also *first people*, who wrapped themselves lovingly around the Anishinabe to their south and fused gently into the Inuit of the north. The borders of the immense Anishinabe territories roughly followed the borders of the watershed of the Great Lakes, where it separates from the watersheds of the Mississippi and Hudson's Bay to the north.

During the 1830s several business interests and government agents on the U.S. side of the border persuaded select Indian leaders to "sell" the real estate upon which the Anishinabe remained, while retaining unlimited access to its resources, free education, and other commodities for their children and children's children in perpetuity. There is extensive evidence that the Indians thought that the purchasers were only buying trees. In exchange, Michigan acquired title to a chunk of real estate that was necessary for statehood. The property was not paid for. The obligations to the Indians were forgotten, the access to resources they had been promised was ignored, and the Indians huddled together in small, remote communities in various states of poverty induced by unemployment, loss of land base and livelihood, and other forms of socioeconomic abuse and exclusion. Originally, the entire county of Leelanau had been set aside by planners as an Indian reserve, but the bulk of the land was subsequently taken away once its value was realized. Eventually the entire Indian population of the region was limited to thirteen acres of real estate. The argument used during the Allotment Era of Indian relations was that it was more land than the Indians needed to survive upon. Modern attempts by local Natives to buy back some of that real estate continue to meet resistance.

In spite of this, traditional Woodland Indian culture survives because the stories, the traditions, the belief systems are all based in pragmatism and are still applicable today. They have remained intact through generations of economic upheaval and religious barnstorming, precisely because human nature is surprisingly uniform. Issues such as domestic violence, sibling rivalry, loss of life, greed, and misuse of resources are universal. Every culture has developed stories about them. Amazingly, the Indians of the northern Great Lakes have managed to keep ours intact, in one form or another, developing, changing, and rising to the occasion to help us cope with life, legal battles, and various insufferable circumstances via humor, grace, prevention, and gruesome example. And we develop new stories and forms of storytelling to meet new cultural and individual crises as they develop. These are as valid and as rich as the old stories and are grounded in our amazing adaptability. They counteract the notions that we are vanquished or vanished or that we are valuable only in historical contexts.

Today's Indians are associated with casinos. Casinos are loopholes in racism. They bring dividends and services to a limited number of Michigan's Native residents. But they do not eliminate the socioeconomic principles of apartheid in America that keep loopholes like casinos essential for those they service. Unfortunately, less than half of the state's Indian population can come up with the paperwork and credentials to qualify for federal programs or casino-related funds. Extirpating the Native population for the purposes of garnering resources did not lend itself to facility of access to promised goods and services. So, thousands of Michigan's Indians are left out in the cold. This does not preclude some members of the dominant culture from assuming that all Indians get free stuff, payments, and services, or from wondering why the half of the Indian population that does get varying benefits can't see fit to share them with the rest of the "Indians" out there. (Although they never seem to ask why they themselves do not do the same thing.) It's like asking someone who is recovering from a harsh infection to share his or her penicillin. It is asking Native people what you have always asked us to do: do more with less.

People who come to buy my artwork and my books often ask me what I think about "per capita" payments, dividends paid to members of two of Michigan's Indian tribes. I tell them about my friend, Mimi. We waited tables together as teenagers. Mimi's family owned various successful businesses. Along with her siblings, she is now a stockholder in various businesses and receives substantial dividends, without doing hard physical labor for them, merely by virtue of her birth. Indians who receive benefits do so by virtue of their birth because their parents and grandparents made contracts, business decisions, and personal decisions that put their offspring in that legal position, not unlike the heirs to America's great fortunes. (Entire families of career politicians involved in the military-industrial complex come to mind.) While many of my neighbors flock to Mimi's social events and enjoy throwing her name around, few of them pride themselves in knowing an Indian fisherman. I am, however, proud of those who do.

By the way, Mimi has owed me about thirty-six bucks for about ten years. She doesn't call me much anymore, probably because when I hear her name, I start to chant, "Me, me, me—whaddaya want for free?" Also, I think she finally figured out that Indian artists in Michigan weren't held in the same regard as Indian artists in the Pacific Northwest, where she'd been living for a few years. And maybe the fact that I was two years older than her finally stopped impressing her once she'd hit her forties. As youngsters, we truly loved one another. As disparate members of dominant and oppressed cultures, we stopped enjoying one another's company. The differences, all socioeconomic, outweighed the similarities.

The receipt of "per capita" payments by only a small percentage of Michigan's Indians has led to various welfare myths about Indians in general, accompanied by some resentment due to perceptions that we're all living high off the hog and are not working for a living. In fact, most Indians I know work about seventy hours a week. We have the lowest per capita income in the state. So many of us work more hours for less money to buy basic goods and services at the same prices as anybody else. No one has offered to honor us with free Toyotas because we're Indians, and we do not expect them to. However, many people each year ask us to appear as guest speakers without pay at events that are designed to honor Native American people, usually at institutions that are designed to serve Native people by educating the public about them, like museums and national parks. They somehow don't put aside money in their grant proposals for paying Indian consultants and speakers—because they're too busy working on programs to bring socioeconomic justice to Indians—or at least maybe just let the rest of the world know that we haven't died out (yet). It always throws them off when I demand access to the right to earn a fair and equitable living. It cannot happen if ignorance prevails, and we are not allowed to voice our concerns. And it definitely cannot happen if good-paying jobs become so few and so far between that they become the birthright of the regionally most powerful.

By the way, Indians do not live on less because Indians choose to do so. Indians do not drive older cars because Indians choose to do so. Sixty-two Fords and Chevies are cool. Eighty-two Hondas are not. Having a busted faucet is not a quaint, ethnic behavior. Losing a tooth is not a spiritual event. Untreated diabetes is not a result of ignorance or stupidity; it is the result of lack of access to jobs with medical benefits. Asking Native American people to fill that niche for the psyche of America and her love affair with a convenient image of self is racism, pure and simple. Today's Indian women are no more Pocahontas than Pocahontas was Pocahontas, if you get my drift. Indian men are no more the Indians of America's imagination than the Indians of America's movies and books were actual Indian men. Those docile women of America's fantasies, films, and literature were too nice to insist upon being hired at equal pay for equal work. Those evil men who provided the caricatures for sports team mascots were too violent to be allowed to remain in the neighborhood, especially since real estate values had risen. Especially since people figured out that those rural Indians were sitting on prime waterfront property—without those mean, cranky, demanding other minorities in the neighborhood—oh, you know, the ones who wanted to eliminate the stigma of separate schools, the ones who struck down *Plessy v. Ferguson.*

People of color make up one-third of the population of the United States. We make up less than 10 percent of most white-collar professions. We are absent in the schools, at the veterinary office, in the doctor's office. It makes us balk at going to the doctor. It makes us less likely to obtain a family pet. Even if the vet is a really nice person, if the receptionist looks down her nose at us, we can't always get appointments for our pets. Even if the doctor is a really nice person, if the receptionist looks down her nose at us, we will not make doctor appointments for ourselves. Please stop writing grant proposals to educate Indians about obtaining medical care. Start writing grant proposals to educate the people who stand between medical care and us. Start making it emotionally and financially feasible for Indians to obtain medical care with dignity. We know it is there—just not for us. Equal education, equal employment, equal health care on paper only are useless; they must be equal in practice.

My insurance agent, Dick, is a friend. He is a professional cartoonist. He teaches art classes. He's a part-time philosopher. I enjoy pulling my farm trucks out of hibernation each spring for a season of hard work. It's an opportunity to share stories with Dick. Dick says that he thinks that it's easier to be African American in Traverse City than to be Indian in Traverse City. I'm inclined to agree. First of all, there aren't many African Americans in Traverse City, and they aren't asking for the implementation of 150-year-old fishing rights that were previously ignored. One or two black folks mowing the lawn here and there are OK. Same thing with light-skinned Mexicans. One or two, as long as they don't talk funny or stand out in a crowd, refuse to streak their hair with peroxide, or run for public office, they're OK. And East Indians. A technician here and there, maybe in a back room. Just as long as they don't have too many children . . .

With few exceptions, Native America is worse off than thirty or forty years ago. Casinos, "per capita" payments, and settlement claims have caused considerable backlash. Jobs are even less available for people who are perceived as the thankless recipients of something for nothing. There used to be Native American teachers and social workers in Michigan, even if they serviced the Indian population only. As public funding for such jobs has decreased, the presence of Native Americans in those jobs has decreased. I am aware that I infuriate people by talking about racism and exclusion in hiring. I am aware that I infuriate people by calling Traverse City and its environs "white-flight" communities. But I infuriate them simply by being here, by refusing to hide under the carpet, by refusing to be either an "invisible Indian" who works the night shift at the most undesirable jobs or a "cute" Indian who does cultural presentations or token Indian blessings or pipe ceremonies for less than a living wage—Indian as entertainment.

More than anything, I think that many of my neighbors would simply like the Indians to go away, so that they can have the land, the views, the sport-fishing, the jobs, and everything else without guilt and without responsibility. As long as Indians are still in the neighborhood, there is the potential that we'll get uppity, that we'll insist that our versions of our stories are more authentic than the cute and convenient ones that are written by white authors, that we'll insist that our versions of our culture and history are more authentic than the cute and convenient ones created by white museum curators. And then there is the biggest horror scenario of all—we'll figure out a way to enforce all those treaties and snatch all of that land back, arriving in bulldozers, snarling, waving tomahawks, and scalping redwood decks off mortgaged homes preciously perched upon waterfront and view lots.

Best keep those myths about Indians as welfare cheats and lazy, undeserving bums intact. . . . Have you noticed how, instead of vanishing, they are buying back their own land and increasing the size of their reservations? Don't give them credit! Instead, plant a headline on the front page of the weekly real estate rag: *Indians to Remove Acreage from Tax Rolls.* Heh, heh. That'll keep folks scared of 'em. And if they're scary, they're expendable. It's worked for generations, and it's worked all over the world. OK, so I infuriate some of you by talking about this stuff. The way I look at it, I infuriate some of you by merely breathing. What have I got to lose?

Indians do not want to be "cottage country" Indians, the ones that exist only in people's imaginations, promulgated by a plethora of children's literature that makes Indians look stupid, docile, and content with a lesser wage and poorer living conditions. That's probably why the larger resorts in northern Michigan often hire Jamaicans to work during the summer. They've got that cool accent, and, if they've got attitude, they keep it to themselves. Attitude. An awful lot of people wonder why Indians have it. I'm not sure. There's been an awful lot of pressure to whup it out of us over the last couple of centuries.

As long as we had a land base to return to—either in the form of a reservation or in the form of vast, unwanted tracts of land (northern Michigan, for example)—we could be docile as heck in public and be hardworking people of dignity at home. But now, even swamplands are considered desirable.

My grandmother's "last" name meant "lives on a slough." I figured it wasn't by choice. Her family had lived on some prime sandy beach before they ran for their lives into some nasty places where there wasn't even a breeze to keep away the black flies. Good enough for Indians, I guess. She never acted like she believed it, though. Neither did my mother. Neither do I. Neither does my daughter. That's one heck of a family tradition. That's a lot of powerful Indian women. Beautiful Indian women. Pocahontas, eat your heart out. Here I come, babies in my arms, ancestors in my back pockets. Formidable. Indefatigable.

Ask any Indian man. They will tell you: Indian women are mean.

Not mean, I say. Tired. Fatigable. Drawing lines in the sands that used to be ours, on the beaches where our children no longer play—partly because we cannot afford the fifty-dollar-per-year parking fee, and partly because we are looked upon as defecating dogs would be looked upon on those beaches. Not our beaches, because there are welfare myths that we do not pay taxes. In Leelanau County, people of color tend to populate one beach at one park at one inland lake, far from the towns full of summer cottages, far from the national park. The Mexican park. Except that the Indians sneak in, too. And a few of those African Americans that my new neighbors thought that they had left behind in the crumbling cities creep in, too, many by marrying those Indians. . . .

Maybe people like the Mexicans a little better than the Indians. That's why the Mexicans get hired at minimum wage to seasonally prune and harvest the fruit trees and to work in the fruit-processing plants: They don't have attitude. They are from somewhere else, someplace foreign—like Texas. They are "guest" workers. They do not have that history of treaties and expectations. They don't plan on owning real estate or sticking around in perpetuity. A man who owns a local fruit-processing plant and who sends the "Mexicans" to work in his hundreds of acres of fruit farms without water or port-a-potties once commented to me that they don't know what it's like to work hard. He had just returned from a vacation with his family in Hawaii. A sixteen-year-old girl who went to high school with my daughter had just quit school to go to work in his processing plant with the rest of her family; they needed the money. For rent. To be paid to him. Not for health insurance premiums. They went without. Not for vacations. They went without.

"They tear apart the trailers I rent to them," he has told me.

"They are angry," I replied.

I tried to apply for a job at the national park once, as a winter interpreter. I used to write a column for *Legacy*, the magazine of the National Association for Interpretation, made up mostly of park personnel, interpreters, and museum personnel. I started out in college wanting to train to be a wildlife biologist, but I was told that the field was not integrated. So I trained as a museum curator but discovered that the field was not integrated. So I trained as a schoolteacher but discovered that the field was not integrated. So I made lemonade. I lectured about what was least desirable about me in the job market: I was an Indian. And I wrote about it, mostly with beauty, because that's all that park interpreters and museum personnel and other educators like to hear about. They certainly don't like hearing about how Native people might actually make pretty good park and museum interpreters and schoolteachers.

I like writing about beauty, not about racism. But the personnel director at the national park refused to give me an application. Easy out for them, I think. No application, no discrimination. No paper trail. Too bad. Professional credentials aside, after several thousand years in the neighborhood, my family knows a lot about the place. Beautiful stuff. Not just my family's loss, financially. Yours, too, culturally. Yours, too, in terms of beauty: The beauty of story. The beauty of history and natural history. The beauty of diversity. But I guess they were afraid that I only knew how to talk about Indian stuff, that maybe I couldn't pick up a raccoon skull and identify it as *Procyon lotor* or talk about hormone induction caused by DDT and PCBs, or talk about my non-Indian relatives who homesteaded here. And because of all those myths about us being defeated and reduced to nothing and losing our language and our culture, I guess that there would be no reason to teach white people the mnemonic device used in the Ojibwe language to recognize the spring call of a male cardinal . . .

The dominant culture also lost out in its ability to see past the concept of "other," in its lack of opportunity to learn to socialize with different people, to do business with different people without bullying and warfare. You see . . . incompetence at home can translate into incompetence abroad. I'm not sure that ignorance can sustain itself, even in northern Michigan, a place that considers itself more provincial than it really is. Unfortunately, those who control public jobs in northwest Lower Michigan don't consider themselves as practitioners of discrimination. They merely hire people they know already, from cultural experiences they know already. And since they don't work and socialize with Native Americans, they don't really know of any in the workplace that they might maneuver into a job opening or use to meet an institutional need. However unintentional, the system, in practice, excludes Indians from equal employment opportunity. Sometimes doing the wrong thing is just so darned easy, that it takes serious, conscious effort to do the right thing.

I have met scholars from all over the country who have come to northern Michigan to vacation and are dumbfounded by the blatant racism and the apparent lack of cultural diversity. One woman who went away for several years and taught at the University of Michigan came home and supplemented her income by adjunct teaching at Northwestern Michigan College in Traverse City. She found herself wondering, "Who sucked all the diversity out of the classroom?" I have been asked, frequently, how do the young people who come out of this enclave perform in the rest of the country? And I respond simply that I doubt if they have to. Our culture is currently set up to provide them with privileges that go beyond their normal abilities, to allow them to succeed with lesser qualifications and lesser effort. Well, here, at least.

Recently I was told by an inebriated young white high school teacher to leave the table at an educational banquet to which I had been invited. The individual who took it upon himself to withdraw my invitation did not like the topics I write and lecture about and consequently frequently discuss when education is the subject at hand. I hadn't really done anything wrong. I'd merely spoken confidently while keeping my head high. I'd quoted statistics from state and federal institutions, a book by a constitutional scholar, and other published studies. I was also told by my "colleague" not to laugh, not to talk, and not to smile. I was told, "I don't want to look at you sitting there thinking that you know anything about anything." Apparently I was not being docile enough to comply with his perception of a female minority. He leaned in beyond the borders of personal space, his fists were clenched, his teeth were clenched, and he had lowered his voice to a hoarse hissing whisper, as though he were experienced in keeping the volume down in a public setting while intimidating someone he thought of as vulnerable. As the situation progressed, he began to rigidly lurch upwards with each "Don't . . ." and he verbally and physically thrust my way. It was not an encounter that lasted a few moments or that would result in embarrassment or apology on his part. It was lengthy enough to display itself as a repeat behavior pattern by a possible abuser. But, since I've had twenty-five years of experience as an educator in both regular and special education, and I've worked with high school and college students, adults, and soldiers, I am not easily intimidated by a twenty-something with a crew cut who might think I am lesser than him merely because I am a woman and a minority.

As a minority in a primarily white profession, I'm used to being dismissed and even attacked. So I hold my own. I do not run. I smile, I laugh, I joke, I quote statistics, and I make it clear that I am not disturbed by the notion that my facts, figures, quotations and sociological theories upset the status quo. I am in fact dissatisfied with the status quo. Shaking things up and making people think is a nonlitigious way of provoking change and thought in a profession known for its poor skill levels and poor sociological performance, in a geographical region that is known for its segregation and its poor sociological performance. It's also a way to get pertinent information out to the public in an era when school newsletters are produced by public relations firms and are sometimes written in such a way as to mislead the public and promulgate ignorance.

However, since this banquet was part of a class for schoolteachers that is run not unlike a kindergarten class, the students were beginning their minipresentations for one another and the visiting guests, and no one was really in charge to the extent of being capable of responding to the fact that a white male had arrived, open beer in hand, staggering drunk, waving a remnant of a six-pack, and was intimidating a female minority under the auspices of a university class for schoolteachers. So I left, not only the table, but the event itself. It was, after all, time for a young blonde in tottering heels to give her show-and-tell-caliber presentation for a predestined A in a class that was based upon keeping warm bodies happy and uneducated for the purposes of generating income for salaries in an institution of higher education . . . in an era when education is less about education than it is about credentials for the privileged.

As I drove from one end of Traverse City to the other, and home to the safety of my own family and farm, I couldn't help but fear for the people this high school teacher is in close contact with. If he is so readily able to justify treating a fifty-year-old woman with several times his experience and credentials that way in front of a table full of witnesses, how is he going to treat the students in his class when he thinks that no one is within earshot? What kind of damage will he do to a teenage girl who is already distressed over something age appropriate, like wondering if she has body odor? Or to a minority teen who has spent five days a week, nine months a year observing the fact that no people of color ever rise to a position of authority by obtaining employment within the authoritarian walls of the public schools he has attended all of his life in northwest Lower Michigan? Or the young man who has seen his father abuse his mother or speak irrationally about minorities and is trying to formulate his own opinions that might be less repressive than those modeled to him? Children are vulnerable, and there is no room for an abuser in the public school system. It is not only against the law to abuse a child physically; it is also against the law to abuse a child emotionally. Who was supervising the young educator of young people in a Traverse City high school, the teacher who cannot tolerate ideas different from his own, let alone teach people to look for new ideas? What impact does his potentially damaging behavior have on the community in which my children and I must function? What is he really teaching?

A fellow "teacher" of this youngster, a twenty-something blonde in crippling heels and tight dress, joined in the attack. "And what school do *you* teach at?" she dangled the participle through a snarl, confident that she had put me in my place, confident that the fact that she'd secured a position in an all-white profession in an all-white school district made her a superior human being over a minority of twice her experience and credentials. And this allowed her to reach out and abuse someone who was surely lesser, surely expendable. And I wondered, once again, who was in charge at that Traverse City high school, and what flaw in his personality made him feel comfortable by surrounding himself with the vicious, the immature, and the culturally incompetent? What lack of professional training and cultural exposure at the university level, beyond that which I had experienced that day, left him unable to break a self-perpetuating chain of abuse and misbehavior? What lack of responsible professional supervision left the gaping holes in cultural competence that made him feel able to or willing to put in charge of classrooms full of young people other young people who themselves thrive upon abuse? And how could students and parents of color possibly survive in such a setting of condemnation, a setting in which their own failure would be a prerequisite for the emotional satisfaction and economic reward of those whose job success came not as a result of academic credentials, but as a result of parental economic success and white conformity?

Oh, that's right, these things are sacred cows. I'm not supposed to acknowledge the fact that teachers are no longer underpaid, that the profession is predominantly white, and that the gap between what the average public school teacher or administrator is paid and what the average Native American is paid is proportionally equivalent to what the average CEO of a major multinational corporation is paid and what the average public school employee is paid. That's right. I'm not supposed to talk about the gap between the middle class and the rest of us, disproportionately people of color. I'm not supposed to talk about the whitening of the field of education now that it's no longer a low-paying profession. And I'm not supposed to talk about education as day care, as opposed to education as edification. I'm not supposed to talk about the fact that, nationwide, the university program with the lowest entry requirements is educational administration, followed by elementary education, followed by secondary education . . . I'm not supposed to ask how this happened, how these jobs stopped being competitive and became gifts of appointment for the well-connected and bullies.

I do not work at Traverse City Area Public Schools, although I was a substitute teacher there for six years, with no hope of advancement from temporary, part-time status. After the first few years, I withdrew my application for full-time employment, in the hope that it would make me less of a threat to the white "colleagues" who chose to be abusive to me. I finally left because of that racism, not by the students and parents, but increasingly by the staff, who grew younger and were made up more and more of newcomers from downstate who were fleeing the urban problems of the places where they had grown up and who had predetermined judgments about people like me. This was long before I had become verbal about minority issues, long before I began writing and reviewing and lecturing about racism in education at universities. I was about as user-friendly an Indian as you could get back then. Docile. "Yes, sir. No, sir." I sat quietly and took verbal abuse back then. I took blame for things I did not do. I bent over backward to help make the status quo move as smoothly as possible.

I spoke up on behalf of a Native American student once, and found myself physically assaulted, threatened, too frightened to go to my supervisors to report the racial epithets and abuse. The school principal who assaulted me, threatened me, convinced me that I was lesser, dirt, worthless, without protection and value within the school system—because of something I have no control over, my color—is still a principal in Traverse City. And another principal, one who stalked my daughter and me, threatened to hurt my daughter, is the superintendent of a suburban school district not far away. They will both retire with full benefits, earning more in retirement than the average Indian earns in a lifetime. They will leave carnage in their paths. Their victims will not merely be the "others," the expendable, they will be the weak, the handicapped, the needy. . . . And this, this is important: they will be you and your children because your family will have been deprived of the benefit of living with diversity, of living in a world that is bigger than that which you can control—because you cannot control everything. So you didn't have the benefit of me and my skills. You didn't have the other minority teachers who excelled against all odds, who attended college and did well against all odds. You've had the lucky, the affluent, the white, and the abusers. And sometimes you get underachievers. Do you feel, under these circumstances, that your children have been well educated, that they can survive in today's increasingly small world, in which white privilege is a dwindling commodity?

Back then, really only a few years ago, not even a generation, I was compliant. I was docile. I was a good Indian. That was before I had opened a Pandora's box of racist books to be reviewed . . . before I had opened my heart and soul to speak out about not only the beauty and grace of the Native people of northern Michigan, my children, my family, my friends, my community, my nurturing, life-giving lakes, hills, and forests . . . but also about the ignorance, racism, hatred, and abuse that threaten that beauty every day. Today I am a different woman. Today I move mountains, and a boorish, boyish, manipulative, self-centered young teacher, Traverse City's high school role model for the region's youth, will not stand in my way, not with his clenched fists, his clenched teeth, his hissed insults, commands, and threats. Not with his white male privilege. Our beauty, our competence, and our motivation to succeed and better ourselves are bigger and stronger than his selfishness and his ignorance. And if that's not an argument for affirmative action, I don't know what is.

I have spoken with the director of Northwestern Michigan College's University Center, the institution that rewarded this young David-without-a-Goliath with teacher recertification credit for showing up inebriated and in need of a victim; I have spoken with the director of personnel at Traverse City Area Public Schools; and I have informed them that it is not acceptable for me (or anyone) to be afraid to speak out or to write about racism in Traverse City's educational circles, that abusive behavior is not an acceptable response to statistics and theories about racism and sexism of which one does not approve. It is not acceptable to assume that, because one is female and one is a minority, one is vulnerable and an acceptable victim or that one is also therefore underqualified, inexperienced, or lesser in any way. I suspect that young David thought I could not possibly be a credible source of professional information because of what he perceived as my lesser socioeconomic and sexual status. This is not behavior I wish to continue to be modeled in local schools. I have to live in this community, and if it is increasingly made up of graduates of an increasingly biased educational system, it becomes increasingly uncomfortable and unsafe. I do not wish to be one of Jim Crow's children. I do not wish my neighbors' children to attend public institutions that teach them how to become the cyclical abusers of Jim Crow's children.

The director of personnel at Traverse City Area Public Schools is a woman. Only a few years ago, her chair was filled by a man. I suspect that she has earned her stripes in a less-than-supportive work environment. Although the field of education is still made up of about three-fourths women, educational administration is still made up of about three-fourths men. This is an improvement over even two decades ago, when there was still about an 80 percent split. Still, the field of education remains one of the least sexually and racially integrated professions in the country. The implications are profound. Five days a week, nine or more months of the year, we model a system of sexist and racist cultural and behavioral guidelines to our children in publicly funded institutionalized settings from kindergarten through graduate school.

Although the personnel director seems to understand my feelings about inappropriate behavior and sexism, she still doesn't understand my charges of racism. And I fear that, now that I have exposed the fact that I am a Native American, her tolerance and patience are dwindling to disinterest. Ah, another disgruntled Indian. And that will be that. She has gone out of her way to point out to me that Traverse City Area Public Schools now has a black male high school teacher. I congratulate her and urge her to go out of her way to make sure that he is comfortable and treated with respect. I do not antagonize her by telling her that one black guy on staff doesn't even qualify as a speed bump on the superhighway of multigenerational racism. But I let her know that racism was a significant contributor to my choice of leaving the not-so-high-paying job of substitute teaching. Too bad, because I was good at it.

For all of her listening and inaction, she cannot take away the fact that my son, who has just completed second grade, has recently witnessed his mother being hissed to like an unwanted dog . . . for the crimes of being colored in public, for not keeping her head down, staying in her place, or accepting a status quo of culturally walking two steps behind, as well as for the crimes of quoting state and federal statistics and an award-winning author of nonfiction. It is unacceptable that people of color in this community remain unseen and unheard. I have watched the gender and racial progress of the sixties and seventies slip backward in my home community. Issues that we associate with the Deep South or with our state and nation's capitals are not far away.

As in the declarations of some of the segregationists Peter Irons quotes in *Jim Crow's Children*, I often hear the claims, "There's no racism here," or, "All the minorities are happy in the schools here," or, "We're meeting the needs of all of the minorities here." In fact, only a few short decades ago, Michigan's membership in the Ku Klux Klan was triple that of Mississippi. Among minorities in the state of Michigan, Traverse City is known as the sister city to Pulaski, Tennessee. It is a joke of sorts, because we know that few if any people in Traverse City are aware that Pulaski, Tennessee, is the birthplace of the Ku Klux Klan. Even scarier, we wonder if enough of northwest Lower Michigan's residents care. This may seem combative, but the fear with which we live is as real as the fear with which you live. Some of you are as scary, irrational, and heartless to us, as people of color are to many of you. When our cars break down, we pray that the next car that stops will contain people like us . . . you know, nice people, the kind that won't rob us, threaten us, take advantage of us. Odd, isn't it? You may have grown up thinking that you have a patent on that particular line of thought.

Looking for fictional characters to give voice to real-life issues can be tiresome. And if I have anything for which to thank Traverse City Public School's young teacher-as-bully, it is for making me indignant enough to know that I have a right to speak openly about ignorance, hatred, and racism, without pretending that it happened to someone else. The young man has, I suspect, ambitions to become a public school administrator, a profession that ranks high among perpetrators of domestic violence. He was wearing the telltale brown polyester suit that has become a uniform for the profession, and I suspect, from things that he said that night, that teaching is difficult for him. Many administrators become administrators because they cannot cope with children and parents. The ones who thrive on community interaction and problem-solving are a great gift to their community. So I worry, worry that unsuccessful teachers and bullies do not make for a comfortable administrative setting that allows anyone but the most affluent white teachers, students, and families to function in comfort. I also worry that racism based upon contention over job resources could be exacerbated even further; that white male students are being given the impression that they do not necessarily have to work hard at succeeding in the workplace; and that white female students are being given the impression that they do not necessarily have to work hard at succeeding in the workplace because marrying a white male is their best career strategy. These are examples of what can go wrong within a community if the educational system models sexism, racism, and intimidation.

Through racism the community at large loses brave and broad thinkers of color. It loses people of color as producers and consumers, as environmentalists and all of the other niches that need to be filled by those who can respond to change by thinking out of the box. By being kept on the bottom, people of color are deprived of opportunities at being philanthropists, conservationists, and all of the other types of leaders that better the lives of everyone. In the long run, sharing opportunity in America benefits everyone, even the privileged.

· 6 ·

Falcon Clan Meets Indian Boarding School

*I*ma Pipiig was like a sparrow hawk dodging past a plate-glass window. There was nothing in her early hawk childhood to prepare her for this phenomenon. Trees. Clear, crisp leaves moving in the breeze, then gone, a glare, loss of bearings in dive and space.

She had grown up in a loving family of sparrow hawks, demure, part of the food chain, honest in their own role in nature. Loving parents who chased down hundreds of chipping sparrows and the occasional young gull as a special meaty treat for their brood. These were good things, and this was a good life.

But they needed more, they were told, these loving parents. They needed to provide more for their children—a *different* life way, a *different* set of values, a *new* way to dive and dip and follow the breezes. ENTER—EDUCATION . . . CATHOLIC PAVE-THE-WAY-FOR-THE-CAPITALIST-RIP-YOU-OFF-FOR-EVERYTHING-YOU'VE-GOT-UNTIL-YOU'RE-DEAD-AS-A-DOORNAIL-EDUCATION, PUBLIC RIP-YOU-OFF-FOR-THE-HIGHEST-SALARIES-WE-CAN-GET-WITHOUT-WORKING-AS-HARD-AS-YOU-FOR-A-LIVING-AND-PROVIDING-YOU-WITH-ANY-SERVICES-THAT-MIGHT-INTERFERE-WITH-OUR-OWN-PROSPERITY-EDUCATION. *MANDATORY* PUBLIC EDUCATION, THROW-YOUR-COLORED-ASS-IN-JAIL-PUBLIC-EDUCATION, YOU'RE-STUCK-AND-YOU-GOTTA-PAY-US-AND-PLAY-THE-GAME-OUR-WAY-OR-WE'LL-TAKE-YOUR-CHILDREN-AWAY-FROM-YOU-AND-JEOPARDIZE-THEIR-SAFETY-EDUCATION. Compulsory cultural abuse.

The toughest part was the glass—reflective, fleeting, shiny but deadly.

And so the sparrow hawk families dived and dipped, adjusting to the inconsistent images that appeared in the plate-glass barriers, varying with the whims of those who had installed them—just as the reflections of the *real* world varied with movement of sun and clouds. Every slight error in judgment resulted in loss of energy, loss of resource, and loss of life, until so many of their spirits were broken, like cold and limp feathered necks. First shocked, then unconscious, then lifeless. Eyes ringed by immobile gray rims of stiffening gossamer skin. Feathers ruffled, but still lovely, singular prizes to be taken home as symbols of vanishing lifestyles and vanishing wilderness by the installers of the new vision.

Ima Pipiig had made a big mistake. She had spoken her heart and soul. She had been brave for a brief moment. She had contemplated doing the forbidden—holding her head up, as though she had civil rights, as though she had the same value to society and the ecosystem as a white human being. Silly sparrow hawk, she had opened her beak and shrieked, shrieked in the language of sparrow hawk, the high pitched and desperate, "Kai, kai, kai!" Eight out of ten times that Ima Pipiig tried to reproduce and fend for her children, to dip and to dive, to keep them merely safe and alive—SAFE, silly Ima Pipiig . . . wanted to keep her babies safe—eight out of ten times, Ima Pipiig failed. The sparrow hawks would only succeed if Ima Pipiig tried ten times or more. Because without this relentless, head-beating-against-the-wall effort toward mere survival, the sparrow hawk part of the Ojibwe culture would die, and thousands of years of success and beauty would die with it.

Stupid, stupid, all-white teachers—they would never know that they had robbed even themselves and their very own prodigious white and irresponsible offspring of something as precious as the tiger, the panther, the passenger pigeon, the last buried, earthen preserve of Tyrannosaurus Rex . . . the last of the sparrow hawk bits and pieces, dips and dives, of the Ojibwe culture. Because, if these white teachers were to have a 100-percent-success-rate at acculturation and were to get the bonuses and the benefits, and the real-estate-at-top-value-with-really-cool-good-fishing-and-hunting-and-historical-FANTASIES-intact, then they were going to have to get rid of the goddamn Indians. Because the goddamn Indians did not have perfect attendance at school and at parent teacher conferences, and they insisted that the Michigan Educational Assessment Program met the needs of the teachers more than the needs of the Indians, and they insisted that having only white people working in the schools gave both Indian and white kids a terrible message about socioeconomic layering in society, and they complained that the books about Indians written by white people about Indians were not as good as the books about Indians by Indians, even though ordering Indian books from the special Indian catalog could take as much as an extra twenty minutes, and the Indians didn't give a shit that the school employees might have to work another twenty minutes over thirty-five or forty hours a week, because they worked seventy hours a week for less pay . . . And dear lord Jesus, didn't they deserve their poverty, those Indians—because they were ignorant and dirty and alcoholics and lived off welfare; and they only had those college degrees with all A's because they got a bunch of scholarships because they were colored and everybody felt sorry for them because they were colored and dressed funny and don't wear spike heels and pantyhose and expensive dresses in snowstorms like we do; and THEY EAT ROADKILL, and they're stupid as hell, which is why they can't get real jobs like the rest of us who work hard, thirty-five or forty hours a week; and if we could get rid of the Indians, we could get the Golden Apple Award, which is the Michigan-State-Find-Your-Butt-With-Both-Hands-in-the-Dark-Award for school districts with high-income residents who score higher in the Michigan Educational Assessment Program tests because affluent parents' children score higher on those tests; and then we can claim credit for the success we had nothing to do with, and I don't have to really work as hard as they do for a living or compensate for the fact that I came from the bottom quarter of my freshman class in college, which is where 75 percent of my peers and I came from, and dear lord Jesus, I really only got this job because I wear spike heels and pantyhose and stupid dresses that no one else in this school district full of stupid working-class people wear, but I looked really good to the dumb white guys in brown polyester suits who go to the right church and automatically get these jobs and like the fact that I wear this bra that shows pointy tits under this bleach-blond coif that doesn't move, even when I have sex; and dear lord Jesus, where do these Indians get off, expecting *me* to work as hard as *them*, because they are different, and dirty and filthy, and they smell like sweat and wood smoke, and who in their right mind would think that wood smoke smells good for anything but roasting marshmallows on the beach?

· 7 ·

Venn Diagrams
(We Are a Subset of America . . .)

*W*here I come from, wood smoke is perfume. We do not divide it up into two words, as you do. We say it as one: woodsmoke. It is a concept, a complete whole, separate from other forms of smoke, mist, or visible entities in our clear, clean air. It is not in the least generic, as are the words "wood" and "smoke" in mainstream English. It is so complex a term, that it actually has subgroups of perceptions and indications. When one of us uses the word "woodsmoke," it immediately invokes the question: *What kind of woodsmoke?* Ah, the nuances. Hardwood smoke versus softwood smoke. Old, dry, and papery versus well-seasoned versus green versus seasoned and wet. And then there are the woods themselves . . . Birch is a personal favorite of mine. But I appreciate the circumstances under which the others are used and when they are perfect for what is going on around a fire that is transforming that particular piece of wood into a certain variety of perfume.

Maple wood used to boil down maple syrup in the sunshine on a bed of snow in February or March. . . . Now, *that* is a very special type of perfume. Applying this type of perfume takes at a very minimum several hours. It involves going out to one of the barns, sorting through boxes and boxes of canning jars, and finding the full box of jars set aside just for this purpose . . . old mayonnaise jars, horseradish jars, and other commercial jars that fit canning lids. It is not about the lids fitting the jars; it is about the jars fitting the lids. We don't use those jars for pressure canning because they are not designed to withstand the same amount of pressure. They could burst in a canner, spoiling a lot of hard-earned homegrown and home-procured food products. So we save them for pickles or for making maple syrup.

We don't have a word in Anishinabemoin for maple syrup. We have words for the sap and for the sugar. Making the maple syrup has history bigger than my own memories of making maple syrup. Making maple syrup is a transitional activity, a marker of historical change in the culture and adaptation techniques of the Anishinabe people. Originally we didn't make maple syrup as a long-term phenomenon. We went straight to maple sugar. Syrup was a fun step along the way. However, the ultimate goal was a finished product that safely stored large quantities of an ample resource that makes itself available for a very short period of time each year. And that time period is broken up into sporadic fits and fizzles. When na sap runs, da sap runs, an' ya gotta make sugar when na sap iz dere, c'z dat zisbaakwit abpoo runz fast n furious til a warm wun turnzit sour. (Translation: make hay while the sun shines.)

So . . . we made sugar, and rarely syrup. And hoo-boy! Did we use da sugar! A whole nuther set of subsets of cultural and linguistic implications would apply here, but I'm trying to be brief, to give you shortcuts, y'know, subsets without contemporaneous knowledge of the other subsets or of where this particular subset comes from, as in what it's actually a subset of. And how often do I get to end sentences with prepositions? So . . . we started making more syrup than sugar. This reflects the socioeconomic and material impact that the Anishinabeg, masters of ingenuity in the field of adaptation, have continued to sustain as a result of dwindling access to our original set of natural resources . . . to which we originally had full access. (Please note the proper use of preposition in that last phrase. I *am* bilingual, and I do fluently speak, read, and write the dialect of the majority culture. Forget fluent . . . are you even moderately familiar with or respectful of my dialect, er, uhm, my subset of the American English language?)

Oh yeah, sugar to syrup. So, we've had increasingly less access to the resource, that is, the maple sap. That's increasingly less access right on up to the present. (Heh, I bet you thought that was back in the nineteenth century, didn't you?) So, Indians have had to take a less leisurely approach to preserving the sweetness of the sap. It's concentrated into an even shorter period of time because we have to concentrate on the few places left where we can do that, and they are not necessarily places where we can do something else during the somewhat slow, tedious process of boiling down hundreds of gallons of a watery substance into a solid form, which amounts to selectively removing a few sparse molecules from those gallons and gallons of sweet water. We can't be in our own seasonal homes to do other chores, sewing, mending, business correspondence, baking cookies for the school bake sale, rotating the tires on the truck. . . . So we sit and visit. And we make syrup instead of sugar. Because making syrup requires less time and less fuel (maple wood, which produces its own particular perfume when burned under a pan of evaporating maple sap, the fumes of which it mingles with beautifully, warmly, and sensuously as one moves one's lawn chair across the crust of snow to catch the moving sunlight as it travels with the hours from morning until late afternoon's blasts of heat then cold).

And jars. The canning jars, preceded by crockery jugs, are cheaper and easier than the old style bark baskets and cones we used to make and store the maple sugar . . . because of, that's right, loss of access to the birch bark via loss of access to the land bases that produce it. (These subsets could be accurately drawn in a series of Venn diagrams.) And the old syrup used to taste not only of maple smoke, but of birch smoke, too. An experienced palette can discern the two, their ratio, their quality within the finished product. Maple syrup, Anishinabe, Leelanau County, 1939. Ah . . . a good year. Light. Maple fuel with a hint of birch woodsmoke, short sap run, cold nights. Maple syrup, Anishinabe, Leelanau County, 1959, Ah . . . another good year. Short sap run, cold nights, maple fuel only. Still strong, clear, and good, with a healthy bouquet of hard, crisp woodsmoke. Maple syrup, Anishinabe, Leelanau County, 1999. Best available under the circumstances. Somewhat elongated sap run, with short bursts of too-warm weather, which caused an almost immediate souring of the sap before sufficient quantities could be gathered for a good boil. Mixed seasoned and wet, rotten maple woodsmoke with a hint of rotten poplar, plywood, and other junkwoods. It hits the palette with an almost aspartame-like-overripe-but-still-hard-as-a-rock-shipped-thousands-of-miles-commercially-mass-produced-nectarine quality. Heavy. A bit translucent, as opposed to sparkling and clear. A cream-of-tartar-like residue at the bottom of the mayonnaise jar.

When it is perfume, it is poetry. At its worst, it is still the best around. It still evokes images of the camaraderie, muscles warm from work, and the perfume, any version of that perfume will do, of woodsmoke in all of its intricacies and the memories of those intricacies—some of which go back decades, some generations.

All that, and I've only described one form of woodsmoke. Maple-syrup-making-woodsmoke. And even that is just so darned full of subsets. But there are other woodsmokes. There is fish-smoking-woodsmoke and getting-ready-to-fire-up-the-sawmill-for-the-season-woodsmoke and hot-cedar-woodstove-cooking-fire-woodsmoke and the-first-morning-fire-of-autumn-woodsmoke and "Mom-can-we-roast-marshmallows"-woodsmoke. And there's my friend Evan's favorite woodsmoke, which is so different from mine and so-gross-that-I-can't-even-tell-you-about-it-woodsmoke. All of these types of woodsmoke have subsets, which are stories and histories. They are not just subsets of material entities. They are subsets of people's lives. They are our culture and our history. They are nuanced perfumes of cultural diversity. They set us all apart from one another and record our interactions with one another.

Sometimes those interactions are pretty stinky. They need perfume to mask them. Racism. Indifference. Being too lazy to look past one's own comfort zone of cultural familiarity. Those things need masking. They need perfume. The problem is, one person's perfume is another person's poison. I like the smell of woodsmoke and human sweat. It is a good smell that evokes hard work and real chores that need to be done. It is a smell that deserves respect. I respect people who walk into a business smelling of hard work. I appreciate that they don't necessarily have the time or energy to go home and clean up before coming in to do brief shopping or business. It's a value judgment that I make and carry around with me, probably because I know what it's like to live in that subset of America.

I am also painfully aware of the subsets of Americans who do not share that value with me. They don't necessarily know what it's like to work that hard or that long. There is a perception about people on the bottom, the working underbelly of our economy, that they work less. They don't. They work more. They scramble more hours for less pay because a gallon of milk and a gallon of gasoline cost at least as much on the bottom as they do on the top of the economic food chain. Some things, like health insurance and health care, cost more. And safety nets disappear. Collision insurance on automobiles becomes cost prohibitive. People squeeze just a little more mileage out of a set of tires. Things get tough, sticky, as margins of error contract and disappear. There are only twenty-four hours in a day. Sometimes our dominant culture asks its subsets to make more out of less. Sometimes our dominant culture forgets the human qualities of its own subsets and thinks of them as just that: subsets. When those subsets are given nonhuman names and qualities, they stop being subsets. They move off on their own and become separate sets, with titles like "different," "expendable," "lazy," and "mascot." For most of America, Native Americans fall within the "expendable" subset of Americans in general most of the time, except once every four years, when we fall into the subset of "voting block."

My neighbor and dear friend, Evan, is upset with me because I indicated a desire to vote for Ralph Nader in the 2004 presidential election. Evan, a John Kerry supporter, wants things to go back to the way they were four years previously. Unfortunately, for me, a Native American, going back to the status quo of four years ago is no different than going back to the status quo of forty years ago. Native American people are still on the underbelly of America's socioeconomic heap. (Since I belong to that subset of human beings who savor the perfume of fish-smoking-woodsmoke, the term underbelly renders an entirely different subset of images and perfumes from that of your typical political economist.) Evan and I will never reconcile on these differences. Our subsets will not intersect on this particular issue. Evan has inherited wealth. I have not. Evan is a white male. I am not. Evan has a full-time job with benefits that is commensurate with his credentials. I do not.

On the other hand, Evan and I intersect, or overlap, in many ways. We both obtained our undergraduate degrees from Oberlin College at roughly the same time. We're both smart. We both work hard. We both consider owning and protecting large tracts of rural real estate/habitat as priorities for which we will work hard and make sacrifices. We both appreciate the perfume of maple woodsmoke floating and intermingling with evaporating maple sap in the aluminum-folding-chair-on-the-snow-sunshine of February and March in Leelanau County, Michigan (his house, his sap, his woodfire, my jars).

Yet Evan's very favorite kind of smoke is not woodsmoke at all. It is the smell of burning garbage. . . . Because that was his initial introduction to the concept of enjoying a fire out in the open air of nonurban America. "Dontcha remember when you were a kid on summer vacation and they would burn the garbage at the dump every Saturday?!" He punctuates his words with body language. He is delightfully alive and moving and gesturing. He is reliving his childhood with such joy that I am happy for him; he is, after all, my neighbor and friend, and I love him. He extends his hands and sweeps his arms toward his nostrils in lanky remembrance. You've got to admire that *joie de vie*.

Yuck! No, I never experienced that. I don't bag up my garbage and send it off somewhere else. I have the good fortune to have the space to compost and store recyclable materials and the will and energy to spend the time doing so. As much as I love my neighbor, I will never completely share his enthusiasm for the stench, rather than perfume, of burning garbage, just as I will never completely share his enthusiasm for merely returning to the status quo of four years ago. It is a status quo with which he is content, and I am not. On these particular issues, our subsets do not intersect.

This could be rendered quite easily as a Venn diagram. One wouldn't even have to bother looking at all the other subsets, such as what constitutes perfume to each of us and whether or not one's hours of toil are worth more than the other's. But ignoring certain subsets would involve value judgments . . . about which subsets to label as "valuable" or "expendable" and about when to do so. My values will not permit me to fall into a subset that accepts the status quo in terms of the welfare of the Anishinabe people; and I happen to think that improving the welfare of Native Americans and all people from the working underbelly of America's economy will improve the welfare of America as a whole, that big set of which I am a member of several different subsets. I hope that my particular subset in respect to this issue is not too small. One of the problems that confronts Indians is that there aren't quite enough of us to initiate a serious bus boycott.

The last couple of years, I have not had the time to share a maple-sap-boiling-maple-wood-fire with my white neighbor. I am working more hours for less pay. The gap between the number of hours I work to pay for a gallon of milk or gasoline and the number of hours he works to pay for a gallon of milk or gasoline have widened for far more than four years. I am angry when he wants to go back to the unacceptable status quo of a mere four years ago, just as he is angry that I do not care enough for him to cast a vote toward bringing his family's comfort level back to that of a mere four years ago. I am jealous when I smell that delicate blend of woodsmoke and maple sap steam on his clothing. When I smell that "Mom-can-we-roast-marshmallows"-woodsmoke on his clothing and not on mine, I worry for my children and the things I cannot give them, including my time. I worry even more when I realize that Evan has been so poorly educated socially that he cannot see downhill, below his own socioeconomic comfort level, to see the extent to which I am struggling—that he cannot see that my children have the right to be educated without my forfeiture of mammograms or dental care or safety on the public roads. You see, in some cases, the smell of woodsmoke carries with it connotations of safety, time invested in one's children, even economic security. How can these things be anything less than perfume? How can this perfume be any less valuable than a white male's introduction to the world of rural America and his own personal transition from urban life to the usurpation of rural America for the benefit of his own offspring, the last holdout of America's unwanted Indian occupants? How can this perfume be any less valuable than the smell of urban America's burning garbage?

• 8 •

Educating Ima

$\mathscr{I}$ma Pipiig withdrew, quietly, after her first few years of unsuccessful attempts at finding employment in the public educational institutions of northwest Lower Michigan. The white-flightists were vicious, often verbally and physically abusive, and the educational jobs were coveted because they were among the highest-paying jobs in the region. So Ima Pipiig waited a few more years, hoping that a higher caliber of white-flightists might have moved into the region and that she might have finally built up sufficient credentials to be considered more than an ignorant Indian to the ignorant educators of northwest Lower Michigan's public institutions of education. She wrote children's books, she wrote scholarly articles, she lectured in museums and universities, and she guest lectured in teacher education courses at various colleges and universities everywhere but northwest Lower Michigan.

Ima Pipiig had made the mistake of believing the myths she had heard about laws and ethics in her public education courses, a post-high-school-extension-of-the-lies-she-had-heard-since-grammar-school. So now, foolishly believing in the Constitution of the United States and its vague notions about equality, she had approached an educator . . . in higher education. BIG MISTAKE. Ima Pipiig had had fantasies of becoming recertified to teach public school—and actually getting a job as a public school teacher—ha, ha, ha . . . or, if unsuccessful, of filing a lawsuit against what had become locally an all-white field of education, the all-white elitist teachers' union—as though anyone cared that the field was all-white, and that straight-A minority candidates like Ima Pipiig got passed up for employment for decades on end in favor of young-and-stupid, young-and-uncaring, young-and-white, young-and-less-qualified applicants for teaching jobs. But come on, no local white-flight lawyer would see the value in a lawsuit that held the credentials of a less-than-human colored person against those of all those white people who made enough money to buy suits and dresses and pointed high heels and pointy brassieres . . . because, after all, they were all on equal footing . . . those Indians must have fantasized the racism and the discrimination. Those Indians must have blown their inheritance, must have proved themselves incapable of working thirty-five or forty hours a week from the very beginning, must have been ignorant and different and out of touch with the basic tenets of the working world around them . . . welfare bums . . . recreational fish thieves . . . always wanting something for nothing . . . All of those dozens of Indians who had obtained teaching credentials and were incapable of finding teaching jobs in the public institutions of northwest Lower Michigan must have all had bad personalities . . .

Ima Pipiig had originally been trained as a museum curator. But she found out that the field was not integrated. So Ima Pipiig trained as a teacher. But she found out that the field was not integrated.

Ima Pipiig worked her way through undergraduate school doing temporary, part-time unskilled labor. Ima Pipiig worked her way through graduate school doing temporary, part-time unskilled labor. Ima Pipiig funded her postgraduate studies doing temporary part-time unskilled labor. She found out that that particular field was integrated. Heavily.

Ima Pipiiig made the appointment by telephone and came to the white woman's office at the University Center of Northwest Lower Michigan at the appointed time. She and her daughter stood only halfway into the office, ready to run, because the chairs were neither empty nor inviting, and Florence Reznik looked nervous, perhaps even in fear of being soiled by their presence. Ima Pipiig presented the white woman with her academic credentials, assuming that they would be of value, have an impact, earn her a respectful tidbit of attention, and even hope, in terms of her future academic success. After all, all Ima Pipiig really wanted to do was to reinstate or even expand her teaching credentials, the ones she had let lapse—not because she was not good at taking the light and fluffy education recertification courses while working full time—but because she could not afford to pay the tuition, earning only minimum wage or less at the temporary, part-time unskilled labor she had been restricted to since she had returned to northwest Lower Michigan from the southwestern United States, where integration in education was less of a phenomenon, though still an uphill battle.

Ima Pipiig had taken the National Teacher Exam, the exam that would, within a few years, be determined by the Michigan Education Association to be too hard for white teachers to take. And Ima Pipiig would score in the ninety-sixth percentile ranking for people who had masters' degrees and doctorates. And she would score in the hundredth percentile ranking in the professional knowledge core area, the one that reflected the basic knowledge taught in all those years of education courses. And Ima Pipiig would not have taken a single course in education . . . because the courses in education were so Mickey Mouse, so immature, so juvenile, so designed for privileged white kids who went to college to avoid hard physical labor, that anybody, even a colored girl from the bush like Ima Pipiig, could do well in them and could score in the hundredth percentile ranking . . . but it didn't count because she was colored and must have gone to college for free, because they felt sorry for her because she was colored, and she couldn't possibly compete with them, because they were white, and they knew what white people expected of people with college degrees, especially educators, who were supposed to educate in the status quo. . . .

Ima Pipiig was the *first* Native American in the history of the National Teacher Exam to pass the exam the first time because it was so culturally biased—imagine that! She was the *first*—just like Rosa Parks was the *first* black woman to hold on in that seat in the front of the bus long enough for the police to arrive . . . All that Ima Pipiig had to get her through the simplistic white test designed for white children of white supremacists was common sense . . . Wow! Just intelligence . . . Wow! She had become a tribute to the low level of expectations in the field of white education. Ima Pipiig did not have to be exceptional, she merely had to find her butt with both hands in the dark . . . the professional standard of white educators in America, the ones who did not expect people of color who were more competent than them to show up. . . .

The woman behind the desk was not to be fazed by a mere Indian. She spoke down to Ima Pipiig most pleasantly, outlining what was necessary to become certified to teach in the state of Michigan, but not really looking at Ima Pipiig. The woman was looking through her, annoyed that she had to give the foolish Indian woman her time instead of just mailing her a list of the course requirements. And when Ima Pipiig finally got the white woman to look at the pages and pages of paper, to see the degrees and certifications and licenses and awards and recommendations that testified to a far more extensive and successful career in higher education than the woman herself had enjoyed, the white woman exclaimed in surprise, realizing that Ima Pipiig had handed her the papers for a purpose. Unknown to Florence Reznik, her initial assumption that Ima Pipiig was without significant credentials, as revealed by her surprise, sank like a knife into the heart and mind of Ima Pipiig's college-aged daughter who stood, almost cowering, behind her mother's arm in the oppressive environment of unwelcomeness . . .

There was potential for certification and recertification in several subjects there in Ima Pipiig's papers, even though there was no hope for a job, because, after all, there were no Indian schools in the area. And like many of the self-proclaimed liberals who had recently moved north to the Twin Bay City region, she suggested that Ima Pipiig move elsewhere, perhaps farther north, to a more remote region, where there might be a tribal school where a teacher of color might be welcome . . . Still, the Indian, in spite of her lack of potential in the teaching profession in the lower peninsula of Michigan, seemed resolved to become certified again; and she would serve well as a warm body in the university center's classrooms. And that was part of what Florence Reznik's job was about—fooling people into thinking that they were qualified to do anything but clean toilets with the credentials she provided, even if one was not white. No matter, Ima Pipiig probably didn't have to dig very deep into her pockets for time and effort and tuition . . . Those Indians probably all went to school for free, and they seemed to spend their whole lives on welfare, at the expense of people like Florence Reznik who worked thirty-five to forty-five hours a week for at least ten or fifteen years before they could retire at 60 percent pay; and if they were really serious about being middle class, those Indians should learn what it's like to work thirty-five or forty-five hours a week instead of what they really do work. So Florence Reznik, eventually, after getting over being soiled and annoyed by an Indian-with-a-bad-attitude and her daughter, would begin to figure out a way that even poor, desperate Ima Pipiig could meet her needs. Instead of looking upon the Indian woman trailing her daughter as a liability, Florence Reznik knew, that in the true spirit of diversity in education, she should look upon her as an opportunity.

Florence Reznik used every opportunity possible to get warm bodies into her classroom, so that she could get funding for her class and stay employed just a little bit longer, while she finished up her doctorate, which would increase her salary significantly and put her on track for tenure . . .

After that visit was over, Ima Pipiig felt less secure in her hopes that the racism in education in northwest Lower Michigan had improved from what she perceived to be an unbeatable low a few years earlier. After that visit was over, Ima Pipiig did not plan to go back to the university center, ever. After that visit was over, Ima Pipiig wanted to bathe. And after that visit was over, and after the Indian and her teenaged daughter had climbed into their big dump truck and driven back to the comfort of the farm, the child did something Ima Pipiig had never dreamed she would do. The girl, herself a freshman and a presidential scholar at the very same college—an overachieving Indian child, cut from the same stone as her overachieving role model of a mother, with several college credits in chemistry and math under her belt before she graduated from high school, in spite of the fact that she worked ten or twenty hours a week or more on the family farm—scrambled under the counter in her mother's never-use-them-much pots-and-pans-cupboard and pulled out a full quart jar of slivovitz. It was a Czechoslovakian type of white lightning distilled from fermented plums and had been presented to the family the previous Christmas by neighbors. And now the girl, who had never had more than a few sips of beer in her life, poured herself a tall water glass of the clear liquid. Ima Pipiig dove and screamed and threw the strong liquor down the sink.

The girl cried and hung on to the faucet for support. "It's been a long time since I've ever seen anyone treat you so disrespectfully, Mom." And she was right. Ima Pipiig had done her best to shelter the girl from her interactions with white educators, had kept her within a comfortable circle of Indians and intellectuals and loving neighbors who would no more talk down to Ima Pipiig than beat a dog. The girl was stunned that someone would treat that way an individual with the credentials and accomplishments of her mother, especially knowing the sacrifices and excessive labor that her mother, a person of color, had had to put in to get her degrees and awards and high grade point averages (because the child had, after all, done the same thing herself—getting college credit through courses on the Internet, having surpassed the skills of her all-white high school teachers). The mother, of course, had been accustomed to it and expected no less than abuse in the form of dismissing body language and tone of voice. But now she'd gotten full of herself and her accomplishments and had put out a feeler within the educational community, and she had brought the child along to show her how it was done; and the child had seen full-face how a white educator treats an adult Indian, one who is not little and cute, one who is middle-aged and potentially a pain in the ass. And it was a blow that nineteen years of protection and praise and pressure to overachieve had not prepared the child for. As beautiful and functional as the Anishinabe culture had been, it could not have prepared the child for the level of ignorance and racism that she would encounter in the outsiders' real world, especially the real world of higher education. In some ways, Anishinabe children were as vulnerable to excessive abuses that were tolerated by the dominant culture as porcupines were to Buicks on pavement.

Seeing that a course in Native American literature, to be offered for the first time during the next year, would meet a requirement for one of her endorsements, Ima Pipiig asked if she could teach the course, in exchange for college credit for the course. She was, after all, better connected in the field of Native American literature than anyone she knew of in Twin Bay City. She and several other Native American authors corresponded regularly, and Ima Pipiig wrote on the topic for textbooks and periodicals. But Ima Pipiig was told no, we'll find a teacher, and Ima Pipiig knew it would be a white person, and Ima Pipiig knew that the course would be soft of content and bland.

Ima Pipiig had fantasized briefly that she could beat the white system in this white-flight community; and the white woman who implemented the university center satellite program for distant Iron State University saw the window of opportunity, the weakness, the visions of grandeur, racial equality, and self-respect . . . It took her a couple of weeks to find the right venue, the right circumstances, but eventually, it happened—and Ima Pipiig was duped into taking part in the higher education system, of wasting her hard-earned, less-than-minimum-wage-more-than-thirty-five-or-forty-hours-a-week-colored-woman-dollars on the education-roulette-wheel. Silly Ima Pipiig . . .

"Ima? Ima Pee-pig?" Florence Reznik mispronounced the name.

"Buh-BEEG." The owner gently corrected.

"This is Florence Reznik, from the university center . . ."

"Hi!"

When Ima Pipiig answered the phone between eight and five, she knew that there was potentially money involved, from people in public institutions who only worked from eight to five. Besides, Ima Pipiig was more forgiving about abuse to herself than Birdie, who loved her mother and hated to see her hurt—just as Ima Pipiig was not tolerant of abuse to young Birdie and her brother. Ima Pipiig even found Florence Reznik likeable in some ways. So Ima Pipiig didn't mind talking to Florence Reznik. She always considered it an opportunity to educate the educator.

Florence had once hired Ima Pipiig to speak at the university center, at her OK-you're-close-and-it's-short-notice-and-you're-not-trying-to-book-me-ahead-for-less-than-a-fraction-of-what-a-white-person-with-my-credentials-makes-so-you-can-have-me-real-cheap-'cause-I-got-nothing-else-on-my-colored-horizons-anyway rate. And even though Ima Pipiig didn't make a living wage that included retirement or medical and dental on the speaking engagement, Ima Pipiig had wooed the whiz-bang out of those folks and had made a working wage on prints and other high-markup artwork, so it had been worth it. Over the years, in an effort to meet the needs of her family, Ima Pipiig had learned how to be an ethnic lawn jockey for the educators of Twin Bay City and northwest Lower Michigan. She gave them the warm-and-fuzzy cute Indian stories that they needed. And she always snuck in a little bit more. She always considered it an opportunity to educate the educator.

Ima Pipiig had learned how to educate educators while being a cultural prostitute for white educators. So now, Ima Pipiig was practically groveling. She was desperate. Her daughter was in college. Ima Pipiig couldn't afford a mortgage and car payments that would qualify her daughter for financial aid.

She lived, instead, in a one-bedroom house that was completely paid for, because it had been homebuilt; and she drove a twenty-year-old-dependable-rust-bucket of a vehicle to be able to pay the half of the tuition and fees that wasn't covered by the "full" academic scholarship. And Florence Reznik knew an exposed neck when she saw one, a tender underbelly, a weak and helpless victim, a colored woman, the lowest-of-the-low colored women—a Native American female, lower even than a black woman, lower even than a light-skinned Mexican. Ima Pipiig was ripe for the picking. Ima Pipiig was desperate, hungry, without options. She didn't have cash, but she had ambition, and she was a warm body.

Florence Reznik had found a federal gravy train in the field of education that was so easy that all she needed was a warm body. She didn't need to really teach, she didn't need to work more than thirty-five or forty hours a week, and she didn't need to meet any criteria, such as proving that her classes actually improved the lives of anyone they touched. And even had there been actual ethical criteria in place, Florence Reznik gave all of the students in her classes an incomplete and made them fill out a positive class evaluation form before they got a grade several months later; and even better, Florence Reznik made everybody in the class write a letter to their state legislator saying how wonderful the class was and requesting that they continue federal funding for the class. This was, after all, higher education, and minorities like Ima Pipiig were lucky that they were given the chance to participate in the system at all. After all, they all had bad attitudes on account of being lazy welfare bums and living off casino money and the dominant culture's hard-earned tax dollars. And ignorant, stupid Ima Pipiig was just that—nothing but that—a warm body. Florence Reznik didn't know anything about the legal concept of fiduciary duty—that one who had greater knowledge had a responsibility to one's partners, a.k.a. taxpayers, to perform honestly; and even if Florence Reznik had had any concept of fiduciary duty, she would have known that it customarily does not apply to the field of education—because in some settings, educators exist for educators, and the notion that they exist for the public is a mere myth that is used to incite a knee-jerk reaction that provides funding, funding, funding for perfect white educators like herself who have been serving the needs of the dominant culture by acculturating land-and-resource-holding minorities for years, since the McKinley era, at least.

The American Writing Workshop was a federal gravy train of the sort that colleges and universities had come to like. It guaranteed teaching positions in a time when college and university enrollments were dropping in response to nationwide income loss. It had nothing to do with finding or solving the root causes of that cultural phenomenon, and to Ima Pipiig, it would eventually seem that it had little to do with teaching writing, either. It was simply a federal gravy train for those who got jobs in the program. It brought administrative income into the sponsoring institutions. It created a handful of teaching jobs and attached lower-paying clerical positions. It did not create new jobs for the students who participated in the program. It did not help them become better at what they did, if they had jobs already. It was simply a warm-bodies-let-the-dollars-flow project. And, as had become the norm in higher education, it didn't matter what kind of bodies they were, as they all generated the flow of income. So nonthreatening minority bodies were acceptable. Indians were acceptable. And sparrow hawks were acceptable. As long as they stayed in their place and did not interfere with the nonfunctioning comfort level of the predominantly white public school educators seeking recertification credits. As long as they did not interfere with Florence Reznik's nonteaching and her field trips to the national park parking lot or some store that she thought was cute . . . because, after all, Florence Reznik was busy working on her doctorate, and, for some reason, universities were requiring terminal degrees from their staff because they had come to the conclusion that undergraduate degrees and master's degrees in the last twenty years didn't have quite the same value as they had had only a generation ago . . . So Florence Reznik had to pretend that she actually gave a shit and was actually learning something and teaching something, because she was, after all, white, and she must have gotten this job because of her superior skills and not because she was white.

And Ima Pipiig, who would come to observe all of this with the warped clarity of an outsider, figured that too many Florence Rezniks out there measured their own value by the fact that their mothers had made themselves available to a privileged white male, and they themselves had attached themselves to a white male, and some sort of relationship to a white penis was all that anyone really needed to work in the field of education anyways—because people of color and women of color were too ignorant and too lazy and too much on the dole to be good teachers. And Ima Pipiig would stay leery of the Florence Rezniks. And Florence Reznik would definitely come to believe that Ima Pipiig needed a leash. And the two women would dance the dance of distance in the uncomfortable spaces of their shared summer.

"Ima, how would you like to team-teach a course on writing with me this summer?" Florence asked. Ima Pipiig was taken aback. The credentials had meant something after all. She and Birdie had misjudged the white educator. Perhaps the white educators were right; perhaps Indians didn't have the social skills to understand how things are done. Perhaps this was an opportunity, this team-teaching thing, an opportunity to learn from a peer, to learn how to be more like a white educator, to be more acceptable to the world of all-white academia in northwest Lower Michigan. Perhaps this was an opportunity for this woman of color, in this environment where opportunities were in short supply for women of color.

"It's an honor to be asked to do this. It's very prestigious." Florence Reznik lied into the telephone. She was trying to drum up any warm bodies she could come up with. Ima Pipiig had published a few small children's books. She had a grown-up book coming out with a university press in a few months. The program could take credit for that. The program would use her name in perpetuity as a graduate, as their product. If they got lucky, Ima Pipiig would get famous. Then they could take credit for it. And Ima Pipiig should, after all, consider herself lucky to be involved in their program at all, because, after all, Indians were dumb and uneducated, and Ima Pipiig had merely gone to some bumfuck private college in Ohio, south of Cleveland; it was called Overland or something like that. And it was small, really small, and had only a four-to-one student-teacher-ratio when Ima Pipiig went there, not like a real state university, where there were hundreds of people in a class sometimes and one could never garner the attention of an instructor; and applicants to that little private college, in Ohio of all places, had to come from the top twenty percent of their high school graduating class, but Ima Pipiig had probably only been admitted out of sympathy, because she was, after all, an Indian . . . and, through affirmative action, the halls of academia had become swelled with minorities with no cultural common sense whatsoever, taking all of the good, high-paying jobs away from the Florence Rezniks and all of the other Americans who worked thirty-five to forty or forty-five hours a week and knew what it was like to work hard without getting something for nothing. They'd put in their time. They deserved the jobs better than the minorities who did not work and expected something for nothing.

Ima Pipiig knew better than to be honored by the request. Ima Pipiig knew better than to respect the word "honor" when it came out of a white person's mouth. As an old tribal elder had once told her: *The only thing better than on 'er is in 'er.* Ima Pipiig knew that she was being bullshitted. But Florence Reznik had held out a carrot. Ima Pipiig could either receive a stipend (which was insufficient to cover her costs) or she could get three college credits toward getting her teaching credentials intact again. And, since she had the power to do so, Florence Reznik would give her the credits in any class Ima Pipiig wanted; and since Ima Pipiig knew that the Bullshit 101 basic education course that was required for recertification would be infantile and boring, Ima Pipiig was willing to forgo it in exchange for showing that she could team-teach a course in writing—which Ima Pipiig could do with one lip tied behind her back, because Ima Pipiig had won awards for her writing, her artwork, her ingenuity . . . because Ima Pipiig had taught a lot of things and had developed teaching materials for a lot of subjects over the years. There was one thing Ima Pipiig knew she could do: she could teach, even the unwilling.

And since team-teaching was the carrot that Florence Reznik had illegitimately held over her head, and since Ima Pipiig had spent decades being a guest instructor at some of the finest educational institutions in the Midwest, before the economic restrictions of the late twentieth and early twenty-first century eliminated frivolities like minority scholarship; and because the reality of racially based unemployment had forced Ima Pipiig to forfeit her teaching credentials, Ima Pipiig thought of this as an opportunity of sorts. She hoped against hope that somehow Twin Bay City had grown in the last few years of its white-flight-community-expansion to accept a person of color as worthy of working in the schools. Silly Ima Pipiig.

By the time she would discover that she was not to team-teach, but to be a compliant colored lawn jockey, a mere "student" in a class that taught nothing; before she was to complete this summer course and experience the racism modeled and encouraged by Florence Reznik; by the time she would have been emotionally battered by the roomful of white teachers who seemed to have been trained in the arts of attacking minorities and those of lesser socioeconomic status; by the time she had run back and forth, jumped through purposeless hoops and meaningless exercises; by the time she had taken precious time away from her youngest child, who would never be a preschooler again, and her garden and her own business of writing and producing artwork and stocking away resources for lean, lean times ahead . . . Ima Pipiig would know better than to continue to seek recertification in the field of teaching. She would have been put in her place: OUTSIDE that institutional system of ignorance and ignorance-based hatred. It would not be the role they would believe they had relegated to her. Because Ima Pipiig, for all of the plate glass, illusion, and misinformation, was a sparrow hawk. She could dip and dive. And she left Florence Reznik in the dust when it came to survival and doing more with less.

Now, glancing out the window at the bluffs above Twin Bay City's Boardman River, sitting in Florence Reznik's stale, hot classroom that first day, before eventually being emotionally coerced into letting go of any pretense of being an educator or a professional, Ima Pipiig smiled at the other "students" in the teacher recertification course. She remembered the statistic she had learned early on in her education courses at the University of New Mexico, the one about how 80 percent of the people who went into the field of education came from the bottom 20 percent of the people in their high school class who went on to college. And she remembered how the statistic had been repeated to Birdie in her sociology course at the junior college only last year. She did a body count. Twenty-three. She wondered which two out of ten would not be underachievers. And then she chastised herself, telling herself that poor expectations could influence the outcome of the students. She questioned her own judgment, began to doubt the statistic, began to question the reality of such an absurdity. By this point, Ima Pipiig had been so beaten down by the system, that she began, in these closed quarters, to see herself as lesser, in spite of her credentials and experience, in spite of the socioeconomic factors that made her academic accomplishments even more worthy than those of the more fortunate. Opening her mind and trying to lift her expectations of the people surrounding her, Ima Pipiig dutifully followed the instructions provided more pleasantly than usual by Florence Reznik in the presence of a supervisor visiting for the day from a distant downstate university.

Now, asked to write and read aloud about her own childhood experiences in school, Ima Pipiig drew a blank. It was assumed, at this time, by the new white residents of Twin Bay City, Michigan, that Ima Pipiig had experienced the same sense of homogeneity and small town all-white comfort that these people had moved to Twin Bay City and created an image of for themselves. And so, because she was a good Indian, and because she was still trying to dive and dip and dodge and respond to the fleeting, always changing expectations of her white overlords, Ima Pipiig wrote, and Ima Pipiig read:

> *I am not a woman prone to amnesia. Yet school brings on such non-memories to me. My parents did not go out of their ways to send us to school. They feared it might interfere with our educations.*
>
> *We read and wrote, clustered by the stove, as eager for one another's company as we were for the experience or a finished product.*

Ima Pipiig's audience of course, at this point, thought that she was talking about a kitchen stove, and that she and her siblings were baking brownies from a box mix. They assumed that reading the instructions on the box was the reading lesson. They all lived in houses with furnaces with noisy electric blowers, and they did not share Ima Pipiig's vision of a silent woodstove, stoked up to fight off the wind and cold of a temporarily inhospitable outdoors in the midst of a six-week-long winter snowstorm, long before the climatic shifts that had made her homeland a haven for the white-flightists from the prairie fringe cities of the industrial southern third of the state. They did not hear the wind over the crackle of the fire. They did not visualize the dim light of the short, clouded days. They did not hear the hissing and popping of the burning logs inside the stove, close to her warm ear, the tick, tick of the expanding and contracting stovepipe, the perfect whistle of the perfect airflow of the perfectly adjusted air intake valve on the cast-iron door only inches from her perfect brown-haired head. But Ima Pipiig saw these things. Ima Pipiig heard these things. Ima Pipiig felt these things. Ima Pipiig lived these things.

There was no television then. No radio. The sounds of our voices broke the silence of endless wind and waves.

Now Ima Pipiig, of course, was no older than her mid-forties, and these people did not fathom her world without electricity. They did not see the small house at the bottom of the hill, with its hand-pounded well, steel pipe forced into lakeside sand by Ima Pipiig's tall father. A cast-iron hand pump mounted at the edge of the sink intercepted the water before it made its underground way to the lake. It always ran cold and clear. Sweet. Ima Pipiig and her sisters and brothers knew the meaning of sweetwater. But these people, they did not taste the sweetwater. They did not know how the adults and the older children checked and stoked that woodstove each time one of them awoke, at all hours of the night, to keep those old metal pipes from freezing. This was technology to Ima Pipiig, who was now reliving her childhood. She could taste the sometimes rust in the pipes. It was not a bad taste. It was a taste of independence and familiarity. She found comfort in the reliving of this, in her mind's flight from the discomfort of this room full of strangers. Strangers in the way they thought. Strangers in the ways they consumed and jostled the Indians out of their way to consume more . . .

We simply read to one another. Heavy hand-bound volumes. Some were for the littler kids, some appealing to adolescents. Mostly I remember the great black volumes of works by Mark Twain. Long after we'd finished Tom Sawyer *and* Huck Finn, *then graduated to the patient, slower action of* The Prince and the Pauper, *we graduated to the stealthier adventures of Twain's poetry. I remember long poems of deer running through the woods. I experienced the crashing of the brush. I felt the panting of the panicked deer.*

Through her own writing, Ima Pipiig was reliving the way that Twain had brought a panting deer alive for her more than thirty years earlier. She remembered how she visualized Twain's deer on the hill behind her own house, how she knew that it was not the same deer or the same woods, but that it didn't matter. Because after the hard-cornered spaces and the constant hurt of schooldays away from home, comfort, and familiarity, there was joy in Twain's running deer. It did not matter that mostly moose poked around the corners of Ima Pipiig's family's small house. It did not matter. What mattered was the reliving of it that took her out of this room, now . . .

I don't know where the quiet for this sort of reading came from. I think it was a result of the freedom to get up and roam. Periodically, we'd go out to dissect a frog. There was no shortage of paper or coloring and writing implements. There were encyclopedic books and journals. These were places to turn for text to copy and learn by rote through the fine motor movements of my hands and arms.

How could my parents, barely literate themselves, have seen fit to create an educational haven for ten children? It seemed their lives were busy enough with mere survival, with the details of being merely alive.

As Ima Pipiig read these words aloud to the room full of white schoolteachers they would not know the hardships that had been brought upon Ima Pipiig's parents by the newcomers before them who had altered their environment and their lives. They would not understand the generations of hurt that had ensued from the tussling over resources—game, lumber, waterfront property, road easements, real estate . . . They would think that Ima Pipiig should have simply gotten over it, that it was done now. They would not understand the hurt that ensued from their intrusion into Ima Pipiig's environment and the damage to future generations of the sparrow hawk portion of the Ojibwe culture that was as essential to the physical environment of this place as was the wind in the trees . . .

My only memories of school are the times in chapel, lost on the long wooden pews. It was there that we'd see siblings and find the comfort that enabled our hearts and minds to open up and learn. There we glanced nervously, like animals in a cage, waiting for butchering. We risked the punishment of daring to be distracted from the liturgical tasks at hand, for a mere glimpse of a familiar outline of a head of a loved one.

They did not see the long, dark halls, harsh and empty. Girls only. Boys only. Rag uniforms. Tennis shoes, flat, unsupporting of growing feet, narrow and pointed, not wide like their free-ranging feet. Holes where those toes worked their ways out the sides. Big empty pointed-shoe fronts. Underclothing loose and without elastic. Institutional. Didn't matter whose were whose. Nothing to read. Those Indian kids might fight over it. Not take care of it. Probably couldn't read, and if they did, couldn't understand it—the Educational Psychology Bullshit One-Oh-One Course Textbook said so—minority, likely to achieve lower on the achievement tests; Catholic-multiple-siblings, likely to score lower on the achievement tests; low income, likely to score lower on the achievement tests. (Who the hell wrote that fucking textbook?)

Long hours of sitting, sitting, sitting on long wooden benches against the walls. No reading. No math. No haptic learning through living in an environment. No touching each other. You had to get permission to talk, permission to walk across the room, permission to look out the window. They didn't want Ima Pipiig to took out the window. No, Ima, if you look out the window you will cry; and then you will make the other girls cry.

The ladies who studied Maria Montessori and her studies of war orphans who suffered from sensory deprivation—they never made the association between what was done to Indian children in Catholic schools in the past and what was done to Indian children in PUBLIC schools in the PRESENT.

When it was all over, when they were home, when they were free, their parents would ask them what's wrong with them. They couldn't move or laugh or look up. They were too used to sitting still, sitting still, sitting still, to avoid the stinging of a cheek, lips numb from the swat across a "belligerent" Indian face. Forgetting about the whistles of the sparrows and the cries back and forth between the hunting sparrow hawks. Separated from the sound of the wind in the trees . . .

All her listeners were figuring out was that Ima Pipiig needed to get over it. It was over and done with. The boarding schools had been long closed, and abuse, neglect, and misunderstanding of minorities were things of the past. They should be used to poverty by now because they obviously brought it upon themselves. Ima Pipiig's listeners did not see the loss of freedom and hope and joy that the sparrow hawks had lived through. They only saw the lone feathers of the roadkill birds that they took home as treasures, as testimony to the fact that they, too, had come to live in the land of the Chippewa; that they, too, lived lives of quiet solitude; and that they, too, understood this place and her people's place in it, far better than Ima Pipiig.

The newcomers did not see the hurt that they continued to impose upon Ima Pipiig and her children, as they moved north, looked down their long noses at her, and tussled with her over the resources, the beaches, the fish, the game, the road easements, the real estate, and the jobs. The white schoolteachers did not see that because of the hardships imposed upon sparrow hawks by their predecessors, that Ima Pipiig and the other contemporary sparrow hawks would always be losers. They were tired. They were weak. They'd been poisoned by the pesticide-like toxins of racism. They were confused by the constantly changing rules, their own changing reflections in the plate glass, the distorted images of their world, their trees, their waters, the sounds of the wind and the waves muffled by the passing cars of the hurried commuters. For all of her diving and dipping and hunting endlessly for her own survival and dignity and self-respect, Ima Pipiig had lost her place in the traditional food chain—now dominated by new predators, predators without a sense of the circular and obligatory nature of the environmental boundaries within which she had once grown and flourished. And she wondered if, when they were done with her, if they would take home each of her feathers, singularly beautiful, as trophies of a vanishing lifestyle and vanishing wilderness.

Before I Offend Most of You,
I Would Like to Thank You for Coming

Boozhou, aniishinaa . . . Lois Beardslee, anishinaabekwe, indiizhinikaash. Wawauzhukgesh dodaim 'nizhiibp, gi' imaa Leelanau County, Leelanau Peninsula, Michigan, *'nizhiibp.*

Hello, how do you do? My name is Lois Beardslee, and I am a Native artist and writer from Leelanau County, Michigan. Before I offend almost everyone in this room, I would like to thank you for coming to this fund-raiser for Channel Two in Traverse City, for supporting local broadcasts of Pacifica Network's *Democracy Now* with Amy Goodman and for supporting independent media in general. When I suggested that I speak about the media tonight, I was told that I would be "preaching to the fold," an already converted audience. If I could, I would name tonight's lecture "Circumspice," after the state motto of Michigan: *Si quaeris peninsulam amoenam, circumspice,* If you seek a pleasant peninsula, look about you. I'd like to concentrate right now on the second part, *circumspice,* look about you—not far away, but close in—because the relationship that I, as a Native American female, have with the local media is very different from yours.

Your schools and universities, the books made available to you in bookstores, libraries and museum gift shops, the exhibitions and lectures selected for you by parks, museums, and history centers, along with your local newspapers and other media have already painted your expectations of Indians like me, and I live with the socioeconomic repercussions of those paint jobs every day. Michigan ranks ninth highest among the states in Native American population, and northwest Lower Michigan has one of the highest densities of Native Americans east of the Mississippi. You rarely see us in your daily lives, although you do see signs for the casinos that have served as loopholes in racism. We live in sort of an underculture, not quite among you.

Within your educational institutions, minority employment continuously vacillates between zero and a fraction of 1 percent. On a daily basis, educators model and reinforce a standard of cultural and financial apartheid that reverberates throughout our community.

Native American women have the highest number of college diplomas of any ethnic group in the state, and, except for whites and certain Asians, nationwide. Yet the group with the number-one highest unemployment in Michigan is Native American women, followed by Native American men. The Ojibwe, or Chippewa, tribe is the second-largest tribe in North America. Our historic and modern territories comprise thousands of square miles. We were and are one of the most successful groups of human beings on the face of the earth. Our sophisticated culture, language, oral history, art forms, and religion remain intact, although this has not been made obvious to most of you. Too many of you have been trained to see us as angry, lazy, ignorant welfare bums who simply won't conform to the cottage-country images of cute, docile, compliant Indians like the ones described in a host of abysmal, financially profitable cultural rip-offs and misrepresentations that have been written by non-Indian authors for non-Indian audiences.

The group of people you have come to refer to locally as "the tribe" is organized under federal regulations as the Grand Traverse Band of Ottawa and Chippewa Indians. By the federal and state definitions that control the distribution of assets, I do not belong to this particular band, although, by traditional Ojibwe cultural definitions I belong to the same tribe and the same community. Dividing our bands up into little competing units has been one of the government's methods of reducing treaty-driven expenditures. Only about half of Michigan's Indians currently meet all of the legal definitions of Indian anymore. I know of families in which one sibling meets state or federal requirements and one does not; one receives help from agency-funded tribal programs to help overcome the socioeconomic burdens imposed by racism, and one does not. Nonetheless, I have watched our bands and communities transform themselves from groups of multicentury holocaust survivors into bands of thriving, though not necessarily affluent, cultural warriors.

Every square inch of new property within the local tribe's "reservation" has been bought back with hard-earned dollars. I understand this, because every square inch of my own family's traditional homeland that is now in my hands has been bought back at a fair market value, in spite of the fact that I have earned less than ten cents on the dollar compared to most European Americans with equal or lesser credentials. Recently, in an effort to expand their per capita ratio of land to a larger square footage than the thirteen acres recent history had allocated them, the Grand Traverse Band bought back several of their own acres at a competitive current price. Rather than recognize the enormity of this accomplishment, the *Leelanau Enterprise*, the county newspaper, ran a front-page headline, "'Rez is growing; Property to come off local tax rolls."

Indians appear to be depriving you of your just and due tax income. No matter that there are Native American families regionally living on a few fragments of property doled out during the allotment era of Native American history who are unable to obtain clear title to their land, will never be able to sell it or transform it in any way, but continue to pay county taxes on it, due to the curious, abusive, and ever-changing Indian policy that has dominated Native people and their lands. Were they not to pay these taxes, the property would revert to various governments. No matter that hundreds of Native people live outside of the reservation, pay taxes, and receive no economic benefits from tribal recognition. No matter that Indians who live off the reservation pay school taxes but represent a disproportionately high number of parents whose children are homeschooled or are privately educated. No matter that we are almost completely excluded from employment in publicly funded jobs. Those things will never make it into the local media because they will not inflame you; they will not encourage you to accept the apartheid status quo that limits Indian access to resources like jobs, real estate, tangible comforts, and intangible comforts that include respect and the benefit of the doubt.

A few years ago, Alan Campbell, editor of the *Leelanau Enterprise*, for reasons I will never understand, secretly joined with the local American Civil Liberties Union to file a lawsuit against the Suttons Bay School District, the district closest to the reservation. The suit alleged that Native American presenters on school premises, even when school was closed, were violating the separation of church and state. The ACLU's legal case rested upon the argument that all Native Americans are unable to distinguish between the real world and the supernatural world, based upon *The Spirit World*, a *Time-Life* book about Native American spirituality. It is a source that would not be acceptable in an entry-level college freshman composition course, let alone in a federal courtroom. Yet Campbell ran a front-page headline and article, indicating that the ACLU threatened to sue the school district for violating the separation of church and state, and that the ACLU never threatened to sue unless it was sure it could win. Campbell stated in the article that there would be a public hearing on the issue before the Suttons Bay School Board but "accidentally" listed the time an hour later than the actual scheduled meeting. When I telephoned Campbell about the issue, he reiterated that the ACLU only sued when they were certain of a win, he discouraged me from writing a letter to the paper in regard to the lawsuit, and he withheld information about his personal involvement in the suit.

This goes beyond poor judgment. This is a violation of the very principles of journalism. I try to find a rationale for this behavior, but I can think of none likelier than ethnic intimidation driven by greed and lust for power. The resources at stake are no more than the equal right to buy a few acres of real estate in a white-flight community that constitutes a public-land ghetto next to a national park, small-scale Indian fishing rights that allegedly impinge upon a sport fishery already weakened by larger-scale non-Indian commercial overfishing, and a few regional jobs that pay a living wage. All that the *Leelanau Enterprise* and the local ACLU accomplished was to bully a small school district out of hiring Indians for occasional speaking engagements, the only crumbs left to us regionally within the field of education, in a corner of the state where minority employment in education is virtually nonexistent. This was not a failure by ultraconservative special interest groups and media monopolies that are funded by multinational corporations and arms dealers in capitals far away. This was ethnic intimidation by local institutions that purport to be ruled by professional ethics. It happens here. *Circumspice.*

Right now, public school administration is one of the most lucrative professions in the Grand Traverse region. Locally, educators receive entry-level salaries in excess of those of entry-level engineers. As public resources tighten locally and nationally, labor unions tend to recruit from the highest-paying professions, and educators are becoming economically separate from the working class. The gap between the earnings of an average working mother and the earnings of a public school administrator in northwest Lower Michigan is proportionally equivalent to the gap between a school administrator's earnings and those of a corporate executive. How can people teach about issues that affect and empower the rest of us if they don't live in the same economic reality that we do? While the teaching profession is roughly 75 percent female, the field of educational administration is roughly 75 percent male. This pattern, as well as our tolerance toward it, reverberates in our communities, but it starts at home, and public education is as close to home as one can get. These issues do not garner the attention of the local papers and the ACLU. But we need watchdogs locally as much as we need them nationally and globally. The usurpation of resources for personal gain does not merely happen far away. *Circumspice.*

A few years ago, my local school district passed up dozens of female and minority applicants (and one androgynous male with whom I was very impressed) with doctorates, high grade point averages, and years of experience to hire as their middle school principal a white male with an abysmal transcript, a highlight of which was a D+ in "elementary arithmetic for schoolteachers." The public school takes on the mantle of media, giving the following message to its adolescent girls, five days a week, nine months of the year: "It's not what's between your ears that counts; it's what's between your legs. If you want to succeed in America, succumb to a white penis, any white penis, even if it's attached to a classic underachiever." Since the only objection came from a minority female, it wasn't taken seriously. Her educational credentials couldn't possibly qualify her to make judgments for white, middle-class children, especially if those judgments challenged those of white males. Besides, he's the coach, and you know, we have girls' sports, too. That Indian lady couldn't possibly have been the first woman in the history of the local college to have participated in varsity sports, could not possibly have earned a varsity letter for her participation on the men's cross-country team, opening up regional sports to girls and women, long before the current school board members moved up here from cities downstate to avoid busing and all that icky *Brown v. Board of Education* stuff. It's not within the domain of what public education as a form of media has trained you to believe about the structure of power.

"Besides, that Indian lady, she went to some bumfuck private college in Ohio, just south of Cleveland; it's called Overland College, I think. She kept muttering something about the Underground Railway and integrated schools.

"Sure, educational curriculum is the softest stuff on college campuses, but, hey, we only gotta be one step above the kids. We've got no obligation to stop teaching stereotypes . . . In fact, the less we teach people the better. We don't want them voting in the school board elections, because we've got the school boards packed with people who will keep our salaries up, as long as we give them the sports program they want and the socioeconomic status quo they want . . . Viva ignorance! Viva apathy! Viva the status quo!"

You are hurting yourselves.

If you have been watching *Democracy Now*, you know that Lawrence Summers, current president of Harvard University, who has a history of undermining sexual equity in hiring, recently announced that women do poorer in science and mathematics for genetic reasons, forgoing countless studies indicating that the reasons are cultural. Do you wonder why this is tolerated nationally, when you do not intervene in such mindlessness at home? (Why can't Johnny read or understand complex issues like race and gender discrimination? Aw, heck, Johnny can't even do long division . . .) *Circumspice.*

A former local elementary school principal was repeatedly accused of harassing, threatening, stalking, and battering women and children. He was given glowing recommendations and became the superintendent of a district not far away. Are you concerned about bullying in schools? What do you do when the bullies are on staff? You won't read about these things in your school newsletter. Today, most school newsletters are produced by a public relations specialist. Often parent-teacher handbooks instruct parents about the behaviors school administrators would like families to give them; but they fail to include student and parent rights. Under these circumstances "family values" become a moot point.

How can we counteract our lack of influence with politicians like Bart Stupak (I don't care what your wishes on the issue are, I'm voting my own beliefs . . .), Candace Miller (all those black folks in Ohio who didn't get to vote are merely crying sour grapes), and the corporate executives who occupy the White House, when we can't exert influence with our local school boards and our school administrators? *Circumspice.*

Recently the superintendent of the school district where I reside became involved in efforts to increase the number of subdivisions near my home, to counteract a decline in public school enrollment. All public school populations fluctuate, and part of an administrator's job is to plan for and respond to those fluctuations. It is a conflict of interest for him to try to influence local zoning issues for the purpose of altering demographics that affect his salary. His insistence that any subdivision would be good for the school district is an assault on the community and the environment. I'd have loved to have complained to school board members, but most of them had unlisted numbers. And the one who showed up with the superintendent and the developer to push for the subdivision owns developable property across the road from the future subdivision. How did this blatant culture of self-service become the status quo in a public school? How do we prevent its practitioners from modeling this socially inappropriate behavior that can then be carried into other, greater contexts? How do we prevent its practitioners from sanctioning this boorish mode of human interaction as history and part of our expectations of one another as citizens . . . or perhaps as *noncitizens?* The superintendent has moved up the coast for an additional fifty thousand per year; the bulldozers are still here. If we can't fight this sort of nepotistic abuse of public funds for individual profit here at home, how can we fight it in our states' and nation's capitals?

When Pacifica Radio's *Democracy Now* first appeared on Free Speech TV a couple of years ago, I wrote to my local public radio station and indicated that I would withhold my support for the station until it carried "Democracy Now" or another alternative to "National Pablum Radio." That was a big risk for me, because, as a Native American, I do not have access to full-time employment here; my income is opportunistic and dependent upon the whims of the local media in regard to support of my writing and my art. I have far less leeway than many of you when it comes to income loss, when it comes to taking chances for the benefit of my community as a whole.

It would take me hours to list all of the people who have dismissed me or threatened me over the years, sometimes for quoting statistics from government sources on education and employment, sometimes for asking questions, sometimes to put me in my place, and sometimes, just because I exist, as a person of color in a place that does not want people of color . . . and simply because people know they can get away with bullying someone who is considered lesser or vulnerable. And you ask why we have allowed Muslims, people who are seemingly different from us, to be demonized, simply because they have resources we want and simply because we can get away with it . . . *Circumspice.*

Some of you know of me as an artist, a safe artist, one who does cute children's stories and illustrations that fall into your expectations of what a Native American in northwest Lower Michigan should be: demure, giving, willing to accept unequal pay for equal work, willing to entertain, willing to follow directions without asking questions. Few of you know that I write nonfiction, too. You will be hard-pressed to find those writings in local libraries. Because, after all, how could a mere Indian, an Indian *woman*, know anything important? Do you wonder why, on a national level, minority yesmen and yes-women are being used as lawn jockeys by the present administration to avoid real progress in civil rights? Isn't that what you have been trained to expect at home? Do you wonder why, on a national scale, we are so receptive to the concept of millions of people of color as *other*, as lesser, as disposable? *Circumspice.*

Don't tell me you cannot eliminate apartheid, economic inequality, abuse of power, and incompetence in the media at home, because you are too busy fighting them far away. These problems exist on a larger scale precisely because you tolerate them at home. I've heard Traverse City referred to as the "Sister City to Pulaski, Tennessee." (That's the birthplace of the Ku Klux Klan.) Take responsibility for the moniker and try to eliminate it. Look about you, but not through binoculars. *Circumspice.*

Now, look at the first part of our state motto: If you seek a pleasant peninsula . . . Pleasant for whom? For those who have inherited wealth and power? For those who are lucky enough to have access to resources? Is it any wonder that you suddenly find yourselves as expendable to the political and corporate elite of America as the people of Bopal, India, are to multinational corporations? Isn't that the same system you have tolerated at home? Radical extremists are taking their cues from you and from me. They learn what we will tolerate nationally by watching us at home. *Circumspice.* Because these problems don't just hurt you or me or those weaker and more needy than we are. They damage and endanger all of us. Don't take my word for it—after all, I'm brown and I'm female . . . I am *other.* For your own well-being, *circumspice.*

＊～ꜱ

Hmmm . . . This isn't going to work. They've already given me three times longer than all the other speakers. It would be rude to go twice as long as I should. There's only so much people can sit and listen to. Too bad . . . I've got so much to tell you. I'm going to have to take a different tack . . .

· 10 ·

Turtle TV

$\mathcal{T}$he old turtle sat on his log in the shallow back bay. It was a particularly warm spot, no matter the time of the year, because it was near the place where the gray-water drainage pipe from the cheesecake factory emptied into the Boardman River, just south of Twin Bay City. In his youth, this had been a wild place. Today it was a safe spot amid the mini-malls and housing developments. The industrial district had become, by comparison, a wildlife refuge of sorts.

Turtle's children, those of many generations and many years on this steep-banked bay, played and rested before him. They dove and chased dragonflies, minnows, and pollywogs, learning the timeless lessons that turtles passed down to one another about how to survive in a back bay, in a corner of northwest Lower Michigan's peninsulas that had not yet been discovered by those eager to garner, hoard, and develop those remnants into their own mistaken expectations of turtle heaven.

Someday, it would be their jobs to teach the newcomers about turtle survival, he supposed. Because his culture, turtle culture, was old enough to know that the environment of the back bay could not function properly without the presence of turtles. These were evolution's turtles, the turtles who learned and taught and learned and taught again, until turtles had become pragmatic survivors in this place. Many of the newcomers would arrive with the notion that the evolution of the turtle was without value in the face of their own belief system, one that gave them automatic superiority and precedence over those who were not of their faith. They would destroy the environment up and down that riverbank, certain that their faith would render evolution useless. After the turtles were gone, they would anticipate, the riverbank would bend to their convictions, and the Great Lakes, the whole of North America, and the world would follow.

But nothing could be further from the truth. There was nothing the old turtle would have enjoyed more than to have lived long enough for the new-comers to have destroyed themselves through the errors of their convictions, but he suspected that his beloved back bay would probably be destroyed with them, along with his children, those of many generations and many years on this steep-banked bay. The dilemma had become a topic of conversation among the various animals and mysteries who found solitude below a great, hollow beech tree that sent its immense branches out over the shallow waters and warm sands of the turtle bay. It was here that Manaboozhou, mysterious, half spirit, half human, spent idle afternoons, listening to the chatter of the generations of turtles. Turtles were his messengers, his newsbeat. Turtles were as good as TV.

He listened to their talk of changes, how their birthrate had dipped, un-til they'd learned just enough about the newcomers to avoid the more obvi-ous dangers. They spoke of the dangers that they could not eliminate. They spoke of the old culture that was being replaced by the new, not because they opposed all change, but because they feared that the old ways and the old knowledge might come in handy some day. The bay was on a dam flooding, after all. It was an artificial place created by technology. And who knew when that technology might fail, might fall to changing whims, changing notions about the necessity of a dam. Or who knew when the river and the lakes and the rain, snow, and all of the mysteries of the environment might take back the flooding. They were, after all, the river and the lakes and the rain and the snow—all mysteries known to offset the plans of men and beasts.

They made him chuckle, those turtles. They sometimes talked in circles. Even the great Manaboozhou, the son of the West Wind, knew that some-times turtles held information that his own brain could not hold. Turtles had been holding up the earth since his young and foolish childhood, and that was so many generations ago that Manaboozhou himself had lost the ability to reckon. It was for this reason that Manaboozhou had gifted turtles with the ability to be in more than one place at one time and with the ability to exist throughout time. It was precisely these gifts that made turtles so knowledge-able, so interesting, such good gossips. Turtles were better than TV.

Northwest Lower Michigan College had purchased the old cheesecake company offices on a hilltop view lot just north of the cheesecake factory. The building had never been used and sat pristine above the river flooding that formed the lake. It rose in multileveled beauty from the center of an asphalt parking lot, just downwind from the dumpsters at the cheesecake factory, where pie dough and corn syrup–infused fruit sat rotting as future pig fodder to be picked up on a somewhat unreliable and too-infrequent schedule by a local farmer. Due south of the entire property, and upwind from the dump-

ster at the cheesecake factory, Ima Pipiig and her family had once lived in solitude on an isolated dirt road. The site of the factory offices had once belonged
to an uncle who had lost most of the allotment, signing it away in illiterate Indian ignorance, thinking that he was signing a paper that allowed it to be
logged. Most of what was left was lost in the dam flooding. All that remained
of the original allotment was a one-room house surrounded by tulip bulbs and
old purple lilacs on the hillside above the turtle bay. Eventually, unable to survive, the Indians left, and the land was sold to compensate the county for the
burden of printing up a tax bill. The old house persisted, windows alternately
broken and boarded by a series of homeless war veterans and middle-class hippie children. Its family memories vanished with the sense of loss that kept its
old residents far from that place.

Manaboozhou liked to walk the scrubby second-growth forest that lined
that hilltop along the river. He liked to remember the place as alive and full of
Anishinabe children, his children, those of many generations and many years
on this steep-banked bay, where they had played and rested before him. They
dove and chased dragonflies, minnows, and pollywogs, learning the timeless
lessons that the Anishinabeg passed down to one another about how to survive
in a back bay, in a corner of northwest Lower Michigan's peninsulas that had
not yet been discovered by those eager to garner, hoard, and develop those
remnants into their own mistaken expectations of Indian heaven.

As he emerged from a scrubby pine plantation that was much in need of
care and thinning, Manaboozhou was surprised to see Ima Pipiig. She wore a
down vest over her hooded sweatshirt. It was soiled from hard work, dark soil
clinging to bits of pitch that had become embedded in the fabric from carry-
ing firewood and lumber. Near the door of the old house, she sat on an old
chrome-framed chair fragment from the 1950s. It was the kind that people
used to have in their kitchens, the kind used to sit around small, square pull-
out tables whose plasticized metallic surfaces usually matched the weak plastic
padding on the chairs. The plastic and the padding were gone now, and it was
impossible to see what color they might have been originally. But Ima Pipiig,
so seemingly tired in her limp-armed posture of rest on the wooden seat fragment, looked up into his eyes, smiling; and Manaboozhou at that moment remembered the bright red vinyl of the cushions and the table in the lamplight.
He remembered the joy of the family that had once occupied the now relic of
a home. He remembered the plentiful meals of panfish and trout that had been
shared with him at that table.

When Ima Pipiig smiled, Manaboozhou remembered all of these things,
as he remembered life details for countless generations of Anishinabeg who
had fed him along this riverbank—his children, those of many generations and
many years on the steep-banked bays, where they had played and rested before

him. They dove and chased dragonflies, minnows, and pollywogs, learning the timeless lessons that the Anishinabeg passed down to one another about how to survive in back bays, in corners of northern Michigan's and northern Ontario's peninsulas that had not yet been discovered by those eager to garner, hoard, and develop those remnants into their own mistaken expectations of Indian heaven. Like the turtles, remnant populations of Indians had adapted and persisted into the present, fearing that the old knowledge that had taken thousands of years to be accumulated would find itself expendable in the faith of the newcomers.

"Ima Pipiig, what are you doing here?"

And the woman raised her head and smiled again in response to the wind in the trees.

"Ima Pipiig, I'd thought this place would be too painful for you to visit."

Ima Pipiig found strength in her pain, and she rose up from the chair remnant. She walked past the holes in the ground where the newcomers had dug up the precious old flower bulbs that Ima Pipiig and her mother had helped her auntie plant on an extended family visit to that wood-sided house on high ground above that now-flooded river valley. She strode past the spot where the drainpipe from the cheesecake factory lay buried deep in the sand. Below this spot she had gathered sweet blue mallard eggs on cool spring mornings, reveling in her success in beating the raccoons to the booty left by immature, young hens. She wrapped her arm around the trunk of a big beech tree for support and leaned way out over the water. From the pocket of the down vest soiled from hard, honest work, Ima Pipiig withdrew a small carved stone turtle. And this she left to rest on a turtle log in that back bay, warmed by sunshine on shallow water and by the effluent of the water pipe that protruded from the cheesecake factory, just across the railroad tracks.

Then she walked back to the former cheesecake factory office building that had been bought by the college and that now housed the university center at Northwest Lower Michigan College, an institution that specialized in the recertification of white schoolteachers for the all-white school systems of northern Michigan that specialized in the reeducation of countless generations of Anishinabeg, children, those of many generations and many years on the steep-banked bays, where they had played and rested with Manaboozhou and the turtles. They dove and chased dragonflies, minnows, and pollywogs, learning the timeless lessons that the Anishinabeg passed down to one another about how to survive in back bays, in corners of northern Michigan's and northern Ontario's peninsulas that had not yet been discovered by those eager to garner, hoard, and develop those remnants into their own mistaken expectations of Indian heaven. Like the turtles, remnant populations of Indians had adapted and persisted into the present, fearing that the old knowledge that had taken thousands of years to be accumulated would find itself expendable in the faith of the newcomers.

Ima Pipiig climbed up into the cab of her dump truck in the back corner of the big asphalt parking lot. Rain began to pelt the windshield. It had become cold and inhospitable for the summer day that it was. Ima Pipiig had had enough of the university center and the teacher recertification course that had been offered through the American Writing Workshop. She had grown tired of futile practice exercises and the bored participants who obligingly critiqued one another's bits and snippets of writing in an effort to avoid becoming anything other than teachers who had no initiative to learn, no reason to exceed, no reason to beat the system that was rigged in their favor. Her only goal for the whole summer had been to prevent these people from messing up her work. Now it was time to go home and to write.

· 11 ·

Public Education as a Form of Media

Boozhou, aniishinaa . . . Lois Beardslee, anishinaabekwe, indiizhinikaash. Wawauzhukgesh dodaim 'nizhiibp, gi' imaa Leelanau County, Leelanau Peninsula, Michigan, *'nizhiibp.*

Hello, how do you do? My name is Lois Beardslee, and I am a Native artist and writer from Leelanau County, Michigan. Before I offend almost everyone in this room, I would like to thank you for coming to this fund-raiser for Channel Two in Traverse City, for supporting local broadcasts of Pacifica Network's *Democracy Now* with Amy Goodman and for supporting independent media in general.

As we discuss the need for independent media to educate Americans, I would like to turn that discussion on its head and talk about how our public educational institutions have already been serving as media. . . .

I don't have time to woo you, to impress you with my credentials. I've got them, and I'm not willing to play the usual northwest Lower Michigan lawn jockey game that requires me, as a local Indian, to stamp them on my forehead before you consider giving me the time of day. I don't have time to entertain you, to prep you for reality, or to sneak up on you with local anecdotes that justify facts and statistical realities. So I'm going to throw out ideas and statistics that you will find dumbfounding, unbelievable. Some of you will curse me and leave angry. I urge you to stick around and listen because the status quo of inequality in America is starting to hurt you as much as it's already been hurting me. . . .

Discrimination in educational institutions and in employment is already so severe that a Native American's likelihood of committing suicide increases by one-third if he or she obtains a college diploma; and we already have a suicide rate eleven times greater than that of the general population. While we have the highest high school dropout rate in the state, we still manage to go on to succeed in higher education. We just don't have much to show for it. The notion that education can actually be damaging to people of color goes against the grain of everything we have been taught about the role of education in society. Education for the sake of education alone is without value and mistaken lessons are relayed by example if the system is not held accountable to society as a whole. . . .

Our museums and our children's literature are insipid. They are dominated by white curators and white authors who depict people of color as a mere adjunct to European American culture. The shelves of our libraries, bookstores, and museum gift shops are loaded with offensive children's books that purport to represent the Native culture of this region, yet portray us as ignorant, cute, docile supplements to a cottage-country culture of usurpation and exclusion. The local college museum refrains from acknowledging local Native American culture in favor of Inuit art—safe art—from cute, safe ethnic people from far away—the kind that don't compete with newly arrived folks for jobs, real estate, public-land access, and other resources. . . .

We need to take back our local institutions. Too many school board members have unlisted telephone numbers. Find them. Bug them. Demand accountability and public accessibility. Don't let them make decisions in private, don't let them hide behind big tables in one end of the room, don't let them make you feel like a stranger in the institutions *you* own, and don't let them make you fear for the safety of your children if you anger them. Make freedom of information requests. Get on school and museum boards yourselves. It's not always easy; in some areas they practically constitute private clubs whose members are as shameless as our state and federal politicians. Our public educational institutions are media resources we must reclaim as surely as we reclaim the airwaves.

State educational retirement boards often have reciprocity agreements with public employee and military retirement programs. This contributes to our growing number of institutions headed by military officers and professional politicians. It contributes to institutionalization of military recruiting and cultural disparities and to the subjugation of free thinking and active citizenship in all but a few limited domains. School boards and administrators are not sharing the realities of the "No Child Left Behind" act with parents. And if they're paid enough that they'd rather endanger our children than jeopardize their jobs, we've let the local economy layer itself too much already.

There, that's short enough. Short enough! Imagine that. They don't have a long enough attention span for me to tell them what they are doing to me and to my people every single hour of every single day. They don't have a long enough attention span for me to tell them that they should not be sorry for what happened to our ancestors, but for what is happening to us right now. They don't want to hear about how letting me be expendable could contribute to their own expendability. I could stand there for hours giving anecdote after anecdote after anecdote, and too many of them would still think I'm talking about someplace far away. No wonder they thrive on ten-second sound bites! I wonder if any of this will make any difference.

I used to be so afraid to talk about these things, afraid of the power that the people in the public schools had over me as a parent, afraid of the power that the people in the colleges and universities had over me in terms of employability. But it's gotten so bad. It's become so painfully aware to me of how dispensable my kind is to them, that I feel like I've got nothing to lose anyhow. I'm turning into a literary suicide bomber.

They would accuse me of biting the hand that feeds me. But what if it's not really feeding me? Who is responsible for the nip of the hungry dog, if not the self-proclaimed master who fails to feed it sufficiently?

I wish these things were happening in strange countries far away. That way we could put the blame elsewhere, the shame elsewhere, and expect other people to do something about it in boardrooms and capitals far away.

Racism 101

$\mathscr{B}$ecause they were basically nice enough people, and because Ima Pipiig was basically a nice enough person, Ima Pipiig would come back to the writing class obediently to visit in subsequent years, when she was called upon to do so. She'd been lured into participating in a writing class by being told that she would be team-teaching. But it turned out that she would be a student and she would be treated no differently than Indian children had been treated in the abusive style of all-white educational institutions, even though she was a full-grown woman. But she came back obediently to visit in subsequent years, when she was called upon to do so.

She could always peddle a few books, and a few of those below-five-or-ten-dollar items of artwork made from bits of birch bark and the other bits and pieces of nature that non–Indians had come to associate with Indians and their role as acquiescent remnants of a lifestyle long past that existed only in the imaginations of those who had come to northern Michigan eager to garner, hoard, and develop those remnants into their own mistaken expectations of Indian heaven. She had given up on the notion of an Indian as an educator worthy of equal respect, position, or pay here on the shores of the Boardman River. But she played the game of showing up. Ima Pipiig had stopped minding that she did not fit in with the faith and plans of the newcomers.

Florence Reznik, who taught the teacher recertification course, was not an especially good teacher. She was busy working on her doctorate in education, so she didn't put much creativity into the class assignments. She was small and found tall, energetic Ima Pipiig somewhat intimidating. Her doctorate was supposed to be about how diversity actually does make a difference in education. Ima Pipiig, aside from being a published author who would lend credence to the American Writing Workshop class she was teaching, was supposed to be her gesture to diversity. But she'd bitten off more than she could chew with Ima Pipiig. The other published authors she'd talked into thinking they were going to help team-teach the course had been much easier to handle. They were standoffish and seemed annoyed at being her students, but they never said the things that Ima Pipiig had dared to say. Ima Pipiig wrote and spoke about racism, racism in education—to a room full of educators! Ima Pipiig was scary. That's why Florence Reznik needed a bouncer.

There was something that was not quite right about Florence Reznik. She could smile and be charming, which was a change for Ima Pipiig, since the faculty in elementary education at the University of New Mexico fifteen or twenty years ago had rarely gone that far when it came to dealing with the Mexicans and the Indians. Some had downright sneered. And Ima Pipiig, a product of an environment of educational abuse against people of color, had practically glowed and swooned under the slightest smile, nod, or sign of affirmation from an educator back home in Michigan. But still, there was something that was not quite right about Florence Reznik. She was dismissive, dismissive in a way that was abusive to Ima Pipiig, in a way that told her outright that her education and her experiences as an educator, a minority, and an author were not merely suspect, but completely without value in this white context. She set up her classroom and environmental factors in such a way that her classroom was a laboratory of dissatisfaction and hatred. Ima Pipiig wanted desperately to identify the problems and their causes, but they were so far from her home and life experiences that they left her clueless. She could not fathom what made so many of the educators who had come to Florence Reznik's classroom so hateful. She suspected that they had arrived that way, and that Florence had merely exacerbated and inflamed the natural tendencies that were already there. And Ima Pipiig suspected that the only reason Florence Reznik did this was because of her own fear and feelings of inadequacy. She struck Ima Pipiig as a woman who was so desperate for a high-paying job that she would dismember a goat with her bare teeth. And this struck Ima Pipiig as odd, because Ima Pipiig lived far below the socioeconomic level of Florence Reznik, who was married to a white professional; and Ima Pipiig had a very hard time reaching out and hurting others for her own financial gain. Yet Florence's teaching methods were primarily those of hurt, interspersed with smoke screens and bubbles that were designed to make it look as though she was creating a nurturing learning environment. Ima Pipiig's worst fears were that the educators in the recertification class, already prone to abuse from at least four years of indoctrination in the profession of abuse, would copy the model of the teacher. As the summer progressed, her worst fears were realized, and Ima Pipiig would leave the experience fearing for the Indians and others who would become the beneficiaries of all that training in the fine arts of discarding the lesser elements of society.

For all of her dislike of the writing class for teachers and the fact that she'd been tricked into thinking that she'd be team-teaching in exchange for her college credit, Ima Pipiig knew that she had Florence Reznik over a barrel. Sometimes Florence would have to treat Ima Pipiig in a denigrating manner, just to keep her in her place, to make sure she didn't get too creative and too comfortable with her role in that room. And the other educator-students in the room, following Florence's model, would start talking down to Ima Pipiig, too. Ima Pipiig found this fascinating. She'd come to realize that she frightened them all a little bit. And this empowered her slightly, allowed her to regain her perspective, to look upon herself as competent. Once she realized why they wanted so desperately to deprive her of self-respect, she was able to redeem some of it, by virtue of her very "otherness" from those who feared their own incompetence as a contributing factor to their own failure or success in competing against Ima Pipiig on equal terms.

And this fear of "other" on their part was causing them to become more abusive than usual. They began grabbing at straws in order to put Ima Pipiig in her place. After all, she had no business accusing them of being less than superior to her. After all, they had teaching jobs and she didn't. The only problem was . . . Ima Pipiig never seemed to fold in response to this logic. She merely quoted statistics that pointed out their own complicity in a system that favored privilege. She even had the audacity to write, as her class project, a lengthy piece of nonfiction, a piece about race and gender discrimination in education. She'd researched it ahead of time, in anticipation of the class. And now she just sat there, twiddling her thumbs or making sweetgrass baskets or writing out her grocery shopping list, while the rest of them edited and sweated over the few paragraphs that would become their own tributes to their families and their desire to be part of their image of northern Michigan that they had sought out by moving here. And Ima Pipiig sat there, thinking that she knew more about Indians and Indians in education than any of them.

She'd had the audacity to write her paper with the intention that it be published in a major educational journal that she'd already picked out ahead of time. She wrote nonfiction—in a writing class of all places! And she quoted statistics in a class that wasn't supposed to be about statistics, but about finding one's self through writing. And they shot down her statistics, too. Once Ima Pipiig claimed that in her research she'd discovered that there was only one Native American teaching outside of a Native American studies program in a Michigan state college or university. But that administrator from Mitten Tip Community College, the one with the big nose who was so good at making people feel like dirt in the classroom, she told Ima Pipiig that she was wrong, that there were two.

And Ima Pipiig only giggled. She found it profound that these people might actually believe that two was a better statistic than one, or that it somehow negated all of the other incriminating statistics that Ima Pipiig had gathered from various studies and governmental agencies. But she actually knew better, knew that they did not find themselves any less incriminated. They simply chose to hide from the fact that they were part of the problem and that discrimination did not occur only in schools and communities far away. And Ima Pipiig knew better than to argue with them about it. She simply let statistics fall like lead balloons within the room. She did not feel the need to bat them about like a child at play. By fighting them, by denying them, these people simply incriminated themselves in their complicity. And this made them easier for her to perceive as "other" and easier for her to write about.

They weren't all bad. They were just people, and Ima Pipiig had her favorites among them. She was most surprised by the one she had initially perceived to be an aging hippie. Silvie had turned out to be the most receptive of all to Ima Pipiig's ideas and suggestions, and she proved to be a good student. She broke with Ima Pipiig's stereotypes about vegetarians, and Ima Pipiig was grateful to her for having opened that door in her mind. Even Gloria, Florence Reznik's assistant-slash-bouncer was fun sometimes. Ima Pipiig enjoyed joking with her the most because she knew that Florence had put Gloria in charge of keeping Ima Pipiig under control. Sometimes Ima Pipiig would pretend to be Gloria's dog on a leash, and she would bark and lick Gloria's hand, just to let poor Gloria know that she wasn't really in control. Other than that, Ima Pipiig was fairly respectful.

Silvie had once suggested that class participants exchange their actual seating place placards with new names that they made up for themselves. Ima Pipiig obediently wrote "Looks Good in a Bikini" on the back of her card. Gloria, sitting directly across from Ima Pipiig, had written "Fat and Ugly Bitch" on hers. Silvie had taken to calling them "Looks Good" and "Fat and Ugly" for short. Ima Pipiig thought that resonated their actual perceptions of their roles in the scheme of things. She imagined that Gloria perceived of herself as a bouncer doing someone else's bidding, and she wondered what this might have done to poor Gloria's self-esteem. Ima Pipiig, who had nothing to lose anyways, perceived of herself as the teacher. So she strove to teach this room full of white educators that Indians had every reason in the world to be self-confident in the classroom, even if they were different, and that maybe that difference could contribute to the well-being of the classroom as a whole. Somebody had to do it. Florence Reznik was still bringing in poems about Crazy Horse.

Besides, Ima Pipiig assured the class, she did not even own a bikini. She swam naked.

So there she was, in a room full of all-white teachers with poor training that left them with bad attitudes about Indians. And she'd only agreed to go there because she'd been told that she would be a teacher. So, in spite of the odds, Ima Pipiig taught these people on a daily basis. When push came to shove, when they were just too tired and lazy to fall out of the comfort and convenience of the racism they'd been raised with, Ima Pipiig would surprise them. Ima Pipiig was a shape-shifter. She could be docile, smiling, angry, and imposing. Some days she could be so soft and gentle to them that she held out in her extended brown hand the image of the docile young Indian maiden that they wanted all Indian women to be in the northern Michigan they were carving out for themselves. But just as they would reach, gratefully, for that stereotype, Ima Pipiig would turn into a fish or a bear or even Ernest Hemingway; and this would disturb them the most, because Ernest Hemingway hunted and fished and wrote about the banks of the Boardman River, only feet from their classroom window, and they did not want to confuse their imposing image of him with that of a tall Indian lady in a light blue sundress, just when they'd gotten her to be the docile cottage-country Indian maiden of their imaginations.

Once, when they all went out to lunch, Ima Pipiig ordered a beer. They all responded with a single, unanimous, audible short intake of air. It wasn't quite a gasp. Because Ima Pipiig looked around the room at all of them with a confident, shape-shifting smile, before they could complete the breath, and she said, "Did you think that all Indians cannot handle even one beer, because we have a natural, genetic, *cultural* tendency toward alcoholism?" And the ladies giggled nervously. And Ima Pipiig drank half of the beer with her burger, even though she did not like beer. She had merely ordered it to measure the response of those around her who had sworn up and down that they harbored no stereotypes about minorities, no, not them, none at all. And she needed on that particular day to hold up that stereotype to all of them as a mirror because someone had to be the teacher of the teachers, and Florence Reznik was rarely up to the task.

It was no wonder that Florence Reznik was afraid of Ima Pipiig, afraid that she would shake up things and disturb the peaceful facade of her kindergarten-like classroom. It was as though Ima Pipiig lived to shake up the status quo, as though she had no stake in it, as though she thought shaking up things was a valid teaching method. Which, of course, it was. And in spite of the fact that she got out of control and expressed her dissatisfaction with the status quo even here, even in her own classroom, Florence Reznik actually liked Ima Pipiig a little bit and felt that she contributed a little bit of diversity to the classroom. It's just that it had to be channeled to meet her own needs, not Ima Pipiig's. Because Florence Reznik wanted her doctorate, so that she could have this job, so that she could be financially more secure than Ima Pipiig and the rest of those Indians, and she could be emotionally more secure than Ima Pipiig and the rest of those Indians, and she could be more a part of this place away from the cities from which she'd fled more than Ima Pipiig and the rest of those Indians . . . That's why Florence Reznik needed a bouncer, and that's why she was glad that Ima Pipiig rarely showed up to American Writing Workshop events in the years that followed, even though her boss at Iron State University kept Ima Pipiig on the mailing list. Surely the woman must understand that the invitation didn't mean her.

Ima Pipiig, of course, did show up one day, at a banquet, much to Florence Reznik's visible chagrin. She pulled her arm backward in involuntary refusal to give the tall Indian one of the packets that she was handing out to the other people who were arriving; and she scowled when Ima Pipiig nodded, smiled, and said, "I'll show myself in," loping beneath the seams of the tailored blue jacket of a business suit that interjected itself between the beaded barrette at the back of her head and her fresh, dark blue jeans. Her hair was pulled back tight and crisp, and the rest of her flowed past Florence Reznik with confidence, effectively pulling the rug out from under the small white woman's intentions of being in charge, of setting a mood of control from the doorway, while her supervisor visited smoothly with various people inside the banquet room. Ima Pipiig, of course, had anticipated Florence Reznik's revulsion, but she had no way of knowing that she was disrupting anyone's self confidence by merely *being* there, *being* there with a uniform that said, "professional and comfortable with it," *being* there with a small box of books and magazines under her arm, as though she had something of value to share. Florence Reznik hated when Ima Pipiig showed up at writing workshop events fresh from the farm, like an unbroken horse; she always stole the show.

The hotel that had provided the university center with the best financial deal for its various banquets was far across town from Ima Pipiig's peninsular home. She had had to wind past both arms of Lake Michigan's Grand Twin Bay, in searing heat, on roads clogged with summer tourists. Normally, she was up in a rural bush camp somewhere in northern Ontario this time of year, far from the people and the heat, but she had clustered together a few speaking engagements in Indiana and Michigan and decided to squeeze in the banquet while she was back in the States. Ima Pipiig was glad to see an acquaintance there that had published several books of fiction. She was a neighbor, and Ima Pipiig had known her for years, because their daughters were both about the same age and were both of mixed parentage. The writer was a bit of an oddball, a remnant intellectual in a community where being an intellectual had become a liability, and her sister had had a child with a local Indian who proclaimed to be a medicine man and spiritual leader in the hopes of getting white women to go to bed with him. It had been a fairly successful strategy, and he had fathered seventeen children by various white mothers, scattered throughout the state. The two girls got along well but didn't go to the same school, so their paths only overlapped when their relatives went out of their way to make it happen. Since their mothers both worked and didn't have much in common, it didn't happen very often. But it was nice to see a familiar face.

By Ima Pipiig's standards, racism in education had gotten even more severe since the last time she'd seen the folks at the university center. Apparently the class methodology hadn't improved much, either. Her writer friend was hostile and condescending to everyone around her, including Ima Pipiig, who hadn't seen her in years, and Ima Pipiig recognized what was going on. She'd gone Hemingway on them, in her own sort of way. And later, they would talk on the phone and vent about the fact that they'd both been tricked into lending their names and credentials to the writing class, by being led into believing they were to team-teach a college course.

But since that conversation hadn't happened yet, things were getting unpleasant at the dinner table. And Florence Reznik, not realizing that her boss had actually invited Ima Pipiig to the banquet because she wanted to talk to her about another project, kept sending Gloria-the-Bouncer over to ask, "Did you bring your invitation with you?" and "Whose guest are you this evening?"

And when Florence Reznik herself tiptoed over, waiting until Gloria-the-Bouncer was safely behind Ima Pipiig's chair, in case Ima Pipiig shape-shifted into a Tyrannosaurus Rex or Crazy Horse himself, Ima Pipiig finally looked up from her plate and asked, "Would you like me to pay for my own dinner?"

"No. Heavens, no." They scattered like flies from a horse's behind.

But, since her writer friend was being curmudgeonly before Ima Pipiig had finished her beef in wine sauce, and her friend Daniel, who was married to an Indian, was sitting at a full table with no empty seats, she took her plate and slipped into one of several seats next to Gloria-the-Bouncer, giving her a quick hug and a kiss on the cheek. She did this because she genuinely liked Gloria. She was smart, and she deserved to perceive of herself as something more than a bouncer. And she did this because she was a shape-shifter, and she knew that they were afraid of her, and that this was not the time to be an angry bear. It was time to be a friendly bear. Because even as a *zhiikwamukwaah*, a friendly bear, Ima Pipiig scared these ladies as much as an angry bear; and Ima Pipiig liked scaring them to death with their own prejudices, in the hopes that she might some day get them to understand that it was their own fears that had frightened them in the first place. She hated to pass up an opportunity to educate the educators.

"How have you been?" Gloria asked.

"I still look good in a bikini."

"You published the new book."

It was one that Gloria had read the manuscript to back during the writing class because Ima Pipiig did not write little bits and snippets like people in writing classes were supposed to do, and Gloria had been assigned to keep Ima Pipiig in her place and to pretend that they were all critiquing one another's work. She'd dutifully written a page of comments about the manuscript, which ended with a presumption that Ima Pipiig would not change a word of the manuscript. She had assured Gloria that, indeed, she wouldn't, and that it was at the publishers already. Gloria had always found it difficult to keep her footing when Ima Pipiig was in the room. Things hadn't changed.

"I published the paper from the class, too," Ima Pipiig informed the bouncer.

This banquet was the culmination of the teacher recertification class. They were going to make presentations. It was cute, and Ima Pipiig was not one to be cute in a situation where Indians were expected to be nothing but cute. So, during the banquet at the end of the class two years earlier, she had sat at a table sipping Jim Beam with the deans of several different downstate colleges who had wandered in to take advantage of the bar. This year, an administrator was a scarce commodity, so Ima Pipiig, feeling like she'd been the only one dumb enough to show up at this event more than once, attempted to mingle with the young teachers who had been sitting at the table with increasingly nervous Florence Reznik and Bouncer Gloria. Eventually Ima Pipiig would leave, but not before the group followed Florence's lead in talking down to Ima Pipiig, who had had the audacity to show up in the guise of a published author, one who wrote both fiction and nonfiction about racism in education; because, after all, we do not have racism in education here, it only happens elsewhere, in places far away. Because Ima Pipiig had, foolishly, told people exactly who she was and what she did.

It had been a couple of years since she'd been in that abysmal classroom at the university center, and Ima Pipiig had forgotten what it was like to be in a room full of people in a profession where at least three-quarters of the people came from the bottom quarter of their freshman class in college. She had taken to giving them the benefit of the doubt of five percentage points or so, because she still found the statistic that 80 percent of them came from the bottom 20 percent of their freshman class to be frighteningly unbelievable. She had forgotten how susceptible they all were to Florence Reznik's teaching and modeling of hatred and fear, and, above all, keeping her good-paying job intact.

A very young bleached blond in an educational-administrator-wannabe-flowered-dress and matching spike heels stood up to give her presentation in the kindergarten-play that would be her emblem of accomplishment commemorating her graduation from the Suzanne P. Creamcheese School for Dumb White Girls. She cocked her head in Ima Pipiig's direction, avoiding the dignity that looking directly at her might convey upon someone as insignificant as a mere Indian woman, and asked, "And where do you teach at?" before tottering off to her designated spot on the rug to recite her little ditty, as though the fact that she had obtained an entry-level teaching job in an all-white profession in an all-white school district in an all-white town had made her somehow superior to a fifty-year-old woman with three times her credentials and three times her professional experience. Ima Pipiig was not surprised by the incident. It certainly wasn't the first time it had happened to her. But she was disappointed by the setting. She had hoped for more from the university center. She had hoped that the infusion of ideas from downstate colleges might have brought a little bit of enlightenment to northwest Lower Michigan. But the downstate colleges and universities were as unintegrated as they were in Twin Bay City, where racism and the hoarding of resources, including human dignity, were not far away.

And before Ima Pipiig had had enough, before she'd had the common sense to walk away from any interaction at all with the white exclusiveness and extreme stupidity of the university center, a young strawberry blond in a crew cut who looked like his steroid intake was at war with his baby fat began to hiss at Ima Pipiig: "Shut up! Shut up! You don't know anything about my school district. Shut up! Administrators are mostly white males . . . you don't know what you're talking about. Shut up!"

And Ima Pipiig could do nothing but smile apologetically. "I don't make up these statistics. I merely research them and write about them and talk about them. It's your job to make them wrong."

"Shut up! DON'T you tell me what my job is! DON'T you laugh at me!" The face was flushed, the teeth and pudgy fists clenched. He alternately made faces like a little boy and a pugilist, depending upon whether or not he wanted sympathy or he wanted to be the aggressor. He looked to Florence Reznik and Gloria-the-Bouncer in his most boylike demeanor. To Ima Pipiig, he squeezed his face into a hiss, he leaned with clenched fists. He seemed oafish in his brown-polyester-I-wanna-be-an-administrator-when-I-grow-up limp suit. She knew the type well, and she knew an abuser when she was in the presence of one. Later she would learn from her writer friend that he'd arrived already drunk, six-pack in hand, and that not one of the professional teachers of teachers who had concocted this abysmal event had had the presence of mind to suggest to the young man that this was not professional behavior and that he might leave . . . "You're lucky he didn't leap across that table and strangle you," the writer friend would say, describing him as a "shallow, broken shell of a human being." Ima Pipiig could understand broken people. She came from a culture that other people tried to break all the time. She just couldn't tolerate the abuser part of broken. That, she felt, was in need of fixing. And she wasn't particularly interested in being the fixer in this particular time and place. But she knew that she would be making a big mistake if she did not refrain from backing down, that this man would do untold damage in a high school classroom if he increasingly got the message that bullying women and minorities was acceptable. And none of the professional teachers of teachers who had concocted this abysmal event had had the presence of mind to warn Ima Pipiig that this man was a ticking time bomb.

Ima Pipiig would learn later that he had played that game of baby face and abuser repeatedly throughout his summer course. Tales of punching people in bars, tales of the tough guy. Then, poor baby. His wife was having a baby. His mom had died recently. Nobody liked him. Everyone conspired against him. Tales of drinking, drinking, drinking. Tales of bullying. Tales of abuse. Tales of angry high school parents. Nobody liked him. Poor thing.

And the young boy, who was named David and had no Goliath but a fifty-year-old Indian woman with a head for statistics to fight against, leaned in even further, looking side to side, lowering his voice even more, to make sure that a room full of witnesses did not hear him, and he pointed his stiff forearm and finger at Ima Pipiig and hissed from his diaphragm, "I want you to get up and leave this table right now. I want you to leave, because I can't stand sitting here and looking at you smiling and thinking you know anything."

Poor baby, indeed. Ima Pipiig looked at the red, fuzzy hairs on the forearm. He was a baby in need of spanking, but not her baby to spank, and a baby who earned as much as a young engineer with the endorsement of an educational system that valued whiteness and masculine gender over competence. She wondered where the school district found these people. But she kept smiling, and she did not back down. She would not apologize for quoting government statistics or constitutional scholars. Even Florence Reznik, who was doing her doctoral thesis on diversity, nodded knowingly at the statistics and ideas that Ima Pipiig put forth. And Ima Pipiig suspected that Florence Reznik was even trying to take mental notes and remember the names of the books and authors and Supreme Court decisions that Ima Pipiig was leaking forth like a nighttime sprinkler on a hotel lawn. In fact, Ima Pipiig had put them forth in a very gracious and polite, though firm, manner. And Ima Pipiig had learned over the decades of abuse and denigration by educators who were older and meaner and more experienced at abuse than this strawberry blond in a limp wannabe suit that she had no reason, absolutely no reason, to apologize for herself.

"*Don't* you smile! *Don't* smile! I don't want you sitting there smiling and thinking that you know anything about *anything*." And then it crept in, that little smile. That abuser's smile. That do-anything-to-anybody smile. She must've shown shock, or fear. And he enjoyed it. It crept into his face and his posture. And Ima Pipiig, who knew an abuser when she saw one, got up and left. She did not just leave the table. She left the room. She left the university center, and she left Iron State University; and she left Florence Reznik and Gloria-the-Bouncer wondering exactly what Ima Pipiig would do and how it would affect their jobs, because Ima Pipiig was a shape-shifter, and Ima Pipiig would no more turn into a willing victim for them now than she had in the past.

The outdoor air had cooled slightly with the setting of the sun. The dashboard lights of the dump truck were a comfortable shade of turquoise green with orange highlights that were softer than the traditional colors on an automobile dashboard. They matched the low glow on the horizon that Ima Pipiig would retreat toward in disbelief. She adjusted the knob that made them brighter and dimmer. She found solace in the comforting rhythm of the big diesel engine that ran smooth and predictable beneath the insulation of the hood. She drove through the eastern fringes of Twin Bay City, a place she could remember in the distant past for its clusters of mobile homes along a rocky and algae-strewn shore, unlike the sand beaches of Sleeping Bear County. Today the eastern bay was crammed full of businesses, each hoping for a claim to waterfront proximity, a testimony to the others who had found this place and found jobs that people of color would never get.

She turned on Interlochen Public Radio, which, ironically, played an interview with an administrator from Twin Bay City Area Public Schools. He had something to do with job training and collecting data on jobs. What kinds of jobs should high school graduates in Twin Bay plan for, he was asked. For boys, introductory level carpentry jobs. And for girls, summer hostesses at restaurants. They had a fine training program for boys to become introductory level carpenters, he said. How did you get a job as an administrator, he was asked. And in her mind, Ima Pipiig chose to ignore his answer about how he competed with fifty other profoundly qualified (white) administrators for the job and got it because he was the most exceptional; instead she fantasized that he answered, "Aw heck, I pulled down my pants and showed 'em my credentials." And Ima Pipiig thought to herself: White. Not exceptional. Just white.

A dumb white guy making eighty thousand dollars a year teaching kids how to look for seasonal part-time employment at minimum wage or slightly better with no health insurance—pretending that he's something more to society than he actually is.

Ima Pipiig turned left at the grocery store where the state highways split and headed uphill and westward, to cross the peninsula that had once been promised to the Indians as theirs and theirs alone, past the subdivisions close to town and the junkyard and the well drillers, the cherry farms, the public dump, and the cornfields. She worried for the safety of the girls who would be cornered in a classroom, in a hallway, around a corner, by the David-with-no-Goliath. If he treated Ima Pipiig that way, in front of witnesses, even witnesses he knew were powerless, like Florence Reznik and Bouncer Gloria, how would he treat children when he thought no one was looking? Ima Pipiig also worried for the safety of the girl who would be having the angry manboy's babies. What would he do when they were alone, without even the threat of others inside the same building perhaps overhearing, perhaps arriving to witness the abusive language and body language. How far would he go? Ima Pipiig thought of the bleached blonde, perhaps only twenty-three, already with hair that did not move, already more involved with self and power to injure than a woman in a room full of teenagers purporting to be their role model should be, and she wondered . . . how would she treat those children, people's babies, especially the children of color . . . But Ima Pipiig already knew. She was more aware of the domestic-violence-like pattern of abusers modeling abuse for the next generation in public education than were the hapless Florence Reznik and her many disciples.

Where did they find these people, she asked herself, shaking her head, as she slid the tall barn door shut behind the massive darkness of the dump truck. The door, big enough to accommodate large tractors and semi-trailer trucks, had been so carefully crafted by Lester that she could close it with one finger. And as she rounded the corner from the last in the row of big barns, there through the trees, she saw the warm glow of the small house where love and competence ebbed and flowed with predictability. After showering off the bile of higher education, Ima Pipiig slipped into a space between the bodies of her husband and her children and a big, longhaired dog, where she dozed off to the constant murmur and flickering lights of the television.

• 13 •

The Lecture They Want to Hear

Boozhou, aniishinaa . . . Lois Beardslee, anishinaabekwe, indiizhinikaash. Wawauzhukgesh dodaim 'nizhiibp, gi' imaa Leelanau County, Leelanau Peninsula, Michigan *'nizhiibp.*

Hello, how do you do? My name is Lois Beardslee, and I am a Native artist and writer from Leelanau County, Michigan. Before I offend almost everyone in this room, I would like to thank you for coming to this fund-raiser for Channel Two in Traverse City, for supporting local broadcasts of Pacifica Network's *Democracy Now* with Amy Goodman and for supporting independent media in general.

Thank you for coming out on icy roads this evening. February is one of my favorite months. It ranks right up there with the other eleven, in that I'm grateful every time I live through another one. *Shigaak bijaagindau giizis.* Sometimes we call February *The Month of the Breeding Skunk.* So I guess it's probably their favorite month, too. But since they sometimes get so excited that they don't look both ways before crossing, they pose an extra road hazard this time of year as well.

Skunks actually come out of semi-hibernation to breed as a response to candlepower, due to the lengthening days. This is also the time of year that chickens start laying more eggs. Onions respond to candlepower, too. Here in the north, they bulb when the candlepower starts to decrease, or when the days get shorter . . . about six months from now. Garlic, which also bulbs, responds to chilling hours. It doesn't bulb well unless it gets frozen early on in its life cycle. Who would've thought that onions would be more like skunks and chickens than like garlic?

I guess that Indians are more like skunks and chickens, too, because we come out of semi-hibernation in February, to attend midwinter powwows. I

97

suppose that a little breeding has always gone on at those powwows, too, but it's none of my business, and none of yours, either; although I guess you could say that Indians respond to chilling hours, too, so maybe we're just as much like garlic as we are like onions. That would make us a little bit more of an enigma than just skunks or chickens.

We have special ceremonies this time of year because the lakes have finally frozen over or have gotten cold enough that they don't cause lake-effect snow. It changes our climate tremendously. The sun comes out and melts down the snow to a harder surface that's easier to travel over. The nights usually get clear, cold, and crisp, and the moon becomes a beacon for night travel. Dawn and dusk tend to be brighter due to reduced moisture in the air. It's just a better time to travel, be it by dogsled, snowshoe, Ford, or Toyota. And people really need to travel because they've been cooped up in wigwams, houses, and barns with the wife and kids, maybe a few cousins and a mother-in-law, for about two months, and the Anishinabe child abuse rate is about to go up if somethin' doesn't give.

Nobody can really afford to go to midwinter powwow. Most Indians don't find a lot of employment in northern Michigan in the dead of winter. Most of us don't find a lot of employment in northern Michigan during the summer, either . . . but we've learned how to take advantage of seasonal resources and we manage to make minimum wage or less. There are a lot of Indian fishermen, basket makers, and casino dealers out there with college diplomas and graduate degrees. And the pain associated with this type of racially based underemployment tends to make midwinter powwow even more necessary today than it was generations ago. You see, racism, and racism in education in particular, is so bad that our likelihood of committing suicide actually goes up if we obtain a college diploma. And our suicide rate is already eleven times higher than yours on a daily basis. So we need midwinter powwow. We need to be in contact with Indians other than the ones who depend upon us, daily, even in the dead of winter, when most Indians don't find a lot of employment, although most of us don't find a lot of employment in northern Michigan during the summer, either . . .

Midwinter powwow is not like the commercial powwows that are held during the tourist season. It's the one we do for *us*, for our own mental health. Traditionally it was also an opportunity to trade essential goods and information. It's always been that way. Because there is inherent value in our millennia-old culture, those needs persist into the present. I can compare our needs to yours, finding similarities between all of humankind—simple things, like the need to adapt to short days and long nights by developing survival strategies, like midwinter powwows and storytelling, and mid-February fund-raisers for public, noncorporate media . . . The similarities are there, in a rudimentary way. But there is a socioeconomic layering to our culture that has been here for so long, right on up through today, and even into tonight, that keeps some of us in the category of "other," as expendable, for the comfort and whims of the fortunate.

There are two basic points I need to make to you today. The first is that, as a Native American, the relationship that I have with the media is very different from the one you have. Here in northwest Lower Michigan, we are often viciously attacked by the media, as individuals and as a group. When Native people try to increase the per capita square footage of the eighty-acre reservation they were eventually left with by saving up and buying back some of their own real estate, newspaper headlines give the appearance that the reservation is growing like an uncontrolled behemoth and criticize Natives for taking off the tax rolls repurchased property that was taken from them at whim by the stroke of a pen, long after treaties were signed. It is somehow alleged that Indians are dipping into the pockets of the benefactors who left them high and dry, homeless and jobless. The editor of the *Leelanau Enterprise* actually initiated an ACLU threat of lawsuit, based upon a Time-Life book about spirituality, against an all-white-staffed public school that had permitted Native American guest speakers on school premises. The editor then published a misleading headline story about the incident, as well as printing the time of a related public meeting as an hour later than it was actually to take place, and gave misleading information to people who called the paper. The pride that those individuals took in intimidating the local Native American population no doubt rivals the pride that members of the Ku Klux Klan once took in some of their most elaborate hooded robes, lovingly hand-stitched with white stars on a field of blue, flanked with various patterns of white and red stripes. No local historical society will acknowledge that during my childhood Michigan's membership in the KKK was triple that of Mississippi's. No feel-good publication geared toward the joys of northern living will document past and present segregation here.

Even the most liberal publications that most of you subscribe to, such as *The Nation, The Progressive,* or *Z Magazine,* are not accessible to Native American writers, because we lack the technology and the "good old boy" connections to get read and published. We are invited as speakers locally in only the most benign, lawn jockey, Uncle Tom contexts, as storytellers and entertainers, usually without pay or for a pittance. We are not allowed to teach, and it is beyond most of your comprehension that we might have skills that would be useful to society. I am as uncomfortable with the lack of input I have with so-called liberal media as I am with conventional media.

The other basic point I want to make tonight is that we've got to start looking at our educational institutions, including state and national parks, museums and historical societies, as forms of media. We've been sweating over how to use independent media to educate people, but now it's time to turn that concept on its head. Educational institutions are public media. Problems we face nationally—economic stratification, racism, sexism, and ignoring the needs of the constituency—have their roots here at home.

Minority employment in educational institutions here vacillates between zero and a fraction of 1 percent. Dozens of Indians have obtained teaching credentials and have been turned away, in spite of the fact that we have one of the highest densities of Native Americans east of the Mississippi. Recently personnel at the Sleeping Bear Dunes National Lakeshore avoided a paper trail in hiring discrimination by simply refusing to let a Native American submit a job application. Native American women have the highest number of college diplomas per capita, yet we rank number one in unemployment in this state, followed by Native American men. If we are able to look upon people around the world as "other" and as expendable for their resources, it is because we have practiced this at home.

Teachers are no longer underpaid. Entry-level teacher salaries locally exceed those of entry-level engineers. This is one reason why the profession is 89.3 percent white statewide. Good jobs have become a rare and contentious resource. And rare and contentious resources don't usually trickle down to minorities. Administrators, mostly white males, receive minimum salaries in excess of $100,000, along with benefits and retirement. The gap between their salaries and those of the average retail worker is proportionally equivalent to the gap between the middle class and corporate executives. While there are approximately fifty applicants for every local job opening, administrators continue to notify the public that there is a shortage of teachers and administrators.

The average public education retiree retires earlier than the average American and receives at least 60 percent of his or her highest working income annually, using up individual and employers' contributions within the first three years of retirement. The balance is made up by retirement fund investments and by taxpayers. Yet most Americans receive no retirement and their future social security incomes remain anything but secure.

Three-quarters of all people who enter the field of education come from the bottom quarter of their freshman class in college. Most state educational retirement boards have reciprocity with public employee retirement programs and the military. It is no wonder that retired Pentagon officials increasingly fill administrative positions in our colleges. If we are lied to in our capitals far away by our lawmakers about expertise and the management of resources, it is because we have allowed the practice to continue at home.

A few years ago the school district in which I reside passed up dozens of female and minority applicants with doctorates and outstanding transcripts (and one androgynous male) to hire as middle school principal a white male with a D+ in his college course on arithmetic for elementary school teachers. Why can't Johnny understand complex concepts like race and gender equality? Aw, heck, he can't even do long division! If you are wondering why Harvard president Lawrence Summers, with his history of undermining gender and racial equality in hiring, recently announced that women are genetically less capable of learning math and science, it is because we have tolerated such ignorance and theft of public job resources at home.

A local elementary school principal who was accused of repeatedly intimidating, threatening, stalking, and battering women and children became the superintendent of schools in another district not far away. Are you worried about bullying in the schools? What if it's the role models who are doing the bullying? If you are wondering how it is so easy for corporate America to militarily bully the rest of the world, it is because we tolerate such behavior at home.

We have modeled racism, sexism, violence, white-collar crime, and usurpation of resources in our schools, five days a week, nine months a year, from kindergarten through graduate school. We have given girls the message that what's valuable about them is not between their ears, but between their legs. We have given white boys the message that they can behave like classic underachievers and still take more than their earned share of resources. Is it any wonder that the educated and formerly professionally employed women of Middle Eastern countries we have plundered don't want to be like us?

All information that your school has collected about your child and your family is passed on to military recruiters, unless you sign a waiver indicating that you do not want to participate in the directory. In this case, your child's information will also be withheld from college recruiters. You won't read about these things in your school newsletter. Chances are, it's produced by a public-relations firm, and the needs of those highest up on the payroll will be represented before those of the community. Ignorance has become an imperative of our educational systems. Comfortable schools have become the exception, rather than the rule. The concept of "us versus them" has come to dominate family and community relationships with our educational institutions.

We need to take back our school boards, advisory boards, and museum boards. These are publicly funded institutions. Their reclamation is as essential as that of the airwaves. It's said that we can't have imperialism abroad and democracy at home. In fact, we've always had imperialism abroad and imperialism at home. They've worn different faces. But imperialism is working its way up the racial and socioeconomic ladder. If your constitutional rights are jeopardized, it is because you have been thunderously silent and compliant in the trampling of the rights of others here at home. The damage resulting from inequality and resource appropriation is not far away.

Racism stopped wearing the face of the Ku Klux Klan a long time ago. Its demeanor is subtler now. It exists in a sense of "other," a tolerance for statistics, for collateral damage, especially the kind that can be kept out of sight, out of mind, out of our education of ourselves and our children. It exists in multigenerational ignorance of "other" as a long-term strategy. That is why we do not permit people of color to infiltrate our school systems, our museums, our children's literature, our theater, our newspapers, our political parties, and even our social movements, as anything less than smiling cooperators, lawn jockeys and cigar-store Indians . . . house butlers and White House butlers. It is no wonder that hatred sneaks locally into the operations of the ACLU and our school boards. It is no wonder that auras of superiority creep locally into our museum exhibits and our writing and funding of grants for arts and cultural affairs. It is no wonder that hoarding of resources for a community of whiteness and safety from "others" persists locally in hiring practices and in people's abilities to socialize or distribute access to publicly funded phenomena. We live in a public-land ghetto. It is a white-flight community. Instead of wearing hoods, the program participants wear all-white schools with all-white staffs, national park backyards at the taxpayers' expense, and armies of expendable poor and minority recruits. These are the pointed hoods of the Ku Klux Klan of the north. These things reflect a culture of sociopathy, but not far away. It is here.

The burning crosses on the front lawns of the expendable have taken on new forms. They are old cars rusting in driveways. They are shorter life spans, due to lack of health care. They are poverty in old age, due to inequalities in retirement accessibility and the dismantling of Social Security for the maintenance of a Wall Street status quo that excludes the poor. They are childhood obesity in the face of soft drink sales in public schools for the purpose of maintaining a system whereby raising money for staff and administrative salaries above those of the community takes precedence over the welfare and education of the children of that community. The crosses burning on my front lawn today are built of ignorance and an educational system that thrives on maintaining that ignorance. We are the Deep South of the North. These illnesses, these forms of cultural and educational domestic violence are not far away.

The far right is taking its cues from us. We are subject to corporate abuse on a national and worldwide scale because we tolerate the concept of abuse at home. Some of you are here tonight because the status quo of inequality in America is starting to hurt you as much as it's already been hurting me. To those of you who fall into that category, I want to say, "What took you so long?" Shame on you. Shame on you for wanting a piece of the story of midwinter powwow without giving Native people a piece of the respect and equality that we deserved long before tonight. You can't simply hunt and peck and pull out the little bits and pieces of our culture that you want and write yourselves cute little children's books that paint pictures of Indians in northwest Lower Michigan without referencing the socioeconomic inequality that has been heaped upon us for years before tonight. We have survived working more hours than most of you for less pay, often with higher credentials. And in spite of those handicaps, we survive and strive for a better future. Our desire to survive is as strong as your ancestors' desire to come here and overtake our environment, not unlike the zebra mussel, the round goby, purple loosestrife, and all of the invasive animal and plant species that have made their way across oceans and continents. Corn has replaced barley in Europe. The American tomato and the peanut rule supreme in the diets of those who have not evolved along with them. Potatoes became so invasive to other cultures that crop losses caused mass famine in the "old world." It is so impertinent of you to assume that only you can have positive impact upon us through educational media, that only you have cultural and educational entities that are of value to the "other." I do not want your concept of "other." It feels dirty and abusive. I no more want to apply it to you than I want you applying it to me. Where do we go from here?

Ok, maybe I got off track here. Maybe this isn't what they want to hear either. I did really good until I got to the parts where I started talking about inequality; until I got to the parts where we do not want our few remaining and newly acquired resources appropriated, stolen by non-Indians for non-Indian consumption, stolen like traditional seed germs and lifesaving biological knowledge, or stolen like traditional stories for white children's storybooks, leaving us out in the cold and without livelihoods. But that's what I really want to talk about—staying alive, physically and emotionally, culturally and individually. It is a biological imperative, and it is a cultural imperative.

Isn't that what racism is about? One group wanting another to perceive itself as useless unless it fulfills the needs of the dominant group? Isn't that one of the tenets of slavery? Beat the "others" down mentally until they give you what you want? Aren't these people suffering from corporate abuse because they tolerate the concept of abuse in the first place? This essay is OK until I get to the parts that they don't want to hear.

• *14* •

Sweetgrass

*N*o one really took the Indians of Sleeping Bear County seriously, except as potential threats in the form of treaty rights. But no one really took the Indians of Sleeping Bear County seriously as scholars or academics, scientists or conservationists, community leaders or concerned citizens to be reckoned with. If an Indian came up with an idea that went against the status quo of the small-town equivalent of corporate greed, it could simply be passed off as a silly idea by someone who was not worthy of acknowledgment. It was an attitude that had hurt the people and environment of the county in a lot of ways that they chose to consider unworthy of acknowledgment as well.

So Ima Pipiig didn't get involved in local politics much. And when she did speak up, it was usually when the self-interest of the violators was profoundly blatant, or when there was the potential for a lot of hurt to a lot of people. It's just that she'd found out over the years that one person really can make a difference. She didn't join clubs or boards or nonprofit organizations. She just did things that she thought made a difference. She gave a handful of bills to a woman who might be trying to escape from a domestic violence situation. She slipped a check to a woman whose trailer had burned down but who did not have the social skills to thank her, ever. She had a policy of picking up at least one piece of someone else's trash whenever she went to the beach. She had a policy of picking up at least one piece of trash from the ground surrounding the trailers where the community took their recycling, next to the river. She spent an hour on the phone with a neighbor who considered herself the graaande daaahme of local politics, suggesting that she disseminate information on how to register to vote in the county high schools, working hard to let the woman think it was her own idea.

Ima Pipiig was like that when it came to being a citizen. She preferred getting things done over making sure that her reputation was intact. She was fairly secure in her image of self as one who worked hard, loved hard, and shared hard. She even ran for school board once, not in the hopes of getting elected, but in the hopes of stirring things up a little bit and getting people to acknowledge a few of the problems that had taken root. She didn't mind that she'd only gotten ninety votes. That was the number of people she had spoken to when she went around getting petition signatures to get herself on the ballot. It was a lot of votes for an Indian in an all-white school district that had scared the minorities out of the district completely in order to keep their property values high. Ima Pipiig didn't mind being the butt of those racists' jokes. She'd been a schoolteacher. One of the ways she'd been successful was by letting the kids think that she was ignorant and foolish—sometimes it was the easiest way to trick them into thinking about what she wanted them to learn. Teaching in one's community was no different.

When local white supremacists filled up the local branch of the American Civil Liberties Union and started attacking Indians, Ima Pipiig spoke up. A few individuals wanted to bully the school district adjacent to the reservation out of letting Indians use school grounds or facilities for any activities. So they threatened to sue on the basis of violation of the separation between church and state. Because Indians believed that everything was spiritual. And therefore Indians couldn't tell the difference between the real world and the spiritual world. So everything they did was religious. So they couldn't do anything in the school. Because the school was public, and Indians were religious. (Not just religious, but defiantly religious. Religious out of the mainstream. On purpose. Against the grain of what they were supposed to do. Against the norm of being lesser and incapable of making those decisions for themselves.)

It was a pretty lame argument. Ima Pipiig did a little poking and prodding and found out that the legal argument was based on a Time-Life book about spirituality, not Native American spirituality as Indians knew it, just spirituality in general. And Ima Pipiig thought that acknowledging all of those religions violated the concept of separating religion from state, and that maybe a book about religions wasn't really such a good legal source. Ima Pipiig ordered the book on interlibrary loan from the public library in Twin Bay City, and she found the book itself to be a pretty lame excursion into the world of Native American spirituality. The text contained some rather unauthentic sources: "A Native American once told me . . ." Wow, that wouldn't exactly hold up in federal court.

The day that Ima Pipiig chose to go to town to run a half dozen errands, which included returning the silly book to the library, the sun warmed the interior spaces of the dump truck, making Ima Pipiig a little lazy, a little more inclined to drive more slowly and enjoy the scenery. There was something about driving the dump truck that made Ima Pipiig want to slow down and take back roads on those days anyhow. Perhaps it was the new perspective of driving a few feet higher off the road than she was accustomed to that made her want to enjoy everything around her. Perhaps it was the feeling of satisfaction she got when she thought about how much she enjoyed owning her very own dump truck. It was useful and fun. Perhaps it was the way the mass of the big machine was slow to respond to the acceleration of its efficient diesel engine and Ima Pipiig's inclination to save gas and save her brakes from wear and tear, but something about that dump truck slowed down Ima Pipiig's mentality, her need to hurry up and get too much done on a given day.

So she swung east, then north, then back east again, before turning the generally southerly direction that would take her to the nearest state road into Twin Bay City. The dump truck crawled past the old Indian Mission Church, tall and white, taller than wide, built to accommodate a tiny remnant population of the region's aboriginal people—a monument to a white man's religion that served to pave the way for business interests in Sleeping Bear County. Ima Pipiig smiled. She wondered why the old Indian Mission Church did not make it into the book on spirituality or into the ACLU's legal argument implying the feral nature of so-called Indian religion . . .

After she'd complained publicly, after she'd pooh-poohed the ACLU's legal source and suggested that they use *Little Black Sambo* as a backup source, Ima Pipiig was approached by a few of the old retirees from downstate who now claimed ownership of the local concept of protecting the civil liberties of those who they believed needed it. And they would start out smiling, certain that they could trick Ima Pipiig and fool her into believing their superiority because of their prestigious attachments to the field of law . . . but they would leave, scowling, after Ima Pipiig would tear apart their legal arguments and then confront them with the fact that the legal arguments were so lame that they revealed ulterior motives—motives that included hatred and racism and that could surely be interpreted as ethnic intimidation. And, for all of her ignorance as a result of just being an Indian, Ima Pipiig was pretty good at pointing out sometimes that people were either being self-serving on purpose, or they were just plain dumb; and people generally didn't like being confronted with such limited choices when it came to labeling themselves.

The dump truck slid past a field that hid a precious patch of sweetgrass, kept secret among the Indians. It was kept secret because it was sacred, they would tell others. But secret also so that the others would not abuse the resource and use the resource to compete with the Indians for that tiny bit of livelihood they had left in a place that excluded them from most employment

opportunities—which always seemed to go unnoticed by the white supremacists who had filled up the local ACLU, who now claimed ownership of the
local concept of protecting the civil liberties of those who they believed
needed it.

As she drove up and around a wooded hill, peering through the too-
thinned maples of an overharvested woodlot, she could imagine them there,
in their red-white-and-blue polo shirts and khaki pants, teeth yellowed from
so many years of coffee-drinking-planning-of-intimidation-as-legal-theory, as
small denizens at home in the overharvesting. The sweetgrass was sacred to the
Anishinabe people. And she could visualize those yellow teeth hissing, "Sacred! Hear that? Sacred! The Indian said 'sacred!'" And she could imagine
them dancing, all of those denizens, among those trees too thin to hide even
their diminutive bodies and souls . . . "Ha! Ha, ha, ha, ha, HA!" Dance, twirl,
wheeze, patter, thump . . . Rumpelstiltskins, all of them. "The Injuns can't tell
the difference between the real world and the one they've conjured up for
themselves!"

The dump truck passed the washed-out ravines that once held water-
purifying seeps, springs, and streams. She passed the treeless hills that had been
clear-cut, then overgrazed, then exposed to eroding elements, hills where even
moss struggled to survive.

The sweetgrass was sacred. The sweetgrass patches themselves were sacred. They were not wild. They were domesticated. Not domesticated in the
way that a narrow thinker like the local dwarves of the ACLU might think.
They were domesticated with a sophisticated understanding of the landscape
that took into consideration the fact that the stuff could not be transplanted
just anywhere by just anyone. They were domesticated with a sophisticated
cultural understanding of the landscape that took into consideration the fact
that future generations of Anishinabe would be there.

The sweetgrass patches were sacred because the Indian women knew the
history of those places. They knew the Indian women who planted them,
who married whom, who brought the sweetgrass from where and when. They
knew and lived the histories of those sweetgrass patches. They knew who said
what to whom and when. They knew what was brought for lunch on a particular cloudy day that suddenly cooled and blackened and resulted in running
for cover, as the ravens swooped low ahead, cautioning, hurrying, urging the
women and children away from the lightning. And the stories would be told
about the thunderbirds who made the lightning, so that the children would
understand and remember lightning as something to be respected and feared
and thankful for in its replenishing gifts of rains and ozone and nutrients.

The Anishinabe women and children of Sleeping Bear County remained
alive as memories in the shade of trees that seemed to have stood there forever.

Grown men would come to that sweetgrass patch, exchange names and chat, only to realize that they had been in that same sweetgrass patch and had played together decades ago, with a mother or a grandmother or an aunt. And they would remember the toys that they shared on that day, or the sandwich or a precious cookie. Ima Pipiig would look upon a particular hummock and see her mother sitting there, decades long gone. And Ima Pipiig would sit by that hummock and reach over with a hand, as though her mother's knee were still there and touchable; and Ima Pipiig would feel, for a brief moment, the safety of being a child, protected by cautious and sometimes outspoken Anishinabe parents. And to the Indians of Sleeping Bear County, these things were sacred.

• 15 •

The Play

$\mathcal{I}$ma Pipiig didn't really think of herself as a Native American children's author, but apparently they were a little bit rare in northern Michigan. So, when she was asked to write a play for kids through the Museum of Ojibwe Indian Culture in St. Ignace, she was a little bit surprised. And, feeling a little bit unprepared to actually put on a play for performance for the public in the middle of St. Ignace in the middle of the tourist season, Ima Pipiig insisted that the museum also hire Katrina Smithfield. She was the only Indian Ima Pipiig knew of who had ever produced a play, and it had been an incredible play at that.

Katrina was only part Indian and took a lot of the standard kidding about, "Which part?" She couldn't pass for an Indian on even her best day. She didn't talk like one, move like one, and most of the time she didn't appear to think like one. But the Anishinabe culture was never one to throw away a perfectly good human resource; so with liberal doses of criticism, chiding, and downright humbling insults, Katrina was embraced by the Native American community with almost the same enthusiasm with which she had embraced it.

Her father had owned and managed theaters in downtown Detroit, and being smart as a whip, she'd studied theater and dance, succeeding at it, until she was brought down by a leg injury. It was all fairy-tale stuff to the Indians of northern Michigan, a significant number of whom had never been to Detroit but imagined it a metropolitan cultureland on a par with New York City, Broadway and all. So Katrina was the local expert on things of a theatrical nature. And she was *their* expert, putting them all just one tiny step above completely ignorant in things of a non-Indian theatrical nature. So Katrina found her cultural niche, as did the artistic wannabes of the local Anishinabe who had been trained by generations of abuse to think that traditional Anishinabe theatrical traditions were of no value whatsoever.

Katrina's play had been taken from a traditional story lifted right out of Ojibwe oral history. It was the story about how Manaboozhou lit his butt on fire. Only the play concentrated on the part that led up to the part where Manaboozhou lit his butt on fire. As a matter of fact, you couldn't even tell from the play that Manaboozhou ever was gonna light his butt on fire. That's actually the beauty of Anishinabe storytelling. The stories come in bits and pieces that accommodate the time frame available. They can also accommodate the attitude of the storyteller. And sometimes an Indian just won't give away the whole story because they don't trust the person they're telling it to. Also, it takes two or three human lifetimes to learn the whole story because it keeps changing, and it's bigger than two or three lifetimes anyhow. So Katrina was doomed from the outset, in terms of getting that whole story, because she didn't grow up Anishinabe, and people were a little tight in terms of sharing the story and the culture with her. You've gotta live it, and, if you're a light-skinned Indian that ain't got family close by, you gotta earn it.

So there was Katrina, just surrounded by all these incredibly talented Anishinabe artistes. And there was probably more talent and culture and history and stories and imagination and talent than one person could wrap herself around. Yet, being the incredible teacher and organizer that she was, she just scooped up all those Indians and made them into one hell of a theatrical troupe. The costumes kicked heinie, and there was even one loon costume that woulda been the toast of Broadway, if Broadway had ever heard of a loon dancing around with a bunch of ducks and Indians. It was the most glittering and professional thing that the twin cities of Sault Ste. Marie, Michigan, and Sault Ste. Marie, Ontario, had ever seen. Richard Sheesheeb's performance as a loose-limbed yet competent Manaboozhou was an inspiration to the Indian children who'd been coerced into being part of the audience, and the bobbing tail feathers on that loon still come up in conversation over many a steaming hot plate of venison pasty or fried whitefish.

So Ima Pipiig figured that if she had Katrina Smithfield on board, she could pull off any sort of performance. Somehow, things fell into place. Funding was obtained sufficient to pull Katrina away from the real estate office, and a date was arranged that wouldn't interfere with hunting, fishing, and life in the bush, so that Ima Pipiig, a bunch of children, and several other essential Indians could converge on the Museum of Ojibwe Indian Culture in St. Ignace for the entertainment and edification of museum visitors and the general public, not to mention the Indians, as well.

Ima Pipiig was adamant about having enough funding and free time to allow the Indian artists and sharers of cultural tradition to interact with and learn from one another, just like academics and professionals should. This would not be half-assed, underfunded, and an imposition upon the Indians. This would not be baby-sitting. This would be a glimpse into how the culture actually functioned before resource depletion and underemployment had wreaked havoc with their time and ability to function as parents, teachers, and leaders. The museum director felt very strongly that the play, along with its creation, memorization, practice, and costume making was to take place in the immense cedar longhouse that dominated the yard outside the museum. And all of this within a week. The longhouse was open. It was drafty. It was damp. OK, thought Ima Pipiig, they're not expecting much. And she put it in those terms: don't expect much.

When the time to produce the play arrived, the student participants turned out to be a very young, very exhausted group of children who had been participating in a summer youth program for a couple of months already and who had just returned from a ten-day camping trip. They could care less about producing a play.

There were other new twists. The play was going to have to be about the clan system because that was what was next in the curriculum of the summer youth program. And there was a possibility that a nature conservancy group might kick in some money, so the play had to be about animals and how they behaved in nature. None of this seemed particularly difficult to Ima Pipiig, because, after all, one of the purposes of the clan system was to teach people about how animals behave in nature. However, it was one of those things that, once again, took maybe a couple of human lifetimes to learn, and even then one wouldn't be especially knowledgeable about it in such a short period of time. So Ima Pipiig was hoping that some of the other Indians knew a whole lot more about the clan system than she did. As it would turn out, they all knew about as much about it as all the other Indians who grew up in the clan system, and between them all, they managed to scrape together two or three human lifetimes' worth of collective knowledge and experience—which is why they call it a culture instead of just a bunch of Indians.

Ima Pipiig knew one thing for certain: This late in the summer, these kids were fried. And they were developing some much-deserved bad attitudes. She knew that the only way to get them to write a play was to make it fun. And she knew that the tribal elders wouldn't mind so much because that's the way a culture works. You mix fun in with everything, especially hard stuff, and sad stuff. And kids like icky stuff, so Ima Pipiig planned on finding something icky that the kids would jump on and enjoy, like roadkill. But there were these two older kids who were being paid to be there to help run the program, and they were, for the most part, a big pain in the butt. They were way more juvenile than the fourth graders, which is what automatically happens to boys once they hit junior high school.

After two days of frustration and no progress, the big boys left for leadership camp, and Ima Pipiig and Katrina Smithfield heaved huge sighs of relief. Because, boy, could those boys lead. And one of them in particular was leading all those kids into violent tumbles that broke most of the props and spilled the fruit juice and pudding snacks. And it looked like the play was mostly going to be about how animals from the clan system pass gas.

Anyhow, in the way that all of these mysterious things happen, it rained. It rained for a week. And the longhouse, which hadn't been maintained and repaired for the last twenty-five years, as a real functioning longhouse would've been, was in serious need of a new cedar bark roof. So the whole for-the-pubic Indians-teaching-in-the-old-way thing got moved to the local junior high school gym, just down the hall from the summer youth program classroom full of computers, art supplies, and cookies and juice boxes. Sometimes it took a little tobacco and a little prayer to the ancestors to get out of that rut that white people had a tendency to put Indians into . . . that do it the old-fashioned way without electricity rut. With only three days left out of a week that was intended for superhuman things, Jackie Adikameg, who was in charge of costumes, sure seemed delighted when she plugged in her sewing machine and her iron and they both worked.

The script from the play was looking pretty good. The adults whose names were attached to it had been getting pretty nervous and had been fairly certain that even the elders, in all their wisdom, weren't going to forgive them if the play resembled one of Manaboozhou's mess-ups without his usual finesse for fixing things and cleaning it up. So they ordered a pizza and threw back a serious volume of diet pop while they took the few fart-free fragments of suggestions that the children had given them and merged them in with the traditional clan system and their own life experiences. They added a few healthy doses of secret cultural necessities in encoded cryptic Indian slang and sprinkled the final product with several behavioral guidelines that they each hoped their own offspring would adopt someday. The result was a contemporary Anishinabe masterpiece centered around the concept of totem animals as roadkill. It would please the children, it would please the nature conservancy people, and it would please the tribal elders, especially the ones who understood the double entendre about the careless massacre of Indian people and disregard for Indian culture. The women returned to their respective homes and motel rooms to collapse and sleep the sleep of the accomplished.

Somehow, somehow they all got through the next few days. At one point Ima Pipiig and Katrina snuck off to pick wild blueberries. At first all they could find were raspberries. And somehow, between the logging roads and the fresh fruit and the wild grouse, they found a little bit of peace of mind. The kids didn't necessarily associate their need to be up on stage with the need to show up every day and practice, or even to show up the day of the play. The moving trees that gave the effect of a car rolling down the road were trained as understudies for the clan animals. Bear claw fuzzy slippers and other props and costume addenda began showing up on the gymnasium floor. Katrina Smithfield used her best downstate accent and theatrical credentials to talk the theater teacher into giving her the key to turn on the stage lights, even though she was an Indian, and even though six out of ten households in the city of St. Ignace had at least one Anishinabe grandparent. Ima Pipiig, along with some of the parents, taught the kids some traditional animal motifs that were worked into the scenery and duct-taped to the back stage curtain. The dancing swamp cedars were outfitted with green T-shirts.

The bear turned missing and had to be rounded up from her grandma's house. The crane broke her leg when she fell off the stage wrestling with the turtle. She was replaced by a tall, willowy redhead who was an actual member of the Crane Clan and who volunteered from amid the forest of trees that looped forward in time to the chorus. When she picked up the script and read perfectly, everyone's heart skipped a beat. She'd never spoken before, and no one realized that she had a speech impediment. The grace and skill with which she came to the task and wooed everyone in the room was a humbling experience that brought joy and satisfaction to the adults who'd been nervously wondering if they were going to look worth their paychecks. The whole thing suddenly fell into perspective.

And then, at the end, when Tony and Artie brought in the big drum and sang clan songs with those kids, Ima Pipiig started to cry. The boy who'd played the lead character, aptly named Little Boy, had been so unable to show enthusiasm to the grown-ups, so programmed not to interact, even though they could all see how hard he'd practiced and learned his lines, even though he could not look out to the direction of the audience to read those lines, even though he read those lines so quietly that the audience had to be given a copy of the script to read along with him; he sat in that circle with the grown-up drummers, and he stared down at that big, humming drum that gave him something nonthreatening and comfortable to focus upon, and he beat upon the drum with the drumbeater that was placed in his hand, even though he would not look at his own hand, and he softly mouthed the words to the choruses of the songs that were being shared with him. After he was done, his mother, who also could neither look up nor smile, slid out of the audience and into the comfort of her own privacy and torture.

It was hard doing the stuff that Indians needed doing in a program that was designed by non-Indians for an Indian audience. And Ima Pipiig and the ladies who had come together to make that short, sweet play happen knew that they had beaten the odds. They had done more with less, as countless Anishinabe women had done in the last few hundred years of generations before them, ever since the beaver felt hat had become all the rage in Europe and copper had been discovered along the shores of Lake Superior.

THE CLAN SYSTEM OUR WAY

Written by Ima Pipiig
&
The Anishnabe Life Circle Summer Youth Program Cast and Crew

Directed by Katrina Smithfield

Costumes Designed by Jacqueline Adikameg

Produced by Eve Martel
Director, Museum of Ojibwe Indian Culture

Sponsored by
Museum of Ojibwe Indian Culture
&
Sault Ste. Marie Tribe of Chippewa Indians
&
Michigan Association of Community Arts Agencies

Special Thanks to Tony Gronden for cutting the cedar trees and for leading
the kids in the drumming.

THE CLAN SYSTEM OUR WAY

Lead Singer: (Faces audience.) *Boozhoo.* Thank you for coming tonight. Before we begin, we'd like to teach you a nontraditional traveling song, so that you might help our main character, Little Boy, on his very special journey.

(Teaches audience song to tune of Woody Guthrie's *Take Me for a Ride in Your Car, Car.* Way hiya, way hiya, way hi. Way hiya, way hiya, way hi. Way hiya, way hiya, way hi. Way hiya, way hiya, way hi. Take me for a ride in your car, car. Take me for a ride in your car, car. Take me for a ride in your car, car. Take me for a ride in your car, car.)

Little Boy: (Drives down road. Children holding up cedar trees pass behind him to give the illusion that he is moving forward. Little Boy stops, gets out of car.)

Deer, Crane, Turtle, Walleye, and Bear: (Lying dead at edge of road.)

Little Boy: (standing) Look at all these dead animals alongside the road. I remember when I was little, how my grandpa got out and put tobacco in their mouths and pulled them off the side of the road. I wonder what happened.

(Little Boy goes to Deer, takes pinch of tobacco out of zippered plastic bag and puts it in the animal's mouth.)

Deer: (Stands up slowly.) It was winter. I was going to the cedar yards down by the big lake. In winter, when the snow is too deep in the hills to paw down to the grass, we go down where the snow is less deep, to eat cedar. Good hunters know to follow the cedar trail in the sweat lodge, to find their ways to providers from the deer family like me—deer, caribou, and moose. It's the same thing out-of-doors. But I had to cross the interstate. (Shrugs shoulders.)

We are providers, because we are predictable, easy to find, and we give you our flesh to eat. We give you our skin to wear and to wrap around valuable things. We give you our antlers and teeth for tools. Even our toenails are used to make beautiful music and old-style jingle dresses.

Little Boy: You won't go to waste, *Wawashkesh.* Here comes Tony Gronden. He hasn't been as successful as usual in hunting this year. Your tender flesh will feed his family. He'll make hand drums out of your hide. It's fitting that you love music.

Deer: (Quietly walks offstage.)

Little Boy: (Returns to car, drives. Trees pass behind him.)

Chorus: (Sings Way hiya, way hiya, way hi. Way hiya . . . Take me for a ride in your car, car . . .)

Little Boy: (Stops car. Gets out. Walks over to Crane.) All of the clans of the Anishinabeg followed Crane here. *Ajiijauk* is a leader. Crane led us to food and shelter, to the whitefish in the rapids. (Puts pinch of tobacco in Crane's mouth.)

Crane: (Standing.) I was passing over I-75 on the way to join my family in a farmer's field after visiting a nearby swamp to feast on frogs and minnows.

I'd known of an Anishinabe woman who was in need of a large feather fan for her daughter's jingle dress. Just then, I saw her car below, so I flew down into the headlights of the car ahead of her.

You see, if I had flown into *her* headlights, she would have felt too guilty to accept the gift of my life.

Little Boy: (Returns to car, drives. Trees pass behind him.)

Chorus: (Way hiya, way hiya way hi . . . Take me for a ride in your car, car . . .)

Little Boy: (Stops car, gets out. Walks over to Turtle, puts pinch of tobacco in Turtle's mouth.) *Mishiikenh,* Little Turtle, how did you come to be here, poor thing?

Turtle: (Standing.) Didn't you see, on your way here, that I-75 is being dug up from here to Kinross? Didn't you see those huge, huge metal claws digging up the swamps, ditches and seeps alongside the road? Boy, those were some hungry, greedy creatures!

I was just minding my own business, burrowing into the mud, when, WHAMMO—my whole world was turned upside down. I was swept up by one of the beasts. I looked it in the eyes—big, ugly glass eyes—they didn't even look alive and caring. It didn't even have eyelids! I'm telling you, it was scary!

But I was one brave turtle. I said, "Hey, pick on somebody your own size!" And sure enough, I saw this huge Shell Oil Company tanker truck coming down the road. I thought, "Now there's a turtle your size, buddy." Then, oops, he dropped me onto the pavement, and the rest is history. (Turtle turns back to audience and points to tire track on shell, looking to audience and nodding.)

But I'm a healer, don't you know. And just by the act of putting tobacco in my mouth, you are healing your own heart and soul.

Little Boy: (Returns to car, trees pass him.)

Chorus: (Way hiya, way hiya way hi . . . Take me for a ride in your car, car . . .)

Little Boy: (Stops car, gets out. Walks over to Walleye, puts tobacco in Walleye's mouth.) What is a fish doing out here in the middle of the road?

Walleye: (Standing.) It's a long story. I was being airlifted from my home in Bay de Noc to Caribou Lake, east of here, near Drummond Island. The lake is always overfished, because walleye are such a popular sport fish. So it needs to be restocked constantly. It seems that some human beings don't know how to take care of precious resources.

The container full of water and fish that was attached to the underside of the helicopter began to sway when we got to a windy stretch over the highway. The lid came loose, and I was sloshed out.

Can you imagine what it's like to be taken from the place where you grew up? To be taken from where you know every rock, every plant, every inch of shoreline, every food source and resource—just to please a few rich so-called sportsmen?

We from the fish clans, we *Giigonhyag,* we are teachers. What I'm here to teach you today is about thinking things through before you use up a resource, even something as small as a fish. The decisions you make today will affect not only your children, but mine as well.

So here I am, a fish out of water! I can't remember how many times my mother told me not to hitchhike, never to get into helicopters with strange men.

Little Boy: (Returns to car. Trees pass him.)

Chorus: (Way hiya, way hiya way hi . . . Take me for a ride in your car, car . . .)

Little Boy: (Stops car, gets out. Walks to Bear. Starts to put tobacco in Bear's mouth.)

Bear: (Growls.)

Little Boy: (Steps back. Looks scared.)

Bear: (Stands up, brushes self off. Yawns.) Boy, I love these sunny winter days, when I can climb out of my hibernation hole, stretch my legs, and warm myself in the sun. It's a chance to walk around my home and make sure everything is OK. It's my job to protect the village, you know.

There are so many new roads through my home, new houses—I lost my way. I got so tired and so scared, I sat down in the sun by the side of the road here to rest. I must have fallen asleep.

It's all so confusing. Can you show me how to get back to a place where we'll all be safe?

Little Boy: Let's put out tobacco for our grandfathers, *Mukwaah*. That will be a good beginning.

Little Boy and Bear: (Both reach into the zippered bag for tobacco and place some on the ground. Then they walk off together, Little Boy guiding Bear.)

(All of the animal actors and several other different animals walk about the stage.)

· *16* ·

Creation Stories

$\mathcal{I}$ma Pipiig was worried. She was worried because she had received two creation stories through the mail in the past week. People mailed Ima Pipiig Indian books—books by Indian writers. But Ima Pipiig did not have time to read. She was too busy being an Indian. Ima Pipiig figured that she made less than ten cents on the dollar compared to a white person with her life skills and experience. Well, actually, Ima Pipiig knew it for a fact. But she humored herself occasionally by pretending that she probably actually made more. Nonetheless, Ima Pipiig had little time to read the piles and piles of Indian stories and books that white people felt obliged to send her. There were Cherokee creation stories by Cherokees. And there were Ojibway creation stories by Cherokees, retold from what they had heard via Ojibways. And Ima Pipiig didn't like that one bit because Ima Pipiig was Ojibwe. And Ima Pipiig was so busy being Ojibwe in small Indian towns that had become somewhat larger white towns that she did not have time to read all of these creation stories. And the most perplexing creation stories were the ones that came from Ojibwes and Ojibways and Zhippeways—Chippewas. Gawd . . . it was awful.

And the most horrendous creation stories were the ones that were adapted or even flat-out made up by non-Indians, mostly white ladies who'd moved into their families' summer cottages as permanent homes somewhere north of Chicago or Detroit or some big city in Ohio and were fairly certain that they had a real grip on the substance of traditional Indian stories on account of having been allowed to play (not work) in the woods for a couple of weeks a year. Those stories made Ima Pipiig's blood pressure get really high because they were the ultimate in sociopathic thievery. She looked upon it as trying to make money off a people who had nothing left but a few intangible traditions that were dangling out there for the taking because U.S. copyright law wasn't designed to protect that sort of thing. If it's legal, it doesn't seem to matter much whether it's ethical or not. And Ima Pipiig even wondered if it was legal because once somebody started making up their own versions of the Indian stories and passing them off as Indian stories, they were violating the federal Indian Arts and Crafts Act. Somebody had mailed Ima Pipiig a copy of that, too. But Ima Pipiig had even less time and patience for researching and filing federal lawsuits than she had for reading all those damned creation stories that were crossing her path. The real issue was that these spoiled white girls were so spoiled, so out of touch with social responsibility, so out of touch with the concept of being a world citizen, that they'd screw anybody for a nickel—hence the plethora of "Ojibway" Indian stories that were pirated from nineteenth-century Schoolcraft racism or just plain ol' manufactured, so that those lil' white girls could earn a pittance over their monthly interest check from the inheritance trust fund to keep up the "good life" in the summer-cottage-within-driving-distance-of-the-national-lakeshore, where they could play Indian, pretending that picking a handful of rose hips was equivalent to trying to survive without an inheritance and without hope of employment now that the new wave of white inheritors had winterized the summer cottages and taken over the economy and the landscape, thunderously silent of the racism that killed the Indians they so cutely fashioned themselves after.

The only thing that Ima Pipiig knew for sure was that she hated the word "puke" because it was so onomatopoetic, and these Indian stories made Ima Pipiig wanna pee-uuuke!

The truth of the matter was that Ima Pipiig couldn't stand having all of those creation stories coming at her all at once. The truth of the matter was that Ima Pipiig couldn't begin to figure out how to tell a creation story to a white person. And that's what all of these things were . . . creation stories extracted from Indian oral histories, histories that were much longer than a child-length book, white-adaptation-stories canned and packaged into Children's Literature 101, ala Dominant Culture Bullshit Curriculum 101, distilled, fabricated, and squished-into-book-format-to-compete-with-white-authors-who-are-stealing-our-stuff format. Whew! What a pain in the butt! Ima Pipiig wanted to pee-uuuke!

The truth was that the creation stories took all of one's lifetime to learn, and even then one didn't get the whole thing. It took several lifetimes to absorb it all—thousands of lifetimes, stretching out in a long chain of lifetimes from the present deep into the past, all the way back to creation itself. And Ima Pipiig tried to imagine what those first observers must have passed on to the first listeners they came across. Did they holler, "Hooooweee! Didja see it? Didja see it? We weren't even here a minute ago, and then, *pow!*" Or did they just squirm and wiggle their pseudopodia? Or were the first voices merely manifested in the wind? Because there was only one truth that Ima Pipiig knew about creation stories, and that was that, no matter what part of the story one individual had, there was always somebody gonna come along knew the part that came before that.

Ima Pipiig was worried. She spread a heaping soupspoon full of bean salad onto a cold piece of slightly burnt garlic toast and contemplated all of these unnecessary creation stories. "Heck, we're here," Ima Pipiig thought to herself, "how much more creative can one get?"

· 17 ·

No, Wait—I Know a Part
That Comes before the Beginning

*I*ma Pipiig was worried. She was worried because she had received two creation stories in the mail in the past week. Ima Pipiig piled a heaping soupspoon
full of bean salad onto a slightly burnt piece of cold garlic toast and contemplated creation stories. Not just any creation stories, but the kind that were
written down—the kind that people had the tendency to mail to her—as
though an Indian would have the time to read a bunch of books by a bunch
of Indians. The truth of the matter was that Ima Pipiig worked as hard and as
fast as her fifty-year-old body would let her, and then she collapsed for a few
hours and slept like a dog—not just any dog, but a dog who had worked hard
all day, or a puppy who had played hard all day. Ima Pipiig didn't see much difference between the two. The major factors were exhaustion and the inability
to move one's muscles even one inch further.

Ima Pipiig took a hurried bite out of the garlic bread and beans. The
bean salad wasn't really conventional bean salad at all . . . It was an eastern European dish—white beans with lemon juice, onions, salt, and parsley, and a
shot of vinegar, because lemon juice was a bit expensive for someone like Ima
Pipiig to use exclusively. The beans had been free. Sometimes Ima Pipiig and
her neighbors swapped big boxes of food. "Here, I got a lotta this. I hope
you're not offended." So food kept going around in big circles until it ended
up with the right people who needed it. Ima Pipiig usually had fish and apples, sometimes venison, sometimes lots of homegrown fruits or vegetables.
And other people usually had fish or eggs or beans or something else. The
Great Depression of the early twentieth century had never quite left the Indian community, and it lingered among the white homesteaders and miners
who would eventually intermarry with the Indians a little bit in the backwoods

areas of northern Michigan where the Indians hunkered down in their largest surviving numbers.

This was the area of the country where the Catholic Church had tended to send nuns and priests who had tuberculosis and other physical and social illnesses that would cause damage to the church's reputation in crowded urban centers. This was the area of the country where trees and topsoil had been used up frivolously, and the exploiters took the money back south, leaving ghost towns and small populations of people who knew how to survive. So the food went around in circles like that, among the older families and among the Indians. It was rare for it to cross racial lines like that. Usually there were Indian food circles and non-Indian food circles. But, after the new land rush, after busing in the inner cities following *Brown v. Board of Education*, after the new white people came in hordes and hordes, a lot of the poorer white folk and a lot of the Indians found a common ground for survival. And then there was the influx of federal designations and federal lawsuits that divided up the Indian community . . . and access to the things needed for survival got even weirder. So people formed circles within circles, whereby need and generosity ebbed and flowed, and people learned to recognize who understood the concept of circles and who didn't, regardless of race. And survival came to take on more importance than creation at certain times. Then the creation stories really got mixed up. Because people were creating new stuff, new traditions, new alliances, and sometimes those old, old creation stories, they had to be stuffed into a back pocket for a while, maybe while somebody went to church or went to a funeral or just had a good gossip with a snack at a neighbor's house.

And, while everybody knew that the old creation stories weren't thrown away, just bundled up carefully with sweetgrass and some old, old baskets and some old, old recipes and some old, old survival skills and some memories that stretched back thousands of years and took more than one lifetime to learn and memorize . . . a few little white ladies now and then would tell Ima Pipiig, "You people threw your culture away; the spirits spoke to me; they made me the real Indian . . ." and Ima Pipiig would sigh . . . There were more white ladies who thought they knew what it was really like to be Indians than there were Indians.

Larry Parmentier had been adopted out to a white family at a very early age, even though he'd always been told he was an Indian. The lack of continuity that came from the circumstances of his birth and his adoption left him with a propensity to put things in order, any kind of order. He was a good organizer, Larry. A really good organizer. It was a gift. He was half white and one-quarter Ojibwe and one-quarter Ottawa. And when he came home to northwest Lower Michigan and held out his hand, the Indians showed him how to put tobacco in it when he had requests, and they said, "Larry, you're not quarter nothin' and not half nothin', you're just a dumb ol' Indian." And now that he was an Indian, the tribe decided to take advantage of that gift that Larry had, that organizing gift.

So one day when Larry called up Ima Pipiig and explained how he had used his organizing gift to obtain a paying gig of storytelling, grown-up storytelling, not cute little children's storytelling, at the Grand Rapids Public Museum, Ima Pipiig was interested. And when Larry told Ima Pipiig that he envisioned a threesome of storytellers that included her, him, and Frank Abisakiishik, Ima Pipiig got out her pencil and her beat-up old wall calendar; because Frank was a good friend, and Ima Pipiig could always use a good laugh. And even though, on the phone and through the letters that began to flow, Ima Pipiig could tell that poor Larry's gift of organization was going to be a real pain in the ass when it came to the joyous experience of a bunch of dumb ol' Indians batting around a perfectly good story, she knew that she and Frank were just going to have to take a deep breath and show that boy how it was really done.

Ima Pipiig was tired when she got to the Grand Rapids Public Museum. She'd been hired to do storytelling earlier in the day at Ferry Harbor Elementary School. And Ima Pipiig had spent a significant part of her childhood back and forth between northern Ontario and Ferry Harbor, Michigan, just south of Twin Bay City, on a narrow strip of land between Crystal Lake and Lake Michigan. A swath of mountain that ran straight up into woods and abandoned homestead and ghost-town wildlife, comprising one hundred and sixty acres, a square mile of homestead by a white man whose son had married Ima Pipiig's mother's sister and had inherited Ima Pipiig and a couple of her siblings when her father had died on the highway further inland. This was the community Ima Pipiig had tried to repay when she'd agreed to do storytelling at the elementary school in Ferry Harbor.

A distant cousin, many times removed, but kind and sweet and gracious, had greeted Ima Pipiig at the door. The administrator, a principal with no experience whatsoever from somewhere downstate who looked upon Ima Pipiig as nothing more than a colored person hired for the day, gave Ima Pipiig a work schedule that was so unrealistic and so hurried and so physically demanding, that Ima Pipiig had not even had a ten-minute break for lunch. She was seven and a half months pregnant with the little boy, and she had been forced to haul box after heavy box of display items and cultural materials from room to room. The young white administrator could not be bothered to offer help. He was, after all, an administrator, and it was not his place to soil his hands or to lower his status by showing kindness to a female, let alone one of lower socioeconomic status. Ima Pipiig did not walk out on the boorish young man, because she was seven and a half months pregnant, and she was trying to save up enough money to have the little boy in a hospital, where the birth might be a little bit safer. So she did the job, and she left for the Grand Rapids Public Museum at least an hour late, because the schedule she had been given by the young and inexperienced boorish white man had messed up her own real-life schedule that took into consideration factors like traffic and wet, fresh snow on the roads.

Ima Pipiig was tired when she got to the Grand Rapids Public Museum. She had driven four and a half hours in a wet, treacherous snowstorm, after working seven hours nonstop without even a potty break, and she had previously driven an hour and a half in a wet, treacherous snowstorm to get to that first job of the day. And with barely time to go to the bathroom in a back room of the museum and grab a cup of coffee that had been brewed for the after-event reception, Ima Pipiig pawed her way through the heavy velvet curtains of the backstage of the auditorium until she saw the wide silhouette of Frank Abisakiishik and the lanky, nervous silhouette of Larry Parmentier, and an empty chair between the two; and Ima Pipiig slid out, in a slinky black hand-me-down pantsuit from the wife of a boy she had dated in high school, and Ima Pipiig raised her head and smiled and began to woo that audience. She'd had enough denigration at the hands of the white boy in charge of administrative denigration at Ferry Harbor Elementary School, in spite of the grace and kindness of the distant cousin and the appreciative teachers and students, and she was ready for an audience that was looking forward to her. Because Larry Parmentier was a good organizer, and having found his Indian roots, he had also found that there were appreciative audiences and not-so-appreciative audiences, and he had made sure he had set up the former for the threesome of Indians. Because Larry Parmentier was riding a fence, and he cared about the opinions of those two Indians on the stage with him as much as he cared about those hundreds of white people in the audience. And because Ima Pipiig had been wooing audiences long enough to know within the first thirty seconds whether or not she had a good audience or a bunch of crackers. And Ima Pipiig felt good about this audience. She was going to give a performance that they would not forget. She had the freedom to cut loose. And she did.

Poor Larry had planned on a round robin—I tell a story, then Frank tells a story, and then you, Ima Pipiig, you tell a story, and then me again. But poor Larry Parmentier, for all of his finding his Indian culture and being initiated into bits and pieces of it by various Indians, he didn't know what was about to hit him—because Frank Abisakiishik and Ima Pipiig had a few more bits and pieces of that culture than Larry knew even existed—several decades worth, with thousands of years of condensed practice passed down in a tight little package of rambling and story expansion to the nth degree . . . and they were both consummate bullshit artists on top of it all. By the time Frank stopped, out of breath, and Ima Pipiig took over, in the very first round robin, Larry Parmentier was left in the dust, long arms hanging limp at his sides, and too nervous to sit in his upholstered chair on the stage.

"Oh, but Frank, Frank, Frank," Ima Pipiig had doubled over her round belly, laughing and gasping for air, "but I know the part of the story that comes before that!" And she told it. And then she told him the part that belonged to Anny that came after that, and the part that belonged to Anny's dad that came before that, and there was a piece that belonged to Charlie Shedawin before that, and she was pretty sure her own grandfather had told her a piece that came before that part or during it or after it. And then she ran out of air and needed to rest her pregnant frame, so she turned, quietly, to Larry, who fumbled and grabbed in the air until he came up with a traditional story that he had read in a book somewhere that he didn't know if it had a part before or a part after or not. And he told, it, and it didn't really fit in anywhere, but the audience enjoyed it.

And then Frank just started talking about his dad. And then he ran out of hot air, and Ima Pipiig told a story about a fat and happy raccoon that was singing to the four directions; and she used the big pregnant tummy with the little boy inside as a prop, thumping it joyfully to each of the four directions, singing, "I'm a fat and happy raccoon, singin' by the light of my grandfather moon . . ." The audience guffawed, and Frank guffawed, and Ima Pipiig danced on that stage, in all of her pregnant exhaustion, washing away the stain of denigration that that young white public school administrator had left upon her early in the day.

And the night went on like that, until they ran out of time, and Larry had learned enough about Indian storytelling, so that he finally knew at least as much as the audience did that night. Then they all went into the staff kitchen and had snacks; only for Ima Pipiig it was the only thing she had eaten all day, and she unabashedly ate all of the honeydew melon and strawberries off the fruit tray. Then she donated a piece of artwork to the museum before she shuffled through the cupboards of the staff kitchen until she found a chipped coffee cup that said "Grand Rapids Public Museum" on it, and she dropped it into her purse. Because it was her policy to ask for a coffee cup with the institutional logo on it from every museum and university at which she was to speak, as part of her contract; and Ima Pipiig had forgotten to make that request before coming to the Grand Rapids Public Museum because Larry Parmentier was such a good organizer. And after several cups of coffee and plates of fruit and cheese, Ima Pipiig was ready for driving home four or five hours or so.

The heavy wet snow had gone away, along with any trace of moisture in the air above the highways heading north. The roads got less and less crowded, and the night got less and less polluted by electric lights. She saw the telltale visual thumping of pale greens and reds in the sky that indicated that a whopping good night of northern lights was ahead. And periodically she would stop on the shoulder of a familiar two-lane on a big flat plateau of a hayfield and stare up at the increasingly bright and pulsing northern lights. They were, according to the old stories, campfires along the pathways of the souls of the departed; and Ima Pipiig saw the faces and lives of those departed folks; and she knew and called out to them all by name: Yvonne and old Charlie her neighbor and her grandpas and some great uncles and aunts, some sweet boys who had died way too young, and even a beloved pet or two. And as she lay on the warm hood of the small station wagon, she patted her round belly like a prop and sang to the cold night air, "I'm a fat and happy raccoon . . ." and she giggled out the rest of the story, the parts about the four directions and the morals and the lessons learned by many, many generations who passed these things down to her in one form of shorthand or another until she had the time to live each and every one of those messages. And Ima Pipiig relived those thousands of years of stories for the next few hours, every time that she hopped back into the car to warm up her toes and to wrap her cold fingers around the still-warm steering wheel. And Ima Pipiig took the new bits and pieces that she had learned and lived that particular day and inserted them into the proper order in the oral history she would never live long enough to learn all of, especially the parts that came before the parts everybody else already knew . . .

The roads got snowier and snowier, until the last ten miles took her half an hour, but she didn't care, because even ten miles from home was home. Lester had left the porch light on, and he had stoked the woodstove, and the big brown dog, who did not wake to come to the door, rolled her eyes at Ima Pipiig as though to invite her into the crowded bed where Lester and Birdie breathed slow and heavy, Birdie pressed up against the sprawling animal. The house was warm, and the blankets were loose enough for Ima Pipiig to slip in between the two human beings, pulling them around her shoulders. She had been as grateful for the welcoming nature of the audience in Grand Rapids, as she had been for the porch light in her own driveway, and Ima Pipiig had been careful to drive far east of the town of Ferry Harbor, so as not to soil her homecoming. She would never again return to this town of her childhood because it had become a cold, white snowbound town without compassion. Even the sound of the dog's breathing, blending with the music of the others created a space where she and the yet unborn little boy could find solace. Ima Pipiig wondered at how that solace could exist in two different spaces, hours and miles apart from one another, one urban, one rural, with such contempt and disrespect pocketed in between. And she was grateful for the organizational skills of that Indian boy, Larry Parmentier, and she marveled at how he had found himself a bunch of Indians from so far away, in spite of the pockets of contempt and disrespect in between. Ima Pipiig smiled. The last thing she felt before falling asleep was pride in being a pocket of solace; that Larry was probably going to be a pretty decent storyteller some day.

Now, as she bit into that bean salad sandwich, as the tang of the vinegar worked its way around the sides of the back of her tongue, Ima Pipiig remembered that day of bad storytelling followed by that night of good storytelling. She thought of Indians like herself, the ones who were all mixed up. Ima Pipiig was one-quarter Polish. She joked that it was a legal requirement on the forty-fifth parallel, which she supposed must look a lot like Poland, given the large population of Polish people that ran in a band from east to west across northern Michigan and northern Ontario. She thought of Larry, the product of two Indians who were themselves both half Indians. It was like that. Even the half Indians were culturally all Indian, because it was mainly the Indian culture that took them in. The dominant culture usually walked away from those offspring of mixed parentage.

People didn't always understand how this happened, how half-breeds could go around claiming Indian culture, and how children of half-breeds could go around claiming Indian culture. And if those mixed-breed offspring could be culturally Indian, how come somebody who had spent all of their summers coming up to the north woods where the Indians used to live couldn't know just as much or maybe even more about Indian culture and write some perfectly good Indian stories? After all, didn't they both get the stories from the same source—from that white guy, Schoolcraft, the Indian commissioner, who had written them down before they disappeared, because those silly Indians couldn't even read or write, and wasn't he doing them a favor by preserving their culture, and weren't they doing them a favor by preserving their culture, since they hadn't even bothered to write it down yet, after all these years; and hadn't they just thrown their culture away? Hadn't they forgone the beauty of the place in favor of tar-paper shacks and broken whiskey bottles and jobs at steel mills in cities far away?

Ima Pipiig chewed the soft beans slowly, moved a piece of crisp onion around with her tongue. She thought of her own marriage to blond Lester, the letters she repeatedly received from her angry white mother-in-law, telling her that she had no intention of leaving anything to Lester, implying that, after years and years of love and sacrifice and hard physical labor side by side, raising children with no help in child care, no hand-me-down baby clothes, no family support from that angry white side, Ima Pipiig was still married to Lester Browning for his parents' money, his potential inheritance, his class status as the offspring of people who considered themselves superior to Ima Pipiig and all of the Indians who had survived for hundreds of years doing more with less. It was no wonder that Indian creation stories took precedence over those of the dominant culture in the lives of those mixed-breed, dog-like creature-Indians. No wonder the throw-away people found solace in the traditions of those who did not throw away people, but who found miracles and humor and loving stories and entertainment in the mere daily survival of each and every one of themselves.

The gifts of individual survival of each and every one of the Anishinabeg had become transformed, over thousands of generations going back thousands of years—all the way back to creation, to when it all began; and it takes more than one lifetime to learn it all, takes thousands of lifetimes, going backward to creation itself, creation of specific people, specific species, specific events, specific interactions, just like they really happened, because we were there.

Ima Pipiig had seen quite a few maps of the Ojibwe migration in museums during the course of her travels. It was the migration story of one band of Ojibwe who came from the east coast of North America and ended up here and there along the way, some of them ending up on the western end of Lake Superior. It was a really good migration story, and it was a really good map. The only problem was that, everybody (not Indians) started thinking that that was where all of the Ojibwe Indians came from, and educated people all over Michigan who knew more about these things than Indians did, kept telling the Indians that they were newcomers to this place, too, like maybe even only a few hundred years before the fur traders came; and Ima Pipiig thought that that was really funny. Because where she came from, the story was different. The Ojibwe people where her family came from had been there as long as the land had been there, maybe even longer, because there were a lot of complicated events and funny and tragic stories that happened even before this particular batch of land got here; and Ima Pipiig's family's story went back thousands of generations for thousands of years, and every time somebody told a story, there was always somebody who knew the part that came before that. And before the new guys showed up six hundred years ago or so and needed a place to crash and maybe a few good-looking women to marry and have beautiful children with, the Anishinabe were there, and those people just blended in and became Anishinabe, too, because it's just not like the Anishinabe to throw away a perfectly good human being when they might have a really good skill that the community could use, like organization or storytelling or something really important like that.

• 18 •

The Lore of the Turtle

*Y*oung turtle's a lot like an ol' bobcat. Bot' draped on a log in d'sunshine, one eye open. Young turtle lookin' fer predators, ol' bobcat lookin' fer prey.

I knew a young turtle once, his mother had had him way up on a hill. There was no sandy shoreline left for the mother turtles to lay their eggs in undisturbed. It had all been subdivided and had become the domain of children with toys, adults with lawnmowers, and docks, condos, personal watercraft, speedboaters, and all sorts of scary stuff to a mere turtle. The only places left for the mother turtles to brace the shore, heavy with eggs, were the backwaters and the sloughs, lowlands and places where the sand was too wet to keep their precious cargos warm and dry. So they'd taken to climbing the cliff-like hills above the sloughs created by distant river dams. There in a band between the bluffs and the industrial part of town flanking the railroad tracks, they found warm, dry sand, devoid of vegetation anymore, suitable for the sunshine growth of turtle embryos a few inches below the strong sniffing ability of predators and the mere curious.

It was here that the young turtle was born, on the upper banks above the Boardman River floodplain, far from water. The job that faced him was one for which evolution had not prepared him. An unnaturally long scrabble to fresh water awaited him. If he could make it across the man-made plains, an occasional puddle, and a strip of muddy service road, the woods and their brushy understory would provide him protection from crows, blue jays, and robins. Perhaps he was too small for even a hawk to bother with.

Then there would be the treacherous, though downhill journey through the underbrush, full of mice, voles, chipmunks, more birds, and who knows what else; only to reach the shore, hoping that that moist stretch of sand would at that particular moment not be occupied by hungry ducks or even a raccoon.

So it was that Manaboozhou, spirit child of Winona and the West Wind, happened to pick up the small turtle, no bigger than a quarter in his big, full-grown human hand. He gently cupped the tiny animal, smiling to himself at the scratching of its tiniest of toenails against his rough palm, and as quickly as he could, he climbed down the steep bluff, through the scratching branches of young oaks and poplars, supporting himself at the water's edge by grasping a trunk of a huge, hollow, smooth beech.

And the big man released the tiny turtle, barely an hour since it had pecked its way from its shell and clawed its way to the surface. He set the animal at the very edge of the water, to find the safety of the lake in his own good time. Then he threw a handful of *kinnigkinnig*, good Indian prayer tobacco, over the surface of the water. Minnows skittered to the surface where it floated, then reformed a tidy school, leaving in disappointment. This, Manaboozhou knew, would distract the shallow water pike who waited among the weeds for an unsuspecting meal to swim past their mouths. This would buy the young turtle time to find himself in the new world that would become his home. He deserved to get there in a timely fashion, without an exhausting and dangerous search.

This turtle is as old as I am now. We sit on that riverbank and talk. Not as frequently as we used to. He has family. I have family. There are chores. It's hard to find the time these days.

We drape ourselves over old logs, bark gone, surfaces worn smooth and silver gray by water in its changing forms—lapping waves, shifting currents, rains, snows, sliding ice. But today the sun is warm and welcome, and we watch minnow schools advance and recede with a regularity they have perfected over thousands of years. And we query about one another's families and activities, the business of being woman and turtle. We share one another's troubles, offer advice and consolation.

Been away, I tell him. To *chimknaak mnaassinh*, these days called Turtle Island. His neck stretches out longer than usual. His eyes open wide. He's heard of this island from all of the older turtles. There is a body of lore among them, about this island. It is named after one of their ancestors, and they feel a sense of kinship to this geographical place by virtue of their oral history, kept alive by distant turtle relatives who have traveled from watershed to watershed, braving the treacherous altered lands in between that have been taken over by strange people. The old turtle remembers the care Manaboozhou took in placing him here, at this shore, and in giving him the advantage of that tobacco and prayer. So he is afraid to leave this place, afraid of losing the kinship and camaraderie of his own kind within a known environment, afraid of losing the thousands of generations of history and adaptation that have made him a part of this place, afraid of offending Manaboozhou and his family were he not to accept the gift of his placement within the circle of life on and around the land left after Manaboozhou and the water people had a big controversy, causing waters to rise and recede, creating the perfection into which the turtle people had been born.

Distracted from the harshness of change, we giggle from our sun-warmed logs at the continuity of story. For every story we know, there is another part to the story that comes before it, that sets it up. Our stories go backward for thousands of generations. They shift and meet our needs. We are the stories. We dance them, live them, laugh them, cry them.

He wants to know about the big "turtle" island. I am not sure what to tell him. It has changed. It's a tourist resort, I tell him. It's a monument to change, I tell him.

Change is good, he says.

Not dat kin'a change, I shift on my log.

He wants to know.

I don't want to break his heart. I don't want to disturb the continuity of his people's story because it's a good one. It's served his people and my people well. It meets our needs.

He thinks I'm being cantankerous.

Well, dey gotta buncha buildings on it now. Big ones. Tourist hotels. An' dey gotta buncha Jamaicans workin' 'ere.

Jamaica?

Yeah. It's another island. An' nuh people dere got beat up about as bad as d'Innyuns, an' ney come over here an' dey work. An' ney're pretty and ney smile when ney work. Not like us, 'cause dey don' r'member how it was all ours. So their hurting is diff'ren'. An' nay wait on da white people all day long, lookin' up, smilin'. Not like us, lookin' down.

He wants to know how I got there.

I was hired by a company that does school field trips in da springtime. An' nay bring boatload after boatload after boatload of schoolkids and teachers and parents to that island in the springtime, when the rates are cheap. And they teach them about history.

Just thinking about it, I slip into that harsh midwestern accent, each word staccato. After an hour of it my jaw would ache, and I would become emotionally exhausted, torn from the comfortable dialect I share with my turtle cousin, when I am in comfortable places.

History, eh? We got a good history, us turtles. Damn! We got a good history.

We giggle and nod knowingly, each on our respective logs.

I was the Indian part of the history. Mixed in there with presentations about the voyageurs and the geology of the Great Lakes. I liked that part. I liked being mixed in with the geology. That's the way our history works. We're mixed in with the geology. Just ask the turtle.

Dija tell'em 'bout da turtle part? Dija tell 'em 'bout da flood part before it? An' 'bout da fight part before dat? An' 'bout da jealousy part before dat? An' 'bout Manaboozhou's brothers an' all da dumb stuff dem boys did before dat? An' na cool stuff dey did too? How long were ya dere? Long enough to tell 'em?

Nah. Not dat long, cuz. I only had dem folks fer'n hour atta time. I had to tell 'em 'bout other stuff, too.

But, but you told 'em 'bout da turtles?

Had to.

Hah!

Had to, because they'd most of 'em read some really awful books dat got 'em all confused.

Had to set 'em straight 'bout us turtles, eh?

Yeah. But mostly I had to set 'em straight about the other stuff.

What other stuff?

The other stuff in the books. The stuff that we're silly. The stuff that we're ignorant. The stuff that we were conquered. The stuff that we're mostly gone. The stuff that we're expendable. The stuff that only white people are good enough to tell turtles' stories to white people.

That's silly. Nobody tells a turtle story better than a turtle.

We shift and stretch on our respective logs. We giggle and nod knowingly. He slides into the water for a snack. My jaw hurts from telling stories in another dialect. I scramble back up the slope, keeping an eye out for young hatchling turtles working harder than nature ever intended to take their place in the turtle story.

· 19 ·

Book Reviews

I want to talk about books for a moment . . . children's books, the ones written by non-Indians in Indian genre, the ones based upon public domain "Indian" stories manipulated and sometimes outright fabricated by wanna-be-writer "ethnologists" like former Indian commissioner Henry Rowe Schoolcraft in the nineteenth century. These books frequently have been especially selected for my youngest child over the years by a teacher or a librarian and sent home to placate me because I am an Indian mother who finally dares to talk about the comfort of minority families in a public institution . . . Usually they are colorful and beautiful, and they are chucky-chock-full of stereotypes about nice, docile Indians that used to live here and somehow cleared themselves out of the way for the predominantly white families and all-white staffs of the local school districts. In the elementary education curriculum of most colleges and universities, this is called teaching social studies by starting close to home. To Native American parents, it is called early indoctrination in the concept of self as second-class citizen; it is called poison.

I remember the first time an editor sent me a box of books to review. They were children's books, all about Indians, and all by non-Indian authors, some thoughtlessly mass-produced series books. All seemed to exist primarily for the purpose of making money for non-Indian authors and editors who sought to exploit America's love affair with either a romantic or a disposable notion of America's first people. I had taken on the assignment only reluctantly . . . partly because it was work without pay, the kind of role Indians are traditionally asked to play in the education of non-Indians about Indians. Yet also, I had known, even then, that putting words to the contempt I had always had for this type of literature would change me forever. I knew that, once I had crossed that line and had been given "permission" to vocalize my anger and the reasons for it, I would end up opening my mouth much more than a dominant and abusive culture would want me to. I knew that, just as Black women like Fannie Lou Hamer who tried to register to vote in Mississippi during the 1960s would be told by their governor, "Mississippi isn't ready for that," a Native American writer criticizing white-produced teaching materials in Michigan in the first decade of the twenty-first century would be told, "The field of education isn't ready for that."

When I opened that Pandora's box of damaging stereotypes disguised as children's literature, I shook, I cried. I hid them out of sight . . . but not fast enough, before my children saw them . . . and I mailed them back straight away, without even so much as a note telling that editor to go to Hell. After several reassuring phone calls, insisting that I, too, am an American worthy of having an opinion, that my contribution to the field of education is, indeed, valid, even though I am a person of color, and an unpaid one at that (think slavery), the dark books were mailed back into my safe home and I was again violated. Ever since, I have been unable to keep my mouth shut. I have been writing, researching, and writing again; researching, comparing, lecturing, speaking out in public; and always, always researching again and again to justify truths about racism in education and in literature about Native peoples that would be accepted more readily if they came out of the mouths of nonminority educators. But they rarely do.

· 20 ·

The Lars Nederstadt Holocaust Museum

*I*ma Pipiig went to see Sherman Alexie at Lars Nederstadt Auditorium in the old Twin Bay City High School. There was nothing about it at all in the local media, but she noticed that there were fliers every place that Indian people usually went. She had never read anything Sherman Alexie had ever written, and she had never been to see any of his movies. She didn't like movie theaters much. They were dirty and smelled bad, they were full of far too many people, and the volume was always too high. But Ima Pipiig figured that if the local Indian tribe had paid the money, and if the local school district thought an Indian was good enough to go through all the effort to bring him here, the least she could do was show up as a form of moral support. She was getting kind of Indian lonesome anyhow, hadn't spoken to any she wasn't related to in days.

Ima Pipiig put on a new–never–washed pair of blue jeans and a matching dark blue hooded sweatshirt. Meant as the ultimate compliment, she pulled a brand–new–hurt–your–eyes–they're–so–white pair of tennis shoes out of the box. Ima Pipiig took along a small sweetgrass–and–porcupine–quill basket to leave as an offering, a way of saying thanks to this Indian boy for getting himself famous enough to get invited to an all–white school district. And he didn't even have to go to jail to do it. She figured she'd go early, to get a seat in the front, to give the boy the basket, so she took along a small basket lid she was working on to pass the time.

Sherman was a pretty good speaker, once he got warmed up. She could see that he was wearing a favorite jacket so that he would be comfortable while he was working, because it didn't hang right to be a dress–up jacket. Mostly he talked about things that Indians talk about at the kitchen table, which made Ima Pipiig feel comfortable for all the trouble she'd gone to to relocate herself for a few hours. She'd made pizza with pepperoni, green olives, and an onion chopped up from the garden. There was a big salad with red lettuce, tomatoes, and Swiss chard in a big open bowl in the refrigerator, where the family couldn't miss it. Now she had her work with her. After she'd visited with some of the other Indians she knew from the front rows, after the long boring introduction by the bald white man who prided himself on his accomplishment of bringing an Indian to an Indian town, rather than the accomplishments of the Indian boy himself, after watching the boy get comfortable and smooth, after getting used to the sound of his voice and the cadence of his humor, Ima Pipiig knew that she could take her eyes off the stage. She could look down at her basket lid. She could work, and she wouldn't have to feel guilty about doing something purely for her own entertainment . . . because Ima Pipiig always had to work. She was an Indian in an Indian town that had become a white town. And for all of her life plans and good intentions, Ima Pippiig worked more hours for less pay than the thousand or so white people stacked up in the rising seats of the auditorium space behind her. Now, she was earning her keep . . . now, she could listen.

Yep, that Indian boy was a pretty good speaker. Just like the things that Ima Pipiig had to say, except that nobody listened. He talked about racial profiling since the two airplanes had hit the towers of the World Trade Center in New York City. Ima Pipiig understood. Ima Pipiig knew. Ima Pipiig had experienced it from day one. It was worse than when security guards followed her around department stores, worse than when shopkeepers became uneasy. The profiling of brown people was bad enough that Ima Pipiig began wearing beadwork in public again. She'd stopped wearing beadwork, stopped out of fear for the anger that people felt for her for being an Indian in a town that had swelled into their own perfect white suburb. But now the beadwork was a form of rescue that allowed her to pass through U.S.-Canadian customs to visit with her family, that allowed her to walk into a school building to pick up her son for a dentist appointment, that allowed her to walk into a branch of the bank where the tellers didn't know her.

Yep, that Indian boy was a pretty good speaker. He said that when the planes hit the towers, he thought, *Please don't be brown.* Ima Pipiig had thought that, too. Being brown was tough enough. It didn't need help.

"Please be Swedish terrorists," Sherman Alexie delivered his punch line.

Visions of Lars Nederstadt loomed up in Ima Pipiig's mind. A large man. Long torso, long legs. Great shock of grayed blondish hair protruding forward over the heavily rimmed glasses. Pouty bottom lip. Holier-than-thou sway to his lower spine and hips as he swooped down to put the pouty lip in line with the small brown faces of those dirty Indian charges, the ones he wished would just disappear and make his job easier, the ones that wouldn't go away, those few thorns among the roses in his fjord-like northern home.

Ima Pipiig remembered little Charlie Pauquin, standing next to her in that hallway outside the cafeteria where Sherman Alexie would be signing books at the end of this warm evening. "So where have you *been* these past several days, *Mr. Pack-kwinn*," the tall man mispronounced his name. Charlie rolled his blue mixed-breed eyes up at the tall man, as if he was going to make the mistake of trying to answer. Ima Pipiig let her eyes gloss over, go slightly out of focus, and stared slightly ahead, but not high enough for it to seem as though she was being bold enough to make eye contact. She had perfected this to an art form. *Don't give them anything. They'll use it against you no matter what. There is no good or bad behavior. Don't give them anything.*

"*Paw-quinh*," Charlie mouthed, soundlessly. Correcting the pronunciation of his name had become a reflex. The French voyageurs had left their mark upon the landscape with their eloquent place names and their odd, non-English spelling of Charlie's last name. His lip quivered. Charlie was about to speak. Quickly, Ima Pipiig bailed him out: "*Paw-quinh*," she spoke, slightly above a whisper. Ol' Nederstadt was distracted. He wouldn't notice if Ima Pipiig focused her eyes and had an intelligent look on her face for just a moment. She took advantage of the window of opportunity, turned her head slightly to his direction, drew her chin up to firm from slack, narrowed her dark eyes and hissed, "*Paw-quinh*. It means hazelnut." And she drew her chin back in and tilted her head back to nonexpression in just that split second, before the big man with the vein-laced face caught his own head pivoting in response to the nothingness of an Indian child. But little Ima Pipiig didn't really seem to have been there, and it was as though a ghost had spoken. He turned his head back to Charlie, "So, where have you *been* the last couple of days, Mr. *Pack-kwinn?*"

Ima Pipiig didn't mind the after-school detention. She didn't mind that she missed the school bus home, that her parents would be working in the sawmill until after dark and just assume that she was spending the night with a friend, that they would be too tired to ask to come get her anyway, even if they did have a phone. And she knew that they'd understand why she had stayed at Charlie's side and had spoken up on his behalf. Ima Pipiig didn't mind sleeping on the couch at Charlie's house in town, even though it smelled like cigarettes and beer and urine, didn't mind that they had arrived at the empty house so late that they had to pick bits of boiled cabbage from the sides of the empty pot. She had saved four saltine crackers from her lunch for the long bus ride home, and now, as she divided them up into two equal piles of crumbs and pieces, Ima Pipiig did not mind sharing them with Charlie for dinner.

   If you were a Chippewa Indian going to school in Twin Bay City during the middle of the twentieth century, there *were* Swedish terrorists.

   When she rose to leave, Ima Pipiig was approached by some white acquaintances. She welcomed the opportunity to chat, while the crowd moved amoeba-like towards the cafeteria, thinning out ahead of her. She ambled out of the building into the welcoming arms of the darkness that wrapped itself around her. Among the lightless old brick houses, she found her small station wagon. There she waited for the pistons to fill the crank case with oil and watched the headlights of shiny SUV's disappear into the new Twin Bay City, a white town full of white neighborhoods. Careful not to touch the muddy interior floor of her car, Ima Pipiig took off the brand-new-hurt-your-eyes-they're-so-white tennis shoes and placed them on a clean blue handkerchief on the seat next to her. She delicately folded in the corners of the fabric over the shoes. This hurt was not worth getting the new shoes dirty for. She pulled away from the stone and brick monument to her own isolation, and Ima Pipiig receded into the warm night, barefoot.

• *21* •

Men in Brown

I feel soiled, so far, by my summer—not by the six dump-truck loads of moist and squishy, well-composted manure I have been using to mulch my immense vegetable garden—but by the foul and squishy, well-composted attitude of the white male administrators and board president of my children's school district.

"Bubbas," I call them . . . wide-bottomed men in shiny brown polyester suits, polyester that hangs like Flaaarida-condominium-wear . . . not a satisfying warm brown, but dark and sickly browns . . . like meconium, or diarrhea . . . like when one mixes together all the odds and ends of enamel paints in the garage to waterproof a project that one doesn't much care about. . . . When given the option of picking out their own custom color for their new automobiles, these aging former athletic directors will pick out "baby-poo brown" or "good-god-gold" 100 percent of the time. It's as though they are still fixated with what each of them has left in the toilet, their mothers' praises from the 1950s and 1960s still ringing in their ears, "Gooood boy! Your poo-poo is the sweetest and the biggest in the whole, wide world!"

So, I grimace, knowing that they have just passed up forty-nine female applicants with years of experience, glowing recommendations, and straight A's and B's . . . to hire another one of them . . . an athletic director with a scant year of experience in teaching, another scant year of experience in administration-slash-sports-stuff, and a D+ in elementary arithmetic.

This is the new middle school principal. This is the guy who will be passing out the academic awards at the assemblies. This is the guy who will be passing out the bumper stickers that say, "I have an honor student at . . ." This is the guy who will be authoritatively passing judgment and admonishments based upon . . . performance? The man can't even do long division; how is he going to grasp more difficult concepts, like gender equity?

I spoke to a middle-aged parent of my youngest child's classmate about it all . . . while she waited on us at Pizza Hut. "But boys need a man in authority to respond to," she insisted. Who told her that? Who *demonstrated* that for her? Her father? Her brother? A boy who held her down by her hair while he grabbed at her adolescent breasts? The president of her school board, whose wife cannot make eye contact with strangers? The wide-bottomed "Men in Brown" who have demonstrated to her all of her life, that she is their inferior, less competent, lower on the pay scale?

I thought about her daughter, already eight, only a few years away from that awkward, hormone-changing period of her life that she will spend under this newest initiate to the world of "Men in Brown." Ground zero is the only term I can fathom for a middle school child's level of impressionability about gender roles.

I wanted to blurt out, "Do you want your daughter to end up as a middle-aged waitress at Pizza Hut?" But I bit my tongue, which I will never regret, because the woman is doing the best she can, and waiting tables is honorable work . . . still, I know that she and her daughter (and son) are but one working man away from poverty. I want better for her daughter. It's my job, as a human being, to do for her daughter what she doesn't have either the real or the social intelligence and skills to do herself.

I can fight this cycle in my home but am frustrated at wanting to break it in my community. The school powers continue to be impediments to progress, for progress might endanger a white male monopoly on high salaries. Even more frustrating is the fact that these wide-bottomed "Men in Brown" (who always counterpoint with yellow shirts the color of baby poo) are well compensated for the responsibility of looking out for the interests of their students. Instead, they give blatant, deadly messages: "Penis good, breasts bad." "We put the *pubic* in public education." *Dare* we include graphics on that "I have an honor student . . ." bumper sticker?

"But Mom, I'm a boy—I only need a D+." "But Mom, I'm a girl—I only need to marry somebody with a D+." Even my own son is cheated by this, and I work hard to counteract the unreality of his public education. Gender does not surpass mind. Race does not surpass mind. Power does not surpass mind. Why is there no parental lockout device to protect my children from the "Men in Brown"?

· 22 ·

Why Ima Pipiig Did Not Vote

*I*t was 1930, she thought. Probably. When Indians got the right to vote. She couldn't remember exactly when. It wasn't celebrated as a holiday, and it wasn't marked with a big star on a chart on the wall of the classrooms she had passed through in her lifetime. It was after women could vote. It was after black men could vote. Finally, Indians could vote. And Ima Pipiig, who wasn't even alive when Indians got the vote, voted. She liked voting. She liked having choices. Even when they weren't very good choices. Even when the choices hurt her or the environment either way. She liked getting to choose between the bad choices. It lulled her into thinking that she had choices.

Ima Pipiig had tried to go the extra mile once. She'd tried going beyond mere voting. She'd tried running for school board. She did all right, considering that she was the only Indian in an all-white school district. Everybody that she talked to was nice to her. And everybody that she talked to voted for her. But she only talked to about ninety people.

She'd answered the questionnaire that was sent out by the local newspaper to all of the school board candidates. But the questions were all silly; and they had to be answered in twenty-five words or less. The questions asked things like "What do you think about the need for a program for gifted students?" And Ima Pipiig didn't feel that it would be polite to answer, "Are you kidding? You just hired a middle school principal with a D+ in remedial math. He can't even run a remedial program, let alone supervise the education of a bunch of kids who are smarter than him." Besides, it was longer than twenty-five words.

Ima Pipiig remembered when the fellow interviewed for the job of elementary school principal. It was the day before they quietly interviewed him and hired him for the job of middle school principal. Ima Pipiig had

145

gotten herself allowed to be present and observe the hiring process. She wasn't allowed to participate in the process, not really, but she was allowed to pretend to participate in the process, so that the white male administrators *in situ* and the chubby white male president of the school board could cover their asses with a paper trail in case Ima Pipiig decided to drag them into a federal courtroom.

They hadn't wanted her to be there for the process at all. She showed up at a school board meeting, and she sat through the whole thing, which was boring and designed to keep the audience uninvolved and at arm's length. At the very end, someone from the school board mumbled into a microphone from way back behind the tables in the front of the room where the school board members were cowering from the public and asked if anybody had any questions and then looked down at her feet and at the back wall, making it very obvious that she didn't want anybody to have any questions. And all of the school board members snarled when Ima Pipiig had the audacity to raise her hand and stand up. All she really wanted to know was if she could be on the selection committee for the new elementary school principal, since the previous elementary school principal had threatened her and her daughter and had stalked them, so maybe she could be part of the process, so that she wouldn't be so nervous about the new one. And the superintendent looked very nervous, and he staggered around the front of the room in his baggy brown polyester suit a little bit, staying close to the board members' row of tables jammed back against the wall of the room, and he even appeared to Ima Pipiig like he might want to crawl under one of those tables a little bit. And he finally stopped pacing, as though he'd finally come up with an idea, and he said that he'd already had too many requests from parents to be on the selection committee, and that he couldn't possibly have a selection committee with nineteen members on it. And Ima Pipiig asked why, if he could have eighteen, he couldn't have nineteen. And he staggered around in the flapping polyester, bumping into the tables behind him and jostling the school board members a couple of times, and he finally said, "Well, I can't."

So Ima Pipiig went home and drafted a letter to the superintendent asking for the names, addresses, and phone numbers and the applications and resumes of all of the job applicants, and the names, addresses, and phone numbers of all of the people who had asked to be on the committee. And then she asked for written justification as to why the process did not belong to the public. Then she sent a copy of the letter to everyone on the school board.

She would have liked to have phoned the people on the school board, but they all had unlisted phone numbers. And before she complained to them about it, they never even used to publish their names on the school newsletter—because being on the school board in the Sleeping Bear School

District wasn't about meeting the needs of the community or obeying the laws; it was about making sure that one's kids were treated better than everybody else's in the school system. Geographically, the school district was very large, formed from several smaller districts years before; so nobody but the people who lived on the southern and northern fringes of the school district had the option of going to an adjacent school district through the state school of choice program. It was a peninsula, so the people on the east and the west and the people in the middle had nowhere to go unless they had the resources to drive a long way. So being on the school board was a good way to guarantee that one's kids got special awards and scholarships and stuff, and it never seemed to dawn on any of the school board members that they might actually have some sort of fiduciary duty to the community. So Ima Pipiig ran for school board. And even though she did not win, and even though the editor of the *Sleeping Bear Gazette* was mad at Ima Pipiig for being an Indian woman who would not stay in her place and tried to make fun of her candidacy, Ima Pipiig managed to bring up a few intelligent issues and to get people thinking about their own welfare, even though they could not be bothered to think about the welfare of people like Ima Pipiig.

And a few days later Ima Pipiig got a phone call from the bookkeeper for the school district telling her that she could be on the committee. And when she got the names, addresses, and phone numbers of the other eighteen parents who had asked to be on the selection committee for the elementary school principal, she phoned both of them. They were nice enough ladies. One was the wife of a middle school teacher, and she had a tendency to yap like a poodle, but she seemed fairly sharp. The other was a mother of two who was upset that soccer was not an official school sport, and she told Ima Pipiig at least a dozen times that she was a lawyer. She genuinely seemed nice, even though Ima Pipiig wondered if she realized that there were students in the school district other than her own.

The envelope that had delivered the names, addresses, and phone numbers of the eighteen-minus-sixteen parents who had asked to be on the elementary school principal selection committee also contained a list of the fifty-two applicants for the job. Ima Pipiig recognized some of them. She even knew some of them. She had actually worked with a couple of them. She was particularly surprised when she saw a woman with a doctorate on the list whose last name was Payment. Payment was an Indian name. This lady was either an Indian or a parent to Indian children. And Ima Pipiig called up Mrs. Payment and had a nice chat and found out why Mrs. Anishinabe Indian lady was not on the list of eleven candidates who had been selected as a finalist by the white male administrators and white male chubby guy who was president of the school board of all-white Sleeping Bear Schools. Because

Mrs. Payment's children were Indians, Mrs. Payment's professional experience was limited to her local tribal school and other Native American programs at various institutions throughout the state . . . And Doctor Payment was very obviously an Indian on paper to the hit men of the preselection committee because her only experience was limited to Indian stuff, and who else would be limited to Indian stuff but an Indian.

Ima Pipiig did not need to see the woman's application and resume that were withheld from her by the white-males-in-charge at Sleeping Bear Schools to figure out that she was an Indian, by birth or by marriage . . . The Indian name Payment came from the Indian town of Payment, once located upon an island in the Shagonabe River, near where it separated the towns of Waashike and Adikamek, Michigan, just before it emptied into Lake Superior. The Indians who stayed in Michigan and did not flee several miles into Canada had been reduced to poverty induced by limited access to resources imposed at gunpoint. So the Indians became dependent upon annuity payments for survival. And the annuity payments were made on an island, which made it pretty difficult for a lot of the Indians to go pick them up. And some of the families that could not travel, because of liabilities and handicaps of one form or another, clustered around the payment site, forming the Indian town of Payment, which was translated into the Indian name of Payment; because the barely literate white clerks who were sent to Indian country could not write down names like Ogemagiigido or Waabakaikai or Zhingwauk or Asaamig or Sheedawinh . . . Some of those clerks who controlled the payments were themselves descended from a white homesteader named Payment, who had taken advantage of the fact that the government had decided that the island was too big a resource to leave to mere Indians, and this facilitated the spelling of the name, as well as the usurpation of annuity payments intended for Indian families. So the Indian name of Payment stayed alive throughout history as a testimony to ignorance, theft, and change.

Then Ima Pipiig read through the pile of eleven resumes that had been picked out as finalists ahead of time by the white male administrators and the chubby white male president of the school board of Sleeping Bear Schools. As a minority professional, she'd been on a lot of selection committees for a lot bigger fish than a small-pond elementary school principal, so she knew how to do it effectively. She recognized some of the names. She knew some of the applicants. She had worked for some of them. She knew people who had worked for some of them. And there were a few she did not know. Most of them were pretty good. All but three were women. One of the men looked good. The other two men had such abysmal resumes, ersatz recommendation letters, and downright embarrassing college transcripts that Ima Pipiig wondered why they had been selected over Mrs. Doctor Payment, other than the fact that she looked like an Indian on paper.

The day before the interviews were to take place, the superintendent phoned Ima Pipiig to come meet with him and the other parents in his office to prepare for the interviews. So Ima Pipiig put off her trip to the grocery store and to run business errands in town; she put off working on mining contracts; she put off filing receipts from the farm; she put off working on inventory for her own business; and she volunteered an hour of her time to join a bunch of white boys who were being paid for their time and a couple of white women who thought that they were sharp as heck; and she showed up at the preinterview meeting, because Ima Pipiig, as a minority, had interviewed far bigger fish than a small-pond elementary principal, so she wondered what those white boys were up to.

The superintendent of schools was there, in a brown polyester suit, and for backup he had brought in the high school principal, also in a brown polyester suit, also a white male he had handpicked and who was at least a foot taller than the superintendent, because he was an awfully little fella, that superintendent, and he was afraid that Ima Pipiig might shape-shift into a grizzly bear, because he hadn't gotten very good grades in social studies, and he didn't realize that there were no grizzly bears in Michigan, and that the worst Ima Pipiig could turn into was a little bitty black bear or maybe a bobcat—leaping across the table with that constant smile of hers on her face and maybe scratching his eyes out. So he had the chubby white male president of the school board with him, too; because the superintendent and all of those white guys were as scared as heck of one middle-aged Indian woman; and they supposed they should be scared of the two white women as well . . . And Ima Pipiig smiled and shook hands with everybody and calmly corrected them when they mispronounced her name.

They were all led into a small room behind the superintendent's office, by the superintendent, who was sweating and nervous, flitting, and avoiding eye contact. Ima Pipiig walked right into that room first and took the alpha seat at the table . . . although anyone who knew Ima Pipiig knew that any seat she took at the table was the alpha seat at the table because Ima Pipiig was an alpha female—which left the white male superintendent and principal and school board president reaching inside of their baggy brown polyester pants and searching to make sure their genitalia were still intact and wondering why they hadn't studied more carefully about the pecking order of wolves and shape-shifters and Indian women . . .

And while the white guys were scared to sit next to Ima Pipiig, and the white women had no choice, and the poor high school principal got stuck sitting next to her, Ima Pipiig whipped out her notebook and pen and wrote down the date and the place and the names of everybody who was present, staring into the Adam's apple of that poor high school principal, and asking, "Do you spell your name with an 'o' or a 'u'?" And the poor man, a foot taller than Ima Pipiig, nearly wet himself. And Ima Pipiig, knowing how easy it would be to intimidate the whiz-bang out of those poor, quaking, white incompetents, wrote slowly and mouthed the words slowly, in time to the pen: " . . . nearly wet himself . . ."

So the superintendent—who was used to huffing and puffing at the pink white ladies of the school district who were intimidated by the professional credentials that the incompetent man kept zipped up in the front of the baggy pants of his brown polyester suit—began to huff and puff and look for a house to blow down. And Ima Pipiig, whose fine motor skills were well-honed from years of making cute artsy-fartsy-less-than-minimum-wage-arts-and-crafts-for-ignorant-white-folks, could write faster than the men could talk, summarizing the superintendents' instructions out loud, clearly, slowly, for the written record, and for the white ladies sitting on the other side of her who did not have the presence of mind to arrive ready to reword the lies and bullshsit . . . And Ima Pipiig wrote: "Set of questions already prepared by white males; women not to ask job applicants any questions . . ."

And the soccer mom who had told Ima Pipiig repeatedly that she was a lawyer just sat there stupidly. And the wife of the middle school teacher who yapped like a poodle and had the sexual appeal of Olive Oyl began to yap loudly, "What? What? The women can't ask questions?" So Ima Pipiig quietly set down her pen, leaned in from the alpha seat at the table, and said, "May I have a copy of the questions?"

The superintendent wet himself. Then he hemmed and hawed and said that they hadn't written them yet. So Ima Pipiig wrote down: "Sup't. wet himself. Hasn't manufactured questions women forbidden to ask," spreading the words across the page slowly, mouthing the words, flourishing the cursive with a cheap Bic pen. Then, to add insult to injury, she looked at her wristwatch and wrote down the time of the quote.

Then Ima Pipiig asked, "Do any of you know one or two of those questions, off the top of your head, so that I can be mentally prepared and listen with a purpose—I believe that's an educational objective you're required to teach, listening with a purpose, so I assume that you can provide me with an idea of what a question might be like?" The superintendent reached into his polyester pants and found his testicles missing. The president of the school board realized that he had never had testicles, so he didn't even bother to feel around. And the high school principal got brave, because he was the tallest, and he said, "Uh . . . Uuuuuh . . . Uuuuuh . . . What kind of experience do you have writing federal grants for special education?" He was not asking the question of an imaginary candidate. He was asking Ima Pipiig if the question was OK.

Ima Pipiig kept looking at the high school principal and smiling. The wife of the middle school teacher squawked and stared at the high school principal expectantly. The soccer mom looked down at the table. The high school principal squirmed in his seat. And the president of the school board scratched his stomach and quietly farted.

"Well, gentlemen," Ima Pipiig announced . . . "The interviews start at nine o'clock tomorrow morning. That's less than twenty-four hours from now." She smiled around the room at each and every one of the white men as though they were stupid. "I've got some errands to do in town. I'll be back at one-thirty this afternoon. You'll have the questions written and typed up and ready for me to pick up then, won't you? Because you've had three years' notice that this guy was going to retire now, didn't you? So you've had three years to prepare these questions, now, haven't you?" And Ima Pipiig nodded yes to the white women on her left. Then she nodded yes to the white men on her right and across from her. And everyone in turn nodded yes. And the superintendent spoke directions through a gap in the door to a clerical assistant who agreed to have the questions typed and available at the hour indicated. And the high school principal reached under the table to adjust his scrotum in his too-tight underwear. And the president of the school board looked under the table to see if he had gum stuck on his shoe. And Ima Pipiig directed all of them out of their own conference room, closing the door behind her because she was the last one out. That's how alpha females behaved after they had the rendered the rest of the wolves belly up and whining.

And at one-thirty in the afternoon, the list of bland and meaningless questions quickly thrown together by the fumbling white guys in charge of unearned salaries at Sleeping Bear Schools and supplemented with questions by the underpaid clerical staff was ready and waiting for Ima Pipiig upon the desk of a clerical assistant. And the superintendent's door to his office was closed, until he heard that Ima Pipiig had come and gone and it was safe to pretend that he was in charge on that particular day. Ima Pipiig knew that the questions would be absurdly irrelevant to the problems that faced the school district. And she knew that parent participation in the procedure would have little impact on the abuse of public resources that dominated the operations of the Sleeping Bear School District. But she knew that the three men who ran the show were well aware of the laws they broke regularly and the public trust that they violated regularly, and that they would always be looking over their shoulders. She liked popping up behind them periodically, not to keep them honest, because they were too bold to be honest, but to make it just that much more difficult for them to violate the people of Sleeping Bear County.

Deep in her heart, Ima Pipiig knew that one person could make a difference. So she showed up for the "selection" process the next day, just to send ideas rolling downhill into the education community, like pebbles on an eroding slope, like loose sand on the dunes of the national lakeshore that attracted people who wanted a big backyard at the taxpayers' expense and a few people who wanted a whole lot more at the taxpayers' expense.

Ima Pipiig's favorite of the eleven meaningless interviews was with the man from Grand Rapids. He walked around the room, looking everyone in the eye—even the parents—and he smiled and asked them what they did. The other parents identified themselves as "just parents."

"And you, Mrs. uh Pee-pig?" he fumbled over her name, slightly embarrassed.

"BuhBEEG," she corrected him, gently, reassuringly.

There was no doubt that Ima Pipiig was an Indian. She'd worn a large barrette made of porcupine quills and shimmering beadwork on birch bark, just to make the powers-that-be at the Sleeping Bear School District on this particular day aware that diversity was among them, whether they wanted it or not. So the gentleman from Grand Rapids did not ask what kind of a name it was. He merely asked, "Ah, what does that mean?"

And Ima Pipiig smiled a little wider and answered, "Between."

"Between what?"

And she smiled a little wider and answered, "Just between."

It did not throw him off. He was experienced, intelligent, erudite, and knowledgeable. He knew how to fill in with information when there were no intelligent questions available for him. But Ima Pipiig knew that the white men of Sleeping Bear Schools would not want him. Because they did not want among them a man who answered questions directly and politely without bravura intended to mislead and intimidate. This disappointed Ima Pipiig because she felt that the school district needed some competent male role models for the district's students to counteract the incompetent male role models the superintendent and the president of the school board had surrounded themselves with.

Long before the eleven meaningless interviews were over with, Ima Pipiig had spotted the two young white men with very little job experience and very poor social skills that the president of the school board had accidentally admitted to handpicking ahead of time at a church function downstate. The superintendent had danced the dance of blatant intentional influence peddling in front of the tables full of committee members—people he had handpicked to be supportive of his predestined choices—a couple of school staff that he trusted, an elementary school counselor who was despised by the community but who regularly nominated herself for awards, a couple of school board members who never said no to him, ever. He twirled his stubby frame periodically in the front of the room, shamelessly finding fault with the amazingly professional women candidates with doctorates and years of experience, good references, and outstanding college transcripts earned under adverse conditions as single parents, and he slurred, knowingly, "If those *laaadies* want to get administrative jobs, they're going to have to go to another district . . ." Then the chubby president of the school board hopped up and spoke on behalf of his white Christian brethren whose only apparent professional credentials were behind the zippers in their polyester pants, and he said, "Whoo-boy! Were those two guys amazing, or what? I mean, wow! What great communicators! What great answers to those questions!" And Ima Pipiig giggled, wondering how "Du-uuh . . ." must have seemed like familiar language to that particular president of the school board who had already surrounded himself with other white Reformed Christian males who said "Du-uuh" quite regularly.

And when the superintendent jumped up and flapped around in the brown polyester again, he decided to throw the killing blow to the only other male candidate, an androgynous middle-aged man with a doctorate and a superb record of improving the status quo in the multiracial urban school district he had supervised for a decade. He put his hand to his hip, held one wrist slightly limp, and said, "I dunno, something about that guy just didn't feel right." And Ima Pipiig giggled again because the pose looked so natural on that poor superintendent, combined perfectly with the swaying brown polyester, so as to condense his very demeanor to nothing more than hot air and fluff, a man who was unaware of the fact that this school district of less than a thousand students graduated at least two homosexual students every year, students who, like the other minorities would leave this community and never return, no matter the gifts and skills they had to offer. And when he puffed up his chest and announced that, "The new administrator must be someone that the current administration is comfortable with," Ima Pipiig had to physically stifle back a squeaking laugh. Because the two white Christian fundamentalist males who had been handpicked by the current men-in-charge were not only babbling idiots, but they had submitted college transcripts that were laughable. No one in their right mind would submit such abysmal college transcripts with a job application unless one considered oneself a shoo-in for the job. Outside of their educational administration courses, of which Ima Pipiig had had several and could testify were the fluffiest college courses on the face of the earth, these guys were pulling straight C− averages, sprinkled heavily with D's in basic courses such as math, science, history, and language skills, supplemented by B's in physical education. Had these young men not been the beneficiaries of white male privilege, had they been forced to acquire employment commensurate with their credentials, they'd have been on the business end of a shovel. But then again, so would have the superintendent.

Ima Pipiig really had no intention of making waves during this process. She merely wanted to make sure that the new elementary principal wouldn't be someone prone to threatening, stalking, and battering women and children—again. But she saw the white Christian fundamentalists who had tolerated this behavior in the past leaning toward white male privilege once again. So she spoke up. She looked around that room, and she smiled, and she spoke the unspeakable. She dared to mention the lack of competence and experience of the two white male Christian fundamentalists who had been handpicked ahead of time. She did not make a suggestion as to which white female candidate would be most appropriate for the job of new elementary school principal, and she knew better than to suggest the androgynous white male from down in Grand Rapids. She merely pointed out that the school district had left an abysmally obvious paper trail in the wake of its long-term practice of sexual discrimination in administrative hiring, and that it was time for the school board to make it unofficial policy to stop breaking the law—because any old parent could just drive down to a federal courthouse tomorrow and file a lawsuit, and that the fees to do so were not cost prohibitive at all. And everyone in the room nodded in agreement, especially the women, whose jaws fell slack.

The only one who didn't really get it was Louise Crawford, an aging woman whose coif was bleached so blond that her entire head of hair had been rendered transparent, revealing an under layer of pink-skinned skull and neck to those nearest her. Ima Pipiig thought that it made the woman look like poultry. Louise Crawford had been recently elected to the school board. She openly spoke about her white flight and racism throughout the course of the day's interviews, as though they were badges of honor. She didn't really seem to understand much of anything that had been said that day; but her husband had been elected to the county board of commissioners as soon as they'd moved up to Sleeping Bear County, and he needed his wife to be a warm body for him on the school board. On the basis of what she had seen and heard, Ima Pipiig perceived that his agenda in both circumstances seemed to be at odds with the needs of the general public. Some people just liked being in charge.

Eventually the powers-that-be hired a female elementary school principal. And the next day, they would very quietly, very secretly interview for the new position of middle school principal that they had especially created for one of their dumb, white, Christian brethren who had interviewed for elementary principal. Knowing that the boy had been hired for life, in this all-white school district where incompetence thrived, Ima Pipiig enrolled her kindergartener in the adjacent school district closest to her home, a decision she would never come to regret. And the new white female principal of Sleeping Bear Elementary School would move into her new, higher-paying job at the all-white school, in the all-white public-land ghetto next to the national lakeshore that provided her with a big backyard at the taxpayers' expense, never knowing that she owed the success of this particular job search to one feisty Native American woman whose child she would never administer to. Indeed, she would never administer to any children who were minorities or had special needs because they would continue to be driven from the school district by ignorance and greed, and the status quo of Sleeping Bear Schools would be held intact by the guardians of ignorance.

And now Ima Pipiig's phone was ringing off the hook because the soccer mom who had informed Ima Pipiig repeatedly that she was a lawyer had decided to run for school board against Louise Crawford, who had become president of the school board by default, after Ima Pipiig had publicly opened up a few cans of worms, causing the longest-standing members of the school board to lose their seats to some younger white Christian fundamentalists who would keep their phone numbers unlisted, in the fear that the people who stood in line to vote for them might actually expect something of them. And now the wife of the middle school teacher was squawking into Ima Pipiig's ear, trying to get her to help, because they had to get rid of that Louise Crawford, who had become the president of the school board. When Ima Pipiig asked why, the squawker had no specific reasons; she simply said, "She's not very good." Ima Pipiig would have been happy with any sort of explanation, even something mean, like, "She's got the IQ of a garden vegetable." But she got nothing.

And even though she would never bring her child back to Sleeping Bear Schools, Ima Pipiig liked to vote, even in the school board election. So now she was curious. Ima Pipiig phoned a longtime teacher in the district, one she trusted to speak honestly. Yes, yes, they needed to get rid of Louise, the teacher echoed. Why? She has an autistic grandson, and she wants the school district to spend the money to hire the child an aide, instead of putting the money into salary raises . . .

Ima Pipiig did not like Louise Crawford. Ima Pipiig thought that it made sense that Louise Crawford had an autistic grandchild because Ima Pipiig, who used to be a special education teacher, suspected that Louise Crawford suffered from similar symptoms herself, and communication disorders often ran in families, where genetics were sometimes exacerbated by the nurturing effect of behavioral constructs within an environment. And this made Louise more understandable to Ima Pipiig. She thought back on one particular class on traumatic head injuries she had taken at the medical school at the University of New Mexico, when she was doing postgraduate work in education. Special education teachers were allowed to take coursework in the medical school, and Ima Pipiig liked doing this because the courses offered more substance than the classes in the College of Education. She visualized Louise Crawford's skull outlined beneath her thin bleached blond hair. It was easy to go one step further and to visualize Louise's brain without the skull, its *dura mater* pulled back, revealing the lobes, in the palm of Ima Pipiig's hand, the pungent formaldehyde dripping down her forearm to her elbow in the summer heat. She remembered the instructor pointing to the area inside of the Broca's and Wernicke's areas of the brain, describing the resulting communication disorders that resulted from blows to the head that caused swelling and damage in this area. "If the blow is at the side here, it affects interpretation of prosody in speech, if damage is more toward the back, it affects motor output of prosody in speech . . ." the instructor went on and on, describing the behavioral effects of damage to the right, damage to the left, the various combinations of damage to various parts of the brain and their correlation with the incarcerated. . . . Ima Pipiig had *loved* that class. When she was a girl, a professor from Harvard University used to summer down the road from her house, and he used to visit Ima Pipiig's father, because he used to pump him for information about birds and wildlife; and Ima Pipiig's father used to love to listen to the man talk about the physical workings of the human brain; and the two men, one educated in the academy, and one educated in the woods and wetlands, shared wine and venison on long summer evenings and talked about Piaget and electrical synapses in the brains of frogs, while she and her nine brothers and sisters bounced in and out of the building, like operational definitions of various stages of brain development. So Ima Pipiig would bring in the Harvard psychologist's books and the articles he'd used as references, and she would have the *best* time with that instructor from the medical school.

And it was because of these experiences that Ima Pipiig really understood that Louise Crawford had limitations beyond her control. Ima Pipiig had tried talking to Louise about discrimination in the school district once, but Louise had whined out loud, "Minorities? Why would we have to worry about minorities? We've hardly got any to speak of!" Ima Pipiig knew that she could insert another word or two into that sentence and find the same mentality being applied back upon poor Louise herself. Autism. Down Syndrome. Handicapped. Other. Why would we have to worry about them? We've hardly got any to speak of . . .

The only difference between the two standards was that Louise Crawford was willing to apply hers to Ima Pipiig and all of the people of color of Sleeping Bear County. And Ima Pipiig was not willing to reciprocate—not even to an avowed racist like Louise Crawford. Ima Pipiig was not willing to vote for Louise Crawford because she was not willing to meet the needs of people other than herself. And she was not willing to vote for someone who would not meet the needs of an autistic child. So, for the first time, ever, Ima Pipiig did not vote. And poor Louise Crawford, years later, still president of the school board of Sleeping Bear Public Schools, tried to put her autistic grandchild in the adjacent school district through the state school of choice program, along with Ima Pipiig's son, the Middle Eastern children, and all of the other autistic children and children with special needs from the northern regions within Sleeping Bear Schools' district boundaries. And she was turned down because those school of choice slots had all been filled up previously by the children whose needs Louise Crawford had seen as irrelevant.

· 23 ·

Jim Crow—Culture of Convenience

𝒯ortilla Bill. Not tor-*tee*-ya. Tortill-uh. Rhymes with Bill-uh. We called him Tortill-uh for short. He was a soft-spoken, genteel sort of fellow. A hard-working white man. Tall, good-looking. Worked more hours than most people. Adored and nurtured his children. Friend and good host to people of all ethnicities. First person one would feel safe to turn to if one needed a hand.

That's why I was so surprised and so curious when he began to speak pleasantly of "broomsticking niggers" during his Georgia childhood. Animated, smiling, he let the stories flow out of his mouth in that soft, beautiful, at peace with the world, slow southern accent that we'd all come to love.

We all lived in a small village outside of Albuquerque, New Mexico, in the Manzano Mountains. It was an odd mix of refugees. There were methadone addicts from New York City and Chicago, frightening characters from the federal witness protection program who never seemed to stay out of trouble and therefore never stayed too long, and the minority poor—the Indians, the Mestizos, the remnant populations of indigenous Indian "Hispanics" who were the unacknowledged direct descendants of the Anasazi—and who, like them, still built and lived in two-room houses of stone, cedar poles, and mud. The sunshine and the months of drought were as harsh as the bullets that ricocheted from one stone wall to the next and the sight of three-legged dogs chasing in packs after old-model cars lurching in the deep-rutted mud roads that almost connected the yards full of dysfunctional wringer washers and old ice boxes converted into firewood boxes. I fit into all of this somehow—of mixed parentage, low income . . . standing out perhaps only in that I was a graduate student. That was back in the 1970s, before we'd learned that Indians with college diplomas would be prevented by the dominant culture from obtaining nontribal employment commensurate with our credentials. Before we'd

159

all come to accept post-civil-rights-movement-white-dominance as fact, as American culture, as convenient. We. Not me. *We.* Because I am outnumbered and I have no choice in all of this. It's sort of an operational definition of being a minority.

But back then, I was hopeful about my role in society. There were so many of us, so hopeful, that an entire educational niche was built around making money off our hope. Colleges and universities opened up to minorities, especially those who had academic scholarships from private foundations—they weren't as much of a drain on the public sources of financial aid. And private foundations were beginning to balk at giving scholarships to Indians, assuming that they were garnering more than their fair share of public financial aid. Even so, it was so hopeful an era that America was willing to put resources into sending people of color to institutions of higher education. Those resources were especially useful when involved in hiring white people to teach and acculturate those youngsters of color. So the ranks of the institutions swelled with white instructors and administrators and a couple of token ethnics, but mostly, whenever possible, token ethnics who weren't too ethnic or too offensive, or too scary, and, in the case of Indians, often people who had only recently discovered that they might be Indians—after all, who knew better what white folks expected of Indians than white folks who had become Indians, nice Indians, Indians who didn't need anything serious for their people—like equal pay for equal work or equal access to the nation's resources—stereotypical Indians. Convenient system.

So there I was, helping to keep those white teachers employed, living without indoor plumbing or livelihood above the federal minimum wage, still scraping and saving and paying out tuition money and gas money and book money, in the hope that one more college diploma and a few more years of overachievement would make me finally acceptable to the white hiring system that dominated America. So there I was, hopeful, expecting the culture of my white college peers to be safer and more user-friendly than the culture of our parents' era.

I was born in 1954, the year of *Brown v. Board of Education.* Tortill-uh was about ten years older than me. He came from that middle ground between our nation's generations, the very onset of the baby boom. Tortill-uh formulated his earliest views of life and cultural interaction during a heinous era of Jim Crow, before there was any illusion of protection for minorities from hatred, lynching, and systematic stigmatization. I wanted to know about the justification he'd felt in his mind for the bold, outright racial hatred he had grown up with. This was something, I knew, Tortilla Bill would never do, broomsticking niggers. Not this man. But here he was, acting it out at the Thanksgiving dinner table, like so many soft and gentle stories about the Deep South he'd told us before.

So I probed. I asked questions until I was satisfied. Tortilla Bill pulled no punches, kept no secrets, misconstrued nothing. It was, in fact, the accepted norm of the day, torturing, denigrating, compromising the safety and livelihood of people of color. They were there, they were weak, and they were easy targets. Targets one could hit without repercussions. Easy. Convenient.

And I probed this aspect of it with intensity. Because this was what I wanted to know: Was it because they were people of color, or was it because they were convenient? Tortill-uh made it very clear to me, that he and his young friends knew that "the coloreds" were the safest targets to hit. There were plenty of whites out there they'd have loved to have done it to, but they knew they'd never get away with it. They equated colored with weakness. They equated weakness with convenient. That was his answer. When it came to reaching out and abusing someone, colored equaled convenient.

Broomsticking niggers. When a black man walked down the shoulder of the road, along the fields outside of Atlanta, young whites would entertain themselves by holding a broom handle out the open window of the passenger side of a car. At the last moment, they would swoop to the right and hit the unsuspecting individual in the back of the head, neck, or shoulders with the broomstick, knocking him off his feet. It was part of the Jim Crow culture of the region. Black men were poorer, more likely to walk than ride. They had no business walking with their heads erect alongside a public road. They were supposed to be invisible, and above all, humble. They were there as easy victims, whenever Tortill-uh and his young friends felt frustrated, or when they felt like victims themselves and needed someone weaker upon whom to take out their anger. Maybe they had just had a fight with a girlfriend, or with their mothers.

Broomsticking niggers. It was a tradition from the 1950s that overlapped with newer phenomena, like drive-in burger joints. Did the broomstickers associate that action with the taste of strong and tangy root beer from a frosted mug? Wasn't it a song from the radio earlier that day that had prompted Bill's memory and inspired the discussion at this multiethnic celebration in honor of the successful arrival of European Americans upon the shores of yet another lesser people whose resources were to be acquired and squandered? At the time I was too young to understand the irony of the role that African Americans were playing in that particular dinner celebration . . . no honor for their successful arrival, except as instruments for the satisfaction of their European American masters.

It was a catch-22 for the "niggers." They were less unsuspecting than powerless to prevent the possible. They had no business going off the road into a white man's field. They had one place to be, legally, and that was on the road easement. But, culturally, they had no rights to the roads. It was a convenient way of life for members of the dominant culture. No one prosecuted the broomstickers. No one spent money on the separate, colored schools. No one forfeited time, money, or effort to invoke equal protection under the law. Local and state authorities were in the convenient position of receiving a paycheck, whether they did the right thing or not. And back then, there was no right thing in regard to people one considered lesser than oneself.

Back then. I said back then, didn't I?

My small son has rummaged through his cupboard of "precious things" to find a toy metal detector he received for Christmas from a big sister last year. He's checked the batteries to make sure it works. He has never used it for anything other than locating quarters his dad has tucked under throw rugs for him. But, starting next Monday, he will use it to check for nails in the shoulder within the road easement where we park the car to wait for the school bus. It is a form of empowerment, because, even though he is only a second-grader, he has been culturally broomsticked by his white neighbors.

I do not send my son to the nearest public elementary school. His sister went there. We lived through years of intimidation that included threats—by white staff, not by students; years of catch-22-type fear that took away our level of comfort and leeway, took away chunks of her childhood; and years of indifference by white school board members who did not want to be inconvenienced by dealing with the safety or the dignity of a minority family. Through Michigan's "School of Choice" program I have the option of requesting that my resident school district "release" my child and that a neighboring school district "accept" my child. I do not know what the criteria are for releasing and accepting, but, after years of ethnic intimidation, I fear that complaining or standing up for my civil rights or inconveniencing white male school administrators may lead to an interpretation of those criteria that will leave me even more frightened for the welfare of my child than before.

So, I will bend over backward to be a cooperative parent, and, when necessary, my child and I will be invisible. When I fill out the questionnaire each year, as to the reason for leaving the school district in which I reside for the adjacent district, I want to leave that question blank, but I am told that the releasing school will not release me without a reason. I am not informed of my legal rights. I am afraid of not being released by the abusers who threatened our lives. I will not put, "Ethnic intimidation, racism, sexism, abuse . . . all leading to visceral fear." I will simply write, "Preference." And it will not be questioned because they are glad to be rid of the people of color, the handicapped, the chubby, the shy, the devout, those who are fleeing for a variety of reasons, all of which might take precious money out of future salary raises . . . There is no money in meeting the needs of the weak. Federal legislation that mandates equality and special services is so riddled with loopholes that morality is the only hope; and it has proved as fruitless in this public-land ghetto next to the national park as it has in corporate America. These are people who want a big backyard at the taxpayers' expense, and they don't care which indigenous life forms they kill to get it. This is a form of American sociopathy that draws crowds to resources, and private lots adjacent to public land are a resource.

My white neighbors know about the intimidation and the scars of fear it has left upon me as a parent. They know that I am the weakest, most vulnerable person in their neighborhood, and they know that I will not speak out and jeopardize my tenuous position as a "guest" in the public schools unless the situation is life-threatening, as it was years ago, for my son's older sister. They were not inconvenienced by the culture of Jim Crow back then, and they are not today. They are the "crackers" that Thurgood Marshall spoke of throughout the 1940s and 1950s, throughout the various litigations that led to *Brown v. Board of Education*. Theirs is a culture that was passed down to them by their parents because it was convenient. It is a culture that was, and still is, modeled to them in their schools, local government, and public institutions, because it is convenient. There is no anger or embarrassment by the bulk of my neighbors that those they consider lesser are evicted from the public school system by intimidation and threats. There is primarily the sense of vulnerability on the part of another, and this they see as an opportunity, much as a predator looks upon prey. And when push comes to shove, they will acknowledge their own forms of broomsticking with the same unabashedness as Tortilla Bill.

My family lives close to the school district line, and I was surprised when I was informed that the bus from the "accepting" school would be able to meet us at the bottom of our steep, winding hill, only a half mile from our home. Our secondary road descended to meet a busier county road at a safe T-shaped intersection, on a slight rise, with visibility in all three directions. If my work schedule made it impossible for me to pick up the child, I knew he could safely walk home after being dropped off there by the bus. The time and gas involved in transportation would be minimal. These things all contributed to deciding to put my son into the adjacent public school district, rather than home-schooling him; sending him back to the district I live in is not an option.

I knew, when I began meeting the bus, that one particular neighbor would not appreciate our presence on the road near his house. He'd located it as close to the road as legal setback requirements permit on the large parcel of land his father had bought for him. Complaints would not come because my presence at the intersection a few minutes a day interfered with his schedule of work and sleep. He didn't need to work. But sometimes people are hurting for one reason or another, a relationship gone bad, or childhood experiences that none of us has a right to speculate about at the expense of a neighbor . . . My presence there, the mere occasional sight and sound of me, triggered a need to be empowered . . . and for whatever reason, my neighbor decided that the road easement was his domain alone this particular winter, not to be shared with someone he perceived as weaker, as one who could be bullied . . . There was probably no premeditated thought about our danger in another spot, or the extra cost of going elsewhere, or the environmental impact of accruing extra automobile miles twice a day by going elsewhere, or the restriction upon my work schedule by not having my son dropped off in a safe spot he can walk home from . . . I can only guess that it was about psychological power. It was this man's equivalent of broomsticking a nigger. And as angry as I am about the ease with which he brushes off my safety and my rights, I understand the cultural ignorance that facilitates his acceptance of double standards. He imposes them with the same thoughtlessness with which one might swat a fly.

During mild seasons my neighbor enters my orchard and buildings without invitation, whether we are home or not, and usually when we are not, sometimes just looking around or even seeming a bit lost, weaving a criss-cross trail of truck and golf cart tracks in the long grass, back and forth between house and barns. Sometimes he has been more familiar with the progress of my own vegetable garden than I am, and he makes no attempt to hide the fact that he goes through our things and monitors our lives. He does it with such a smugness and acceptance of it as normal behavior, that we chuckle about it and ask him to remember to run the sprinkler if things get dry. It's pretty much become a joke in the community, because neighbors would be scolded, were they to set foot on that fellow's family's farm; and as double standards go, this one seems harmless. And in small towns, people chuckle at one another, and we put up with one another's idiosyncrasies. Pointing them out would just hurt someone's feelings unnecessarily. Idiosyncrasies sometimes are the result of negative experiences, and one has to give one's neighbors leeway, just as one needs leeway oneself. It is part of what makes a community work.

And because idiosyncrasies are sometimes predictable, I anticipated complaints over my presence in the legal road easement at the bottom of the hill. I did not use my high beams when I approached the intersection on dark winter mornings. I parked on the other side of the road. I did not play the radio. I kept the boy as quiet and unobtrusive as possible. We tried to be invisible. We stayed within the legal road easement, like those roadside pedestrians in Tortilla Bill's Thanksgiving story. We tried to keep our heads down, like those pedestrian "niggers" of Tortilla Bill's youth, and things went smoothly for a year and a half.

My neighbor had a falling-out with a friend, and he seemed to suffer. By mid-February, I was informed by the morning bus driver that I was forbidden to meet the bus at that particular location because my unhappy neighbor had complained that the bus made his dog bark. The school buses from another district stopped and turned and dropped off children in that particular intersection a few minutes before I arrived, and the milk truck from the dairy farm applied its air brakes at that intersection a few minutes after I left. None of these things seemed to make the dog bark. Perhaps for some reason, the dog was sensitive to our presence alone, even when we changed vehicles or arrived on foot; however, I suspect that the real culprit was the fact that I retained a practical relationship with his ex-friend.

We were instructed to go past the end of my neighbor's real estate, to another intersection. There was no reason not to give it a try. This particular location was down in a swamp, flanked by curves, hills, a stream, and water-filled ditches. We were in the midst of one of the largest snowstorms we'd had in years. For more than a month, we had not had a single day without snowfall, and it was to continue for at least two more weeks. The new location was rarely plowed at in the dark of early morning. I was nearly struck by other vehicles almost daily.

There were no parking lots or driveways nearby, except across the road from the gentleman who had complained. After a few weeks of close calls, the owners of that driveway came to my rescue. And eventually I began to use the road easement again, because it was, after all, the road easement, and I did not feel that anyone else owed it to me to let me use their private property day after day. I was also developing a bad attitude about equal access to public road easements and public education and other services that I pay for. And I was remembering what Thurgood Marshall had said about the "stigma" of separateness when he worked so hard to strike down *Plessy v. Ferguson's* heinous notion of separate as equal. My child and I were no more responsible for my neighbor's unhappiness than were the black men of the outskirts of Atlanta's roadsides every time Tortilla Bill and his friends were angry and inconsolable . . .

As much as I am willing to put up with my neighbor's idiosyncrasies, being broomsticked because of a broken relationship goes beyond my level of tolerance. I equate it with being a victim and with teaching my child to be a victim. There is something visceral, biological in my rejection of that role in society. *Plessy v. Ferguson*, separate but equal, was not overturned solely on the basis of the discrepancy between physical entities of the white schools and the colored schools in the Brown decision of 1954. *Brown v. Board of Education* was about social stigma, the social stigma of being designated as other and expendable and convenient to ignore. As an Indian in northwest Lower Michigan, my entire family history with the dominant culture has been almost exclusively one of stigma. I know the damage it does firsthand. Its damage is measurable, in higher suicide rates, in underemployment, in poverty, in poorer access to health care, in poorer access to the safest and most cost-effective places on the public roads . . . I will not instill acceptance of stigma and its repercussions into my child as young as the second grade. Other children watched knowingly out the bus windows. Questions from white parents at the school were reaching us. We were beginning to be seen as people that it was all right to do this sort of thing to. We were becoming "other" in a community that did not have a history and skills to enable it to blend comfortably with "other."

One late March afternoon, when I went to meet the school bus, wooden stakes had been inserted into the road easement where I normally park. I squeezed past the stakes and parked past the intersection. After the bus arrived, I was still able to turn and drive up my road, although with increased difficulty. As the days passed, the stakes would be moved to increase the difficulty of my use of the road easement. It had obviously become an intentional game, and the goal was to drive me away from the part of the road where visibility made it safe to park and turn.

I thought about trying to calmly discuss it with my neighbor, but I've known him for a lot of years, and I knew that if we discussed the issue, a wedge would be driven between us. Were the issue to be resolved by a third party, there was the possibility that he would somehow save face, and things would go back to normal. The issue would never be discussed. He would eventually wander in and out of our yard, barns, and lives, and the rest of us would stay on our own sides of our respective roads. Some people just need a white male in a uniform to tell them what is OK and what is not. It has to do with how they were brought up and who was allowed to draw boundaries for them. Nobody wants to admit it, but it's part of the problem of Jim Crow culture. There are different sets of perceived behavioral boundaries that go beyond the law. That is why the law has to be interpreted. Some people think that separate is equal, and some people could care less about equal; they're just used to getting their way.

By the time the road easement problem peaked, it was the onset of spring break. Business offices for the school and the county road commission were closed by the time I got my son home and settled in and tried to make phone calls regarding obstructions in the road easement. Over the weekend, the stakes had been blown down by high winds. By Monday, the stakes were replaced in a sturdier fashion, even though school would not be in session that week. I feared that I might be in for a difficult fight for my legal right to use the road shoulder—not because I doubted that right, but because I could see that the double standard was being pressed into service again. And I knew that inaction in the face of that double standard would be the option of convenience for the public employees I was going to have to deal with. But this is the nature of double standards. This is the nature of racism and exclusion. It is simply easier to let it happen than to actively do something about it, and my neighbor is not only well aware of this, he is emboldened by it.

The hoops I jumped through seemed endless. Eventually I filled out the state paperwork for homeschooling and pulled my son out of school, anticipating that it would take months to resolve the issue. Various public employees on the local, county, and state levels blew me off. Those who simply did not ignore my letters and calls for help either threatened me, bullied, me, or told me that it was not their responsibility. Eventually, after repeated requests, I got a deputy sheriff to intervene, clear out the road easement, and have a talk with my neighbor. Except for tire tracks around my yard, and the occasional deposition of bags of feces on my doorstep, my neighbors have left us alone.

It seems silly to have to work so hard to use a road easement. I didn't make that choice frivolously. I made it on the basis of safety for my child and the environmental impact and cost of driving extra miles on a regular basis. I made it on the basis of safety for my child in the face of a Native American suicide rate eleven times that of the national average. I made it on the basis of safety for my child in the face of Native American unemployment that surpasses that of all other Americans nationwide and locally, even though our ancestral home has absorbed and employed hundreds of thousands of new white residents in the past few decades.

Unemployment for Native Americans in the state of Michigan, in my chosen profession of education, is outrageous. While writing about the problem may help improve the situation in the long run, or for generations to come, what do I do about right now? If my car is struck and damaged while I fumble in an unsafe intersection away from an unhappy and angry neighbor's property, who will pay? How will I transport my child? How will I make a living? What if we are hurt? Will the racists at the school district I am fleeing reach into their pockets to help? I doubt it. And the county road commission employee who told me to forfeit my use of the public roads and do what my white neighbor (who he had to rush off and meet for lunch) told me to do—will he pay any medical bills, any damages? Of course not. Jim Crow culture is, after all, convenient for the abusers, not for the victims—even when the reasons for the abuse are frivolous.

So the boy has gotten out his toy metal detector, and we are going to check for nails in the public road easement tomorrow. For now, the barriers are gone. It took several trips to the school and the sheriff's department. It took months of effort. It took homeschooling for a while, until the situation was settled. It took certified letters to the road commission and the county prosecutor's office. In the end, the state department of education claimed it was not their domain, the superintendent of schools claimed it was too controversial, and the deputy sheriff tried his best to avoid getting involved. But eventually the issue went away for a while because my neighbor is the kind of guy who wouldn't run through a stop sign once someone pointed out that he'd get in trouble for it. It's like that with broomsticking a nigger, too. He just needed a white male in a uniform to tell him that it wasn't acceptable anymore. Because he wasn't going to take a colored woman's word for it.

In the course of those trips to the county sheriff's office, putting many uncompensated miles on my car, using up unpaid hours of my time, the dispatcher at the county sheriff's department, the one with the high school diploma, the one who has never been educated about *Brown v. Board of Education* or any of the statistics that pertain to the socioeconomic phenomena that dictate my life, took it upon herself to chew me out for pulling my child out of school. "The boy belongs in school," she insisted, as though it was the safest option for an Indian child at that particular time and place, as though his brown mother could not possibly have academic and professional credentials that match or exceed those of his white schoolteachers, as though these off-campus field trips to the county racism facilitation center were any less informative about the boy's designated role in American culture than the field trip to Burger King and the local Ford dealer that his third grade teacher would eventually subject him to. None of them would ever be forced to confront the laws about compulsory school attendance that could provide loopholes for punishing a woman of color who did not do what she was told on the county roads of this white-flight community.

There were kind people in all of this, too. There were the neighbors who offered to run over the stakes with their pickup trucks. (No thanks, I insisted, I'm a farmer; I've got stuff bigger than a little ol' pickup truck to run over a few stakes with; it's about something bigger. For all of their kindness, they do not necessarily understand what the big deal is about equal rights.) There was the second grade teacher who was as emotionally distraught by the situation as I was and who volunteered to drive to my home to pick up the child. But it wasn't about being able to drive the boy to and from school. It was about something bigger. And in all fairness, the superintendent of Leland schools did, repeatedly, respond to my neighbor's frequent incoming calls by claiming that it was a public road and that the bus could legally stop there . . . after I got pushy and decided to exercise my right to use the road easement. If there is anything to be learned from this, it is that racism affects nonminorities, too, even if not with the same immediate intensity.

So we will check the road easement for nails because we have interfered with one neighbor's sense of empowerment over someone perceived as weaker and therefore a potential victim. The calm that follows legal intervention is not guaranteed to continue in perpetuity. That extra bit of caution is a price we pay for being Native Americans in a place that has wanted us to disappear, to disappear from jobs and property ownership, from schools and public places, even from the road easements. My son and I were forced into a situation where we had to choose between dangers. Broomsticking, lynching, and all the other manifestations of racism are big issues. They take many forms, and their repercussions affect our mortality, our very survival. For every Thurgood Marshall, for every Martin Luther King, for every well-known advocate for civil rights who makes it into the history books, there are a thousand little boys with metal detectors looking for nails in the road easement, looking nervously over their shoulders for broomsticks, in various and shifting forms. And their parents ease them through these social minefields, helping them decide when and where to fight or flee, when or where to spend precious resources for the betterment of humankind. For the victims, there is nothing convenient about the culture of Jim Crow.

• 24 •

The Chair

$\mathcal{T}$he chair was over one hundred years old. Small, light, and strong, its joints were still tight. Her father had had fifty or more of them, had bought them, cheap, because he was the fire chief, and he needed them for the meetings. This, long before she was born, as she was the youngest child in the family, and the others were much older than her by an unnaturally long gap for the early 1900s. Her father was a well driller and the family ran the village ice-cream parlor on the ground floor of the big house. The carriage house was now reduced to a rotting shed, and a garage was now attached to the back of the house, on the side facing the railroad siding. The general store next door sat empty for decades until a nice young couple converted it into a home, hoping to use the front room with its walls of glass for a beauty parlor someday, perhaps when the kids were a little older, in school maybe.

The dirt road that wound snake-like through the high ground flanking the creek ended abruptly at the four-lane state road, now a major trunk line, that mowed the small village of Williamsburg into two disparate halves, one the funky mill pond village of refurbished homes in the hollow below, the other an unnoticed enclave of Indians and Mennonites spaced out quietly around the silent cemetery. Both halves of the old village merged silently into a patchwork of wooded swamps with orchards gracing the hilltops.

The old lady had been a teacher, junior high, high school, and even at the junior college in Twin Bay City, where she'd been recruited from her position as high school teacher in River Rapids to teach college English in the newly transformed military Quonset huts nestled among ancient pines of the flats comprising the base of the Old Mission Peninsula that divided the east and west arms of Grand Twin Bay. She'd never had to apply for a job in her life, she'd once bragged to young Ima Pipiig. She'd been recruited to teach the

171

farm children of Old Mission in the one-room schoolhouse out on the peninsula, recruited to manage the junior high and high school nearer her beloved
ice-cream parlor home, then wooed to commute through the empty hills, past
the trailer-park village of Acme along the bay, to teach chubby white college
hopefuls who commuted in to the freshly painted barracks from the surrounding hay, potato, and fruit farms.

She spoke to Ima Pipiig about the farming, the logging, the fall potato
harvest that closed all the schools annually earlier in the century. She took the
girl upstairs to the sitting room and let her touch the precious china-headed
dolls of her childhood. She wound up the old Victrola and let the child listen
to the same scratchy recordings over and over. It was the only commercial music Ima Pipiig had ever heard outside of a church or a school.

She was one of ten children, and her mother had died in Canada, shortly
before her father returned to northern Michigan, to breathe new life into the
farm that had been left years before by his father-in-law, Ima Pipiig's only
white grandparent, a man she scarcely remembered. She had been sent to the
old lady to be tutored, one of a parade of needy and poor, mostly dirty little
Indian children, too big a challenge for their already challenged teachers. Except that Ima Pipiig was never dirty. When the busy morning house was
churning with people, Ima Pipiig would break the ice on the top of the prim-
ing water bucket next to the old metal pump, plunge her hand into the cold
water, and empty coffee canfulls of water into the pump mouth, until the air
was forced out of the pumping apparatus, and a good suction could be created
by pumping as hard and fast as she could. Then she washed her face and hands
with the frozen bar of pumice soap, and if there was no harsh and biting wind,
Ima Pipiig pulled the collar of her sweater back and put her head under the
flow. The groundwater was often warmer than the air, and the girl held her
head in the relative warmth of the fresh water until she had completely rinsed
away all remnants of the handful of powdered laundry detergent that Ima
Pipiig had carried outside in her jacket pocket.

Long before they reached the hilltop halfway mark on their mile-long
walk to the school bus stop, the children would laugh and compare the frozen
states of their own heads of hair from under the hats and hoods. And at the
hilltop they would, in turn, each give a mittened swish at the blackberry bram-
bles that had provided them with morning and evening treasures only two
months ago, when the daily trips to and from the school bus were still made
in the daylight.

When the snow would come, Ima Pipiig's father would put chains on the
tires of the tiny two-wheeled Massey Ferguson tractor that counterbalanced
and pulled a two-wheeled wooden cart. The oldest child in the family, actually Ima Pipiig's mother's younger brother, would be allowed to drive. Each

morning Wally pulled open one of a pair of heavy sliding doors on the side of the barn closest to the house where his older brother-in-law was already building a fire in an old parlor stove next to his workbench. Then he wound the handled pull rope around the flywheel and tended the gas lever on the steering handles until the small engine chugged independently. He swung his long limbs up on the board that served as a seat, pulled the noisy carriage to the door of the house, and waited until the children piled themselves and their books and lunches into the small wagon behind him. The eldest took the guard seats in the rear, that is, they hung their feet off the back, making snakes and diamonds in the snow behind the tractorload of children, and they made sure that the youngsters did not fall out or leave a mitten or scarf behind. Ima Pipiig loved to hop off into the soft snow between the tire tracks to retrieve lost items. She hated when Wally wouldn't slow down for her to catch up and hop back on again, forcing her to run in snow that crept up her leggings and over the tops of her flapped rubber snowboots, causing chill and numbness along the middle of her calves. She threw snowballs at the back of his head and screamed at him until her head hurt. The tractor would be hidden away in the woods at the edge of the farm. Then the children walked the rest of the way up a plowed road with modest homes where the school bus ventured.

Sometimes, before the snow was too deep, when the tractor approached a recently logged clearing on the trip home, Wally would let the tractor coast to a stop, put a finger to his mouth, point, and slowly open the glove box on the engine to retrieve a pair of heavy leather work gloves. Then the children would pile out, muffling giggles, and, following Wally's silent hand signals, they would fan out in a circle then begin walking slowly, stiffly toward one another. If their endeavor was successful, they would emerge from the clearing with one or more grouse freshly strangled in Wally's leather gloves. Once home, the grouse would cool outside until homework was done and snacks were eaten. Then the children would clean and pluck the birds. Their father would work in the woods until dark, and they could hear the comforting chunk of an axe or the distant roar of a chain saw as he generated saw logs and firewood.

Sometimes the school bus took Ima Pipiig to the old lady's house after school, for tutoring. It wasn't that Ima Pipiig needed tutoring, but she just hadn't wanted to read out loud to the teachers. The teachers had all agreed that Ima Pipiig was probably brighter than average and even suspected that she could read much better than her brothers and sisters, all of whom would eventually be referred to community volunteer tutors at some point, not because they could not read, but because they did not want to read out loud in an environment in which they were lesser, Indians, "underpeople." Silence remained a safety mechanism for Indian children even by the middle of the twentieth century.

It didn't matter to Ima Pipiig. She enjoyed the time with the old retired teacher. She enjoyed the cookies with chocolate. Chocolate was a rarity in her home. She enjoyed the peace and quiet that provided a perfect counterbalance to the equally enjoyable chaos of the time she spent with cousins and siblings. She enjoyed reading books that were different than the volumes in her home that they had read to one another over and over and over. She loved the Victrola, she loved the elaborate pressed tin that covered the ceiling of the ground-floor living room of the house that had once served as the ceiling of the old ice-cream parlor, and she loved the railroad cars that sometimes mysteriously appeared on the siding. Eventually, she loved the old lady. And the woman had come to love Ima Pipiig as well. So the tutoring sessions continued for years, lasting often past the dinner hour, when they shared a meal by candlelight, and the old lady drove the girl home, deep inland, deep into the woods, where the real estate was cheaper and less desirable to the new people who were moving north to escape the cities, where a few Indian farmers still worked well beyond dawn and dusk to keep a land base for their children. When the snows got too deep, the tutoring sessions would end.

One summer evening, when the rain was falling in sheets and the visibility was poor, Ima Pipiig's father and uncle would die on that four-lane state highway when their pickup truck would hit a lost and frightened horse that would roll up and over the windshield, crushing the two men and leaving fifteen children homeless. The aunt, the one surviving wife, would eventually give up, abandon the farm and the children's hope for staying together in a paradise of the family's own making, and the land would eventually slip away to pay bills, long after the children would have been dispersed among unwilling relatives and strangers. So, for a few years, Ima Pipiig would live with the old woman, and they would comfort one another. The girl missed her family and the quiet spaces of the farm that her father and uncle had revived. The woman missed her husband of thirty-five years who had taken over her father's well-drilling business and had renovated the old ice-cream parlor.

After the old lady's death, after distant nieces and nephews had laid claim to the house, the old dolls, and the Victrola, Ima Pipiig would be sent down to nearby Benzie County to live with relatives she did not know particularly well. She would be delivered by the department of social services, a small cloth bag of clothing clutched in one hand, and a small, sturdy wooden chair in the other. For months the girl refused to sit in any other chair.

Now Ima Pipiig stood in near darkness on the small chair. It was pulled up next to one of the wood ricks full of firewood that lined her narrow driveway among the pines. It had finally stopped raining and snowing, and the air was dry and crisp. Ima Pipiig had wanted to use the plastic lawn chair that had been sitting outside the door to the house for the past several months, but

Lester had just yesterday taken it over to a distant barn for the winter. One sleety night a stiff wind had blown it into the driveway, and he'd nearly run it over. So he took it to one of the barns at the same time that he'd towed one of the kids' old red wagons full of summer toys over there to clean up the yard. Then he'd used one of the farm's hand-pumps to fill the tanks on the big diesel dump truck and brought it over to the house for Ima Pipiig to drive while her car was in the shop getting a new exhaust system. It had been awfully nice of him to do those things for her, she thought. Normally, she wouldn't take the chair outside, but it was dry and her sneakers were clean. She had been too busy all day to take care of this final chore, and now, after ten or twelve hours of steady, though not exhausting work, Ima Pipiig did not have the energy to go to the barns after an unsteady plastic chair to facilitate the tackling of one final pinch of work that she knew better than to put off.

Only last night, Biggie Waldo had arrived from his orchard across the road with a dead porcupine. Gun season for deer was rapidly coming to a close, and no one in the neighborhood had been particularly successful this year. The new hunting rules required that a buck have at least three points on one antler. But bucks didn't have a tendency to stop and pose before the hunter in a position that allowed one to count tines on either side, as Lester had pointed out. Probably frustrated and dying to shoot something, Biggie took out an unsuspecting porcupine, knowing that he could justify the kill by giving it to Ima Pipiig for quills for her baskets and jewelry. So the animal had been set aside on top of the metal roofing tin of a wood rick the night before, out of reach of curious house pets, coyotes, and her own third grader. Lester had assured her that it was a large and beautiful animal that would yield to her a good supply of much-needed quills.

The weather had hovered above freezing for much of the day, so the porcupine now sat in a pool of its own blood that had settled into the valleys of the corrugated metal and had oozed out, soaking one piece of firewood at the top of the stack. It was cold, so the animal did not smell, in spite of the fact that a large bulge of intestines emerged from its side. Biggie had shot the animal at close range with something designed to bring down a much larger animal. Even so, Biggie had not accomplished the good, clean head shot that Lester would have waited for before bringing home a porcupine for plucking. Ima Pipiig knew that it would be easiest to pluck the porcupine from the top of the rick, before the heavy black clouds that had dominated the afternoon potentially dumped their load onto the animal. The huge hole in its sides would make it difficult to remove it from the rick or to return it there when she was finished. She knew that she would only be able to pluck for about an hour or so, before the porch light failed to provide her with enough light to do the job, before her limbs grew cold from beneath the paint-stained down vest she'd snapped over the paint-stained hooded sweatshirt and paint-stained hole-in-the-knee blue jeans she saved for just this sort of dirty job.

She'd gone to the barns to fetch an empty five-gallon plastic bucket. She'd filled it with manure from the composted heap that stood next to her garden, still unfrozen for at least another day, and she'd emptied its contents around the base of the house where her snowdrops, crocuses, tulips, and other bulbs would bring her joy in a few months. She'd rinsed the bucket and placed it in front of the old wooden chair.

Ima Pipiig pivoted the dead porcupine by its quill-less front paws, positioning its rump in front of her. Then, while the liquid light lingered refracted in northern Michigan's humid horizons long after the sun itself had gone beyond the southwesternmost hills, Ima Pipiig gritted her teeth and began the most difficult part of plucking a porcupine. There on the rump, where the quills were the stiffest, sharpest, and most deadly, she had to create an empty space that would allow her to insert her hand underneath the quills and pull them out easily. It was something she had done so often, she could still do it in the almost dark. So she reached in among the quills, as they punctured her fingertips, stuck into them, and caused her to wince time and again. The animal was fresh, and the quills did not come out as easily as they would tomorrow, after another thaw and freeze to loosen the hair follicles within the skin. She separated the quills from the fur that came out with them, plucked out the ones that stuck in her fingers, and dropped them straight down into the bucket. There was not even a slight breeze, and the quills would fall into their target for the next two hours, until sheer darkness and fatigue caused the woman to miss her mark.

She knew it was time to stop. Lost quills in the leaves and grass of her yard would not make for a safe environment for children and pets. The boy had forgotten his library book on the school bus and had been watching cartoons for too long. It was time to scrub away from her hands and forearms the grease from the quills and the germs they carried to insert into their predators, time to add wood to the parlor stove in her living room, time to pull dinner from the refrigerator and begin heating it, and time to take a long, hot shower, so that her hair would have time to dry overnight, before she drove the boy to meet the school bus in the comforting, embracing darkness of a late November morning.

· 25 ·

F-ed by the V-Monologues

$\mathscr{I}$ 've been getting a lot of phone calls lately from the ladies who've claimed ownership to the Traverse City, Michigan, contingency of the *Vagina Monologues*. They put on a show last year, featuring Eve Ensler's celebrated work honoring women and their anatomy, interspersed with essays by local white women. Ensler's essays include pieces in the voices of women of color as well, written not by women of color, but by Ensler herself.

The first phone call was from a woman asking me to try out for the part of the Native American woman who would be reading the Native American portion of Ensler's monologues. It was put to me in such a way that I felt I was expected to prove that I was good enough for the distinction of reading the words that a white woman had written for me, a Native American woman. Since I've probably had more experience with public speaking than most of the community leaders and staff at my local junior college and university center, it was an odd request, to my mind. And since I've probably written and published as much as Eve Ensler, it was an even weirder request.

I suggested to my caller that I might have as much to say about the sexual roles of Native American women as Eve Ensler, because I, unlike Ensler, am a Native American woman . . . and—what a bonus!—I happen to share my strong opinions on the topic through the written and spoken word. Alas, it was not her job to consider giving me my own voice. She had merely been instructed to invite me to the " tryouts," as though the ladies were putting on a high school play, and I were one of so many wistful young Native American maidens wringing my hands and hopeful for the part that Eve Ensler, and subsequently my white neighbors, had determined it was appropriate for me to play. It's a phenomenon I encounter every day of my life. My friends and neighbors from the dominant culture expect me to live up to their stereotypes of a docile young Indian maiden, not unlike Pocahontas, or perhaps some young, sweet girl in a beaded headband and buckskin fringes who no doubt handed the deserving Pilgrims a basket full of venison tenderloins and wild blueberry corn muffins. People often get downright huffy if I don't act that way. So I didn't join the nonexistent line of Native American women trying out for the part, even though she was a really nice lady.

The second call came from another really nice lady, younger than the first. She'd taken on the task of finding artwork for the back cover of the performance program and thought maybe Native American women could be represented by my contributing maybe the artwork and maybe a little poem for the cover, to show that maybe they had, like, you know, taken Native Americans into consideration. Suggestions were made as to the nature of the new original piece of artwork I would be expected to create for this volunteer assignment. And so . . . being the teacher that I am, and having a receptive and intelligent audience, I began to explain why, why, why . . .

I cannot be Uncle Tom for the women of Traverse City, Michigan, any more than I can for your school districts, your museums, your parks, your churches, your families, your children's literature, or your fantasies. And at the end of it all, I agreed to provide a signed, limited edition print for scanning, and a copy of it to be sold to fund the project, along with a quote from a book I'd written and a no-way-definitely-not-short poem that would address women's issues pertinent to the northwest corner of Michigan's lower peninsula . . . Because, oddly enough, I was as competent as the local white women whose pages were to be interspersed throughout the program. My friend the printer found a male business sponsor for the extra pages I had generated.

But, alas, the poem was left out, and the benign illustration and quote were proudly displayed on the back catalog cover of the Traverse City, Michigan, production of the *Vagina Monologues*. I'd been Uncle Tommed, and the white ladies of northwest Lower Michigan patted themselves on the back for giving the impression of being culturally sensitive and compassionate and inclusive, while I tried to wipe the experience of my interaction with them from my mind as though it were offensive goo on the heel of a boot.

A week later, I heard one from that selective group of civic-minded women on the local public radio channel, congratulating herself for developing the ability to say "vagina" out loud. I was saddened, because the women of this region would never know that the Ojibwe—Chippewa you call us—have a tradition so respectful of women, that we only use anatomically correct terms for human body parts, counter to every European language I have ever learned. We are genteel, intelligent. We have a wealth of traditional stories that deal with women's roles, verbal abuse, domestic violence, transgender issues, and every other social issue that any society would need to function for millennia . . . as we did, and still do. Outside of your public schools, we have our own social institutions that teach mechanisms for avoiding dysfunction because dysfunction happens in all cultures. Some address it more freely than others. Yet the ladies of Traverse City, Michigan, did not have the opportunity to learn this because they could not fathom a Native American voice bigger than their own stereotypes of ignorance and docility, perhaps mirroring their own culture's attitude toward women. Just as importantly, it voiced their culture's attitude toward people of color.

And then the third call . . . months after I had put my denigration to rest. . . . Again, this woman was smart and nice. She identified herself to me as one of the women who had put on the "V-Monologues," as though it were an emblem of accomplishment. And I suppose in some ways it is. Would I pose to be the token Native American for a calendar featuring pin-up drawings of women over forty? For some reason, they were having a hard time getting an Indian woman to do it.

Now, if you're an Ojibwe woman who's grown up on a remote island with all of your family, bathing and drawing water from the same lake, changing clothes in the same small rooms where family members are cooking, oiling boots, or playing pinochle, it's not a big deal to be a naked woman over forty. The older women of my family have grossed out our fair share of young white canoeists and kayakers over the years, which is precisely why the calendar has its place in the artistic expression of the non-Indian women who are putting it together. But for the Indian women of the northwest corner of Michigan's lower peninsula, the issue is not one that meets our needs. We jumped on that one centuries ago. Right now, we have bigger fish to fry. As a spokesperson for the civil rights of Native Americans in my area, I cannot afford to throw away my credibility to make the point to a non-Indian audience that Indian women over forty are beautiful and socially acceptable when I'm still trying to convince that audience that Indians in general are beautiful and socially acceptable.

"Don't write about the V-Monologues, please. My name is attached to it," the caller insists, after I have made my points. But I cannot protect her. She has been part of the problem, not the solution. She is one of thousands of white escapists from Chicago and Detroit who have worked their way up the coastlines and the interstate highways into the ancestral homelands of the Woodland Indians of the northern Great Lakes. In our neighborhood, the existing sparse populations of whites and Native Americans had begun to make their peace and intermarry one another just when the white flight began in the 1970s, after that messy bussing/integration/poverty-driven-race-riots thing that nobody wants to take responsibility for.

These new neighbors have been so glad to be part of the *new* nouveau riche, glad to be part of the new public-land ghettos next to the state and national parks, that no one has spoken out about the local public school administrator who threatens, stalks, and batters women, especially the vulnerable ones, the poor or the minorities—or about the corrupt system that makes it acceptable, or the local battered women's shelter that lives culturally under the carpet, like a virus. You see, those women, they're trash; they bring it on themselves. Like the Indians: they're trash; they bring it on themselves. Violence against women, minority women in particular, takes on many forms. I feel myself under no obligation to make it cheap or easy or without embarrassment to the "prominent" citizens and "leaders" within my community.

The phenomenon of white flight into this area happened with such speed and intensity that we could not overcome the fear and ignorance you brought with you. Perhaps we should call it "white blight."

Last week, I was mailed a copy of the part of Ensler's monologues that are written in the voices of Native American women. It was an act of friendship, from that caller who genuinely wanted to know, after the fact, if the monologues met my approval. No one had originally considered that the monologues might not meet the needs of the Indian women who were "included" as a form of political correctness. It's hard teaching you all of this, one at a time, at the expense of many of my own unpaid hours. I would much rather be paid what a white woman with my credentials makes, or better yet, what a white male with my credentials makes—but minority employment in education in this corner of the state runs at, oh . . . around 0 percent.

I would have liked to have had the opportunity to have spoken out before the damage was done, before Ensler's damaging words and stereotypes pertaining to Native American women were performed, celebrated, espoused as the gospel by a white schoolteacher from Traverse City, Michigan, who will take those stereotypes back into the classroom with her. You see, public education is one of the least integrated professions in America today, and the option of educating you in groups is not available to me in the mainstream press, in the public schools, or in any format other than as a token Indian. . . . So I will be reluctant in the future to let my artwork be used, giving the impression of consensus for the status quo, consensus for the bizarre forms of racism, sexism, and ignorance that you have brought with you while you've been busy fleeing from those awful colored folks down in those awful big cities you've left crumbling. I do not like Ensler's stereotypes of me any more than I like the ones you brought with you.

Ensler "researched" the Native American part of her monologues by visiting and speaking with women from the Pine Ridge Indian Reservation. In some ways Pine Ridge may well qualify as one of the nation's armpits, as well as a life-giving vagina, but it is not an armpit of its residents' own making. It is a space full of hardships still imposed upon Native Americans by an outside economy that does not equally distribute resources or opportunities. Any cultural incompetence demonstrated from that space needs to be put into that context, and it cannot possibly be expected to be a salient representative of its people's traditional cultural systems—especially when the dominant culture is already expecting negative and incompetent sound bites.

Ensler did damage to Native American women. Her essays in Indian voices spoke only about domestic violence, in contrast to the essays in white women's voices. Ensler did not make clear to her audience that, in fact, the bulk of partners who abuse Native American women are not Native Americans themselves, but non-Indians who have sought out a weaker, vulnerable element of society—as abusers do. You see, Native American women who are abused, by domestic spouses, neighbors, employers, big business, and even suburban escapees are not deserving-trash as depicted by Ensler and interpreted by my neighbors . . . we are wasted human resources.

Even worse than Ensler's stereotypes is the fact that today, in this twenty-first century, when Native American authors, artists, and activists are educated, outspoken, and available, she took it upon herself to tell our stories for us, as though she could possibly be a competent substitute for our own voices. By wearing the hat of a writer rather than that of an open-minded editor of contemporary Native American women's voices, Ensler has trivialized us and presented us as stereotypes within a vacuum. The end result is as damaging as Barbara Kingsolver's writing a novel suggesting that Indian women get drunk and give our babies away. While Ensler and dozens of other non-Indian authors who write about Indians reap the economic benefits of giving the dominant culture what it needs and wants to think about the competence of Native American people, Native scholars find themselves waiting years for the publication of materials contradicting those stereotypes. Posing naked for a calendar isn't a cultural move a serious Native American scholar can afford to make.

Native Americans have found through the years that we must, of necessity, be very conservative. We cannot afford to be wild among you, different among you, opinionated, uneducated, or even briefly incompetent among you, or we will pay the consequences. We must achieve higher in school, in the workplace, in culture in general, or we will be considered as less competent, excluded from employment, jailed more frequently, considered as liabilities in the public schools and parks we share, be unwelcomed in your restaurants and stores, in any format where opinion contrary to your own might be expressed. . . .

Native American women in Michigan have more college diplomas per capita than any other group, yet we have the highest unemployment in the state. Our children's schools are staffed almost exclusively by whites. Public school administration has become a highly paid white male gravy train that models racism and sexism to our children. We are followed around your stores by security guards. White women tighten their grips on their purses when we or our family members enter the room. Ears close to our concerns. We fear for our safety, and the safety of our children. All this, because you have found our neighborhood to be more desirable than your old neighborhood, and you have reinstituted the policy of Manifest Destiny.

These lakes, fields, hills, jobs, and schools are ours now. Find your own institutions in which to educate your children and to work . . . someplace else, you have told us. *You've got casinos to take care of you now; you don't need civil rights or meaningful integration/inclusion.* Ah, casino money, that loophole in racism that services less than 50 percent of the Indians in the state . . . that new big pie you keep trying to stick your fingers into . . . that alternative to competent civil discourse. . . .

After a lifetime of such battles, I cannot permit the limited success I have achieved with more and better credentials than my employed white peers to be thrown away, simply because you need a token Indian. Your culture has not progressed to that point. I cannot take off my clothes and swing them over my head freely, like Kiishigokwe, the Fog Woman of the Great Lakes who has danced freely along these coasts for hundreds of generations, to the fear and delight of the men of my family. So, instead, I offer up to you the poem that was left out of the Traverse City, Michigan, performance of the *Vagina Monologues*.

A LOVE LETTER TO MY COMMUNITY

I took elementary arithmetic for schoolteachers once, because they told me that *you* need teachers . . . Not bothering to explain that they meant that an Indian could only teach Indians . . . and *never* white children.

I sat flanked in the class by blue-eyed strawberry blond men, one a math major, and the other a high school math teacher . . .

Fuzzy-chubby arms on either side of me. They laughed, snorted, rolled their eyes, and thrust backward in their seats whenever I asked questions. Did my homework.

Their eyes popped out of their heads when they both leaned in to see what the big red star at the top of the page meant *every* time my exam came back.

"Class High." Big red star. Highest grade in the class. "Have you thought of getting your doctorate in math?" the teacher would ask . . . older woman, ready to retire, damned good teacher . . .

"How could she get the best grades *every* time?" the boys thought. "After all, I've got a white penis." They didn't try harder though . . . just did the same old . . . went home and impregnated their wives. Guaranteed jobs, white males in education.

This year Glen Lake school district hired a middle school principal with a D+ in Elementary arithmetic. He had a couple of B's in his educational administration courses . . . to balance out his abysmal performance in *real* college classes . . .

But I'd had those 500 level courses, when the 100 level courses wouldn't fit into my schedule. You see, I took 57 credits in one year, instead of 24 . . .

While I worked 30 hours a week, and my educational administrator spouse worked 34. He couldn't be bothered to share childcare and laundry with a lazy gold digger like me.

And those 500 level courses in educational administration were Mickey Mouse compared to elementary arithmetic . . . or even grocery shopping.

During my first semester, I was taught that 80% of the people who go into education come from the bottom 20% of their freshman class in college.

Not me, not me, I thought, with my 3.9 GPA and my 4-year academic scholarship . . . the fourth daughter of the ninth (and only surviving) son of an Indian fisherman/farmer . . .

I, with my 96th percentile ranking on the National Teacher Exam. And he, from the bottom fifth of the bottom fifth.

I, from the top four percent, stringing beads for a living at less than 10 cents on the dollar, compared to his salary . . . he from the bottom four percent . . .

"Why can't Johnny understand complex subjects like racial and gender equity?" "Are you kidding? He can't do long division . . ."

"Give the guy a break. He's got 4 kids." Ah . . . he's a breeder, a *spermchucker.* If he was brown and female, we'd have called him irresponsible. We'd have called him a welfare mama.

I think about one woman they passed up for the job: 5 foot even, jumped higher than the rest of the cheerleaders, because she was not svelte and blond.

Never lets a 5-foot-7-inch fifth grader push her around. Meets his gaze. Outsmarts them all. Scares the hell out of their fat lazy daddies; knows football in and out.

"If those *ladies* want to be principals, they'll have to go to another district to do it." I can't believe we pay Bozo the Clown a hundred thousand in salary and bennies to fart in the face of Titles VII of the 1964 and 1972 Civil Rights Acts.

"It's got to be someone the present administration is comfortable with . . . " He makes his justification from under the bulbous red nose.

And the other wide-bottomed men in brown polyester suits nod in agreement: Darned proud of the fact that they're not comfortable with brown folks and tits! Willing to bet our children's futures on that class action suit in the waiting . . .

I fantasize about the overly funded boys' sporting events: "Whaddaya do when the Glen Lake team can't get ahead by enough points to guarantee a win?"

"Ya bring out the Glen Lake girly girly cheerleaders, and they 'Spread 'em!' 'Spread 'em!' 'Spread 'em, spread 'em, spread 'em!'"

"Why do Polish butchers in the Glen Lake school district put duct tape in the meat case next to the kielbasa?" "So that job applicants can tape sausages to their thighs . . ."

"I have a daughter who is an honor student at Glen Lake Schools. She gives preference to white penises." (Bumper sticker graphics borrowed from a truck mud flap.)

"I have a son who is an honor student at Glen Lake Schools. He doesn't need to study math." (Oops, it's a secret that every one of those Golden Apple Awards is under scrutiny by the state.)

(News like that could jeopardize the salaries of the highest paid white men in the Traverse City region. Oops, oops, oops.) (Gotta keep the people in our school district ignorant.)

And then there's the one-semester wonder, the 21-year-old white male Spanish teacher with no coursework in either Spanish or education . . . Much better choice than those female language teachers who applied, don't you think?

It was just a Little White Lie fudging that paperwork to the state board of education to hire him on a waiver. (Think of all the money we saved toward my salary . . . oops. Oops, oops, oops.)

I think about my local school board . . . the bellied middle-aged men, and the sad, silent Women who can't be bothered with the message modeled for those adolescent middle school girls . . . whose mothers they asked to spend a half an hour voting for them . . . especially the one who waits on them at Pizza Hut . . .

There's a 2½ × 3 ft. poster of the Good Shepherd at the door to my son's public school. I gently correct him, when he announces that the Lord Jesus Christ is his savior,

Because my merely quasi-Catholic Ojibwe mother never tried to convince me that I had a Savior or that it would be male or white . . . or even human, for that matter.

I distrust them and suspect that they might have found Mr. D+ at a downstate church function. "Praise the Lord and pass the White Penis."

You see, they moved north to Chippewa Country to get away from coloreds and liberals, jumping into local politics in every new suburb along the way.

And the teachers are going to elect to the board of education whoever they think is going to keep their salaries the highest in the region. Can you blame them? High pay, low ethics. Better than working at Pizza Hut.

I envision the middle-aged women on my school board, in a table-seated chorus line, at the front of the school library, baring their breasts to Master D+, singing, "We can't live without your white maaa-yon-hood!" (They have hair that does not move.)

I say to myself that they are victims, that they were taught to be *dependent* upon a white male . . . by their white men, teachers 80% female . . . administrators 80% men . . .

The victims are manufacturing new victims, training them while they are young. Discrepancies in race and gender equity are higher in public education than in any other segment of our society.

They vote overwhelmingly to hire the white penis with a D+, because they must hurry Home to bleach their roots and throw up the pizza they just ate.

My math-nerd daughter moans when she hears the news: "He was the most incompetent teacher I ever had! Why am I going to college, Mom? Should I waste my time with this academic scholarship? Like *you* did?"

I snap out of my fantasy and I hang my head in shame. (This wasn't done by strangers far away.) And I cry, and I scream out in pain as I claw at my maligned Injun breasts . . . We are three years into the twenty-first century.

If we cannot fight abuse of power and public funds at home, how can we do it in our capitals . . . Where the people who control the money and policy meet elusively and tell us that we are special interest groups whose opinions do not matter?

Oops, wait a minute . . . That's what's been happening in our own small school district right here in Leelanau County. Oops. Oops, oops, oops . . .

Remember, girls, it's not the size that counts . . . it's the color.

· 26 ·

The Throw-away People

$\mathcal{I}$ma Pipiig was feeling caught up on all of the harvest-it-or-lose-it and other short-term emergencies in her life. There were milk and bread in the refrigerator, the bills were paid, nothing was mildewing wet in a laundry basket, the freezers had been defrosted, the garden was picked clean, and the household was in general working order. The outdoor temperature had dropped twenty degrees, and the sky and the air felt of impending, but not immediate, rain. It was a good day to pick sweetgrass. The only unharvested resource she was neglecting at this time was the wild patch of raspberries flanked by seedy blackcaps, and she knew that today's clouds would buy her a respite, and that tomorrow she could pick and bake a pie.

The sweetgrass itself was in need of harvesting in a timely manner. It had already passed its prime, and it would require a little extra work to harvest and clean it now, but it was a good year for sweetgrass. The stalks were longer than the towels she used for wrapping and storing it. Ima Pipiig had already picked a reasonable amount of sweetgrass for the winter, but she knew that it was a resource not to be wasted, and she could always sell her baskets cheap, come dead of winter, when she needed the money the most. Self-employed insurance premiums, car insurance, and phone bills did not go away just because northern Michigan's warm-weather tourist industry dried up and blew away like an autumn leaf.

Ima Pipiig, for all of her education, was dependent upon that economy. She kept museum gift shops supplied with "bread and butter" items, small, under-five-or-ten-dollar items for impulse buyers. So she made tiny pins, cards, and jewelry out of birch bark, porcupine quills, and all of the other bits and pieces of "nature" that the summer tourists had come to expect and to associate with

Indians. Cute Indians. Friendly Indians. Gosh, we-really-like-living-in-tar-paper-shacks-and-having-unequal-access-to-the-nation's-resources Indians. Ima Pipiig wasn't really one of these. But she'd learned when to keep her mouth shut and be one, just to pay the bills. When push came to shove, Ima Pipiig knew that she could wholesale her over-the-ten-dollar-impulse-buyer-range sweetgrass baskets to those various merchants of the "nonprofit" organizations. She would make half of the federal minimum wage or less, but money was money when there were no other options. And by January or February, Ima Pipiig would feel less the soreness of her thumb and the sourness of her nostrils from the plucking of a dead porcupine, she would feel less the tired legs and the sore back from picking the sweetgrass, and she would forget somewhat the numbness of her tarsals and her elbows from the repetitive stitch-stitch-stitching of those superb, tight baskets. Come winter, Ima Pipiig would feel the pain of being unemployable, in spite of her credentials. She would feel the pain of being without place or function in the economy of the newcomers, except as a token Indian. And Ima Pipiig would cry for her own uselessness in those quiet hours of the day, alone in front of the woodstove, wondering what an unwanted Indian could do to be productive, now that her freezers were full, the shelves of canning jars bent heavy, and several days' supply of firewood was stacked inside the house. How could she do something to contribute to her future livelihood in her old age, after her stiff arms and back would no longer rest up and become useful for a few more hours?

Ima Pipiig shifted on the couch and took one last swallow from her cold coffee cup, her favorite cup, the one with the loons on it. She drank from it at least once a day, not just because she loved looking at the loons and the tamaracks and that they made her think of life in the bush. It made her think of the proud way that Birdie and her dad had looked the day they had given it to her for Christmas. Picked out just for her. A special gift just to make Ima Pipiig's heart go pitter-pat. And it did. Ima Pipiig also drank from the coffee cup daily because she was superstitious about it. It was sort of a lucky coffee cup.

Ima Pipiig did a lot of small gestures that she knew would be deemed as superstitious, just for luck. It was something she had started to do early on in life, perhaps at about the age of ten, just after her mother's death. Ima Pipiig learned at that young age that she had no control over her own life. She could not work hard, try hard, or be good hard enough to make life comfortable and right. So Ima Pipiig fell back upon the only determiner of her own fate that she knew of—sheer, dumb luck. Even into adulthood, after she knew that it was racism and economic injustice that kept her from getting ahead no matter how hard she worked, Ima Pipiig continued making small, hopeful gestures, in a lifelong, almost innate attempt to get a hold on her own survival and her own future. She touched things with her right hand first. She touched things twice. She drank from that loon cup once a day. Ima Pipiig had tried everything else. She had tried college. She had tried getting straight A's in school. She had tried being docile. She had tried being pushy. She had tried throwing her dignity to the wind. She had tried working harder and faster, harder and faster, harder and faster . . . but there was no harder or faster left possible. So Ima Pipiig drank out of the cup . . . every single day, even if it was just one gulp of water. She did so every morning, first thing in the morning, so that she would not forget, would not fall asleep, exhausted, without having blessed her day by hoping that fate would send her the living wage that white America had denied her.

Ima Pipiig washed the cup and set it in a safe position on the already full dish rack. She procrastinated a little bit. She was tired. She'd cut heavy sheets of birch bark with thick scissors until 8:30 at night. The family had been away swimming for a few hours. After she pulled the venison pasty from the oven and pulled the small paring knife toward her thumb in several repetitive motions that let delicate shavings of huge, overgrown radishes fall into the just-picked spinach salad, she sat down in front of *Democracy Now*, her favorite alternative news show on Free Speech TV, and she earned her keep . . . while high gray clouds swept in, and the muggy air shifted and cooled slightly, before the man and the boy were back and eating their supper as their last gesture to the day, and the television was switched to a movie that would lull them all to sleep on the big bed in the middle of the small house. Ima Pipiig was too tired to move, even if her mind were to will her to do so.

She woke the boy, beautiful and round-faced in his sleep, and told him where she was going.

> "I'm going to pick sweetgrass . . . So you don't wake up and wonder and worry where I went."

> "Uh huh."

> "Where am I going?"

> "Hmmm . . ."

> "Hey, tell me where I'm going, so I know you know and you won't cry while I'm gone."

> "With Sammy Jim Boy."

> "I'm going to pick sweetgrass. Not with Sammy. Just me. But I'm glad you know where I'm going."

> "Do you wanna hear about the dream I had last night?"

> "Sure."

And then he was off on a long one, a little-boy story, a little-boy dream, rambling and without climax or purpose. But he eventually settled back under the covers, and Ima Pipiig was off as well. She rounded up towels, one for the sweetgrass, and the other to wrap around her purse in the car alongside the road. The road closest to this particular sweetgrass patch was used almost exclusively by white people, not like the other patches, the patches so deep in Indian country that she did not have to worry about her wallet. Ima Pipiig put toilet paper in her pocket. She double-checked to make sure that a bottle of water was between the front seats. Cat out. Dog out. Cat in. Should she take the outgoing mail to the mailbox? Naw . . . Ima Pipiig was off, finally. Choke out. The beloved old truck sprang to life. The gravel on the road was loose and fresh, so fresh that she felt like she was driving on velvet. Ima Pipiig crawled along to protect the paint job on the ancient vehicle. In northern Michigan, gravel nicks meant rust.

The clouds kept the light low. Ima Pipiig liked driving under these conditions. Seven a.m. was midmorning to her, and she appreciated the lack of traffic so that she could drive slowly and "rest." The roads were empty. It was too early for the bedroom-community commuters and way too early for the summer vacationers. Ima Pipiig loved the peace of early morning driving. Eventually, after climbing the big hill out of a small harbor town, Ima Pipiig noticed a familiar-looking van behind her. Sammy must have been returning from driving John to "work," dropping him off at the harbor next to his fishing tug. She must have been later than usual, probably from chatting with Mr. Erickson, the distributor who owned the fish market. Ima Pipiig was glad that some members of the fishing family that had dominated the industry during the era when Indians had not been allowed to claim their treaty rights were still able to cooperate with the local Indian fishermen. It was a matter of necessity, but there was no reason why it couldn't be pleasant for them all. And Ima Pipiig knew that if anyone could pull it off, it would be Sammy. She was physically beautiful and open-hearted, and she chattered constantly.

When she turned and slowed to pull off onto the road shoulder, Ima Pipiig was glad that the van turned and slowed with her. She was glad for the company and knew that she would pick twice as much sweetgrass if Sammy was there with her. Sammy hadn't intended to pick that morning, but there was Ima Pipiig, and Sammy knew she could get twice as much sweetgrass picked if Ima Pipiig was there with her to keep her company. Sammy picked in fishing swampers—big, rubber chest-high pants with boots, and Ima Pipiig picked in dirty sneakers and blue jeans, soaked to the knees in the heavy morning dew. Sammy picked sitting down, and Ima Pipiig picked standing up. Sammy snipped, and Ima Pipiig pulled each long blade individually. The shallow-rooted grass could not survive without other grasses, so the women each searched, separated, and plucked the valuable Indian resource one blade at a time, finding the treasured single pieces of sweetgrass, perhaps one among a thousand blades of tall grasses. The women talked and picked for hours like that, out of sight, but within earshot of one another, isolated from the rest of the world, hidden by farm fields, brush and trees, piped at by kingfishers, and sniffed at great distance by cautious foxes and bears. And there, there in that lush green, the two women melted in with the universe, and all was well with their lives and their families for those two hours.

When the women decided that they had picked enough to justify the stop and had begun to worry about their children and their other tasks for the day, they walked back to their cars; and just out of sheer loneliness from being Indians surrounded by non-Indians, they sat on their bumpers between the two vehicles and passed another hour, while the stiffness from picking sweetgrass drifted away from their bodies. Sammy had chickens to fry. She needed to wake and feed her children, finish the dishes, and feed and water the rabbits. Ima Pipiig had to buy bread and make sloppy joes. (This was her day off from venison or fish.) She wanted to pick wild berries while it was cool. She wanted to can some sweet cherries now that the harvest was over, and the orchards were gleanable. She was behind on her orders for the gift shops. Both women would spend hours cleaning, processing, and curing the sweetgrass. There were not enough hours in the day for Indian women.

As they congratulated themselves on their vast accomplishments in such a harsh human environment, they both traveled mentally to some of their toughest experiences in childhood, not the ones that their parents had given them by choice, but the ones America had given them by choice. And the words flowed out of Sammy's mouth uncontrollably, until Ima Pipiig cried.

"I don't want to talk about this anymore," she said, leaning against the dusty bumper for support. She was on her knees now, helpless, as children are, remembering herself as small and helpless. Even if she was looking right at Sammy, Ima Pipiig still saw her as a child. It was as though Ima Pipiig was looking in a mirror. She was numbed by the similarity between all of their stories. She still felt disbelief that such concerted efforts had been made to exterminate and acculturate Indian people, that the phenomenon had lasted into her own lifetime. Even though she fought battles to keep her own children from being treated the same way, as an unwanted commodity in a white world, even though she fought them without hesitance and with limitless energy, her teeth got numb when she tried to picture her own self as a child worthy of the same defense. This was what being an Indian in northern Michigan had done to Ima Pipiig. The unspoken thoughts raced through their heads, as the two women were frozen in that hour-long pause between chores in the misting rain that slowly floated across the Sleeping Bear Peninsula . . . they would protect their babies, just as their mothers had protected them, in the most adverse of circumstances, until they were either dead or battered and broken.

They spoke of boarding schools and foster homes, of being taken away from their families by social workers. They spoke of being separated from siblings. Sammy talked about going to a grocery store and seeing her little sister. The white woman whisked the child in the shopping cart away from bright and friendly Sammy. The social workers and the nuns had given her away, and the white woman was trying to adopt Sammy's sister. She did not want the girl to encounter, and therefore remember and long for, a loving older sister. Sammy's mother lay broken and recuperating in a hospital. It would be a year before she would get her children back, before they would return to the then-remote Indian community they had been wrenched from, by a social service system that had been trained to see them as somewhat less than human and most certainly lesser than whites.

Sammy was running behind on her chores this week. She'd been caring for her ailing mother. Ima Pipiig and Sammy relived the older woman's pain for her, her loss of her children and her minute-by-minute fear for their welfare each and every moment that they were out of her range of sight and hearing, away from her touch.

"I don't want to talk about this anymore," Ima Pipiig insisted, finding a kind of comfort in the dust on the cool silver bumper of the old truck, a comfort in the dust against her tear-swelled cheek, dust that came from her rural home and the road shoulder within walking distance of the sacred sweetgrass, far from the foster homes and detention centers where unwanted older Indian children had been thrust during the twentieth century. Detention centers were indistinguishable from Indian boarding schools. They were throw-away places for the poor, uneducated, and unwanted of America.

The two women talked of being hungry. Ima Pipiig had known such hunger after the loss of her parents. It was a common subject among Indian women of her generation. She talked about how the family had known a white man who was mentally ill and collected a disability that allowed him to sit all day in coffee shops, smoking and drinking cheap coffee. He used to collect sugar packets and sugar cubes. He stored them up in a white paper bag. When Ima Pipiig had the opportunity to go to town, he used to offer them to her, if she would sit and visit with him, help him pass a few minutes of his lonely days of anguish with himself. He would lose his bearings in time and space, and suddenly he would utter garbled noises from the back of his throat, holding his lit cigarette close to her slim brown arm. Trained from early childhood to be afraid to move away from or resist a white person, Ima Pipiig would sit, motionless, hoping and praying that the man would not burn her arm this time. And after he pulled the cigarette away at the last moment before touching her, he would apologize and hand her the bag of sugars. Ima Pipiig would grab it and run back to the dime store, to wait for her ride home. Sometimes those sugar cubes were all that Ima Pipiig and her brothers and sisters would eat for days on end. She could still remember their roughness and the loud crunching sound from chewing them as fast as she could, wolfing them, trying to overcome her hunger, wishing for something more substantial. But her long, teenaged body was grateful for the calories.

And now, Sammy Jim Boy and Ima Pipiig stood up, stretching their legs to recover from their hunching and cowering in the safe space between the two old vehicles, lost in the pain of their memories and their fear for their children's futures. They talked of canning fish, canning cherries, filling freezers with wild and domesticated vegetables and fruits, and fighting off that fear of hunger that never goes away in a lifetime. These two women talked with amazement of their own parents' strength and praised themselves once again for becoming powerhouse protectors of their own offspring to the extent that circumstances and the dominant culture would allow them. And these two involuntary members of the *Ogitchiidaakwe,* the ancient Chippewa women's warrior society, hugged hard, separated, and drove off in opposite directions. In generations to come the two women will be known as *Ogitchiidaakweyag.* In Ojibwe it simply means women who do big things.

· 27 ·

Laughing Man

*H*e was a happy baby, with a beautiful smile. It only made sense that everyone would eventually settle upon the name, Laughing Boy. It suited his demeanor.

The corners of his mouth naturally curled up into a smile, forcing his cheeks up and out, as though he were eternally contented. The slight protrusion to his cheeks exposed them to just a little more sunlight than the average person's cheeks, and they were eternally rosy. The cheeks forced his eyes to crinkle, giving the impression that he was eternally laughing at the positive side of life. And in the colloquialisms of the Ojibwe language, to make someone laugh meant to make them wrinkle, so the name suited him even more.

The natural tendencies of the muscles in his face caused people to smile at him more than at most babies, too coo at him more than most babies, and to sing, coddle, and spoil him more than most babies. And he responded by developing a contented demeanor that was unusual in its eternal presence.

Sometimes, by virtue of his contented demeanor, people leaned toward taking advantage of him, but his grace and generosity always seemed to wear off on them, to change them, to make them better and more loving. It was as though his smile and its repercussions grew in ever-expanding circles, like a pebble dropped into the status quo of a calm lake. He gave as graciously as he received, and the phenomenon seemed to dominate his interactions throughout his life.

He worked hard, even as a child. And because of this, he was allowed to play just as hard. And this created a behavioral cycle that was to be envied by all of the Anishinabe people in all of the villages along all of the waterways, lakes and rivers and stopping places of the whole of the Great Lakes and the dense woods and muskegs that surrounded them. By the time he reached adolescence, people began calling him Laughing Man, in the hope that he would

195

transition as smoothly from childhood to manhood as he seemed to transition through all the daily challenges of life. And, indeed, he did. He was wild and boldly experimental, but always forgiven for any errors and mishaps, because of that darned smile.

He was not tall, but he was strong and beautiful, beautiful even in old age, when his teeth wore away, skewed and yellowed—because of that smile, that omnipresent smile that made him loved and therefore want to love back. He always seemed to surround himself with contentment and goodwill, and his family always flocked to him for the sheer comfort and delight of being near him. And they worked contentedly, all of them, usually with smiles on their faces; and they played and fought hard, all of them, usually with smiles on their faces—always better off for having known and loved him.

He was born on the mainland, on the north shore of Lake Superior, in the log cabin of an aunt, only feet from the water. And his childhood was divided up between the mainland cabins of the Indian harbor of family and friends that enveloped him and the offshore island cabins of the family and friends that enveloped him. It was a place full of fish and game and beauty and life. The history of the Anishinabe people was abundant in this place, in the paintings on the rocks, in the ancient copper mines, in the places where various tool rocks and foodstuffs had been found and stored, in the stories and songs that accompanied every rock, cliff, hill, valley, crevice, lake, pool, breeze, large wave, and phenomenon of the night . . .

The island upon which he seasonally spent much of his life, with parents and siblings, was close to shore, among this cluster of islands, some of which were habitable, some of which were not. Its thirty acres were comprised mostly of rocks and cliffs, with just enough flat and sand beach for one Anishinabe family to retreat among the moose and caribou. They were visited by beaver, otters, and bear. The suckers, whitefish, trout, and lush practically threw themselves from the waters into the arms of Laughing Boy and his family. Life was hard. It required following the resources. But the house and outbuildings of his beloved family home always waited for him.

Summers he spent hours scouring the pebbliest part of the beach. There the agates washed up in abundance. Although he would eventually learn about the geology and the physical forces that created the minerals and stones that were the crown jewels of the Anishnabe people, as a child he was told that the sturgeon flipped them upon the shores for him when he slept or during storms when he fled the beach. And Manaboozhou himself, son of the West Wind, would visit the boy when the sun warmed his back on the beach, while he hunched over, searching, searching.

The boy swore that Manaboozhou had told him stories. He had told Laughing Boy how lucky he was to be here, with these agates, these prizes that Indians from far away sought to inlay their pipes, to entertain their children, to understand the lengthy process of geology in which they played but the tiniest part and were therefore to respect . . . And one day the two of them devised a plan . . . It wasn't right that the beautiful, colorful, sun-catching agates were located only on this beach, in this place, beyond the reach of all of the Anishnabe children in all of the villages along all of the waterways, lakes and rivers and stopping places of the whole of the Great Lakes and the dense woods and muskegs that surrounded them. And so they spent hours hunched over on that beach, gathering agates, large and small, of every color and shape, filling baskets and birch-bark bowls. Then youthful Manaboozhou and his protégé, Laughing Boy, threw the stones into the air, all at once. Before even a single agate returned to pelt them or make a hollow scrabbling sound against the other pebbles of the beach, each and every one sprouted wings and silently flew off to the east, to the south, to the west, and to the north, to all of the Anishinabe children in all of the villages along all of the waterways, lakes and rivers and stopping places of the whole of the Great Lakes and the dense woods and muskegs that surrounded them. And, for years, even after Laughing Boy had transitioned to Laughing Man and was known by his children and grandchildren and nieces and nephews and great-nieces and great-nephews as Laughing Old Man, whenever he saw a butterfly, he would hold out his finger, still and smiling, proud and content when they would land upon it, and he would say, "See? They know me. I made them."

The rest of the agates were set aside over the years by Laughing Boy in baskets and bowls of birch bark. And he entertained himself during inclement weather or on warm, sunny wind-free winter days, when the pebbles were deep under snow and ice, by dipping each perfect stone in water or licking it to bring out its shine. And he marveled at the geologic miracles he learned about, and he reveled at the voyeuristic opportunity of looking through stone, into the history of the land that nurtured him and his family and kept that constant smile sincere upon his lips.

And when the government sent the Indians away, called their homes illegal occupations, Laughing Boy cried. When the Indians smelled the smoke from the burning of their homes, so they would never come back to the islands and mountains and streams and underwater shelves and other life-giving phenomena that they knew with an accumulated knowledge of generations that could easily vanish within a lifetime, they cried. And it is said that when that happened, the rivers swelled with the tears of the Anishinabe men and women and children, and that they overflowed their banks, toppling the largest of the pines and maples that the lumbermen claimed for themselves, eroding great crevices into the very bedrock that would confound the wealth-seekers and require great bridges and engineering. So great was the ecological damage wrought by the removal of the Anishinabeg from this biosystem.

Decades later, Laughing Man would build great fires on this beach, with Ima Pipiig, the only one of his sons and daughters and nieces and nephews and grandchildren and great-nieces and great-nephews who would make the time to bring the old man here; and they would sit, until long into the night, while she held her own children against the cool of the darkness that wrapped its arms around them lovingly; and Laughing Man would tell her all of these things. And he would tell of his years of youth and adulthood as a logger, the only way he could remain on this land that had once been his family's. And he told of the joy of simply being there, being there, among the songs and the stories and the memories . . .

Laughing Man, the logger, would talk to the men who owned his mother's island, one by one, as they enjoyed it and passed it on to another buyer. The first had been an executive from General Motors who had bought it from the Crown for $100—a fortune back then, and a hundred dollars more than his widower mother had gotten for it. And as he saw the last in a long line of white men grow tired with the place, seeing it as a rundown fish camp that was harder and harder to get to, and the fishing wasn't so good anymore anyhow . . . Laughing Man would visit that white man and smile that perpetual smile. He would explain that he had grown up here, that he lived and loved here, that he wanted to die here; and if you ever want to sell it, gee, let me know first . . .

And he smiled a smile that was bigger than his perpetual smile, cheeks reddened from the sun reflected off the water, contrasting like blood on snow against his white shock of hair, revealing the teeth, now worn, skewed and yellowed. But he was beautiful, always beautiful, because of that darned smile, and Ima Pipiig giggled the giggle of the giddy and the contented with the old man. He had been allowed to buy back the island. And Ima Pipiig, although she had already bought and preserved the fish camp of another old Anishinabe uncle, had bought from him and preserved this island home that the old man could no longer transport himself to alone. And as hard as it was for her to justify the taxes and the upkeep and the time away, she and Lester kept coming back to the bush. They kept teaching their children the geologies and the histories and the stories and the knowledge of these places. Sometimes Lester would leave Ima Pipiig alone with the children and the old man for weeks on end. These places would wrap themselves around the family like songs in the night. It was as if there were not enough of them to go around, to learn and absorb it all. It was as if books were burning. These were places that were hurt by the loss of the Anishinabeg, the human parts of them that they had coaxed into symbiosis over thousands of years. Sometimes the very rocks cried out for this family to come back. "I was the first person to own it who wasn't a millionaire," the old man had exclaimed, grateful in the knowledge that written title had somehow given back what could never really have been taken away from him.

Ima Pipiig was cutting back the sprouting balsam and mountain ash that constantly tried to take away any open space that the family cleared next to the old cabin. They needed the openness, the sunshine, the breezes that kept away flies, the berries—the strawberries, the raspberries, the thimbleberries, the currants, the rose hips—that called out to them every summer day and begged to sweeten their dispositions. And when she tugged upon a particularly endless root of thimbleberry next to the sagging ruins of an old smokehouse, she saw them there, as hummocks of humus and pebbles . . . There were the baskets and baskets of agates that had been saved and loved and left behind by Laughing Boy, and she called out to Laughing Man. And he was giddy again. He was Laughing Boy again.

The stones were scooped up from their early graves, put into aluminum bread dough bowls, and hauled down to the beach for scouring with sand. They were rinsed in Superior's potable beauty, swished about in a plastic spaghetti strainer that was usually used for rinsing fillets of pike and lake trout; and they sat together, these Indians, on the beach, swishing the crown jewels of the Anishinabeg in water, or licking them, to enhance their shine, and marveling at the beauty, the history, the geology, the wonder of being able to see inside and through a piece of the earth that gave them life . . .

Since he had returned to his childhood home, Laughing Man had accumulated so many buckets of agates that Lester kept a large rock tumbler rumbling year round on his workbench in the barn back home. The family spent hours and hours looking at rocks. Some were so distinctive that their finders could remember when and where they found them, the weather, the circumstances, who was with them. But no one enjoyed the agates as much as the old man.

Some days when the old man was on the beach finding agates to fill bowls and buckets and baskets, the boy was harvesting plump little boy fistfuls of the precious stones from their containers and heaving them straight back into the lake. And whenever Smiling Man caught the child throwing away his treasures, he would chuckle and say, "Sharing the butterflies, eh?"

When Ima Pipiig would leave to fish for dinner at Indian Harbor with Lester and the kids, the old man would stay behind, bundled against the cold of autumn or spring, in knee high rubber boots, contentedly scouring the pebbled stretches of the shoreline for gifts from the great sturgeon thrown up while he had dared to sleep. He would smile that eternal smile, and he would have long conversations with his old friend, Manaboozhou, about the rocks, about the weather, about the butterflies; and they would share hundreds of anecdotes between them. All the while, Laughing Man's coat pockets would droop heavy with agates and smooth bits of Lake Superior's copper and crystals and stones that told stories from his childhood and his parents' childhoods and childhoods that it had taken his family thousands of years to accumulate the stories from. He would periodically return to the picnic table next to the one-room cabin to transfer his treasures into the plastic ice-cream buckets that Ima Pipiig brought for him to fill and for Lester to haul back to the mainland and the electrical miracle of the rock tumbler in the barn back home.

It was a good life, and it suited his disposition well, the old man thought, as he lay down on a sunny stretch of pebbles to duck below the rising afternoon breeze and to soak up the warmth of the stones. He wiggled his toes in the rubber boots and listened to the hollow musical sound of the pebbles close to his ears and went to sleep, still fingering a large, smooth agate with concentric rings of clear glass and white that created especially sinuous shades of dancing gray. Ima Pipiig's big brown dog cuddled up with him.

Laughing Man was still warm from the sunshine and still smiling when the family motored home with dinner. Ima Pipiig walked over to wake the old man. She took the big agate from his hand and put it in her coat pocket, then walked over to Lester and whispered something into his ear. While Birdie and her little brother cleaned the trout, Ima Pipiig and Lester rolled the old man onto a tarp. They dragged him across the pebbles and up into the boathouse.

Not wanting to leave him in plain sight for the children to come across between an Old Town canoe and the gas refrigerator, they dragged him into a small room in the back of the building that had been sectioned off by a previous owner. It contained an ancient cast-iron bathtub with griffin feet that was once gravity-fed with hot water through copper pipes from a woodboiler uphill from the building. Today the bathtub held nothing but cobwebs and an antique Sea Gull outboard motor, imported from England, that still fired up even after sixty years or so years of storage. Somehow putting the old man in the bathtub seemed somewhat grotesque. So Ima Pipiig and Lester sat him up behind a couple of hundred-pound propane tanks, figuring that would give them time to break the news to the kids—maybe tomorrow, when it was brighter and sunnier and they'd had a good supper and a good night's sleep next to the comforting crackle of the woodstove.

About halfway through dinner, Birdie asked, "Where's Laughing Man?"

"In the boathouse."

"What's he doing?"

"Smiling."

• 28 •

I Wanna Be a Delicacy

They were sick of morel mushrooms, you know, those wild mushrooms that are considered a delicacy. The whole family was sick of them. Ima Pipiig had cooked them in every way imaginable . . . sautéed in margarine, with just the right sprinkling of garlic salt . . . cut in half the long way, then sautéed on both sides until crispy . . . an absolute delight to the summer tourists . . . But not a delicacy—an overabundant renewable resource for a resourceful woman who was pretty good at finding free food in the same places year after year.

She had pureed the mushrooms with tomatoes from the garden to make spaghetti sauce with venison that she chopped by hand, because she could not afford hamburger this particular winter. She had pureed them with store-bought cream of mushroom soup and made a casserole with home-canned French-cut green beans from the garden. She had used them pureed or snipped, from a pint canning jar, as the liquid in venison round steak—whacked from blood-shot shoulders and deer butts—cooked slowly on the woodstove all day in a cast-iron pan. She had thawed them and stuffed them with blue cheese and with onions from the garden, dipping them in batter, just like she did with daylily buds, and had fried them up on the days that she had a pot of oil going for fish, because they caught an awful lot of fish. And she had chopped them up small and disguised them as store-bought mushrooms on pizza, in lasagna, in pasta dishes of every sort imaginable . . .

The boy loved to help her find them; and the restaurants did not pay much for them these days, because everybody else had them; and she didn't get enough in a day or two to justify the gas to take them down to the big cities; and what the hell was she going to do with all these damned morel mushrooms that incrementally built up into sixty pounds or so—you know, those wild mushrooms that are considered a delicacy? She found them and found them and found them, because she had no job-to-match-her-credentials this year again, had nothing in her life that earned minimum wage or better, in spite of her college degrees that had kept white American "scholars" employed and fat-and-happy-and-steered-toward-early-retirement—retirement that their colored "students" that they treated like soil-on-the-sidewalk would never know . . . She'd found those damned mushrooms and found them and found them because that is what the poor and the unwanted, the Indians do. And those morel mushrooms still in the freezer, along with the pending morel mushrooms that were going to spring up and force themselves upon her in another month, because she could not help but gather a resource so bountiful and beautiful, all ganged up on Ima Pipiig's mentality and put her in a bad mood. She did not want spring. She wanted a couple more months of winter to eat up all of those morel mushrooms. Then she could really, really enjoy finding and preserving those morel mushrooms, justifiably spending lazy hours with her children . . .

And they weren't even her favorite wild mushrooms, not even the best, not like the chewy stumpers that she found in the fall, by looking up in the trees so that she knew where to look down, not like the *wabadodashzhashkwedawan* that were strong-smelling and soft and begged to be sliced, not like the delicate chanterelles that were Birdie's specialty and favorite. But, gawd, they were there and considered a delicacy by urban- and suburbanites who considered going to restaurants that served morel mushroom sauces a sign of socioeconomic stature. And silly Ima Pipiig had nothing but that farm with all of those wild things and garden things on it, which kept her happy most of the time; but this year she was sick of the morel mushrooms.

They were there as they had been during every great depression that America had known because they followed logging and clearcutting and abandonment of family farms and orchards. And cutting down trees that had taken lifetimes to produce in order to supplement one short lifetime and one short ideology was a great depression survival mechanism. Beg from Peter to pay Paul. Borrow from Peter to pay Paul. Steal from Peter to pay Paul. Cut the trees. Harvest the mushrooms that grew like molds and germs on the corpse. Morel mushrooms-as-delicacy were a phenomenon of overharvesting of forests, at least today, in Ima Pipiig's overworked mind. This really, really bothered her, because people were not changing the landscape wisely, not thinking in the long run about the safety of the resource and the implications of so many wild mushrooms on the environmental futures of generations to come.

Even the local school board members and superintendent had taken to trying to facilitate the creation of new tiny-lot subdivisions within their jurisdictional boundaries, to generate new children and subsequent state income to keep their honoraria and paychecks and power structure intact. It involved cutting only a few trees, surrounding only a few adjacent farms with farm-choking urban development . . . Ima Pipiig saw it as a violation of responsibility to the very ecology of the place. The economy of greed was eating up the very landscape, transforming its life forms and culture into saprophytic consumers—those who live off the dead and dying. These were people she had perceived as greedy and unconscionable even when the American economy was rolling high. . . . What bad times was Sleeping Bear County facing now, now that the offenders' sources of inequality were gradually drying up, and the gap between the income levels of the affluent and the lesser was not growing as fast as it had recently grown? The schools had changed the time of year when taxes were collected, so that they could double-dip one year, the same year that the farmers in the school district had suffered a 100 percent crop loss. They had logged off the hundreds of acres of woods that belonged to the school district. And now it was time to link up with the developers and skim more income off the thin veneer of glacial till that differentiated the high and dry parts of Sleeping Bear County from the surrounding lakes.

Ima Pipiig knew, that if the more affluent around her were paining and stretching their resources, that so much less would be trickling down to the voiceless wildlife and soils of Sleeping Bear County, and even less would be trickling down to the underpeople of Sleeping Bear County and America in general because they were considered even less valuable than the wildlife. That whole issue of lack of cultural and socioeconomic flexibility, lack of breathing room for financial error and ineptitude crept into Ima Pipiig's psyche. And all this because she had to eat up some very delicious wild mushrooms so that she could totally enjoy seeking, finding, joyously squealing over and putting away for lean times those darned morel mushrooms that would be peeking out from under the leaves, hiding and blending in with the shadows and shades of gray and brown that made up the moist and fertile mat of the forest floor . . . all the while spreading their spores by her very activity.

Finding those mushrooms was a skill that had lost its value by the early twenty-first century. It had become relegated to the entertainment category; and Ima Pipiig felt so financially unsuccessful in the face of her neighbors' growing need to maintain a status quo of inequality at all costs that she sometimes begrudged herself entertainment. It took away from work. This was part of the psychological damage that accompanied the real physical damage of racism. It swam in and out of the Indians' consciousnesses, leaving weeping sores and flesh-rending gashes in place of the self-confidence and competence that had been perfected by the Anishinabe culture over thousands of generations. To Ima Pipiig, it was a form of cultural thievery, to leave people so vulnerable that they thought so frequently of shelter, health care, and food, so vulnerable that they even feared the very notion of spending pleasant hours unproductively.

Food had become cheaper than ever before in history—at least in America, where vertical integration into food processing had kept the largest farmers alive and buying up the smallest farmers. Food had become cheap by virtue of the fossil fuel bonanza that allowed mankind to produce food at a calorie-loss—not just a temporary calorie-loss, but a long-term calorie-loss that gambled against long-term survival, that gambled against the hope that one's offspring might be more inventive than one's self. And Ima Pipiig felt as powerless in this respect as she felt in her inability to earn credentials sufficient to overcome her socioeconomic liability of Indianness.

Food banks still existed in abundance, but they were useless to people close to the bottom of the socioeconomic scale, people like Ima Pipiig. And suddenly being willing to work more hours for less pay became moot. There was no bottom to the middle class of America, no reason to work sixty—no, seventy—no, eighty hours a week—just to make ends meet. Because there was no making ends meet. And today Ima Pipiig conjured up anonymous abusers who never knew when to quit, blending in her mind with the real abusers she was acquainted with, who also never knew when to quit, never knew when to stop squeezing those on the bottom, relegated to the category of consumer, never knew when to stop watching their victims writhe and die. Just as viruses and virulent bacteria that killed their hosts never knew when to quit. . . It was biology. And today Ima Pipiig felt like she was on the bottom of that biological chain of socioeconomic events, at least in America. She emotionally compared her place in the economy to a florescence of fungi upon the death of a forest. It was not a pleasant way to approach the upcoming meal, which really would be made up of delicacies. It's just that Ima Pipiig wanted to be a delicacy, too. She wanted to be valued and employable and inoffensive. She wanted to strike the palette of America as something more than lesser.

Deep in her heart, Ima Pipiig knew that she was a delicacy; and she knew that the Anishinabe people were a cultural delicacy. It's just that she sometimes found herself tired of trying to teach this to the rest of the world. She was painfully aware of the people who refused to be taught, for one reason or another . . . sometimes-understandable reasons, sort of. Economic reasons. Hog-the-resource-of-good-jobs-for-me-and-mine reasons. Not honorable reasons. Just somewhat-understandable reasons.

Those who were better off than Ima Pipiig would complain to her that they only earned this amount, or that amount, completely ignorant to the fact that they were making many, many times what they were willing to let lesser people earn, what they were willing to let Ima Pipiig earn. It was knowledge they intentionally hid from themselves. Those who were better off than Ima Pipiig would tell her that she was lucky to be better off than those who were dying much more quickly than the emotional death of being a minority in America; and they would tell her that if she would just work for little or nothing to raise awareness and the standards of living of those above her, they would, because of their good nature, let enough trickle down to her that she should be satisfied. And Ima Pipiig would not be satisfied with a wage or nonwage that was good enough for her, but not equal pay for equal work and equal skills . . . And sometimes she would look those people in the eye and ask them why they expected that of her. And they would hem and haw and say that they didn't really expect it of her, but by the time they got done distributing all of the culture's socioeconomic resources to themselves, they didn't have anything left to share . . . only they left out the parts about taking *everything* for themselves, so what they ended up mumbling was usually pretty empty.

Her family was growing sick of the morel mushrooms that had once been a delicacy, but that were no more a delicacy because they thrived on the death of trees, and the death of trees was a major phenomenon during the late twentieth and early twenty-first century, when men were starving, and they would cut and harvest everything available to survive. It was the legacy of a third-world America. And Ima Pipiig could no more discuss it with her neighbors than she could discuss the fact that they had educated themselves in the most secondhand manner, had promulgated ignorance in their educational institutions, had dumbed themselves down to the point of destruction of so many delicate and wonderful things around them—except they had not obviously endangered themselves quite yet, and they had a few years of leeway, even though minorities and endangered species and big trees had no leeway. There were always benefits to usurping the suffering and death of the most vulnerable—cheap lumber from the big trees, cheap delicacies from the wild mushrooms that thrived upon the death of the big trees, and cheap real estate and the means to live upon it from the Indians who were made to feel worthless and who were deemed unemployable by the children of the summer vacationers of the 1950s and 1960s who came north to Ima Pipiig's home to winterize their parents' cottages and take everything left that the Indians who had lost most of their land had to offer.

Even the stories, the traditions, and the histories—cultural delicacies of the most extraordinary and palatable sort, mixed in with the mundane, the bland, the sour, and the zesty in a renewable, biodegradable format that had originally accommodated the first people of this place—these were harvested, altered, and their values optimized and vertically integrated into the now dominant culture.

The morel mushrooms had become so cheap, as a result of the cutting, cutting, cutting of the trees for lumber to hold people through the great depression of the late twentieth and early twenty-first centuries, the one that people dare not refer to as a Great Depression, because, God forbid, we already had one. They grew like weeds—the mushrooms, they grew like weeds. OK, maybe depressions, they grew like weeds, too. But nobody was supposed to talk about it; because if they did, they were suffering, and nobody was supposed to admit that they were suffering, lest they be blamed for their own suffering; because then they probably deserved the depressions that came their way. And three-fourths of the public educators, the ones who came from the bottom three-fourths of their freshman class in college, would sit stiffly in their polyester clothing that was designed to separate them from the working people of the school district, and they would blame the poor for being poor. They would say, "We learned in our educational psychology textbooks that minorities perform poorly; so you are responsible for your poverty by making bad choices and performing poorly; and we will not broach the subject of imposition of poverty by those of us who work fewer hours than you . . . because we believe in our own superiority that was dictated to us in the educational psychology textbooks, the authors of which inadvertently left out the part about the poor performing poorly *because of* the poverty we impose for our own convenience and pleasure . . ."

And the Indians and the poor people who picked those damned mushrooms beyond what pleasure and common sense should justify could not garner a living wage sufficient to pay for their time for gathering and their fuel for delivering. So Ima Pipiig canned the morel mushrooms. She froze the morel mushrooms. And she was years ahead of herself in terms of what her family could eat. But she kept canning them and freezing them, figuring that if things got worse, she would eventually be thrown off the land that she lived upon as had happened to so many Indians in the past. And she considered herself lucky, and she ate the morel mushrooms because they were there and they were free, and for some strange reason, she really enjoyed finding them and picking them and preserving them. Because, in a time and place where resources were few for an Indian woman who had frittered away her time and labor on academic credentials, everything was to be garnered, preserved, put away—for lean times that could change their form at whim—and someday those damned mushrooms would be a treat, a delicacy—just as Ima Pipiig was sure that someday she, too, would become a delicacy.

And what would people think of her, this woman whose shelves were full of morel mushrooms, once a delicacy; and her shelves were full of powdered milk and oatmeal and tuna fish and all of the things that the currently most powerful corporate food producers had in excess and that entered the chain of food commodities that Ima Pipiig did not quite qualify for, but the people who did qualify, whose resources were greater but less obvious than Ima Pipiig's, would trade to her for morel mushrooms and green beans from her garden, still leaving her with more morel mushrooms than she and her family could eat . . . And Ima Pipiig wondered how the hell corporate fishermen could possibly have a large crop of tuna fish and need a government food commodities purchase to bail them out, especially since Indian fishermen were starving and hoping that the casinos did OK in spite of the economy, so that they could eat something besides morel mushrooms when they were not allowed to fish. And then there were the Indians who did not have the paper trail that allowed them to fish or to benefit from the trickle-down of gambling revenues, or who had a flaw in the paper trail, or had pissed off somebody in power and would never get a paper trail . . . and they had no casino good times to hope for. Those people were eventually cut off from the tribal system of sharing with relatives and friends by the mandates of the government entities that wanted to save dollars spent on the minority poor; but no one stopped discriminating against those paperless Indians in employment and in the schools; and no security guards, trained so well in the all-white-staffed-schools, stopped following them around department stores; and no white museum curators and park superintendents, self-unassured and wanting to benefit themselves at all costs, would stop treating them like vermin who did not represent the cute little "cave men" that modern American culture had so efficiently replaced.

And Ima Pipiig got so angry that she found herself running along the soggy, snow-melting path to the barn—that same soggy, snow-melting path that had often been the only location for her big brown dog to relieve itself—and Ima Pipiig stepped squish—right into a waterlogged brownish mess that spattered and fanned out ahead of her. "Aw, shit!" she exclaimed, "I've stepped in pooo!" And she ran off the path into deeper snow-mush to clean her fouled sneaker. The wet snow came into her shoes and fell under the arch of her foot. She ran and ran and ran and grabbed at the fresh air over her head until she had done three laps around the workshop barn that held her food-hoarding freezers. Then she stopped, her lean middle-aged body heaving, and Ima Pipiig found herself sweating in places she had forgotten she could sweat.

Today's temperature was over fifty degrees, and no breeze. April fools. April Fool's Day. No joke. The boy was home from school sick, and this week it seemed like he was always sick, and she did not want to take him to the doctor and say, "Why is he always sick? He's got plenty of food. He's got lots of love." Because, really, he just had a cold.

And Ima Pipiig realized that this, too, would pass. The boy would get better and go out to play in another day or so, and maybe her nerves would be less frayed. She sloshed through the wet snow to pull a package of morel mushrooms out of the freezer, because there in the barn and back at the house in the shelves full of canning jars, Ima Pipiig stored her excess energy, her wont to survive, her eagerness to overachieve; and she worried that someday, someday she'd be forced off the land and be forced to live in a place where morel mushrooms would someday once again become a delicacy, for her family at least.

When her eyes adjusted to the darkness of the barn, when she put on the pair of mittens she left on top of one of the freezers for pawing through the boxes and shopping, she was actually surprised at how much of a dent her family had made in that big box of morel mushrooms. She even contemplated taking the time to make new labels and tape them onto the boxes, instead of trying to remember that the asparagus was in the box that said "corn '98," and that the corn was in a box that said "fruit '04," and that she should eat the fish that was in the box that said "veggies '02" before she ate the fish that was in the box that said "fish '04."

Spring was on the horizon. And Ima Pipiig was not sure what spring had to offer her, except another batch of wild morel mushrooms that she would harvest and not feel like using for a while, mushrooms she would harvest in excess and not be able to sell, to turn into value for her labor. And she thought of it as the artwork that she did for the pleasure of her white neighbors who had usurped the land and the right to be on it and the fish and the game and the fresh water—unable to earn her a living wage—and the taste of the morel mushrooms, you know, those wild mushrooms that are considered a delicacy. The whole family must be sick of them, she thought—as sick as she was about worrying about money and about being an Indian in a time and place where Indians were not considered delicacies.

Ima Pipiig knew that she should not think about dinner, not think about the mushrooms that would soon be taking over her life, after the melt of winter's snows, because they were free and they were food, even though free food had over-lived its usefulness in this place at this time . . .

And Ima Pipiig thought that maybe she could write, in this quick span of time before the snow completely melted and the mushrooms grew and the boy was asleep from his cold; because she had been identified now and then as a writer, and maybe she could write and make money, because these days she could not do much else and make money . . . But she was trying to avoid writing—because writing garnered her even less than mushrooms. It did not even provide food that the family did not like but that maybe they could trade for something palatable or at least healthy. Writing was like a great big hole.

And this week Ima Pipiig had to avoid reading. Because reading made Ima Pipiig want to write. Ima Pipiig had read an article in an Indian newspaper that had gotten her perturbed, and she figured she ought to write about it; but Ima Pipiig did not like writing for Indian newspapers because by the time Indian newspapers finished paying the white editors and finished paying the white printers and finished paying the white people who worked at the post office, the gas station, or even a pizzeria somewhere, they did not have money left to pay the Indians who wrote for Indian newspapers. And the Indians did not have much place else to get themselves published, because they were, after all, Indians, and who-in-god's-name wanted to read whatever a dissatisfied Indian had to write, after all? Except the other Indians, who really enjoyed reading about one another's plight and even seemed to find less pain in their own plights when reading about the plights of other Indians. It was almost as much fun as picking wild mushrooms. It was almost as much fun as a good blueberry crop. It was almost as much fun as a good smelt run.

The academic media was busy publishing stuff from the academics, who pretty much happened to be white, and the liberal media was busy publishing stuff from the white liberals. And the white liberals were so busy being white liberals that they did not have time to consider the Indian liberals, who were, after all, not half as educated as the white liberals, who had gone to white liberal colleges staffed by white liberals, geared toward teaching the white liberal children of white liberals . . . Because that's what being a white liberal was all about—helping those who are less able than one's self. And since none of the white liberal teachers ever bothered to explain that white liberalism was part of what was making people of color unable to fend for themselves, second- and third-generation white liberals just figured that people of color were just dumb and couldn't fend for themselves without white liberals *in situ* in the institutions of education and publishing . . . So Ima Pipiig knew that if she was going to get anything that she wanted to write and get said to actually get published and get said, she'd have to send it to an Indian newspaper or one of the other publications that had figured out that Indians were so desperate to have their opinions heard, that they'd write for free, in the hopes that somebody might think that they were good enough to be paid, just out of the generosity and kindness of their hearts . . .

Ima Pipiig put a quart freezer bag full of morel mushrooms sliced lengthways into the front pouch of her hooded sweatshirt. She stuffed frozen juice into the side pockets of her down vest, which now hung open. Satisfied that she had sufficiently shopped for the day, she put the mittens back on top of a freezer, she propped the barn door open to let in the fresh air of springtime, and she headed back toward the house with its endless array of chores and puttering.

While she picked her way along the path, where the snow was still icy enough to support her, avoiding the places where the sun had hit the ground and the mush was ready and willing to swallow her up, Ima Pipiig thought about all of the stuff she had seen on Free Speech TV and had read in the so-called liberal media lately about Ward Churchill. And finding a parallel

between picking her way through the slush and doggy doo of the path to garner a frozen package of free mushrooms that nobody wanted to eat anyhow
and the hubbub surrounding the question of Ward Churchill's Indian pedigree
(with a side order of academic indignation over his comments about contemporary politics and fear for the presence of minorities and wild-eyed thinkers
in the world of public education) Ima Pipiig was ready to put in the unpaid
effort of expressing herself.

This is what Indian ladies did during that early spring interim between
survival and comfort . : . they lost their cookies. They got really, really pissed
off. It was a cultural phenomenon they had perfected through the centuries in
response to the long, cold winters of the north. The kids, the elders, the repetitive diet, the looming prospect of a few weeks in constricted quarters made
even more tight by slush and soggy terrain . . . these were the catalysts that
made Ojibwe women into whopping good storytellers, creative cooks, and occasionally really mean and frightening forces to be dealt with. So during early
spring Ima Pipiig sat down and wrote.

And she hoped that somebody out there might listen and understand—
even though the universities were full of white people with equal or lesser credentials than people of color that they would not hire; even though too many
of the people of color who had been hired by the colleges and universities and
museums were the really, *really* light-skinned and light-mentalitied people of
color, especially the Indians—like the Churchills and the Highwaters and the
Quick-to-Exploits—and plenty of other folks who decided during the late
1960s and early 1970s that being Indian was a real bonanza.

America had briefly opened itself up to the concept of Indians and other
people of color as necessary in academia, creating an incredibly small window
of opportunity. And suddenly there were a lot of opportunists saying, "Hey!
Unlike everybody else alive, I can seriously trace my heritage back sixteen or
thirty-two generations, maybe even sixty-four, on just that one side, that Indian side, and, by golly, I found an Indian! That's right, uh huh, heard you were
lookin' fer some, and by golly, here I am. Not sure about the tribe. Always
wanted to be one." And since those white folks who saw that window of opportunity to succeed easier than they could succeed if they competed against
other white folks, began to be colored, well Indians in particular . . . and those
are an awfully disproportionate share of the ones who got themselves ac-
knowledged and hired by universities and other liberal institutions in the late
1960s and 1970s . . . because, they were the ones, after all, who knew *exactly*
what white America wanted from its minorities, especially the Indians; because,
after all, even Natalie Wood could pass for Indian in the Hollywood TV movies
upon which these wannabes had been suckled and nurtured and trained.

And Ima Pipiig watched a little drivel on Free Speech TV while she mended a hole in a bedsheet. (She had wanted to replace the thin bedsheet with a used one, but the urban poor of Twin Bay City had beat her to the best selections at the Salvation Army.) She had watched as an interviewer, a light-skinned Asian, the most socially acceptable minority in America, a gay woman (the second-most-socially-acceptable minority in America?) tried, tried very hard, to include Native Americans and Native American issues in her programming. And the interviewer turned to academic institutions expecting to find Native Americans, because, after all, that's where one could find environmentalists to talk about environmental issues and economists to talk about economic issues, and one could even find a few African American scholars there to talk about African American issues. But, for some strange reason, it was pretty darned hard to find a lot of Indians. So, when the opportunity presented itself, and he became controversial for his politics, that well-meaning soul interviewed, gawd, Ward Churchill, as a Native-American scholar. And Russell Means sat off to the side like a poodle and spoke only when spoken to . . . And everybody, everybody missed the point—that Ward Churchill should not be sitting in that wood-paneled office earning one hundred thousand dollars a year, when Russell Means and Dennis Banks knew volumes, volumes more about being an Indian and how to tie historical events into the present than ol' cowboy-boot-wearin' Ward-Churchill *would* ever, *could* ever know—because part of bein' an Indian in the late twentieth century, part of bein' an Indian in the early twenty-first century, was having credentials, college degrees and professional credentials earned under the most adverse of circumstances and still, still being followed around department stores by security guards; still, still being scared to set foot in a public educational institution, let alone apply for a job in one, lest one risk having one's precious and beautiful children taken away from one for being different, for being colored, for not keeping one's head down, for being an Injun and a Nigger; still, still watching the wannabes of the free-love-slash-hippie movement pretending to be spokespeople for Indian culture—in that aw-shucks-we-don't-deserve-it-don't-give-us-nothin' soft manner of people-who-did-not-grow-up-desperate-from-birth voice . . . And Russell Means and Dennis Banks (and a lot of Indians *hyphenize* that as one word: Russell-Means-and-Dennis-Banks) and Ima Pipiig, and Sammy Jim Boy and Joan Soaper and Winona LaDuke and a hundred or more Indians really belong in those university and college and liberal-institution jobs and have more, better credentials and higher IQ's and broader social sensibilities than the yuppies-who-had-the-freedom-to-choose-Indianness of the latter third of the twentieth century. . . . But the white people who hired the wannabes—because they found them so much more comfortable a fit than Indians—could never, never fathom an academia which succumbed to skill over birth; or to intelligence, creativity, and natural ability over inheritance . . .

Among Indian scholars and academics—yes, they existed outside of America's colleges and universities and museums and institutions of ignorance-with-a-degree-attached—to be plagiarized came to be known as to be Ja-makied . . . to appropriate another's culture came to be known as Quick-to-Rip-Off, to get a job for the government came to be known as becoming a Ward of the State . . . and the issue of these people's credentials became moot in the eyes of Ima Pipiig; because Indian people had had no choice but to be hangers-on and tolerant of the cultural faux pas of the newly found members of the tribe-of-the-week, giving them authenticity by their very presence. That was the role they had been taught to take on in the world of academia. Supplements. Unpaid consultants, hoping for a few bits and pieces of success and survival to trickle down from the new tribal members who would some-how discover that Indians were OK, all right, good enough to be a part of America. All those Indians, going to college, being nice, working hard, being gracious, giving away the last of their resources—their ideas and stories and cultural identities—in the hopes that they would be good enough to get a job . . . were still waiting for the wannabes to share.

Except for Ima Pipiig. Because Ima Pipiig was not a quick study when it came to being told what her role in society would be. So, in early spring, af-ter the maple-sap run and before the morel mushrooms taunted her, Ima Pipiig sat down and wrote. Even if it wasn't always productive. Even if it was a gam-ble of her precious time and resources. Ima Pipiig sat down in early spring and wrote about the Anishinabe people, who were cultural delicacies and threat-ened resources . . .

And, like a lot of Indians, she walked away from academia because it was invalid. And she walked away from education because it was a waste of time and effort and scarce money. And very, very few Indians are pulling in a hun-dred thousand dollars a year, Ima Pipiig would remind herself, especially in the field of education, which prefers "ethnic lite" over fresh-from-the-trenches-and-potent ethnic a good deal of the time . . . unless it's cheap or free and can be dismissed with the wave of a hand.

Those academic wannabe Indian-lites had done damage beyond measure to Indian people. So what else was new? The so-called-liberal-media had done its story, had interviewed ol' Ward, with Russell, yapping like a poodle (so out of character!), only when called upon to speak (in favor of Ward). And ethnic security of sorts, the demand for "doggie papers" for "real" Indians would probably increase. And real Indians who lost their records, who never had records, because of the swamps and the snow and the black flies and the fires in the churches and because of nepotism celebrated by the banana republic nature of new forms of tribal government imposed by a white and stingy culture, might be cut out from Native American academic culture in North America—because weeding out the wannabes could become more important than including the backwoods urban and rural Indians and the marginal Indians and the Indians who never-in-a-million-years-dreamed that keeping records about being an Indian would be important, since being an Indian sucked, and being an Indian was a source of pain and suffering and an elevated suicide rate and rotting teeth and death-by-lack-of-health-care . . . The Churchills, the Quickies, the Highwaters—they could well kill off half of the Indians in northern Michigan, a third of the Indians in the United States and Canada—all because they saw a window of opportunity; and white folks thought that Indian wannabes who knew so much better what white folks wanted to hear about Indians as expendable, replaceable commodities would be a whole lot better to hire than Indians-who-had-chips-on-their-shoulders and could not possibly understand what academic America really needed and really wanted from its Indian scholars . . .

Ima Pipiig sidestepped a fresh stool in the path. She knew that the old cultural phenomena that were threatened into extinction could not survive without economic viability. And she worried that the culture of "Indian-lite" might replace Indian culture. She saw continuity between the past and the present. She saw value in the old traditions as coping mechanisms for the present. She saw lessons in history. She recognized that modern Native people were more valuable to the present than were stilted imitations. She saw herself, her family, her friends, as culture-building delicacies. She saw a difference between her own notion of Indian-as-delicacy and the dried-up, exploitive notions of Indians that were still thriving in America's institutions. And it caused a pain as sharp as the little boy's earache. So the woman turned back to the barns, in the hopes of finding a Popsicle from last summer to soothe the symptoms of his cold. And she wondered if she would ever find the time to write about someone she did not particularly care to write about; because it would require the emotional strength to open up one of the jars of pain and indignation that she had stored away when she found herself in possession of more than her family could consume.

There were rabbit tracks crisscrossing the path between the house and the barns, now melting down and widening into obscurity. Ima Pipiig had raised rabbits once. She had fallen in love with some gray rabbits that belonged to an anthropology professor at the University of New Mexico. He had given her a pair. But Ima Pipiig found that the gray was a recessive gene. When she crossed the gray rabbits with white rabbits, she got only white rabbits. When she bred the gray rabbits with grays, she got gray. And she tried to apply this lesson to the dominance of white academia over minority academia. She knew that gray minority academia might never survive in America's colleges, universities, libraries, and museums. She knew that radical ideas, different ideas, would only survive outside of the accepted norm.

So Ima Pipiig avoided the hubbub and the hullabaloo about ol' Ward Churchill, just as she avoided museums and colleges and universities, and all of the institutions of white-middle-class-entertainment that passed themselves off as educational institutions dealing in Indian phenomena, but which did not hire Indians to do the teaching. She had learned the hard way, the expensive way, that education was not for education; it was for degrees—for the fortunate— and it was about having a piece of paper that guaranteed superiority for the fortunate. And ol' Ward, ol' Ward Churchill and the clones and the pretenders were as significant to the survival of Native America as were dem museums, wit' dere pup tent wigwams an' dere ideas dat innyuns was gone an' dead an' widdout value, 'cept fer dem innyuns dat sold beadwork at da local historical museum or on da sidewalk in Santa Fe or along da railroad tracks for a century before, 'cause dem white folks, dey gotta have cheap culture at all costs. And once dey get done payin' nemselves an' hirin' one or two dat wanna be what dey think an innyun' is s'posed t'be, dey don't have enough to share.

And one gets what one pays for.

·29·

Dead Horses, and How to Beat Them

It's like beating dead horses, I tell her. It's been done. It will not move mountains. It will not get a dead horse to rise up and move a few inches along the dusty trail of miles. It will not make a culture change, will not make the consumers who are consuming the remnants of Indian culture and socioeconomic strongholds in northern Michigan stop consuming rubbish in the form of children's literature that promulgates damaging ethnic stereotypes.

End of conversation. End of reviews of books by those people without consciences, what the heck are their names? . . . Indians don't care. We go on with our lives of economic and cultural exclusion, and we consider ourselves lucky for having been exposed to the real thing, as opposed to the stuff these people have openly admitted to making up—as though it is OK to remanufacture our cultures and histories into their own convenient formats.

No, no, no, the editor has insisted. We've got to review this one, too.

Why? In case they've stopped behaving like sociopaths? In case they've grown consciences—as unwillingly as growing tumors, bunions, or facial scars? Ripping off Indians is ripping off Indians! They vacationed and then moved into a place where the Indians had lost everything: land base, job opportunities, perceptibility as human by the dominant culture . . . So they took the intangibles Native peoples still had left—their stories, their histories. And when they ran out of Indian stories that were recorded by the old Indian commissioner, they began making up new ones. (Because the Indians sure-as-shit weren't going to tell them any!) Doesn't that qualify as a violation of the Indian Arts and Crafts Act—making up something and then passing it off as Indian? Wouldn't it be a hoot if somebody who could afford to do it got off their butts and dragged those cultural appropriation whores into a federal courtroom? (There's supposedly a half-million dollar fine for producing something and pretending that it's Indian . . .) We know the local ACLU won't bother with it; they vacationed and then moved into a place where the Indians had lost everything: land base, job opportunities, perceptibility as human by the dominant culture . . .

No, it's not an Indian story, that new book—or books—I don't keep track. But I'm so used to being told that I don't know nothin' about nothin' by the newcomers who want everything that I've got, that I think that maybe I'd better check with an elder, and she says—JEEZUZ, I mean Jeezuz. How DISRESPECTFUL, I mean disrespectful! How disrespectful to make up a story about those Petoskey stones. They are special to us. They are among our crown jewels. They are so precious that we do not have a story about their origin. How DISRESPECTFUL to just make up one!

But I'm so used to being told that I don't know nothin' about nothin' by the white people who want everything that we've got, that I think that maybe I'd better check with some more of my elders, and they say—JEEZUZ, I mean Jeezuz. How DISRESPECTFUL, I mean disrespectful! How disrespectful to make up a story about those Petoskey stones. They are special to us. They are among our crown jewels. They are so precious that we do not have a story about their origin. How DISRESPECTFUL to just make up one!

And the editor keeps bugging me and keeps insisting that she should buy a copy of the book from the white publishers who have no respect for anything but their own bank accounts, and that she should mail it to me, and the padded envelope just sits there unopened. And I try to explain to the editor that the damage has already been done to at least one entire generation of Anishinabe children by those publishers who have no respect for anything but their own bank accounts, and that I don't need to see the book about the not-really-Ojibwe-legend of the Petoskey stone that was written without conscience or knowledge of the federal Indian Arts and Crafts Act or the Ojibwe culture, and that they had a cultural illiterate illustrate for the sole purpose of selling to ignorant cultural outsiders who prefer fake Indian stories over real ones any old day of the week. Because *this* is a real Indian story. And if I was a cultural appropriation whore who didn't care if I did real socioeconomic damage to real Indian people by making their stories and culture and perceptions of them look simple and docile and sweet and ripe-for-the-ripping-off, I'd prefer abysmal fake Indian stories, too. And the padded envelope just sits there unopened.

I think that I would like to send the unopened envelope to the local historical museum. They could use it to furnish their pup tent Indian wigwam built by a white guy originally from Chicago or Detroit who did not feel that it was an appropriate use of the taxpayers' and benefactors' money to hire an Indian at a living wage to build something that actually resembled a functional wigwam that a real Indian family wouldn't mind living in for more than a few days at a time instead of just giving the impression that we were camping out for several thousand years . . . They could use the envelope as an artifact of real Indian culture, maybe hang it next to the bunny skins that are hanging outside the door of that dysfunctional wigwam for no good reason whatsoever.

Naw . . . they'd just open it.

• 30 •

Toxins

$\mathcal{I}$ma Pipiig picked up brush in the orchard every spring, as soon as the snow melted to the point that she could extricate the branches from the frozen crust. She worked with huge nippers that took two hands to operate and that were strong enough to cut off a man's limb. She walked the miles and miles of rows where Lester had pruned his blocks of fruit trees all winter long on bear paw–shaped snowshoes that allowed him to maneuver under and around their branches. With the nippers she removed the thickest pieces of tree branch from the tangles of fine limbs. She tossed the woody chunks into piles under the trees for gathering and stacking as workshop firewood at a later time. Then she gathered and intertwined the fine fruit branches she had cut apart, placing them in quarter-mile-long connecting rows on the grassy stretches that separated the rows upon rows of even trees. They had been planted with precision in holes that had been laid out with surveying equipment. And thus the sprayers and spray materials were calibrated and mixed to accomplish the maximum benefit with a minimum amount of chemicals and fuel, usually landing with an accuracy that brought them within inches of their target organisms.

It was a work of art, that orchard; and every bit of labor that was done within it was done with precision planning. The finest of the branches that lay intertwined in the grass were woven together so that they would not blow away in strong spring breezes off Lake Michigan, while waiting for Lester to find the time to attach the Brush Hog mower to the John Deere tractor. They would be chopped and scattered, becoming mulch and organic material for the growing fruit trees. Anything larger than a fifty-cent piece would be gathered up into an open trailer and hauled to a barn where it would be cut into firewood and then stacked inside the workshop for winter fires. There was no waste on this small farm. There was no room for it in Ima Pipiig's life because Indians

219

lived on the socioeconomic edge of society, without leeway; and Lester, having fallen head over heels in love with an Indian woman, had condemned himself to the same fate. Ima Pipiig would never earn as much as a white woman with her credentials. Neighbors would look down at Lester for his choice of life mate and take advantage of the fact that he was married to a woman who could garner minimum wage at best. Even his own father and stepmother would take advantage of him. They would leave him without inheritance for his poor choice—an Indian whose credentials brought neither income nor status, whose circumstances brought neither inheritance nor dowry.

To this day, after twenty years of marriage, the old woman still sent Ima Pipiig letters telling her that she would leave nothing to Lester. And Ima Pipiig could only scoff, knowing that the pretentious daughter of an alcoholic miner who had married into money would somehow think that she and Lester were anything less than soul mates, because of her own inability to understand the concept of a soul mate. The very first day that Lester had seen Ima Pipiig he was smitten, and he had wandered his way through women and relationships until she finally showed up at the right time and the right place, ready and willing. And Ima Pipiig knew that Lester, even though he was not an Indian, was everything that she was looking for in an Indian man; and she loved everything about him, good and bad, handsome and homely; because that was the way it was when people fell into deep, deep love. There was no room for thinking about consequences and racism and hateful neighbors and family. So Ima Pipiig and Lester Browning were bound together like water and fish, like tall trees and sky, like flesh and flesh . . . and nothing, nothing, not racism, not hatred, not financial stress nor lack of leeway, could tear them apart or make them hate one another for more than a few hours out of even the worst day.

Ima Pipiig worked in the orchard a few hours at a time, as best as she could with a toddler close by. She carried the deadly nippers in one hand and a large toy truck in another. The boy wandered along behind, playing in the mix of melting snow and warm spring mud, waving sticks, and singing bits of songs he'd heard on audiotapes in the car or when his family cuddled him in bed. Ima Pipiig wouldn't pick up brush in the part of the orchard that touched the road, for fear that the boy would wander onto the pavement in one unseen moment. So Birdie had done that first hundred feet or so of orchard alone, not enjoying the fact that her parents made her work on the farm and had done so since she was as young as she could remember; but she did that section because it kept her little brother safe. And even though this was a somewhat safer environment, slightly removed from the traffic that had grown from the milk truck twice a day and one or two cars at best into the frightening frequency of a couple of cars per hour, Ima Pipiig never really took her eyes off the boy or the dangerous tools she brought with her. Now she saw the child change path suddenly, duck forward with determination, and squeal with delight, and Ima Pipiig raced across several rows of trees to shriek, "No!" and to reach down to intercept the boy's prize, while the child's hand was only an inch away from one of Biggie Waldo's empty pesticide containers.

Bastard.

The stuff was so concentrated that each two-gallon jug was mixed with several hundred gallons of water. By state law, farmers were to triple-rinse each jug, pouring the rinse water into the spray tank before recycling the plastic containers. But Ima Pipiig knew Biggie Waldo. Biggie was too lazy to rinse out those jugs even once, too ignorant to care about the potential environmental damage of misplaced concentrate, and too financially comfortable to care about using every drop of the costly concentrate. A loophole in state pesticide handling laws allowed Biggie's older brother to take the pesticide-licensing exam for him. Lester had told Ima Pipiig how he'd watched Biggie dump old bottles of long-outlawed chemicals into his spray tank without even measuring. There was a sort of machismo in it, mixed dangerously with lack of knowledge and lack of necessity for obtaining the knowledge. If Biggie's parents had still been alive, she could have called them, made chitchat, and then graciously, sweetly, pointed out that the boys had been so exhausted and so busy that they had forgotten to take care of this particular detail. And the parents, out of embarrassment, would have sent Biggie to clean up the containers right away. But now he just left his garbage blowing about the barnyard and onto adjacent farms. Swaths of plastic, Coke bottles, and cookie wrappers skittered across frozen fields and deep into the woods. Only months before, pesticide drift had traveled these same paths of wind, as Biggie insisted upon spraying every Thursday, even if the wind was too strong, and even if it blew toward the small cluster of houses next to which his family's orchard had been planted. Ima Pipiig and Lester had learned to shut their house windows against Biggie's ignorance and lack of concern, even on hot summer afternoons; but they could not shut up their entire lives or their entire environment from the potential damage that came from a life lived doing as little as one could get away with.

That was the way it was with Biggie. His dad had wanted him to work and had bullied him into working. His dad had referred to him and his older brother as "Fattie" and "Piggie." But Biggie had become exhausted, exhausted from the mere effort of moving his immense body mass from one side of the room to another. He was exhausted by the effort of lumbering out to his car or his golf cart. It had not been his choice to have been nurtured on pure butter and sugar and sweets. It was one of the ways his father had abused his mother, one of the ways his father had abused him. And now Biggie refused to work. He found gadgets and gizmos that simulated work because his frame could not support his three-hundred-plus-pound body and an honest day's work as well. He found a machine in a catalog of farm supplies that operated on propane and sent the sound of a gunshot rotating around a gas cylinder. That would scare off the deer that nibbled the young fruit trees that the Waldos had hired the less-fortunate in the neighborhood to plant for them. It would replace the presence of an actual human being, along with his wife and children, working out in the orchard all year long. Biggie had a twenty-four-hour mercury light installed just outside the barn. This would discourage theft and break-ins at the pole barn because Biggie did not have either the energy or the inclination to scare off potential thieves by actually being there and working, as if thieves were really an issue in this patchwork of interconnected fruit farms. No matter that the barns had been built on the corner of the property, at the minimum legal setbacks from the roads and from neighbors . . . no matter that the light traveled across the property lines into the homes of the farmers adjacent to that farmland, those who actually lived on and worked their farms. No matter. It made it look like Biggie was actually doing something. It was an excuse for not being there. There were a dozen other gadgets—a tape recording of a young deer, dying and in distress; distress calls from dying crows; flashing lights; battery operated radios . . . anything, anything at any cost, to simulate work . . . because part of the cycle of abuse that had brought Biggie Waldo to the point of morbid obesity and irreversible immobility was the money that had flowed his way under the controlling strong arm of his father—Big, Big Waldo.

Ima Pipiig was frustrated. She felt that the last person who should be handling Biggie Waldo's empty pesticide containers was a woman who was still nursing a toddler. But she ran around the orchard ahead of the boy, grabbing up a half dozen empty containers that had blown across the road onto her farm. Biggie mixed his toxic chemicals on a corner of his property flush against the property line, and he had left the pesticide-laden jugs out on the ground all through the previous late summer, fall, and winter. Eventually every single one of them had blown onto the neighboring farms. The southerly spring breezes had brought most of them to Ima Pipiig. She knew better than to call any of the surviving Waldos about it. They would be in no hurry to hire someone to walk around and pick up after themselves, and the chances were that they would become vindictive, angry that someone as lowly as Ima Pipiig had taken it upon herself to make a demand of them. After all, Ima Pipiig was still working for a living and had inherited nothing. So Ima Pipiig bagged up the pesticide containers and threw them into the back of her dump truck, where no children or pets were likely to come into contact with them before she got them to a recycling center, rinsed or not. She washed her hands and arms up to the elbows repeatedly in the cold wash of her outdoor pump, and then she and the boy wandered back into the rows of trees for another half hour or so of work. This was the amount of time she had left, before she knew he'd need to be diapered and fed.

The boy sang, and the woman worked. Lester had tried to cut the largest branches into chunks that his wife could comfortably manage. His standards for comfortably manageable were not quite the same as hers. He was a good half-foot taller than his wife, and even though Ima Pipiig had done little but hard physical labor all of her life, she could not match her husband in strength. As she shoved a large, unruly branch away from her, another, springier branch flew back and snapped at her upper lip. She kept working, trying to avoid thinking about the pain, but eventually she stopped and rubbed some crusty snow onto the stinging lip. She already had a purplish slash above one eye from two days before.

She was supposed to give a presentation at a school in a few days. It was always a challenge for Ima Pipiig to get the teachers to treat her with respect anyway. She did not want to go in limping and bruised and looking like an old farmer. It's not that Ima Pipiig had anything against farmers. She was a farmer. Lots of Indians had been farmers. Her father had been a farmer. Farmers were closer to Indians in their need to work hard than were the newest neighbors, the ones who had followed the new interstates north to Vacationland.

And Ima Pipiig respected everything there was to respect about working hard. But she also knew that schoolteachers lived in a different world than farmers. It was a world that Indians like Ima Pipiig had been closed out of, except as parents, and usually unwanted parents at that. The teachers were, in Ima Pipiig's opinion, so out of touch with the people of the rural communities they taught in that they did not even dress like the rest of the population. They were clotheshorses. They dressed differently, had bigger houses, drove newer, fancier cars, and thought themselves somehow superior to the rural population that provided them with a paycheck. Most of them had moved into northern Michigan from somewhere else, usually downstate, and had chosen the region because they had vacationed there and could obtain employment in a profession that would still allow them to vacation there. There was a distinct division between the older farming families and the newcomers. It was as strong as the division between the old farmers and the Indians. In fact, it would eventually become stronger, as the newcomers changed their new environment. They seemed to have arrived just at the time that the old homesteaders were coming to terms with the Indians and were even starting to intermarry with the migrant farmworkers. To Ima Pipiig, the teachers were the most crucial part of the transition from adaptation back to racism. They modeled to the rest of the growing community how to behave toward people they considered "other." Ima Pipiig didn't like being "other" to anybody, especially somebody who didn't quite get the knack of what it was like to do hard physical labor from dawn to dusk, no matter what your credentials were.

And while she patted at the stinging upper lip, Ima Pipiig tried to prepare herself mentally for the school presentation. The presentations she gave were warm and fuzzy. Ima Pipiig had learned to be sneaky when giving presentations in the public schools here at home. She'd been away and had taught in big cities and in minority school districts, so she knew how to teach. She knew how to get the attention of a crowd. She knew how to get it so quiet in a room full with hundreds of children that you could hear a pin drop. And she knew when she had pushed their patience to the limit and it was time to get them to jump up and move and sing and recite and do all of the whole-body learning experiences that she had planned for them. Ima Pipiig was a hell of a teacher.

The public school employees would usually be rude. They would not bother to look up at Ima Pipiig, a mere Indian presenter in a white-run institution like a school. They would have mail to read or paperwork to fiddle with. They would not model polite behavior or appropriate social skills to their students. Some of them would even chitchat among one another, if they stayed in the room at all. But Ima Pipiig was sneaky. She would woo those teachers into paying attention and listening and enjoying and learning, right along with their students. And then, when she knew that she had them eating right out of her hand, Ima Pipiig would start showing those teachers how all that Indian stuff worked right into their regular curriculum for each specific grade. She'd talk specifically about teaching landforms to those third graders and prime factorization to those fifth graders, and the whole time she'd be talking about Indian baskets and Indian words and numbers and Manaboozhou and all of the stuff that they thought was cute little Indian lore. It was a hard job. Those teachers were really hard to teach. They'd been taught that they were better than the people of color they were supposed to teach for so long that Ima Pipiig had to unteach at least as much as she taught.

Ima Pipiig remembered the educational psychology course she had taken to become certified to teach. She'd always gotten a big red star at the top of her paper, with the words, "Class high" circled in red. It must have been a policy within the Department of Education because Ima Pipiig got that exact same red star and the exact same words in every class she took in her teacher certification program at the University of New Mexico. She remembered how her application into the student teaching program had been lost behind the filing cabinet for months on end, one semester after another; until she'd called the Dean of Student Affairs and said, "I don't care if they don't like Indians; I don't care if they don't like *me*; the minimum requirement is a 2.0 grade point average—I have a 3.97—bump somebody with a 2.0." And they made room for her. And they made her student-teach three times as long as a white person. This, although she had already earned a master's degree, summa cum laude. This, although she had already worked in public education for five years as an educational assistant in the classroom, the only job available to colored women in education in a state where more than half of all people were people of color.

And Ima Pipiig became the first Indian in the history of the University of New Mexico to earn teaching certification on the main campus. Although a few had been trained and certified on the Navajo Indian Reservation hundreds of miles away, it was precisely because they were safely hundreds of miles away and would never venture into the white world to compete with white educators or to try to upset the status quo that they were allowed to do so. So Ima Pipiig did the impossible. She'd fought them all, performed superlatively, and even ended up getting a job off a reservation. But she ended up fleeing for her life when the institutional forms of the Ku Klux Klan and the John Birch Society came knocking at her classroom door. She "abandoned" the teaching job with medical and dental benefits and flew north in a compact car, expecting something better from the north than she had encountered in the south. She'd expected the world to have responded to the hippie movement of the 1970s with something more than a usurpation of Indian land and traditions. She had not expected the post–*Brown v. Board of Education* world of intercommunity urban busing that would have sent racists northward in hordes beyond the imagination of even Thurgood Marshall himself. Ima Pipiig did not know that the vast unwanted public lands and shorelines of northwest Lower Michigan had become the Deep South of the North.

Ima Pipiig would have loved to have gotten a job teaching in a Michigan school. She was homesick for her own classroom whenever she had the opportunity to present to fifth graders in her new capacity as someone who did cultural presentations in the schools. It would have been easier to sneak in a little more information about being respectful of other people and other cultures if Ima Pipiig could've been in the same school building with those white teachers every day, every week. But she had to settle for what she could get, and that meant teaching them a little, just a tiny, little bit about the value of people who were "other" than them. She could only penetrate the homogeneity of the all-white school system periodically. She would never know the longevity of her impact. She suspected, as the communities around her swelled increasingly with white-flightists from the integrated cities to the south, that it was a losing battle. Her little swipes and pawing at the beast of racism made Ima Pipiig feel like a frightened kitten venturing out periodically from under the floor of a feed store. But there were no big hands of government to reach down and rescue her from predators and dominant beasts. Ima Pipiig would fight and snarl for every morsel of food that was to enter her mouth. She was to battle for every scrap of firewood that would heat her home. She was to battle for her very existence, for her very right to live and breathe in the territory that the newcomers were claiming for their own, based upon the historic right of summer cottages fueled by childhood fantasies.

Eventually Ima Pipiig would give up on trying to interact with the schools. She would come to know better than to try to get a job with medical benefits for her family, even as a custodian or an educational assistant. And she would grow tired of one-day field trips into an educational world that grew increasingly hostile to people who were originally from this place, especially those who had been from this place for thousands of years and thought that they had some sort of ties to it or a version of its history that varied from the one the newcomers invented for their own convenience.

The rejection of Native American traditions that did not meet with the storybook ideals of these newcomers pained Ima Pipiig as much as anything else. If she was too "other" for her equal or superior educational credentials to qualify her for equal work at equal pay, at least she could find value in that sense of "other." At least she would have this to pass on to her children, in exchange for the hours she did not spend with them while working more hours for less pay, in exchange for the times she did not take them to the doctor for illnesses and scrapes and cuts and sore spots, in exchange for the clothing and toys they wanted, but she knew that they should not have—because she wanted them to be better than the people who knew them as "other." At least Ima Pipiig would have the stories and the traditions. But the schools and the teachers increasingly rejected those stories and those traditions in favor of their own—white stories and traditions about Indians that kept them in their places, as servants to the others. There was a growing sensation that the newcomers were not content with looking upon Ima Pipiig and her children as "other," but that they were now looking upon them increasingly as "lesser" and "disposable."

Ima Pipiig dipped for more snow. The lip was growing numb. Her sore limbs were growing numb. She leaned the nippers against the trunk of a peach tree, as alike as all of the others around it, memorizing her row and place in the homogeneity. She coaxed the boy away from the toy truck and scooped him up. She would swallow her pride and do her best to try to teach these white people in the schools something, even though she had stopped enjoying the interactions of the public school jobs. On her way back to the house, Ima Pipiig spotted another one of Biggie Waldo's stray pesticide containers. She memorized its row and place, so that she could protect her son from it later. She weighed the various new toxins in her environment, both physical and psychological, that threatened the welfare of her children. Ima Pipiig was tired, and she didn't know where to start.

· 31 ·

Gambling for Dollars

$\mathcal{I}$ma Pipiig picked up brush from Lester's logging operations on the farm during late winter and early spring. He felled the trees into the open fields and the tractor-driving-and-turning-spaces that surrounded the woodlots within his hundred and twenty acres of long-used farmland. Several acres consisted of "pine plantation," plots that varied in size from two acres up to several hundred that were planted with baby pine trees during the Works Progress era of the 1930s and 1940s that followed the first great depression, the one known as the Great Depression . . . because people thought that there would never be one like it again. But Ima Pipiig lived in a constant Great Depression that was reserved for minorities in America . . . one that started before the Great Depression that affected whites and finally attracted the attention of government officials and official photographers and historians . . . one that lasted through the civil rights-slash-hippie-slash-free-love-eras of the 1960s and 1970s into the twenty-first century without break or hope from a booming stock market or cheap-third-world-less-than-minimum-wage-kiddie-meal toys from a minimum-wage-paying-burger-joint-slash-multinational-corporation.

So Ima Pipiig picked up brush from Lester's logging operations on the farm during late winter and early spring. Because the Great Depression that affected Native American people for generations on end did not take a socio-economic break in white racism for Ima Pipiig or her college degrees and her professional credentials. She didn't mind because it gave her a break from doing beadwork and cutesy Indian-artsy-fartsy-stuff for hours on end until she was in pain from her elbow to her fingertips. And even her legs and feet were starting to hurt from sitting still and bracing herself into precise stillness for so long while she made porcupine quill necklaces and earrings for minimum wage or less. A white neighbor who did sign painting and suffered similar symptoms, but could afford to go to a doctor, had relayed to Ima Pipiig the proper exercises for remediating the muscular over-abuse; and Ima Pipiig, unable to spare the free time to do exercises or anything that did not involve making or saving money, had figured out which large motor activities on the farm mirrored the doctor-recommended exercises to counteract and lessen the impact of the fine-motor-less-than-survival-livelihood that had been imposed upon her by racism.

So Ima Pipiig stacked firewood and picked up brush from Lester's logging operations on the farm during late winter and early spring. He felled the trees into the open fields and the tractor-driving-and-turning-spaces that surrounded the woodlots within his 120 acres of long-used farmland. Several acres consisted of "pine plantation," plots that varied in size from two acres up to several hundred that were planted with baby pine trees during the Works Progress era of the 1930s and 1940s that followed the first great depression, the one known as the Great Depression . . .

It was essential that the parts of the trees not usable as lumber be lifted and dragged back into the woods, where they were stacked into piles, not too deep, so that they could compost within a reasonable number of years and render the rest of the woodlot walkable and driveable. They had to be removed from the open areas so that the farm equipment could come through to mow or spray or simply drive by to inspect the growth, development, and pest damage among the various crops, or even to drag through a large log of pine or maple or bass. There was no reason to wait for warmer weather to do this task. Ima Pipiig's schedule would be as full in a few months as it was now, and who knew when illness or possible cash income might interfere with the moving of brush. So Ima Pipiig did not let the brush build up, if she could help it, and she worked on it for an hour or so a day, from late winter to early spring, until early spring wet snows came deep and fast and froze during cold nights to make a heavy crust on top of the brush. When the crust became too heavy, and extrication became too muscle-straining and difficult, Ima Pipiig would find something else more productive to do for a few weeks. Eventually, the warm spring sunshine that spaced out the snow-bearing clouds would weaken the layer of snow, and then Ima Pipiig could walk out on the thin crust and the bare spaces of sod to extricate the long-needled branches of red pine and long-limbed, supple, fight-you-with-every-attempt-to-move-them spruce boughs and drag them into the spaces between trees that Lester did not need open for driving the tractors and dragging out logs.

It was idiot work, but it needed to be done; and if Ima Pipiig did not do the work, then Lester would not be able to earn a working wage. So she supplemented him. And when this job was accomplished, she went back indoors to her beadwork and barkwork and cute artsy-fartsy Indian work that did not match her credentials or her intellect, and she supplemented Lester even further. Because this was the profession that white America had dictated to her, during the late twentieth and early twenty-first century . . . Ima Pipiig supplemented America's racism and sexism and the divisions between the haves and the have-nots. It was the socioeconomic slot that fell between the cotton-grower and the cotton-picker, between the vegetable-and-fruit-grower and the vegetable-and-fruit-picker, between the upper middle class and the lower class, between inherited wealth and the poor and the people of color. And Ima Pipiig was embarrassed for America.

But she facilitated, she supplemented, and she dragged the unwanted branches out of America's perception of itself, so that she could survive and procreate and fulfill her basic biological functions. And sometimes, when she was painfully aware of the role that she filled in American society, Ima Pipiig felt like nothing more than a germ . . . something that lived off the waste products of a dominant society, another organism. But there was something missing in this socioeconomic byproduct of racism—it was symbiosis. Both organisms were not thriving. And Ima Pipiig knew that it could not last. This is probably what kept her going, enabled her to get out of bed every morning and hit the ground running, wondering if she would operate at a profit or a loss on any given day, guessing at what might be the most likely path to survival and financial gain, gambling for livelihood, gambling for dollars.

Ima Pipiig pulled at a springy branch of red pine that was buried under six inches of crusty snow and, unknown to her at the time, buried under several other branches of springy red pine. When a crucial top layer of pine snapped, and the piece she was pulling on gave way, Ima Pipiig reeled backward, but not before a slim branch whipped upward and hit her upper lip. Grateful that it had hit her lip and not her eye, she kept working, trying to avoid thinking about the pain. But eventually she stopped and rubbed some crusty snow onto the stinging lip. She already had a purplish slash above one eye from two days before. She was supposed to give a presentation at the Sleeping Bear County Historical Museum in a few days. She did not want to go in limping and bruised and looking like an old farmer. It's not that Ima Pipiig had anything against farmers. She was a farmer. Lots of Indians had been farmers. Her father had been a farmer. Farmers were closer to Indians in their need to work hard than were the newest neighbors, the ones who had followed the new interstates north to Vacationland.

And Ima Pipiig respected everything there was to respect about working hard. But she also knew the museum employees lived in a different world than farmers, and it was always a challenge for Ima Pipiig to get local museum staff to treat her with respect. It was, in general, a challenge for all Native Americans to get museum staff to treat them with respect. The profession was primarily white. Ima Pipiig figured that this was because people liked to think of it as a socially high-ranking profession, one that required intellect, a broad knowledge base, and creativity, as well as social connections with potential donors. It was a system that worked well for white America, but not necessarily for the minority cultures within America that were supposed to benefit from the educational outreach and cultural preservation of the institutions. In the eyes of Ima Pipiig, who was originally trained as a museum curator, and who had worked with a hundred different museums as a supplemental lawn jockey, most museums served no other purpose than to provide jobs for a handful of white people and to promulgate damaging stereotypes about Indians along with a plethora of other self-serving cultural myths.

Ima Pipiig did not enjoy dealing with the Sleeping Bear County Historical Museum. Her negative response to going there was as visceral as the response she had to stepping inside a public school or putting her children on a bus headed for one. Her history of interaction with the museum had been nothing less than denigrating, even though the museum featured paintings they had commissioned from her (hung exactly as she had asked them not to be hung), and the museum gift shop carried her cute artsy-fartsy Indian work (that did not match her credentials or her intellect and usually garnered her less than minimum wage).

The museum had decided to go Native, interpretively, and had procured grants to exhibit some old baskets and to do presentations for the local schoolchildren. Ima Pipiig did not like that the museum staff did presentations about Indians in the local schools. They effectively cut off Ima Pipiig and the other Indians who had supplemented their incomes doing in-school presentations from one of their few days of work each year at a living wage. And the white curators, for all of their certainty of their own expertise, did not present the Native people and the Native culture in a perspective that met the needs of the Native people; it treated them like cute, artsy-fartsy artifacts.

The new museum director, who had been hired for his carpentry skills because the museum board had decided to expand the structure, had procured a grant from the state and was intent upon having a small birch-bark wigwam built inside the museum. He had tried to hire Ima Pipiig to build it but she knew from previous experience that he would be so untrusting of her judgment, so intent upon squeezing each nickel "so hard that the buffalo pooped," and so insecure in his position of authority over her, that he would call her back, needlessly, time and again, twenty miles or more, for five-minute interactions, until Ima Pipiig would earn less than minimum wage on the project. She had given him the name of an Indian from Sault Ste. Marie who had created wigwams, longhouses, and wigwam-like interiors for several museums and who she knew had enough work options that he would not have to put up with less than a living wage. And having encountered yet another Indian who would not put out for cheap or free in the name of educating America about Indians so that Indians would not have to live in poverty, the scholar-*cum*-hammer fashioned a little bitty wigwam of sorts out of cedar bark. It sat empty, stark, sad, and without humanity just inside the front door of the building. When a few local Indians suggested that the mini-house might be furnished, he obligingly hung a few animal pelts outside the structure. And the Indians sighed, realizing that the poor man thought of Indian people as nothing more than historical figures whose only significance in the manifest destiny of corporate America was their ability to provide furs for The Fur Trade. The Indians began to refer to the wigwam as "the pup tent." So much for dignity. So much for the museum meeting the needs of anyone other than the museum staff and what had become the dominant culture . . .

Ima Pipiig tugged at what she thought was going to be a short pine branch, but it was a long and limber spruce bough, whose bulk was under at least a foot of snow. She realized that she had come out too early to pull at the brush, that her efforts at this time were being wasted. She rubbed at the sore spot on her lip with a wet, stiff mitten, bent down and rubbed more snow onto her lip. She could feel the swelling, in spite of the cold, and the soreness of her ego and sensibilities compounded the injury.

While her body was warm from the exercise, and her joints and muscles were lubricated and moving smoothly, she picked her way through the small woodlot behind the house until she came out behind the barns. There, where the snow had piled in deep drifts on the north side of the woods, there was no sun-made crust on the top of the snow, and Ima Pipiig sunk up to her knees with each footstep. She worked her way to the edge of a ravine and checked a live trap next to a brush pile. Lester had baited it with apples from the barn in the hopes of catching one of the young porcupines that had settled in the brush pile for the winter. It was snacking on the tenderest branches at the tops of the closest trees. Several fruit trees and fairly large pines had been damaged. Lester had simply been too busy to burn the brush in the fall, and now there were consequences. He had gotten out a rifle and a box of dove shot and had given his wife a review lesson on the use of the firearm as well as the proper distance and stance for shooting a porcupine in the head without destroying the expensive live trap or hurting her shoulder from the backlash of the rifle butt; and then he turned over the responsibility of the trap to her, while he worked from dawn past dusk on other projects.

The wind and blowing snow had forced the trap shut, empty, and Ima Pipiig took off her mittens and knelt down in the wet snow to reset it. It was a task she completed frequently, and only one young porcupine was caught unawares. Lester had checked the trap that evening, and he shot it and brought it to Ima Pipiig to pluck for quills. It was tiny and fuzzy, a porcupine equivalent of adolescent. Its quills were too small and underdeveloped for Ima Pipiig to bother with, so Lester burned its body in a big barrel with scraps from the wood planer where he churned out high-quality finish lumber in a backroom of one of his barns until eight or nine o'clock every night. Ima Pipiig was glad that the trap was empty again. She remembered the incredible softness of the young animal, with its thick winter coat, the shine of its eyes, and the beauty of its feet and claws, so perfectly designed for climbing. She had marveled at them with the boy and had used the opportunity to teach him about what a special creature the porcupine was. If it had been large enough, she would have cut out its hocks and cooked them until tender, not out of need for the meat, but to teach the child that nothing, nothing was worthy of waste or to be taken for granted.

Now Ima Pipiig worked her way through the snowdrifts to the workshop barn where the freezers held fish, produce from her summer garden, and every opportunistic food source that came her way. She found some lunch meat that had been on sale and tucked it into a pocket of her pitch-and soot-coated down vest. Then she headed down the well-worn path back to her house, where she grabbed an armload of firewood from a nearby rick and added it to the dry supply inside the door of the house. She washed a load of dishes to warm up her hands, folded a little bit of laundry, and tried to prepare herself mentally for the multihour task of reading, sorting, and reproducing materials for her presentation without pay at the museum next Saturday afternoon. She did not want to be wasted or taken for granted any more than she already had been.

Ima Pipiig had come to equate the Sleeping Bear County Historical Museum with that same live trap she had checked only minutes ago—a place where the museum director would rock on his heels, look down at her, and refer to everything she was and had accomplished academically and professionally in the most denigrating of terms, scoffing at her degrees, her awards, passing off her body of published fiction and nonfiction as worthless and irrelevant. He had done it before, he would do it again, and he would use that manipulation of his power over the jobless Indians of Sleeping Bear County over and over again to leverage his own position and his own stature in the community and to garner matching-fund grants from the state by listing his Indians as "volunteers" and "consultants" . . . He would tell Ima Pipiig to her face that he simply would not write a grant proposal that would pay her as much per hour as he made, and she knew that it applied to all the other Indians as well. And the bullet of that intentional denigration would pierce Ima Pipiig's skull as surely as the dove shot had shattered the skull of that young porcupine. But the death would be slower, preceded by writhing, unlike the clean head-shot that Lester had used to somewhat mercifully terminate the animal that had caused his family a thousand dollars worth of damage in a time and place where survival did not provide him with breathing room for error and loss.

As the nation's economy sagged during the early twenty-first century, opportunity and dignity dwindled for the Indians of Sleeping Bear County. They had always depended upon the trickling down of affluence, and they constantly altered their various strategies for filling survival gaps caused by error and loss in a time and place where leeway was a valuable commodity for those on the bottom of America's economy and cultural ladder. It was an era for swallowing pride even more than ever. It was an era for taking blows to one's dignity and sensibilities as debilitating as dove shot to a small, fragile young skull.

The Indians had formed a loose, unofficial cooperative of sorts and had begun to have an Indian Art Market at various locations that would have them. By the time Ima Pipiig was convinced to join the group, the others had already put in countless hours of unpaid time and labor. It was done with the same hope and desperation for betterment that Ima Pipiig knew firsthand, the same wont for joy in culture and self that had been wrenched from the entire community in effort after effort to destroy their will to hang on to each and every resource as it was deemed valuable by the white newcomers. The group of Indians had been shuffled from one location to another, and Ima Pipiig was grateful when it had found a semipermanent home at the historical museum in Twin Bay City, even though she did not want to deal with the historical museum in Twin Bay City; because the staff at the historical museum in Twin Bay City could not understand why Ima Pipiig was so darned uppity and insisted upon being paid what a professional with half of her credentials would make; because it was, after all, a nonprofit organization, and it was all they could do to come up with the money to pay the salaries and benefits of the white staff at the historical museum, let alone some Indian who ought to be grateful that they were exhibiting tidbits about Indian culture from the region, which would be a great financial boon to the Indians of the region who for some reason were always so darned poor; and why couldn't Ima Pipiig get a job, like they had, and work for a living, for Christ's sake, so that she could donate her time to the museum like they wanted her to . . . like the white volunteers who pulled in comfortable retirements from their jobs as teachers and government employees and businessmen . . .

But Ima Pipiig showed up for the Indian art market because opportunities to freelance in educational institutions that would not hire her full-time had dried up; and she and Lester could put off their own medical and dental care and gamble against their own longevity, but they had to take care of their children. So Ima Pipiig made posters and signs and showed up the designated Saturday of every month to talk and demonstrate and woo people into buying artwork and buying books and respecting the local Indians and donating a dollar to go through the tiny exhibits of the tiny museum, even though this was something she had previously been paid to do in museums, colleges, and universities throughout the Midwest. And a mutual respect and level of comfort began to develop between the Indians and the staff of the historical museum in Twin Bay City; and the Indians made minimum wage or less while they were at home making the artwork, and they made nothing when they talked and wooed and sold the artwork; and they survived one more winter in the harsh environment of a northwest Lower Michigan that had stripped them of most of their resources long ago.

The clubs and other groups that rented the museum space on the other Saturdays complained that the Indians were getting freebies; and the Indians explained that they did not have the luxury of clubs and hobbies because they were working for free and for less than minimum wage and to keep alive a culture that was more endangered than the skeletal remains of *Tyrannosaurus Rex*; and an uncomfortable sort of equilibrium fell into place, while the Indians danced the dance of slave and master with the people of northwest Lower Michigan who needed low-cost culture at all costs.

She didn't remember when, but Ima Pipiig had invited the woman who ran the gift shop for the Sleeping Bear Historical Museum to come to the Indian Art Market to see what the other Indians had to offer. She was hoping that the gift shop might stop handling cheap goods from Southeast Asian sweatshops and start handling cheap goods from Indians' kitchen tables. And the idea for a one-time Indian Art Market at the Sleeping Bear County Historical Museum was born . . . which was fine with the Indians, because they were looking for a location back in Sleeping Bear County, after the white lady who took over supervision of the Indian Health Center had decided that no more Indian activities would be allowed at the Indian Health Center. Besides, it was the dead of winter, and they were looking at near-zero income for the next several months; and try as they might, no amount of frugality facilitated the saving of funds for a winter of poverty, when their best hope at the peak of the summer tourist season was to make minimum wage or less, and this was if they sold everything they ever made, which they didn't; because that's the way it is when one does artwork instead of a real job . . . one gambles that one's labor will turn into dollars.

As they had done in Twin Bay City, the Indians surprised everyone at the Sleeping Bear County Historical Museum by being erudite, intelligent, informative, and entertaining, bringing surprisingly large numbers of people through the doors of the usually quiet institution. So the idea for a more-than-one-time Indian Art Market at the Sleeping Bear County Historical Museum was born. And the ignorant museum director, seeing the enthusiasm displayed by the financially desperate Indians, got greedy—not just greedy for in-kind labor to justify his state grants for the Indian exhibit he was already doing without the Indians, but greedy for self-gratification and the need to talk down to people like Ima Pipiig who did not know their place in the nature of culture and academia. He presented the Indians with a written list of demands . . . demands for free labor in various forms, demands for large donations of traditional, labor-intensive artwork to the museum, and demands for a promise that the Indians would get the heck out of the museum come summer, when the tourists would be showing up in Cottage Country Sleeping Bear County, the affluent backyard of Sleeping Bear National Park, where beauty and historical tradition belonged to people who really knew how to appreciate it. After all, one could not soil the beauty of the place with a welfare-dependent people who just couldn't get it together to get decent paying jobs like everybody else. Those Indians, they were so disrespectful of their own history and culture that they did not know to stand back from soiling that image with their own poverty, ignorance, and self-incriminating public grubbing for the almighty dollar, to say nothing of that icky casino several miles up the road. . . .

And the oral history among those Indian women is now replete with how that white man walked funny after the oral reaming he received from those Anishinabe mothers and grandmothers who had taken their responsibility to the generations that followed them too seriously to be full-time slaves, when they knew they could get by as part-time slaves, or by walking away from the Sleeping Bear Historical Museum completely. So they hunted up alternative locations and argued and bargained, until they were allowed to use the museum space, supposedly all year round, the first Saturday of every month, even when the tourists came; and in exchange, they would each give a presentation at a designated time and sing and shuck and jive and work for free, even though they were already working for free by just being there trying to sell the traditional artwork and prints and cards and jewelry that they earned less than minimum wage manufacturing for a public that normally shunned them and would not hire them with equal pay for equal work . . . Without other options, they would gamble their time and effort toward potential livelihood. They were informed that their use of the building during the summer, the only time it was really of value to them, was tenuous; that they were being watched for quality of performance. And the Indians nodded and smiled and kept their mouths shut because they knew better than to tell the self-centered white man that his presence there was tenuous; that he was being watched for quality of performance.

Once again the Indians were maneuvering and adapting to the changing environment that had taken away the fur trade and the fish and game upon which they had depended through generations of postcontact unemployment. Now they fought for their very right to exist publicly as a reminder of the greed that continued to make the soil and climate of Sleeping Bear County among the most valuable in the world.

So, after a full day of work, after supplementing Lester's logging activities by hauling brush, after supplementing America's love affair with Indians that it perceived to be valuable only as relics of their own accomplished past, after stringing porcupine quills and beads until her arm hurt from elbow to finger-tips; after checking the oil on an ancient car, after sorting out canning jars, defrosting freezers, checking live traps, and all of the little things that most housewives in Sleeping Bear County did not add to their days, Ima Pipiig worked on the presentation that she was going to have to give for free at the Sleeping Bear County Historical Museum, even though she used to do this for pay at colleges, universities, and museums throughout the Midwest.

This was a time to have a sense of responsibility to community and to respect the hours and hours of unpaid labor by the other Indians who had laid the groundwork and put the Indian Art Market together and were gambling for just the slimmest chance of improved survival. This was not a time full of leeway for those on the bottom of America's socioeconomic heap, the ones that Sleeping Bear County took for granted.

And, just as a dog tugs at a leash, just as an animal claws at the inside of a steel cage trap whose door has slammed shut, just as a beast nips at a hand that teases but does not feed it, Ima Pipiig put together a cultural presentation about racism and stereotypes and the use of Indians as lawn jockeys by small historical museums, libraries, and school districts. When the day would come, when Ima Pipiig would grit her teeth and grab at her writhing gut, she would smile, stand up as though an "on" switch had been struck, adjust her accent to accommodate the mainstream Midwestern listening ears of her audience, and she would talk and educate and woo. And, as they always did, the audience would strain to hear her every word, and they would nod, and the librarians would take notes, and the people would applaud and gave her compliments when she was done. And they would buy a few books and a little bit of art-work, and they would take the tables full of Indians and Indian stuff more seriously and respectfully, and they would probably come back again and buy more stuff at prices that reflected minimum wage or less, allowing the Indians to buy groceries and clothing and gas, but not quite enough to buy medical care and comfort in old age or an inheritance for their children . . . because that was what gambling for dollars was all about.

• 32 •

Big Waldeau and Pork Patty

$\mathcal{T}$he Waldos were an odd lot. But Sleeping Bear County was full of odd lots. The other odd lots from the county who knew them, whether it was as cherry farmers, restaurateurs, or karaoke bar bunnies, referred to them as the Waldeaus, with a heavy emphasis on the last syllable, as though it were a fine French wine, rather than a litter of unmarried, obese siblings in their late forties and early fifties who had never had children, never really worked for a living, and never put themselves into a social context that required humility within the community. They were, in essence, a county-wide joke. But then again, most of the county was a county-wide joke. This was the nature of small communities. People thought of themselves as superior to their immediate neighbors, by virtue of whichever idiosyncrasy made them different from their immediate neighbors. It's just that the Waldos thought that they were superior more than other people thought of themselves as superior, and not just in one or two ways. They tended to speak down to their neighbors, not just when they were in a hurry, in the middle of once-a-year-harvest or some such other temporary state that made everybody bad neighbors now and then . . . they tended to do it all the time, and without even the slightest semblance of sound reasoning.

Patricia was the worst of all. She was the educated one of the bunch. She'd gone to Bum-Fuck-College-of-Art-and-Design in some big city or another and had gotten herself a job with an advertising agency for a few years. And if, if you listened to Patty talk about it with more than half an ear, one would have gotten the impression that she was the bright and shining star of the advertising agency, an unofficial executive of sorts, and that half of Hollywood could not have survived without her as an intermediary between the superstars and the ignorant upper-class white fools of the advertising agency.

237

She'd changed her last name to Waldeau, since it sounded much more "Bohemian" than the family's original Bohemian name of Waldovik, and she'd fashioned herself as a young French woman; because she'd learned in her art history survey class about a painting by a French painter entitled, "La Bohemme," "The Bohemian;" and not realizing that the model for the painting had been a Bohemian peasant prostitute, as was the fashion for impoverished young French painters to hire as models in that particular time and place, she got herself confused and figured she must be French, instead of Czechoslovakian. And classy. So she became a Waldeau, rather than a Waldo(vik). This, in spite of the fact that most of the other Czechoslovakians in Sleeping Bear County thought that being Czechoslovakian was perfectly acceptable, and a few even realized that it was something to be proud of, especially in the kitchen.

Patty retired and came home young, in her midthirties, taking the early inheritance that her father had bestowed upon all of the Waldo children in the form of real estate and a house. She bought a condo in Twin Bay City, since that's what sophisticated young sophisticates did, bought a computer, and started her own advertising business, which petered out just about the time that both of her elderly parents died, leaving her enough stocks and bonds to not have to try to drum up a little part-time business as an advertising executive, especially since computers were getting cheap, and everybody else was getting into the business, too. She had also worked as an *artiste*—not for money, but she had painted everything that her mother owned, including the washer and dryer, with lovely acrylic trailing flowers. Before their deaths, she spent the rest of her rare and precious spare time keeping her parents company, carefully lettering the family's fruit-harvesting boxes with the family name and printing return address labels for her family's correspondence in various curlicue texts.

The Waldos were related to a large proportion of the county. There were even several other families who shared the name Waldo, along with some remnant Waldoviks. Most of them refused to admit that they were related to the Waldeaus, but as it is in small towns, everybody knew who was related to whom and didn't admit it. There was Bigelow Waldo and a first cousin, just up the road, named Bigelow Waldo. People referred to the first Bigelow Waldo as Big Big Waldo and referred to the other Big Waldo merely as Big Waldo because he was not obese and did not have delusions of grandeur. To complicate the issue even further, Big Big Waldo decided to name his youngest son Bigelow Waldo, too. So people called him Biggie Waldo, in an attempt at diminution. The other Waldos in the area had children named after themselves, too, but, as is the way in small communities, every one seemed to know the difference between the various branches of Waldos. No one else shared the moniker Waldeau. It was reserved for this particular batch of Waldos because they were downright mean. They tried their darnedest to fit in, and they tried their darnedest to do the right thing, socially, when they thought they might gain positive attention for it, but when push came to shove, and they thought nobody was looking, the Waldeaus were just downright mean.

Their patriarch, Big Big Waldo, had been mean. Neighbors politely referred to him as a "son of a gun." Except when they were in the presence of close friends . . . then they openly referred to him as an "asshole." Nobody really understood his meanness much. Because his parents had moved away when he was young, there were no surviving older generation siblings close by, and the cousins didn't really remember much about the family before they'd moved downstate. His name was Bigelow. Bigelow Waldo, just like his cousin, Bigelow Waldo, who went away but came back much younger. People called him Big Waldo, except behind his back, because they had to distinguish him from the other Big Waldo. So people just called him Big Big for short, or sometimes Big Asshole. Because that's just the way it is in small communities.

He'd been in the military in his youth, retiring quite young and moving back to Sleeping Bear County, where he'd been born, into the house on the land he'd inherited, after his father died in prison for beating his mother and younger brother to death with an old axe handle just after moving downstate, outside of Detroit. It was not information Big Big shared freely with the neighbors. Northern Michigan had had a tendency to make men go mad and kill their wives and children. Big Big Waldo figured his mother and brother were lucky that his father had not killed them right away with an actual axe. He'd been away in the service when the incident had taken place, so it seemed pretty abstract to him. And since he'd grown up watching his father abuse his mother and everyone else he could get away with regularly, it just seemed natural to him. The only thing his father had been guilty of was getting caught with the bloody axe handle. And he hadn't quite had it together to deny the murder. After all, they'd deserved it.

Anyhow, the headstones in the old cemetery in the woods simply said, *Wife of Benjamin Bigelow Waldo* and *Son of Benjamin Bigelow Waldo*. It was as if no one could acknowledge that they had had names or personalities separate from their murderer. People might have spoken of them, spoken of their fate, spoken of their failure to help the woman and her children out of the abuse that they routinely ignored. But in small towns, those things tended to be hushed away into anonymity within a generation.

Ima Pipiig knew about the headstones because she liked to drive slowly and stuck to the back roads. She had a tendency to stop in the old, lost cemeteries, surrounded by the state land that had once been settlers' homesteads and dreams that had gone back for unpaid taxes after the land was used up. That was why the state owned so much land in Sleeping Bear and Benzie Counties; much of the land was not suitable for farming, and the people who had thought of former Indian land as something-for-nothing often worked themselves to death if they accidentally homesteaded and worked a particularly unsuitable piece of farmland with anything less than the respect it deserved.

Ima Pipiig was related to several of the old settlers in those old graveyards, through her one non-Indian grandparent, and she found comfort in their gravestones. She wondered if she could ever find comfort in the fact that so many of them had died young, of outright hardship, after they had so eagerly taken the land from the other three-quarters of her ancestors, leaving them to die of starvation and exposure, while they misused the stolen land base until it was overgrazed and the smallest of its lakes and ponds had filled with silt. She knew that she shouldn't, but she found comfort in the fact that these people did not understand the sandy and fragile nature of these recently glacier-deposited soils. And every time she found a gravestone of a child who had not lived as long as her own had, at least up until that particular day, Ima Pipiig wondered about the Indian children in unmarked graves, if they made it to graves at all, graves that had never been considered worthy of inclusion in the landscape, that never earned a fence or a headstone or a freshly mowed perimeter. In spite of all this she felt a sense of survival for the Anishinabe people as a whole. And then she would feel guilt for her lack of sufficient guilt, and she would sprinkle offerings over the irregular graves that had rocked and heaved from a century or less of freezes and frosts. She could not visit her own mother's grave because it was distant in a remote and overgrown patch of woods. No road passed by, and no township-paid sexton showed up to mow around the Indian graves.

And there was, whether she liked it or not, history in those settlers' gravestones. And the history of the Waldos remained intact in the almost-oral history of those, like Ima Pipiig, who knew of the gravestones and simply did not talk about them because it was not the polite thing to do in a small community.

By the time he was in his late forties, Big Waldo had been in the service long enough to get himself transferred to a radar station near Sleeping Bear County, where he could check out the old family homestead and current real estate values. He soon realized that, with his veteran points, he was better off pulling retirement from the military and getting a job for the postal service. Within a few years, he'd accrued enough time at the post office to pull a second retirement, had married one of the very young Kluska girls, from a family of lithe and hard-working Czechoslovakian immigrants, and had had his first child, Doug. Between the inheritance and the two retirements, and a couple of other inheritances from widowed uncles whose offspring were left in the tiniest of hummocks in those woodland graveyards, Big Waldo was able to get into farming.

Four more children were born, and the Kluska girl managed to work as a dental receptionist between babies. She'd lost her figure and was aging, and it was all that much easier for Big Big to keep her in her place by convincing her that no one else would have her. Big Waldo had put on a few pounds by his midfifties and was no longer handsome, and he became ever more abusive to his wife. She, in turn, became ever more tolerant of the demands of the children because Big Waldo used them regularly to intimidate and bully his wife. Insisting that she indulge them in every way possible was one of his ways of abusing her. And abusing was the only method of interaction with women Big Big had ever known, aside from the whores he'd bought and paid for in big-city ports. So Sylvia cooked and cleaned and baked with real butter for Bigelow's sons and daughter, who grew fat and complacent and knew no different. Sylvia spoke of Big in only glowing terms, as that is the only way that Bigelow had allowed her to speak of him, and that is how Bigelow spoke of himself. And when Big Waldo died, hooked up to oxygen tanks, complaining of the inefficiencies of modern knee surgery, rather than blaming his four-hundred-plus-pound body, Sylvia and the children put on a funeral and a display of loss that reflected the fantasyland in which they had all been forced to live, to cope with the abuse that made them what they were—an island of angry souls in excess of three hundred and fifty pounds each and every one, without social skills and unable to interact for more than a few minutes at a time with anyone other than themselves. . . .

The mother died quite young, only months after the father, of untreated cancer. Because, after all, he was so godlike in his demeanor and command of the household, that Sylvia dare not speak out about her own aches and pains and frivolous needs. Her only value as a human being had been to take care of Big Waldo and his offspring, and duly trained by their father, the offspring had viciously demanded of Sylvia that she nurture their every needs before she consider considering herself. So she was bloated like an obese mother giving birth to quadruplets before she dared to go to the doctor and speak of the pain, and she died within a matter of days, in her own bed, undermedicated and delirious from the pain induced by a tumor the size of a small watermelon. It happened so fast, so soon, within only weeks of the great funereal celebration of the grandiose life of the mean and abusive Bigelow Waldo, that neighbors didn't have time to spend with Sylvia, to bring food and magazines, help her pass the time, give her a sense of self-worth. And neighbors had had enough of Big Big Waldo worship and shied away from the funeral when poor Sylvia died a few weeks after the frantic harvest season. Since Big Big Waldo had set up the boys in the fruit-farming business, all they knew were other fruit farmers. Everyone else had long since shied away, except for an aunt on the mother's side and a few cousins who came out of a feeling of obligation.

The children were angry. They did not understand why the turnout at their mother's funeral had been so slim. They had frolicked in the father-worship of Big Big Waldo's funeral. They had told story after story of his greatness, wisdom, and magnificence. They had told story after story of the joys of their own childhood. But, the neighbors had watched the abuse of those big children's childhood, intertwined with the spoiling of those big children as a means to abuse the mother, and they only half-smiled at the hero-stories. They had been abused and cheated by Big Big Waldo themselves over the years; had turned the other cheek to his intentional insults that he thought himself so glib for tossing about; had been abused and cheated and insulted by Sylvia on his behalf over the years; and had endured the same behavior from Big Big's obese, lazy, and self-indulgent children over the years . . . and now those neighbors turned their backs on the surviving mean children, in spite of the fact that they understood the history and the self-perpetuating nature of abuse that made them what they were. Because that was the nature of small towns. People knew what made people what they were. They understood hurt. And they also knew when to distance themselves from it when they could. Or when to turn their backs on a lost cause.

The first year after the death of the adult Big Big Waldos, the middle-aged children put on a pig roast to celebrate the end of cherry harvest. Business associates and a few relatives turned out. Everyone knew that the "Waldeaus" could put out a spread. They roasted an entire pig, flanked by various fowl, and the meat flowed in great proportions, along with a half dozen or more types of macaroni salad and two dozen cakes and desserts. There was a keg of beer and a karaoke machine. Biggie Waldo was the first to perform on the machine, and he flawlessly sang the one number he had practiced for a hundred hours or more for just this moment. A half dozen portly karaoke bar acquaintances also sidled up to the mike throughout the afternoon.

Ima Pipiig had been there with Lester and the kids. The farm that Big Waldo had coerced the lazy Waldo boys into operating was across the road from the farm that she and Lester owned. Sometimes she and Lester supplemented their incomes by helping to harvest the Waldo's cherries because they would procrastinate until the fruit was nearly spoiled; and Ima Pipiig and Lester were tired but finished with their own orchard. They didn't like doing it, but sometimes the Waldos' laziness left them ripe for the picking, just like the fruit, and they were not too proud to walk away from a fast buck. Besides, pork was her favorite meat, a welcome change from the venison and fish that they procured for themselves; and there would be a few other cherry farmers there with whom she could chat. Ima Pipiig and her family left early. They did not care much for music and were not much for socializing after they'd had their fill. There was always work to be done at home, and the Waldos hadn't really earned more than an hour or two of Ima Pipiig and Lester's family's unpaid time over the years.

Ima Pipiig had driven a truck for the Waldos once, after finishing her own cherry harvest. She was exhausted from weeks on end of twenty-hour days. But Mother Sylvia had called and pleaded, and she was the most likeable of the Waldos. Lester was shaking their cherries for them, faster than they were used to, and Biggie could not drive them to the processing plant fast enough. Sylvia and Patty stood all day in the dark barn, where the water ran through the cooling pipes into the tanks and splattered over their swollen ankles for hours on end, and they sorted the bad cherries from the good. Big Big Waldo was at home most of the time, although he would periodically arrive in his big pickup, drag out his big oxygen tank, and circle the barn repeatedly in a big, noisy, gasoline-powered golf cart. He barked out orders. The women cowered over the cold water tanks, until their fingers were numb from pulling leaves and twigs and scarred and damaged cherries out of the icy water, and their knees buckled from the pressure of their immense bodies pushing downward toward the hard concrete floor. Except for Biggie, who drove the occasional truck of cherries, the boys stood around and barked out orders to the work crew, mostly heavyset friends from the karaoke bar who didn't seem to need anything more than seasonal work themselves.

Whenever Lester and his crew of local teenagers had accumulated enough tanks of cherries for a truckload, and the fruit had cooled enough to be transported without falling apart from the jostling ride, Ima Pipiig would strap down the load, while the entire Waldo family sat and watched. She untangled the nylon truck straps from the dirty pile where the Waldos had left them, coiled them up for throwing, and pitched them over the tall flatbed, with its load stacked two tanks high. Occasionally one of the large man-boys would holler, "Clear!" from the sagging couch in a corner of the barn when Ima Pipiig tossed the straps over the truck; and this seemed to give them the feeling that they were actually participating in the physical labor; or maybe it just made them feel that they were tricking everybody else into believing that they were participating in the physical labor.

Ima Pipiig was several months pregnant with her boy then, and it was hard for her to throw successfully. Sometimes she had to scurry around the other side of the truck, roll up the straps, and toss them again. The Waldos guffawed and had several suggestions as to technique, but none of them ever rolled up the straps or threw them or helped her attach the buckles or ratchet them into place or tie up the loose ends. This had been a major flaw in their upbringing—they thought that watching a pregnant woman work hard was a manly thing.

Weeks later Sylvia would mail Ima Pipiig a check for her time, based upon the current federal minimum wage of slightly more than three dollars an hour, even though the Waldos claimed that they usually paid twelve dollars an hour for harvest labor, because it was so hard to find people that time of year. And she didn't pay Ima Pipiig for the hours she spent strapping down the load in front of those fat, lazy Waldo boys. She only paid her for the estimated time she was away on the road and at the receiving station, sitting in the big flatbed truck, sinking into the overused upholstery that had succumbed to the Waldo frames over the years, before they had become too big to even comfortably climb into or drive a flatbed.

Sylvia's sense of desperation and urgency that had caused her to call Lester begging for help was long gone by the time the time she made out the check. The fruit was harvested, and she'd lost her reason to be accommodating. There was no appreciation for a strong, feisty pregnant woman who could strap down a truckload of fruit that weighed as much as a dozen Ford Broncos or who could drive a big truck with a split differential. Once she had agreed to take on the role of temporary employee, Ima Pipiig had become nothing more than an adjunct to the large people's sloth. But Lester told Ima Pipiig not to feel too bad. Because of her driving, he had been able to work faster than usual, and they'd agreed ahead of time to pay him by the pound. And Ima Pipiig giggled, because she knew exactly what he meant when he said he'd charged them by the pound. Lester had agreed to let his wife drive the truck because he knew that she could facilitate the entire process in a way that the Waldos would not. He wanted this job over with as fast as he could. He would rather be off fishing with Ima Pipiig or making love with her.

So, after her family had eaten its fill at the pig roast, they walked a half mile uphill from Patty's house through a trail in their woodlot. Patty's house on the corner of her family's farm was the one she had bought from one of her brothers after he had lost most of his inheritance at an Indian casino, a few months after their parents had died. It was next to Doug's and Biggie's. Somehow Patty was going to feel safe there, among her relatives, because she didn't have many friends in Twin Bay City; and once she lived there and was in their face, everybody in Sleeping Bear County was going to have to admit that they were related to her, even the ones who didn't want to admit it; because she was, after all, better than them, and they were lucky to be able to admit that they were related to her.

It felt good to walk away from the blending food smells, the grease from the pork drippings melding into the egg smells from the various macaroni salads. It was a short turn up the slope before the trees muffled the poom, poom, poom of the karaoke machine that they were too polite to acknowledge that they did not enjoy. They leaned in and huffed on the steepest slope before crossing the road to their own farm. Where the land that had been sprayed with defoliant for power lines veered away from the road, the trees narrowed in, forming sort of an archway. It was as though they were being welcomed as royalty, steadily working their way up into the paradise of privacy, of blue sky and farmland, away from the forced pleasantness of the obligatory feast. There was light enough yet to work off the meal, to work for the love of work and for the love of providing for themselves without pretense, with pride. The boy would be cuddled, bathed, and cuddled again; and Birdie would stack some wood in a barn workshop, where she could wait to bait Lester into a game of darts, just after it became too dark to work outside, and just before he stumbled along the path through the woods back to the house, the teenager twisting and twirling at his big hands, while they laughed with the warmth and comfort that only family could share.

The Waldos considered the first pig roast such a smashing success that they bought the pig roaster from the fellow they had hired to roast the pig. He didn't mind. He made enough money now and then driving tractor for Biggie that he didn't really need to roast pigs. Besides, there wasn't that much of a market for it. Most of the old farmers knew how to roast a pig without a propane-fired pig roaster. That's the way it was in those old farm communities. And the Waldos were the only people who had ever hired him to roast pigs anyhow.

The second annual pig roast wasn't quite the success of the first one. The sympathy that people had felt for the Waldos' loss of both parents within a year seemed to have petered out. Without their parents around to impose some sort of social restraint, the Waldos had alienated most of their neighbors and business associates within a few years. Eventually they alienated one another. The pig roaster sat in Patty's driveway for a couple of years. She kept asking her brothers to move it, but they did even less work now that their parents were gone.

The old man had insisted that the farm make money. But now, with his stocks and bonds generating monthly income, the kids didn't need it. The farm would be operated with as little work as possible these days. Overseeing employees was such a chore. It required actually going out into the orchard in a pickup truck and looking to see what had to be done. And since no one could possibly perform with the grace and skill of a Waldo, the employees would have to be observed every day or so.

Meanwhile, there was so much leftover pork in the freezer that Patty was baking chickens stuffed with cooked pork every Sunday for her brothers' supper. She fell into a niche of serving the boys' needs by cooking and eating, cooking and eating, not unlike that her mother had occupied, perhaps to justify her very existence, and perhaps to console herself over her loss of something to do now that Big Big Waldo was not around to give her orders. She grew from somewhat mobile obese to immobile obese, and she grew from marginally pleasant and sociable to backstabbing and mean. People began to refer to her as Pork Patty. And the jokes within the community that abounded in regard to the Waldeaus coursed and varied and responded to their every folly and their faux pas, because that is the way it is in small towns.

• 𝟥𝟥 •

Shiigawk

𝒥ma Pipiig's immediate goal for the moment was to wash the wineglass without breaking it. Wineglasses were made for wine, which cut grease—so, except for wiping away the occasional fingerprint from the last consumer, there wasn't much to washing a wineglass—in white-lady terms . . . swish, pass with the cloth, swish, rinse. . . . But the boy had been making potions in the glass . . . first clear pop with yellow food coloring, then water with deeper yellow food coloring. And once Ima Pipiig told him that it looked more like pee than brandy, it was poured into a cokie-cola bottle and given a construction paper label of the rudest and crudest kind that would satisfy an eight-year-old. And at some point the wineglass had been used to make chocolate milk with green food coloring, then red, then cashew nuts, pressed gently with an old silver spoon (because the family could not afford matching stainless steel), so as not to break the delicate glass. Now Ima Pipiig had the onerous job of applying enough dish soap to wash the grease from the glass without making it too slippery to safely hold in the old, hard sink. It was a challenge that took all of Ima Pipiig's concentration, and she was grateful when the sweet old wineglass ended up in the dish drainer intact. But then she was confronted with dismay when she discovered that a heavy glass baked-macaroni-and-cheese casserole pan and several free, heavy, logoed coffee cups were yet to rest upon the precariously balanced load in the dish rack.

Ima Pipiig wondered if having a dishwasher like a white woman would have made a difference . . . Or, did the delicates merely get swaggered back and forth and broken, to no consequence to the happy white housewife who probably wanted to replace her wineglasses anyways. Ima Pipiig had been offered some perfectly good wineglasses in such a circumstance, by a hospital administrator's wife who'd been "forced" to replace hers, because of a party she

247

was having. Ima Pipiig had had to turn them down because she had not had room in her 1800s dish cupboard for one more single little dish. Nothing. The plastic kiddie tumblers were pretty much taking up all the space. Besides, Ima Pipiig did not drink wine. She only used it to sauté smelt with garlic. She only *had* two wineglasses, for the kids to play with, and she only *needed* two wine-glasses, for the kids to play with.

Thinking about wine made Ima Pipiig think about smelt. So Ima Pipiig called the dog from her late-morning slumber on the living room couch, and when the big animal paused wishfully at her empty food dish, Ima Pipiig twisted the knob and pulled the door open expectantly.

"Exercise first, you lazy thing."

The dog ran past Ima Pipiig to urinate in the path ahead of her. Ima Pipiig swished past the spot, into the cool, long wet grass off to the side. It was still too cold mornings to spend much time out-of-doors barefoot, so Ima Pipiig broke into a sort of running trot through an acre of forest toward the barns and the freezers full of venison and fish. It was on cool mornings like this one that Ima Pipiig half expected to find a skunk waiting around the bend. Neither she nor the dog had been skunked yet, in spite of the homey collection of windowless steel car bodies that hunkered in the trees to one side of the path, always providing comfort to Ima Pipiig's favorite striped cousin of the weasel.

One such morning last fall, Ima Pipiig had broken into such a barefoot run, the dog still asleep, filling up one whole end of the couch, not there to spook all wildlife in advance of her arrival. It was there, by the lichen-covered wooden seat swing, resting from chains among the twisted catalpas, that Ima Pipiig had surprised a young skunk. He was not quite a full adult, surely one of this year's offspring, no doubt the culprit who had been feasting from the tall plastic cat feeder in that closest barn. He had wandered out from his temporary summer bedding of sawdust, in a back lean-to room of the old workshop barn where the wood planer sat among stacks of to-be-planed and already smooth and sized lumber. Where the greens of the once-blooming jonquils, irises, and daylilies kept the soil moist between the trees, the young skunk had taken to clawing for fat night crawlers before first light. "One man's fishing bait is another man's snack," Shiigawk, the skunk, would tell Ima Pipiig later, in the warm barn, with a sweet, but menacing smile.

But this skunk, this young one, was one of Shiigawk's offspring—young and careless, used to the movings-about of buffoon-like people during the long summer and dwindling autumn days. The young skunk buck sprang upright and alert, involuntarily, at the sight of Ima Pipiig out of the corner of his eye. Then he hopped sideways with all the beauty, grace, and absolute stupidity of Pepe Le Peu, leaping upward at least a foot off the ground with each bounce, legs rigid, moving only with the force of his long, powerful toes. Ima Pipiig's initial response was to sniff the air, then feel a sense of gratitude that neither she nor Lester's workspace had become contaminated. The poor youngster had not even had it together to stand ground, tail aquiver, threatening to spray. Not even one little poof was sent forth from those villainous glands.

Then Ima Pipiig stood, stunned, in the path, laughing with relief and laughing at the absurdity of the skunk himself, laughing at the gifts of observation that those early animators had had. No one could have drawn Pepe Le Peu without having observed skunks considerably. Ima Pipiig began to wonder what kind of person would do such a thing. A wave of true respect for the animators came over her. Even given her own proximity to entire families of skunks, she did not think she had picked up that sort of familiarity.

But things would change. As the days grew shorter and colder, and early snows began to affect the skunks' foraging, Ima Pippiig began to see more and more of them. Eventually, when the barn doors were closed up for the winter, and great stacks of firewood were balanced against one wall of the workshop, the skunks were deprived of their auxiliary diet of generic cat food. The skunk youths scattered, leaving behind no one but the old man, Shiigawk. The cat was relieved, but Shiigawk was not. With a boldness that comes only with age, he began scratching at Ima Pipiig's barn door.

"What do you want?"

"A little company. A little food. A chance to sit by your warm fire."

"Beat it."

Scratch, scratch.

"You think I'm stupid? I can tell it's you scratching at my door."

"I'm a skunk. You want I should knock?"

"Get a life."

"I'm old, Ima Pipiig. Let me in. If you don't I'll lose my life."

Ima Pipiig was not sure what it was about her upbringing that had prepared her to be kind to those in need, even the offensive, but Ima Pipiig weakened, and Shiigawk was relieved to hear the metallic grate of the hundred-year-old door handle being turned to pull back its inner bolt. He stepped stiffly over the doorsill, sniffed at a basket of carrots, and settled in on a white plastic lawn chair next to the woodstove.

"Smoke with me, Ima," Shiigawk rolled his small shiny eyes up at the ammunition cupboard, high on a wall, not even in the same building as the locked-up hunting rifles. Ima Pipiig flipped up the hand-hewn cupboard flap and pulled out her grandmother's old clay pipe, the only remaining artifact she had of the woman's very existence. She shuffled among the boxes of dove shot and found a small zippered plastic bag filled with sweet shavings of red willow root, a form of Indian tobacco that she had tucked away in a moment of peace, just for such occasions. The nerve of this skunk, she thought. The boldness, the blatancy with which he made it clear that he had observed her life for years, that he had known where the precious pipe was stored, that he had seen her patiently shave that fresh willow root, long before. Had he also observed Ima Pipiig and Lester having sex in the barn on warm afternoons, standing up, using the woodpile for support, while they had a few energetic moments away from the kids? Damn skunk!

"So, Smelly . . . Manaboozhou, my old cousin, gave you a gift, your stench, and with it you have become bold, cocky, bigger than yourself. Who are you to observe my life in its most intimate details?"

"Just a neighbor with an overlapping range of territory, my dear Ima." Skunk farted, lifted his tail, and resettled on the chair. "When you closed up those barn doors, it made for a rather sudden change in my diet." Shiigawk did not even look sheepish.

"After all these years, you should've known it was coming."

"I'm tired, Ima. Let me stay the winter. I promise not to stink up the place." Shiigawk farted again.

"Jeez, is that the best you can do?" Ima Pipiig thought maybe he could try a little harder at not being stinky.

"Are you going to light the fire?"

"Boy, are you pushy."

Ima Pipiig cautiously brushed past the old skunk, rummaged under the workbench, and produced an old copy of the *Sleeping Bear County Gazette*. She separated and crumpled a few pages of real estate ads, threw them into the rusty woodstove, added tinder, a few small, dry scraps from her sawmill, and palmed a used tissue that she found stuffed into one pocket of her jeans. She struck a wooden match against the box and touched it to the tissue, tossing it into the stove.

"Ahem . . ." Shiigawk held up the pipe in one long-clawed front paw. "A light, please." And Ima Pipiig leaned in toward him with the still-lit match.

Shiigawk leaned forward into the proffered match and puffed away at Ima Pipiig's grandmother's pipe.

Shiigawk puffed and puffed away, as though he had all the time in the world. He eventually offered Ima Pipiig a draw at her own tobacco, in her own pipe. But Ima Pipiig declined, not wanting to take into her own system strange saliva from those strange, dark lips. Shiigawk puffed and stared. Ima Pipiig stood at the worktable in the middle of the room, staring back, at first, hoping that Shiigawk would sense her impatience, finish up his bowl, and move on. Instead, he adjusted himself on the hard plastic seat, using his long, fluffy tail as sort of a cushion. Again, Shiigawk farted, this time a long and squeaky one that caused him to shift slightly and readjust. She looked away, mournfully, stared at the pile of newspapers, then tried to concentrate on the other items on the low shelf. There was nothing interesting to focus on really, just a box full of paper bags from the grocery store and boxes full of old bent silverware and dishes that the kids had played with in the garden over the years, making mud and sawdust spoon-shaped cookies in long, careful rows on the edge of the concrete in front of the equipment barn. Sometimes they'd cried, when the faux baked goods were inadvertently run over by an eighty-five horsepower tractor.

She turned to the skunk, "Do you want me to light that again?"

"Not yet."

"Listen, Shiigawk, I've got a long day ahead of me, and you're not helping any."

"So leave. I'll be fine right here." Another poof escaped from Shiigawk's rear, and a bit of his tail fur wavered in the breeze.

Ima Pipiig exhaled sharply through her nose. "Do you think you could go over to the door before you relax your sphincter muscle like that?" she asked.

"I'm a skunk. My sphincter muscle is always relaxed."

"That's just my point. You're not like us. You're different."

"Different customs? Different expectations?"

"Exactly."

"So you don't want my kind living among you?"

"You're different from us. You don't belong here." Ima Pipiig shook her head at the skunk.

"You'd adjust, Ima Pipiig. That's what we did. We got used to you living here."

Shiigawk slid down from the chair and began to sniff around the barn. He pawed at a pile of sawdust in a far corner and urinated.

"See, this is what I mean," Ima Pipiig walked over to the damp pile, scolding. "You're different."

"What would you like me to do, Ima? I've got basic needs."

"Outside!" Ima Pipiig motioned to the door.

"I don't have to go any more."

"Not just to pee, for good!" Ima Pipiig gestured to the door.

"I'll die. My resources are gone. This was my home, right here, right where this barn sits today."

"You old liar. This barn is older than me."

"It was our home, all of our homes, all of us Shiigawkwag." He was calm, insistent.

"Get out of my barn!"

"Our barn."

The old skunk half walked, half hopped with his long claws scratching noisily on the hard concrete. He headed straight for the warm seat by the stove.

"You're practically a rodent."

"Sticks and stones . . ." He lay down.

"You're not human."

"I am as important to the one who created me as you are to the one who created you."

"I pay the taxes."

"We were here first."

That one was a tough one to answer to. After all, it's not like Shiigawk and his family had gotten a treaty or anything. And they certainly had nothing to show for relinquishing the property, except for several bellies full of cat food. The neighbors were doing a good job of providing seasonal housing as well. All the vintage rusting hulks of old automobiles had remained unmoved for decades, except for the old Packard body, which had fetched a fairly good price. Ima Pipiig tried to imagine setting up housekeeping in an old Chevelle that had been emptied of its upholstery by industrious mice. Seemed good enough for a skunk. She looked at the old skunk. He had gray around his muzzle, like an old dog.

> "OK, here's the deal . . ." Ima Pipiig found an old canning jar box, tore off the top flaps, and cut a low door out of one of its four upright sides. She filled it with sawdust and wood shavings. "You potty here."
>
> "It will have to be emptied regularly," the old skunk stated somewhat indignantly.
>
> "Shiiiiiistaa!" she exclaimed in Ojibwe, "You're worse than the cat."
>
> "Treat me with dignity, and I will behave." Shiigawk hunched upward a bit and motioned to the box of matches.

Ima Pipiig struck a match and lit his bowl again. She shook out the match and dropped it in front of the stove door, where she'd remember to throw it in later. Shiigawk was sitting so close to the stove, that she was afraid of opening the door, because a spark from the dry pine might catch his fur on fire. She wasn't sure what one might do with a flaming skunk.

Shiigawk offered up the pipe again, and this time Ima Pipiig took it and drew, subtly wiping the mouthpiece on her sweatshirt sleeve first. She didn't like smoking much, but it was a social thing, a polite custom, and an advance signal of acceptance toward calm interaction and camaraderie. Just one puff was all it took to partake in the ritual observance of mutual respect, for the barriers to break down, and for conversation to begin . . .

So the hours passed, and they would pass often again. Shiigawk learned to leave Ima Pipiig alone mornings, when she was most productive. He waited until afternoons for his smoke, when Ima Pipiig could sit and rest and visit with him. She was a busy woman, and there was much to be done in the name of survival if she was to justify the time with him. She had taken to burning her trash first thing in the morning, throwing in a few scraps from the lumber mill, just to take off the chill on his day. She used the excuse that she was just getting dinner from the freezer, to thaw throughout the short winter day. It was not until afternoon that she would build a larger fire with hardwood, in anticipation of Lester's return to the barn for an evening of hard work, after his long day of hard work. The days were growing shorter, and, after a time, it was almost dark when she'd come to light the woodstove next to Shiigawk's favorite chair.

It was one such afternoon, close to winter solstice, when she'd reached down to stroke his center stripe and found him cold and stiff. At first she cried at the loss of this friend. Then she was perturbed.

"What the heck am I gonna do with a dead skunk?" she thought to herself. Tossing him into the stove didn't seem right. Besides, it would really stink up the place, and Lester would be home in less than an hour. He'd gotten used to the skunk, and had even taken to referring to him as "the cat," but he wouldn't appreciate the stench of burning fur while he was trying to plane lumber in a closed up barn.

She couldn't just toss him on the compost heap or any place nearby, because those heinous stink glands that Shiigawk had benignly refrained from using all winter would stink up the whole neighborhood once they thawed and started to break down. Ima Pipiig had had a great-aunt under whose house an entire family of skunks had dwelled without incident, much to the delight of the old lady. Then one of them died, and all of the surviving members of that skunk family moved out as the stench increased in intensity. They left without so much as a thank you or a consideration for taxes and real estate values. For decades, the stench rose from under the house whenever the temperature got above eighty.

Ima Pipiig sighed. Just as she had suspected would happen, months ago, Shiigawk was finally causing problems, by virtue of his very presence, by virtue of his very difference, by virtue of his sustained and obstinate nature. In death, he had managed to live up to her worst expectations. After riffing through an old phone book without benefit of her glasses, Ima Pipiig dialed the cold rotary wall phone and called Joan Soper. Joan only lived about twenty miles away, but it was long distance. Already Shiigawk was costing her more money than just a little cat food.

"Do you know any special ceremonies or anything for dealing with a dead skunk?"

"Doesn't he have any family?"

"I think they're hibernating in the orchard."

"Oh."

"Any suggestions?"

"Do you think the BIA's got a special skunk department or something?"

"Get real. I don't want the government to get ahold of him. They might do something offensive. He deserves a little respect."

"All skunks deserve respect."

"Yeah, I know . . . Do you think they have a special way of doing it— disposing of them, I mean? You know, they're different from us. They've probably got their own skunk religion and everything."

Joan laughed. "Maybe they're Catholic."

"No, c'mon, Joan, he was a really cool skunk, I want to treat Shiigawk right."

"I'm not coming over to help."

"No, no, I don't expect you to. I just thought maybe you knew. Sometimes you know stuff I don't know. You know, it's a culture. It takes a whole bunch of us to know all of it. I wasn't there for Skunk 101."

"I don' know nuthin' 'bout buryin' no dead skunks, Miz Scarlett."

"Show-off. See ya."

"Good luck."

Ima Pipiig flipped up the flap on the ammunition cupboard above the woodpile. She took out her grandmother's old clay pipe and the zippered bag full of red-willow-root tobacco. She stuffed the bowl, lit a wooden match, and sat in a white plastic lawn chair across from Shiigawk's. She smoked the whole bowl, carefully blowing the sweet opacity across her friend's cold body, smoothing it into his fur. Then she tapped the ashes into the cold woodstove and set the pipe on the edge of the worktable in the middle of the room. As she rose from her chair, the corner of Ima Pipiig's red down work vest caught the mouthpiece of the old pipe. She reflexively dipped and grabbed at the air, but the pipe hit the cement and shattered.

Ima Pipiig walked across the room, singing softly to herself in Ojibwe, "Come in, my fellows, my friends, come in . . . Way hya hy, way hya hya ho . . . " Without even the competition of a wood fire and subsequent draught in the pipes, her softness echoed in the empty workroom. She took a pair of snowshoes off the wall from above her head, bound them onto her heavy boots, and clomped over to Shiigawk's chair, dragging a light-blue baby sled across the cement. She'd bought it at a garage sale for two dollars. These days, she used it to carry groceries back and forth between the barn freezers and the house. Her babies were all too big to fit in the sled now. Shiigawk fit in just right, and she curled his long, soft tail around his nose. He fell out when she tried to drag the sled over the high barn doorsill. It was hard maneuvering through the tight spaces of the workroom in long snowshoes, dragging a dead skunk. She resettled him back into the snug baby sled, closed the narrow door against the yellow of the electric lights, and faced into the cobalt blue of a growing darkness that did not yet yield stars.

Ima Pipiig shuffled out past the equipment barn and the fuel tanks. She followed a set of deep tractor tracks to where Lester had piled scraps from the sawmill in the middle of an empty field for burning next spring. With a prayer, she flung Shiigawk by his strong tail up to the top of the heap, high above her head, where only the front-end loader of Lester's tractor could reach. Then, in the silent cold, in the silent whiteness of the empty, darkening farm field, she sang out loud to the ravens and crows of winter, "Kaa, gaah, gii . . . kaa, gaah, gii . . ." Ima Pipiig cried out into the cold, this clear night more crow than woman, more raven than woman, more night sky than woman . . .

Ima Pipiig sang the Ojibwe song of her childhood with beauty and with grace, dancing and swooping like a free spirit in her snowshoes, in an ever-widening circle around the pile of wood and brush and broken children's toys, until the cold night air soothed her hot and tear-swollen cheeks, until she knew that the Crow Song had brought them from their roosts, just before the darkest of darks. The woman needed those ravens and crows to know they had a job to do, come first light—that they were to guard old Shiigawk through that night. Then they were to do several days of clean-up work, their tidying up with flesh-tearing beaks, their part of the chain of life they had taken part in for so many generations on these sacred hilltops of Shiigawk's old family homestead. "Kaa, gaah, gii . . ." she cried. And they called back and alighted in the pines and poplars of the windbreaks flanking the empty field, one by one, until woman and birds, they cawed together in one great voice that shook the night sky and scared the dickens out of Lester when he pulled up next to the workshop barn in his pickup truck.

Chilled, Ima Pipiig shuffled back to the warm light of the barn. There she gave Lester a quick kiss, lit the stove, and swept up the broken bits of the old pottery pipe. It was a small price to pay for such friendship and joy, and Ima Pipiig would recall Shiigawk the skunk with the same intensity with which she remembered her own grandmother. And just to make sure that everything was done right, she would continue to sing and dance in her snow-shoes for three nights more before lighting the evening fire . . . only a little bit earlier, so Lester wouldn't think she was crazy when he came home from work.

· 34 ·

On Warriors, Living and Dead
(In Respectful Memory
of Charles J. Meyers)

$\mathcal{I}$ am disconcerted. The normally joyous ramblings of my mind have been interrupted. I have seen, more than I care to, military recruitment posters and signs addressed specifically to Native American youth. They misuse our ancient and cherished notions of warrior as a method of manipulation, to try to draw our youth into wars they have no business fighting, to fatten the pockets of the business elite who have traditionally been our enemies, those who have led to our socioeconomic lynching and emotional suicide.

I have grown up with the veterans' songs of our powwows bringing a tightness to my chest, a sense of pride that we protected our country, in spite of the fact that it wanted to throw us away. And underneath that pride was always a sadness in that we had to work so hard to try to gain your respect, to try to gain acceptance into your economy and culture, to be less than disposable. So we sent off our husbands and fathers and sons and daughters to die. They willingly treated themselves as disposable commodities in the hope that, through their valor, their mothers, fathers, wives, little brothers, and little sisters would be held in higher esteem by the dominant culture—in essence, less disposable.

I want to tell you about a little Chippewa girl who lives in Sault Ste. Marie, Michigan, with her grandmother. Belonging to the military reserves had become a part-time job of tradition in her family, part of the tradition of working more than one low-paying, part-time job to survive in the state's sparsely populated upper peninsula, a land of overharvested fish and lumber and empty, polluting mine shafts. By the time she was three years old, her grandfather had gone to war, her maternal uncle had gone to war, her father had gone to war, and her mother had gone to war—all on the same day in the first wave of the second Bush administration's war for oil. It was a selective draft of the poor and the disposable. And all of those Indians went and left that little girl behind because it was what they were expected to do in a modern tradition dictating that they jeopardize their own lives and livelihoods in the hope of making that little girl less disposable to the American people.

I have issues with that expectation of us. I am more than disconcerted. I am angry. So in my anger, I begin to redefine the notion of warrior as it has been bent and twisted to suit the needs of the wealthy over the past hundred years of U.S. bloody history. It never meant aggressor until the upheaval associated with land appropriation and the fur trade forced us into dysfunction. It meant protector. It is one of only five essential occupations of the Ojibwe: leader, teacher, healer, protector, and provider. None surpasses the other in importance. These are the groups by which we align ourselves. These alliances are so important, so ancient, that they are the means by which our *dodaimig*, our totem brethren, the animals of our environment, also align themselves. This notion of protector is so sacred, so essential to our survival as a people, that we hurt ourselves by letting it be reinvented and abused by outside agitators. It took thousands of years to perfect but only decades to toss aside.

I want to talk to you about my friend, Charlie Joe. Charlie was Ogitchidaa, a warrior. O is a prefix. It means that someone does something. Chi means big. Gitchi means great. Ogitchidaa is someone who does great things. Great is bigger than the wars of a nation, especially a nation that based its growth and future upon our exploitation and loss. And apparently continues to do so today. We have been and continue to be among the most highly represented groups of Americans in the military.

To be sure, Charlie was in the armed services, flying for both the United States and Canada. He served in multiple wars. I can't remember the details of his enlistments and his accomplishments. It is hard for a younger person to absorb the details of something they have not lived. It is not my place to remember his war record in the political conflicts of nations. I remember him for his deeds in other wars—the wars for dignity and economic equality, the wars for cultural preservation and the arts, the wars that ensured that Anishinabe children have a solid footing in time and space, even if their grandparents, parents, siblings, spouses, and children are sent off to fight military wars.

These are good fights. In his old age Charlie picked the best of fights. He had the best war stories. In one of the world wars he flew cockpit to cockpit with an enemy pilot. He'd seen things and absorbed information that no other American soldier had seen. So he was sent off to a base somewhere to teach the planners and the pilots about the enemy's resources. I don't remember the details of that military accomplishment. What I do remember are the details he told me about how he was treated, as an Indian, by those white military commanders. I remember those details because they are details I have lived in other contexts. That's how real learning works. And so, through firmness and patience, Charlie taught me how to be Ogitchidaa, a protector, one who does great things. The title has no nuances of trying. It implies success. It is a cultural imperative. He taught me and countless others that we fight wars by being historians, artists, and writers. We find our skills and we apply them to the five basic needs of our culture, in all their nuances.

So Charlie Joe was a turtle. Turtle was his dodaim. Mine is deer. Turtle is a healer. Deer is a provider. But we have both been protectors and teachers, and through our accomplishments we have healed future generations and provided for our offspring. This makes us leaders. And to redefine this notion of ourselves is blasphemy. I am here because of the Ogitchidaag who preceded me, and each time one of them passes on, the imperative rears its successful head.

Note: The Charles J. Meyers Collection of Contemporary Woodland Indian Art is the largest of its kind in the world. Art from this collection has been used to illustrate numerous books by and about the Anishinabe people and has helped to preserve the visual format of our cultural language. Charlie left us on February 8, 2005, at the age of eighty-six.

• 35 •

The Shirt

"No. You can't have the shirt."

"But I want it."

"I know. But you can't have the shirt."

"My friends will think it's cool!"

"I know. But you can't have the shirt."

"It's on sale, isn't it?"

"Yes. But you can't have the shirt."

It is a camouflage design in muted shades of military beiges and greens. The corporations that control America want to go to war again. And they are marketing children's clothing as early recruitment . . . groundwork. The shirts are cheaper than any other shirts. They are in all the stores, and they are cheaper than all of the other shirts. It comes in other colors, that camouflage pattern. Oranges. Reds. Muted. Blending. Bloodlike.

"It comes in other colors, too. Look."

"I know. But you can't have the shirt."

"Why?"

She wants to tell him.

"Why?"

She wants to tell him. But she knows that he is still too young to understand modern military operations. He is too young to understand death.

He is too young to understand permanent loss of faculties, of limb. He thinks it's cool. Blood and gore and stuff like in the horror movies. Like a Hallowe'en mask.

"It's cool."

Like a Hallowe'en mask.

"Mom. I said, it's cool."

"I know. But you can't have the shirt."

But nothing like a Hallowe'en mask.

"I could wear it for Halloween."

"No, I wouldn't let you."

"Why not?"

"I don't want you to be a soldier for Halloween."

"I could put fake blood on."

"It's called Hallowed Evening."

"What?"

"Hallowe'en. It's short for Hallowed Evening. And that means Holy Evening. It's supposed to be a Holy Evening."

"Who cares . . ."

"I care."

It's supposed to be about honoring the dead, she's fairly sure, not just about gruesome ceremonies and an association with all things gory. It's supposed to be about loving the dead, loving their memories. And scaring the kids is just a bonus. Because scaring kids a little bit is important to keeping them alive and safe. That's why we've got stories about bad things. They are preventative stories. They are the true warriors' stories. And it's fun scaring the kids, too. It's fun hearing children squeal with delight.

Ima Pipiig's mind is wandering. It is taking her away from the urban development fringing the once-small town of Twin Bay, Michigan. She is in small graveyards in the woods. Small patches of history and intertwined lives. She is sprinkling tobacco on the graves, following her mother, glad for the opportunity to toss and scatter something wildly with her young arms that beg for wide and simple motions without consequence.

She is hiding bundles of fresh sweetgrass behind the gravestones of Indian soldiers, where the white people will not see them and take them away, as sou-

venirs attesting to the quaintness of northern Michigan's remnant Native inhabitants. The boy is sprinkling tobacco on the graves, following his mother,
glad for the opportunity to toss and scatter something wildly with his young
arms that beg for wide and simple motions without consequence.

"But I want it."

"No. You can't have the shirt."

"Why?"

It is a camouflage design, in muted shades of military beiges and greens.
The corporations that control America want to go to war again. And they are
marketing children's clothing as early recruitment . . . groundwork. The shirts
are cheaper than any other shirts. They are in all the stores, and they are
cheaper than all of the other shirts. It comes in other colors, that camouflage
pattern. Oranges. Reds. Muted. Blending. Bloodlike.

He cannot have the shirt because, because . . . there is nothing in our oral and writ-
ten history prior to the advent of the fur trade that refers to protectors being recruited as
warriors. There is nothing in our stories, no cultural precedents for the concept of children
recruited for future disposability in the form of corporate warriors. Once enlisted, these
children are endlessly deployed until death or dismemberment. There is no Anishinabe
word for this. There is no Anishinabe concept for this. This came with the fur trade, and
our success at adapting to the warfare you brought upon us is being used to recruit us
right now.

Ima Pipiig has seen the government posters, distributed in the Native
American communities, the ones that talk about Indian warrior traditions. Ima
Pipiig knows at this time that the boy is to be protected from the idea of protector as warrior, until he is old enough to know that dead is forever, until he
is old enough to know that dismemberment is not cool, until he knows that
one must carefully choose what one protects.

"Mom. I want the shirt."

"I know. But you can't have it."

· 36 ·

We Did Not Come Over Here
on the Mayflower, by Ima Pipiig

We did not come over here on the Mayflower. We did not come up the Cumberland Gap. We did not follow Daniel Boone or De Soto or a black-robed priest. We came from the tops of tall trees that softly bent down and laid their boughs upon the earth so that she would not be lonesome. We came from the clouds, life-giving mist and sky. We came from the soil itself, from crevices that opened up and gifted us to the open air. We came from the rich mud at the bottom of the waters to mingle with the other life forms and make them complete.

We followed Cranes here. We followed Turtles here. We followed Ravens and Frogs and Catfish and Sturgeon and Deer, Caribou, Moose, Otters, Bears . . . We followed the stars here. We followed the Northern Lights here. We followed rivers and streams and shorelines and horizons here. We followed the wind and the very air we breathe here. We did not follow you here.

So you stop telling those stories about us not traditionally being here. And about us being only a historic presence here. Like we were too dumb to fill up this place with life and culture, until after you nearly killed us off and then let the survivors linger, huddled together for warmth and solace, in the tiny, cutoff hamlets that you call our historic presence here. Yeah, you, lady from the Park Service. I'm talking to you.

You've got to stop telling the Indians the stories that you white folks at the Park Service keep telling yourselves. For instance, that one about the Ojibwe migration myth. You see, it takes a whole lifetime to learn that story about the migration myth, and even then, one only grasps a piece of it. Because it takes many, many lifetimes to learn that story about the migration myth. And the only way one can even begin to understand that story about the migration myth is to be in a room full of people who have spent lifetimes learning that migration myth and to be in a community full of people who have spent lifetimes learning that migration myth and to be in a culture full of people who have spent lifetimes learning that migration myth. Then one can understand it, a little bit.

But simply pulling out tiny snippets of that migration myth is ignorant and dangerous behavior. You pulled out the little pieces that sounded good and that met your needs. You took the parts that suggested that we were not always here and did not always use and need this place. First of all, you suggested that we all only got here a few hundred years before you did. And you left out the part of the migration myth that says that most of us were already here before those Indians whose latest migration myth you borrowed got here. Like they came to a giant empty space. Like there was this archaeological record just chucky-chock full of cavemen without caves and hunters without decent homes and storage facilities and accumulated knowledge about survival in this place . . . and then, poof, some Indians arrived who really aren't from here anyway and have no greater claim to this place than recent migrants like you have to this place. Convenient. Very convenient.

You left out all of the parts of the migration myth that included merging and scattering and forming new groups and identities, as the environment demanded of us. You left out all of the parts of the migration myth that included following the Cranes, the Turtles, Ravens and Frogs and Catfish and Sturgeon and Deer, Caribou, Moose, Otters, Bears . . . You left out the parts about how we followed the stars here. We followed the Northern Lights here. We followed rivers and streams and shorelines and horizons here. We followed the wind and the very air we breathe here. We did not follow you here.

We came from the tops of tall trees that softly bent down and laid their boughs upon the earth so that she would not be lonesome. We came from the clouds, life-giving mist and sky. We came from the soil itself, from crevices that opened up and gifted us to the open air. We came from the rich mud at the bottom of the waters to mingle with the other life forms and make them complete.

You need to stop telling those stories you tell about how we got public education from you white folks through treaties. We already had public education. We had it in our teaching lodges. We had specially educated and certified specialists, teachers. Teachers were such an important part of our society that we deemed them one of the five categories of people that communities and cultures need to survive. We had a special curriculum for those teachers; and the body of that knowledge took up an entire fifth of our totem system. We had special buildings, special teaching tools, even books with written lessons and important historical events. But you continue to rename these things as spiritual, as paraphernalia to a lesser religion, rather than what they were, schools and books and tools, fine arts curricula, literary curricula, math and science and medicine. You rename these things as archaeological sites and as mythology and as artifacts. How absolutely ignorant and boorish of you!

To continue to force your versions of our history upon us is oafish and uncivilized. It forces us to unteach what you teach. It challenges your concept of public education (which still fails to meet the needs of minorities), and it elevates ours. It challenges your terminology, and it elevates ours. It challenges your version of one tiny slice of our migration story, and it elevates ours.

We did not come over here on the Mayflower. We did not come up the Cumberland Gap. We did not follow Daniel Boone or De Soto or a black-robed priest. We came from the tops of tall trees that softly bent down and laid their boughs upon the earth so that she would not be lonesome. We came from the clouds, life-giving mist and sky. We came from the soil itself, from crevices that opened up and gifted us to the open air. We came from the rich mud at the bottom of the waters to mingle with the other life forms and make them complete.

We followed Cranes here. We followed Turtles here. We followed Ravens and Frogs and Catfish and Sturgeon and Deer, Caribou, Moose, Otters, Bears . . . We followed the stars here. We followed the Northern Lights here. We followed rivers and streams and shorelines and horizons here. We followed the wind and the very air we breathe here. We did not follow you here. We are the very essence of here.

· 37 ·

The Ladies Sat There Patiently

*I*ma Pipiig was on autopilot. It had not cooled down the night before. Lester had not gotten out of the house until almost seven-fifteen. Now she sauntered over to the barns in her nightshirt, enjoying the breeze, hot though it was, and the fact that the sun had not yet climbed over the woodlot to the east of her garden, or the block of tall sweet cherry trees east of her garden, grateful for the fact that a row of even taller poplars separated the five-thousand-square-foot patch that Lester plowed for her from the two-track that ran from the road to the back of her farm.

She thought of how she had a hard time getting her neighbors, mostly two-acre-lot dwellers, to understand the concept that not all roads are public, that the no-trespassing and no-snowmobiling signs and the private-drive signs meant them, too, even though they were very nice people, and even though their parents had given them everything they ever wanted, even if it didn't belong to them. And Ima Pipiig longed for winter, because one could dress for the cold, but one could not undress for the heat past one's own sticky, sun-browned skin. And Ima Pipiig longed for the cool of autumn and spring, the times of the year that the farm was snow-free and she was safe from the snow-mobiling youth whose parents thought nothing of sending their children off to play in someone else's yard, in someone else's thoughts and privacy. Because the facility with which her white-flight neighbors trespassed in winter made her love less the snow that she had once loved with every cell of her being; made her feel even more like an unwelcome Indian; made her wonder how these people, these takers, could take not just the land and the identity of the place away from its aboriginal inhabitants, but how they managed to thought-lessly take away even joy in winter, her very thoughts, her very satisfaction with a pristine new snowfall void of motorized tracks, to give the very clear message that she did not dare even to be an environmentalist, a keeper of a small pocket of habitat, a woman who dared to dream of meeting the needs of any creature other than the newcomers . . . because their parents had given them everything they ever wanted, even if it didn't belong to them.

And she loved the autumn—late, late autumn, leaves-gone-from-the-trees-autumn that did not attract tourists. A pocket of time before the bow hunters arrived for their early deer season, the ones who trespassed, too, because they had saved up and bought themselves two whole whopping acres of "up north," and thought that it entitled them to the territory of the mere farmers, since they were, after all, nice people, and because their parents had given them everything they ever wanted, even if it didn't belong to them. They were an odd lot to Ima Pipiig, those bow-hunting city boys, the ones who used live animals for target practice, the ones who bragged that they had wounded six or eleven deer in one season, they were so good at scouting out the deer trails and finding the deer. Not like her Lester, who could bring down a deer almost always with a single shot, who had patience to wait for the right moment, the right animal, the right distance, the right angle, the right thing to do . . .

That was one reason why she married him, this white boy; he was an awful lot like her Indian father. He did not bring home flowers. He plowed the driveway. He did not bring home flowers. He came to get Ima Pipiig to help him lift his one-shot deer into the front-end loader of his favorite tractor. He did not bring home flowers. He taught his children how to fillet a fish. He did not bring home flowers. He spent hours changing the implements on his favorite tractor and plowing up and smoothing her big garden. He did not bring home flowers. He brought home eight dump-truck loads of composted stall sweepings from a neighboring farm. He did not bring home flowers. He brought home strawberries.

And now, while the top layers of all eight immense heaps of stall-sweepings that sat evenly spaced about the garden were cool, Ima Pipiig carefully scraped them off with her wide shovel. She danced up and down the paths of her careful garden in the shade, in the breeze, in the worn and torn flannel nightshirt; and she delicately lifted the leaves between the rows of lovely peas and snow peas, between the bushy potatoes, the Chinese greens, the spring onions, the tall corn sprouts, the cool-sprouting sunflowers that would become so immense that they would hang upside down as fall food for upside-down blue jays. And she would imagine how the boy would delight in these things, just as both he and his sister had in years past.

In spite of the shade, in spite of the breeze that evaporated the moisture of toil from her long limbs, the salty sweat would eventually run down her forehead and into her eyes. The nightshirt would become soaked, would cling to her in a compelling way that Lester would not even be around to enjoy. And eventually Ima Pipiig would retreat to the house, to shower, to feed the boy, to fold laundry, to make little porcupine-quill necklaces for the tourists to greedily gobble up, because they were so cheap, and they did not mind that the Indians were forced to compete with labor from Southeast Asian sweatshops for their dollars; and they did not dream that the strain of earning a dollar might someday work its way up the food chain past their inheritances and their jobs of privilege; and they did not dream that their obvious delight in her willingness to work for less than minimum wage would color her perceptions of them; and they did not dream that Ima Pipiig was being as tolerant of their presence as they perceived themselves of being tolerant of hers; because their parents had given them everything they ever wanted, even if it didn't belong to them.

She stood naked in front of the refrigerator and drank cool catnip and mint tea from an old canning jar, gulping in her attempt at rehydration. She threw on a clean nightshirt and began to wash the dishes, began to plan an evening meal, mentally took inventory of her beadwork and small, under-five-dollar impulse-buy items that would satisfy the newcomers, satisfy the status quo of an unequal economic system, and generally brooded while she waited for her limbs to cool from the heat of hard labor.

It had been a hard week. No, it had been a hard spring. A hard winter before that. A hard year. Birdie's tuition at college had gone up, but not her scholarship. The cost of feeding a family had gone up, but not Lester's income. The cost of gasoline had gone up, but the price on Ima Pipiig's beadwork had dropped. The prices on her beautiful baskets had dropped. The cost of educating her children had gone up. The salaries of the government employees around her had gone up. But Ima Pipiig worked her way down. She did not work her way down because she was incompetent. It did not happen because she was a fool. It simply happened because the hard economy of the early twenty-first century hit those on the bottom first, and it hit them hardest. And Indians were on the bottom.

She had thought of this while she had been shoveling manure. She joked that, by shoveling manure, she was living up to her potential. And most of the time, she enjoyed it—unless she was fighting time itself and was frustrated by a long heat wave. Then she thought of all the Indians at the Indian art market, the ladies who sat in the heat patiently beading, because beadwork was portable and easy to pick up and put down. She thought of the Indians who wandered in and out of the art market, bringing children to and from the artists, bringing a chair, a cold drink, a snack, a message from a mother, a sister, a husband. And the ladies sat there patiently beading, beading, beading. Waiting for the next dollar. Waiting for the greedy white-flightists who so obviously delighted in the fact that the Indians were willing to work for less than minimum wage. But they came a little less frequently now, now that the economic hardships of the early twenty-first century were working their way up the ladder, past the Indians, into the working class, almost into the middle class. And the ladies sat there patiently beading, beading, beading.

They stopped caring about the beauty of their work. They stopped caring about the beauty of tradition. They stopped caring about the beauty of keeping culture intact. They stopped caring about rare baskets and quillwork and rare birch-bark cut-outs and bitings and rare mittens and slippers of soft-tanned deerskin and moose hide and rare handmade drums that begged to be held over an open fire for shrinking and tuning and the bending of a soft ear for perfection. They just sat there patiently beading, beading, beading. Beading, while the white people with jobs that allowed them to rest and recreate wandered past the tables and into the casinos. Beading, while the non-Indian corporate executives who managed America's casinos pulled in medical and dental benefits. Beading, while the lobbyists who controlled what Indians could do demanded hundreds of thousands in bribes. Beading, while the schoolteachers and county and township managers and museum and park employees and environmental stewardship organization staff wandered in and out of their lives, trying to decide if the Indians had lowered their prices enough on their beadwork yet, so that they should buy, because their parents had given them everything they ever wanted, even if it didn't belong to them.

Those Indian ladies, some of them, they called themselves the Underpeople. And they said to take pride in themselves as the Underpeople. Even though they had names like Ogemagiigado and Dibaajimaadkwe, which were names of honor and knowledge with linguistic and cultural roots far older than the mere few hundred years of imposition upon the Indians by the newcomers of the concept and sensation of underpeople. And Ima Pipiig had been angry while she had shoveled all of that manure, the sweet-smelling stall-sweepings of cedar and urine and digested grasses and grains—and the foul-smelling cultural stall-sweepings of northwest Lower Michigan's newcomers' racism and hatred and abuse of the fellow human beings they designated as the Underpeople—because their parents had given them everything they ever wanted, even if it didn't belong to them.

And now Ima Pipiig sat at her worktable, sorting out her beadworking materials, trying to second-guess the whims of her potential buyers. It had been a hard year. She had been approached by someone from the state arts council, wanting her to volunteer her time for a website about Indian artists, even though most of the Indian artists do not know how to use the Internet, do not have hours and hours of free time to learn how to use the Internet. She had been approached by someone from the National Park Service who wanted her to volunteer her time to get her off the hook for not including Indians and Indian input in her interpretive exhibits, even though Indians do not have free time to go to the park visitors' center, even though Indians cannot afford the $50 per year parking fee to use the park, even though Indians no longer live near the park, because they are driven out after a few weeks by the racists in the public schools every time they try to come back. She had been approached by someone from the Twin Bay City Area Public School District to volunteer her time reading a poem by an Indian author (but not by her) because the "educator" felt guilty that Indians do not do this in the schools, even though Indian writers do not have the time to read books of poetry by other Indian writers and even though the Twin Bay City Area Public School District has traditionally refrained from hiring Native Amercans to do these things. She had been approached by someone from each of the local historical museums to volunteer her time to be a consultant on some exhibits about Indian stuff that were conceived of and planned and already put into place by the white intellectual keepers of their white-flight institutional racism, even though they are not the kind of exhibits that the Indians really want to see and even though the Indians would have no input except on paper, for the purposes of funding, duly recorded as having been grateful and fawning, due to the fact that the white intellectuals had finally, finally done something, anything that even acknowledged that the Underpeople had ever accomplished anything but the sweeping of floors and the cleaning of toilets in the casinos. . . . She had been approached by a man from a nonprofit environmental conservation organization who wanted her to volunteer her time for a project that had already been conceived and designed, so that they could get funding from the state for including minorities, even though Ima Pipiig and Lester had already spent their life savings buying and preserving the largest unbroken tract of virgin timber on the shores of Lake Superior, the largest of the Great Lakes, and that she could not afford to volunteer for people who made more money than she did, if she was going to be able to keep the land away from the real estate developers and the commercial loggers.

And Ima Pipiig bit her tongue and did not tell these people that "volunteer" comes from the same Latin root word as "volition"; and that involuntary servitude continues to take on many forms and that it is facilitated today, as it was in the sixteenth and seventeenth and eighteenth and nineteenth centuries, by the use of books and classrooms and exhibitions and websites and other publicly funded traveling snake-oil shows that promulgate the concept of one people as lesser than another, justifying contemporary physical and emotional lashings in the form of exclusion and unemployment. And all of these people, who measured their value of self by their titles and their nonprofit status and their supposed value to the welfare of society as a whole, would explain to Ima

Pipiig that they do not have money in their budget for paying the Indians . . . letting themselves off the hook for inviting an Indian to volunteer, which is more than their predecessors had done . . . while they took home their paychecks and used their medical and dental benefits to ensure that they live long enough to take advantage of their retirement plans . . . while they cursed the Indians for not being willing to volunteer in their community on projects that are designed to honor and benefit them . . . while they cursed the Indians for being cranky and wanting more and for accusing them of never doing anything right—because their parents had given them everything they ever wanted, even if it didn't belong to them. And none of them admitted openly that it was their volition that the Native Americans of the northern Great Lakes would know that they were perceived of as immigrants in their own land—to give the newcomers greater claim to the place and its history and its resources, because their parents had given them everything they ever wanted, even if it didn't belong to them.

Ima Pipiig bit her tongue, because talking back only got Indians in trouble for not staying in their place, and Ima Pipiig was not willing to jeopardize potential maybe sort-of income possibilities for the other Indians in her community by speaking out, even as those potential maybe sort-of income possibilities shrank away to nothingness. Ima Pipiig did not tell these people that they were not the only ones passing judgment. Ima Pipiig did not tell these people that they were not the only ones who practiced tolerance. Ima Pipiig sat at her worktable, trying to sort out the things she would make time for of her own volition—her children, her husband, her extended family, her history, her culture, her garden, her farm, her bush camps, virgin timber that could never again be virgin once harvested, and her environment. She raged against her own inability to perceive of herself as one of the Underpeople. She raged at her parents and her grandparents and all of the people in her life who loved and despised her in ways that made her incapable of being docile and quiet and compliant and lesser. And Ima Pipiig sat there patiently beading, beading, beading.

About the Author

Lois Beardslee is the author of *Rachel's Children* (2004), a novel about the Ojibwe of northern Michigan, and the essay collection *Lies to Live By* (2003). She is an instructor in communications at Northwestern Michigan College and is an Ojibwe artist whose works are in public and private collections around the world.